blissfield.

heather neff.

heather neff.

Cover design by Cassie Lentz
Photography by Heather Neff

ISBN-10: 172643317X
ISBN-13 9781726433174

blissfield.

To you,
for telling me not to start things I can't finish.

author's note.

The characters in this book, the town that serves as its setting and the historical circumstances that form the backdrop of this narrative are all fiction. This tale was born in a dream that floated on the edge of my sleep on a summer morning some forty-five years ago. In the dream a man walks toward the ruin of a house that once gave solace to a woman he loved. In the dream, which has come to me more than once over the intervening years, the man walks through a sweet summer morning, always approaching, but never reaching the door. The woman waits inside, listening to the sudden silence of the dawning birdsong, but never manages to see his face. For over four decades I have wondered why.

Perhaps the answer lies here, in these pages. Perhaps the dream will desert me, now that the man and woman are real.

But then again, they are not real. Their resemblance to any living person is coincidental, except, of course, to those who people this novel, called *blissfield*.

I.

blissfield, north carolina.

2016.

before.

I never managed to remember his name—the Old Man with the white hair—whose stillness kept me from coming apart in the beginning, when I couldn't even tell if it was night or day.

For weeks we sat in silence, my gaze on the snow outside, his breathing the only proof that I was almost alive.

See, coming back from the dead is a crazy thing.

It hurts.

Probably more than being born.

It took a good long while, but finally, and almost by mistake, I made it.

One single thought pierced the fog of grief and pain.

One single thought.

one.

The air awakened as I crossed the Virginia line, emerged from the darkness of a long night of driving, and entered North Carolina, the land of blood earth. Morning glories thrust wildly from the misty drainage ditches bordering the highway, and the asphalt began to steam in the rising sun, even as my escort of shadowy pines, ever-present in the black of the night, surrendered to the coming day.

People die.

I know this; everyone does. Some die in my head, yet keep living in my heart. That's what happened with Grandma. Others get taken by a different kind of death: they thrive in my thoughts, though their physical absence shrivels my heart to stone.

That would be Nina and Gideon Price. How can people die and not be dead? That's easy—I've been murdered, yet I'm still here.

Well, at least I'm pretending to be here.

The doctors said it was a twisted miracle. I should have died for good when my heart quit, after losing enough blood to fill a bathtub, breaking six bones, suffering internal injuries and a very serious concussion. Then there was that stab wound grinning across my chest. The doctors guessed it was lying outside in the sub-zero cold that kept what was left of my brain alive. Rather than taking me out for good, the hypothermia put me into a coma until I was discovered, rushed to a hospital and Frankensteined back together again.

Of course, it took me five more years to fully rejoin the living. And even now, ten years later, I still get sledgehammer headaches, odd blank-outs, and periods of intense, blinding rage. The Old Man said there'd be a lot I wouldn't remember—that the subconscious acts as a kind of padded cell against painful memories—but once I got the Dilaudid out of my system, my memories returned with laser precision. They were so intense that if I wasn't my father's daughter, I'd probably have checked out and let Social Security put me up in a halfway house for the rest of my life. Instead, I chose to fight my way back to—well, I'm not so sure to what.

I guess the Castle in me just needs a fight.

I pressed the pedal to the floor and a road sign blew past me, flashing in the dawn. Two more miles of I-95 to Roanoke Rapids, then thirty on Route 158 to Blissfield, my home. Or, at least the best approximation of a home I'd ever really known.

Restless and carsick, I switched on the radio. I'd had nothing but static for the past two hundred miles, but suddenly a song I'd loved since my childhood crackled out of the speakers: *"Oooh, child, things are gonna get easier..."*

I cranked open the driver's side window and paint-blistering, spongy heat blew my hair into my eyes and mouth, chasing a bee-sized fly around Ruby, my growling, near-vintage Jeep. The windshield fogged up, and not wanting to slow down, even for a second, I leaned forward and bladed my arm back and forth across the glass.

The Five Stairsteps went on, "*Oooh, child...*"

The truth is I hate driving, but I love my rusting red Ruby. I hate highways and swaying, boxy semis, rest-stop latrines, the gasoline and asphalt stench of rusting pickups and the ruler-sharp mind-snatching ribbon of endless highway. But I love the way flooring it with Ruby gets me out ahead of my chaos.

Jesse Brantley, the cop who tried to keep me safe, always warned me about thinking too much. So did Paula, the woman who wanted me alive, even when being alive didn't mean that much to me. Maybe they both had a point. But then, watching someone you love being murdered right beside you, and then going on to die yourself makes you a junkie for sights and sounds and smells and touch. You sort of *over*think, just so you can be ready for the next slap, fist, or thirsty knife blade.

The exit ramp from the highway led me onto the double-laned 158, where I passed a field of lowing brown cows. I took a deep, deep breath and the drenching came on me all at once, and just as if I was still sixteen, I released myself into it. Unlike ordinary sweat sneaking between my breasts and staining the lower cups of my bra, this was the moment when every cell of my northern self melted into the sticky weightlessness of cotton blossoms in my palms, the toe-sucking mud of snake-swirling swamps, and the odd, sausage-smelling cold of the Piggly Wiggly. I sensed, even before seeing the stars drifting loose from the cotton-silk trees and the peony bushes dipping under their heavy burden of scent, that I was almost home.

Yes, this was as close to home as I'd ever been, because this was the last place left to look for the girl I used to be, or the woman I might—well, the woman I *should* have become.

You see, there's nothing like the loss of that last illusion of love. When I got the message, left by an unnamed attendant in the coroner's office of Roanok Rapids, North Carolina—that my grandmother, Corinthia Bibb Castle, had slumped over in the middle of a service at Holy Redeemer Baptist Church, I stood very still, looking into nothing.

Though it was way too late to matter, Grandma had been driven to the red brick Urgent Care office inhabiting a former gas station and now staffed by an overworked nurse practitioner, because the nearest hospital was thirty miles up the two-lane highway.

Still staring into that void, I tried to tell myself that she'd gone the way she would have wanted, in the church she'd attended for nearly a century—but I wondered if she really would have wanted to transition without making things right with me. Even though—let's face it—she'd avoided making things right for the past fifteen years.

Fifteen years. Nearly half of what passed for my life.

So I stood there, staring into space, and played the message again. And again. After the thirdfourthfifth listen I'd made my decision. An hour later I was on the road, starting the stupidlong drive away from my exile and back to Blissfield.

* * * * * * *

The last fifteen miles were not so easy: The fields stretching away from 158 became vaguely familiar, and then I thought I recognized the sagging-roofed farmhouses and raw-slatted barns, some that dated all the way back to slavery. I shot past Holy Redeemer without so much as turning my head, because seeing it was almost too much to bear. And then, before I even had time to prepare myself, our land, our cemetery, and the little town lay before me, with every street, sidewalk and building haunted by the ghost of my younger self, staring back at me without a clue of the darkness to come.

Ruby knew the route like she'd been here a hundred times before. She swung off the road and onto the hard-packed unpaved street, past the remnants of a shack once inhabited by sharecroppers and the adjacent plot of yellowing corn stalks standing much taller than me.

And then we were pulling into the gravel drive of the house where my Grandma raised her three sons, including my father, her youngest—and I switched off the radio. After the jeep clicked, stuttered, and tweeted as if calling to the sparrows in the eaves, the restless southern silence surrounded us.

The house. *Her* house. Corinthia Castle's castle.

Compact and balanced, the one-floor structure was entirely surrounded by a wide-planked porch, with Greek-style columns supporting the shining metal roof. The wooden-slatted walls were painted the yellow of sunshine at dawn, with pure white gingerbread latticing the porch and oval-paned oak door. Grandma nurtured her roses, keeping beds of pink, scarlet, golden and ivory blossoms around the porch, while twin apple trees marked the boundaries of the yard.

But now the porch was splintering. The yellow paint beneath the once shining, corrugated roof was faded, and though she'd only been gone a couple of weeks, weeds had already colonized the flower beds. Had Grandma really let things get this bad, or had my memory—the Old Man warned me about this—fashioned a fantasy of what the house used to be?

I climbed out of Ruby and stroked her roof gently to thank her for bringing me here in one piece, then moved stiffly up the pearl-stoned path to the wide oak door. Automatically I leaned down and placed my fingers in a nearly undetectable niche in the wood, just beneath a window. The key was exactly where Grandma always kept it, and, when I placed it in the lock, the door swung open. Drawing in a breath, I stepped across the threshold, watching dust rise like magician's smoke and swirl lazily downward in the blades of sunlight.

Thousands of times over the past fifteen years I'd tried to imagine myself coming back here. Some days I could smell and taste every detail of the place. Other days it was nothing but roiling grey static without any shape or clarity.

But standing there that morning, it felt like I'd never gone away. The dark flowered runner vaulted straight through the house, from the wide front foyer to the kitchen at the rear. A parlor behind glass doors opened to the right, the formal dining room was on the left, and three silent bedrooms flanked the hall behind them. The bathroom was entered through the kitchen, and a screened porch led to the wire-fenced backyard. Everything smelled of mold, summer heat, and Estee Lauder Youth Dew perfume, as if Grandma had just left for Sunday service.

Like many women of her generation, Grandma purchased a set of furniture when her marriage was young, and grew old with it. The high-backed sofa, with its matching burgundy-brocaded armchairs, was covered with a knitted white afghan. A glass case beside the door contained the porcelain figurines I loved to polish, her gentle hands guiding my fingers, back when I was a kid. The spinet, now sporting a coat of dust, stood open, the keys yellowed. I touched one and listened to the uncertain sound swallowed whole by the house.

Once she would have wanted me to play it in her honor, but it had been years since I'd touched a single key. Fifteen years since I'd stood in this room. Fifteen years since I'd heard Corinthia Bibb Castle's calm, teacherly voice.

The dining room was prepared for guests, with Grandma's Belgian lace tablecloth, a wedding gift from my grandfather, spread across the wide mahogany table where my father and his brothers had eaten as boys. I wondered whether her friends had gathered there to celebrate her in death, or if someone had emptied the credenza of the crystal and silver to prepare it to be sold.

I made my way carefully down the hall, listening for the tale-tell creak in the planks just adjacent to her bedroom. The kitchen was perfectly ordered, with Grandma's ancient silver toaster leashed by its thick electric cord, the fridge humming loudly in the corner, and her decorative plates with images of Dr. King and the Kennedy brothers hung in places of honor over the sink.

Standing stock-still, I peered through the kitchen window into the yard. My gaze fastened on the picnic table beneath the enormous oak, and the tire swing hanging from a branch. The image came back of the elfin girl and her boyish best friend playing football with a muscled young man. Howling with laughter, we tugged at his arms and legs, trying and trying to stop him as he out-ran us in the summer sun.

Nina. And Gideon. And me. Years ago. A lifetime ago. Can you really love someone, more than anything on earth, your whole lifetime long?

Stupid question. A child's question, because Gideon was gone. His sister was gone. Nina and Gideon Price, like my Grandma, were fifteen years of gone.

And shit: I was done thinking. After six hundred miles of August asphalt, my clothes were glued to my sweat-soaked body, my head ached, and I couldn't manage another moment of the memories that were already strangling my heart. Unzipping my jeans, I dropped my pants and stepped out of my panties, using my left foot to disentangle them from my right. I peeled off my tee shirt and bra in one wrenching shrug and stood for a moment, my skin sticky and damp, before walking to the bathroom sink. Removing a towel from a drawer, I wet it in the thin stream of lukewarm water and began to scrub.

It didn't take long. There really isn't all that much to wash, and like a lot of people who've been through some crazy brain shit, I really don't care if I stink. The exhaustion brought on by the bludgeoning Blissfield heat, the long drive and the deepest sadness I had ever known—even deeper than my anger—led me straight to Grandma's bed. Ignoring the dust, the cobwebs, and the smell of wet rot, I stretched out on the chenille spread, my face in her pillow, my arms flung wide, and wept until sleep buried me.

* * * * * * *

The sky, a sharp silver-blue, is ripe with birdsong. We're riding our bikes to school, and Nina is peddling beside me, talking about how stupid Bill Sikes was for killing Nancy in *Oliver Twist*. Gideon, all jeans and faded red tee-shirt, rides a few feet behind us, ever silent and attentive. I haven't read the book, so I'm listening hard, figuring that whoever she was, Nancy must have been real stupid to let herself get beaten to death by her boyfriend. I mean, women mainly get killed when they don't have the guts to fight back, right?

I open my mouth, intending to explain this to Nina, but instead I woke up. Confused, it took me a few seconds to realize I was back in Blissfield, soaked in sweat in Grandma's bed, and that it was already dusk.

The lamp beside the bed wouldn't work, so I went around looking for a fuse box. I finally found it behind the photographs crowding the credenza. I turned on a light and sat in the silence, smoking a Camel, listening to the crickets and looking at the black and white images of my grandmother's face. *My* face. Hearing her throbbing laugh as she tucked me in at night. Seeing her hands as she guided Nina's fingers beside the needle of her old steel Singer.

Retrieving my duffle bag from the trunk of the jeep, I changed into a pair of oversized black running pants and a loose navy tee-shirt with a neckline that hid my scar. After rinsing my face in the sink, I smoothed back my hair, which had frizzled like bacon in the August humidity, wrapped it in a red bandana, and without make-up, headed back to the jeep. I knew I looked just one ladder rung from homeless, but I needed to eat, and had to find food before Blissfield shut down completely. I also knew that if I was going out at night it would be easier—and safer—for me to look like I just quit picking tobacco in one of those fields along the highway.

Driving the half-mile into town was strangely satisfying; so little had changed that I might have been my kidself again. The air was hot and thick with the scents of cut grass and hot asphalt and damp earth, yet there was a blessed end-of-day coolness that promised mist the next morning.

The brick post office, hardly bigger than a garage, still had parking spaces for only two cars. The whitefolks' high school, coiffed with low hedges and shuttered for the summer, dominated the town's one boulevard. The surrounding plantation-style houses, maintained a masterful white, were the oldest and most elegant homes in Blissfield, some dating to well before Emancipation. Peonies surrounded the Methodist church, hydrangeas the Episcopalian, and every blade of grass was trimmed and well-watered, like the set of a Hollywood movie.

Then I crossed the invisible barrier and entered East Blissfield. No family restaurants here—just as in years past, white people hung out on Main Street, and brown folks frequented two or three establishments on the eastern edge of town. Peeling cinder-block buildings with hand painted signs: *Bobbi's Bar-B-Q, Wings-2-Go* and *Candace's Chitterlings*—enticed a few rusting detroits and battered pick-ups,

11

their windows down and Kool and the Gang chanting "*get down on it!*" to their carry-out customers.

At last I rolled into the weed-and-gravel lot outside Whelan's, a square, poured-concrete roadhouse that had welcomed generations of Black people to fraternize after dark, when no other public facility in Blissfield would do so. I knew this because Grandma often talked about the fights and shootings and corn liquor and cheap cognac consumed at Whelan's.

The place was a legend.

Of course I had never been inside: I was on a bus and being shipped out of Blissfield before my eighteenth birthday, and no one, and I mean *no one,* would have dared to serve Corinthia Castle's granddaughter any liquor. Well, no one Black, that is.

Ruby coughed as I pulled up the handbrake, then stalled beside an ancient orange BMW with round taillights and a rusting license plate wired to its frame. A battered Impala and a small herd of trucks nested haphazardly on the grass and gravel lot. Earth, Wind and Fire—"*ohhh, after the love is gone"*— poured through the open screen door, along with the heady scrum of frying lard and blue cigar haze. Lighting a Camel, I locked my wallet in the glove box and climbed out of the jeep, touched her roof for luck, and made my way to the door.

To me, bars are like snake pits: if you're dumb enough to end up in one, something shitty is guaranteed to happen before you get out. Every woman on earth knows there's an asshole in every corner of every establishment dedicated to getting drunk and getting laid; add to that my small frame and unwillingness to flirt, which drunks always mistake for fear. It took me years of therapy, and several serious self-defense courses to find the guts to go out with my co-workers. And even when my girls were close to the table, and right beside me on the dance floor, I was always aware of every glance in my direction, every hand aiming to grope me, every man who wanted to—

Flickering tea lights on Whelan's battered tables, and neon lights behind the bar, welcomed a crowd that seemed to include random folks from the entire Black half of the county. There was no question I fit in: lots of the men were still sporting their soiled work shirts and trousers, while others were stylin' in stained jeans and wifebeaters. One or two even had on jed clampett overalls. But then again, the thigh-blasting hot pants on the women, whose hairstyles ranged from video-vixen weaves to sixties-defiant afros, guaranteed that no one would pay any attention to me. I was so unremarkable I fit right in.

Heat sizzled from the kitchen, which was visible through a small window at one end of the counter. Though it was against the law, cigarette smoke wafted between the tight shoals of drinkers, and the sudden shush of the taps, followed by the sharp click of glass on zinc, added punctuation to the scene. A couple of men looked my way, sized me up and lost interest instantly. The music changed: "*Seems like everything good is bad, and everything bad...*"

"Hello, Cuz."

The bartender, a sweating, heavily-muscled, burnt-sienna man with the eyes of a cop, greeted me. He swung down the bar, a damp towel over his shoulder, and slid a plastic ashtray my way. I saw the holster strapped bandit style over his

Santa belly, beneath a loose-fitting denim vest. This man was no Jesse Brantley, whose cool left an ice-blue sheen on everything he touched. This man didn't waste time on making peace.

"Hey," I replied, slipping one hip up onto the edge of a barstool. He quickly assessed my bandana, tear-bloated face and nondescript attire. Single women rarely walked into a bar like Whelan's alone. That is, unless they were looking for a man. Or money. Or trouble. Sometimes unknown women were followed by unknown men with plans of their own. The bartender just needed to decide whether the baseball bat beneath the counter, or that gun nestled over his heart might need to come out anytime soon.

"Everything good is bad, and everything bad is good..."

"You from 'round here?" he asked, sounding just like a cop, too.

"Yes and no," I answered, lifting my face to the neon. "Can I still get something to eat?"

"Barbeque alright?"

"Sure."

"Fries and slaw?"

"Even better," I said.

"Drink?"

I paused, knowing it was a mistake even before I said it: "Water."

His eyes narrowed suspiciously.

"I'm driving," I explained. His eyes became a squint. I dug in my pocket. "What do I owe you?"

"Four-fifty. Five if you believe in tipping."

"Throw in some cornbread, I'll make it six."

He laughed, liking that answer, and moved away to put in my order.

The fries, thick chunks of potatoes covered with coarse-chopped cole slaw, came out first, followed by a white bread bun heaped with shredded pork.

"Extra sauce?"

I shook my head.

"Where you from again?" he asked, brows raised.

"Ohio."

"Girl, we got to fix that!"

I laughed and his eyes smiled, so I broke down and ordered a beer. Though I was still fucking scared of alcohol, I'd taught myself to sip a little brew when I needed to build a bridge or break some ice. Paula often commented that it was a miracle that all those months of intravenous opioids hadn't turned me into a junkie, but watching my father get high and kill my mother a little bit every day—before finishing the job and going to work on me—seemed the perfect argument against me doing anything that might loosen my grip on reality.

The bartender returned with a High Life and a bottle of shit-brown, home-brew hot sauce. As I ate, I surveyed the room's reflection in the mirror behind the counter. Many empty dishes and beer bottles covered the small tables, and from time to time a customer gathered them up and carried them to the kitchen window. The customer then returned to the bar and, paying for another round of drinks, carried new bottles and glasses back to the tables. A woman got up and took a seat on a man's lap, and he moved on the spindly chair to better appreciate her hips. A cry went up as someone lost a card game in the back. The only people who seemed to be working in the place were the cook and the bartender.

After a crackling pause, Randy Crawford, with her hen-scratch voice, started bringing a little street life to this outpost in the tobacco fields. I smiled, listening to her words. The bartender returned with a hunk of cornbread, swimming in more of the sauce. He hovered as if he wanted to see if I could take it. I thought I recognized him. He recognized me, too.

"You Miss Corinne's babygirl," he said with absolute certainty.

"Wow. You're good."

He laughed like a man who enjoyed laughing. "Naw. You look in a mirror lately? Thought I seen a ghost."

I shrugged, knowing I'd already lost that battle.

"*Dayum*," he continued, whistling through his teeth. "It's been a good few years. In fact, you was wearing maryjanes last time I seen you."

Concentrating on my plate, I managed to avoid his eyes. He leaned on the counter, his face inches from mine. "Come down to close things out? They say nothin' but death'll bring some people home." He paused, bringing his face a little closer. "Sorry 'bout your grandma."

I finally looked up. "Me, too."

He pulled his hand-towel from his shoulder and began wiping down the counter. "Loved that woman! Miss Corinne taught me to read and write a million years ago. Always found me something to do 'round her house when I needed a coupla bills. Wrote a letter to get my cousin out the joint. Didn't work—he still got four to go—but she was willin' to try."

I sipped my beer and let tears crowd my eyes. I figured he wouldn't see them in the semi-darkness, and would understand completely if he could.

"I guess the place coming to you?" he asked.

I shrugged.

"You gon' sell?"

Chewing, I shrugged again.

"Nice house," he remarked. "Probably needs some work."

I looked pointedly away.

He chuckled. "Private type, huh? That's alright." Someone called him from the other end of the counter and he trundled off, the wet cloth again thrown over his shoulder. My eyes went back to the mirror behind the bar, but instead of eyeing the other customers for signs of trouble, I carefully appraised myself.

He was right: everything about me was Castle, and I couldn't for the life of me understand why. My mother's high breasts, small waist, tapered hips and long, shapely legs made her a haunting African talisman. Her smooth black skin welcomed bright yellows and reds, and her eyes, a shade or two lighter than her skin, were impossibly loving.

My father, by contrast, was lean, coiled, fisted, mean. Copley's gaze was sharp and watchful, and his hands could as easily defend as destroy. I shared his small, fleshless frame, mistrustful eyes and curlynappy hair.

Not one single ounce of my mother had made its way into me.

In truth, both Copley and I were molded from Grandma's blend of Africa and the high cheeks, almond eyes and strong jaw of the local Chowanac people. I wasn't sure if that made us attractive or not. I only knew one thing: for better or worse, it sure made us strong.

Because indeed, Corinthia Bibb Castle was one strong woman. One evening, when I first came to live with her, I watched her back down a drunken redneck who staggered out of a bar on Main Street as we came out of the pharmacy. He looked at me and opened his mouth to put into words what was in his eyes. The problem was that he made the mistake of looking at Grandma first, and when he met her steely gaze his mouth closed. He leaned heavily against a lamppost and watched in silence as my grandmother, whip straight, face calm, walked right by him, with me, like her chick, right behind. From that moment I knew I was never in danger when surrounded by the force field that was Corinthia Bibb Castle.

Yet Grandma also had an inner calm that made everyone around her speak quietly. Even if you were dedicated to kicking somebody's ass, when Corinthia Castle was nearby, you behaved like you were in your Sunday Best.

Of course, with my father it was a different story. All the qualities that made his mother strong were out of proportion in him, so her courage became his cruelty, her passion his gunpowder temper. She wanted others to live better lives, and he only cared about himself. How else can you explain what he did to my momma and me?

Randy Crawford's voice faded and the bar voices blended into a heavy sea, the baritones drowning her soprano, the trilling, birdlike laughter of alcohol turning words into indistinct music. The rich darkness of the place encouraged folks to try what they might think twice about trying in the daylight. This was the kind of place where simple slights quickly exploded into violent rages. I didn't need to be in the mix when those storms broke, 'cause I'd made it out of that place once and sure as hell didn't want to go back.

Harold Melvin began singing *"the love I lost was a good love; the love I lost was complete love..."*

"Listen up, babygirl," the barman said, reappearing across the counter. Reaching below, he flipped a handle and beer swirled into a glass. "It's good you came back. Blissfield's part of your blood."

"No doubt."

"So you down here from—" he chuckled as he topped off the foam—"was that New York?"

I shook my head.

"Chicago?"

I shook my head again. Someone shouted with laughter behind us and he shot a look over my shoulder into the drinking darkness. When his eyes returned, he leaned even closer. "D.C.?"

"O-hi-o."

"That's right." He knotted his brows. You from Cleveland? They got a good team."

"They've got LeBron, and no."

"Then where?"

"Akron," I said.

"Never heard of it."

"LeBron's from there."

"Okay: heard of it once."

He stood tall and pivoted away, throwing an imaginary lay-up and chuckling. Gracefully he slid the beer the length of the counter to a man staring up at the TV.

Suddenly I remembered his name: *Bruce*. I had seen him in my grandmother's yard on Saturday afternoons all those years ago, helping out with repairs. He'd been thinner then, but courteous and pleasant to her and completely uninterested in me. It surprised me that he remembered me at all.

I lit another Camel. I hadn't smoked in years, but I'd blown a wad of my dwindling cash on a whole carton of Camel non-filters at a rest stop somewhere south of D.C. I hate the smell, but love their taste of liquid death, and I'd had to shove the carton deep beneath the opposite seat to stop myself from smoking nonstop the rest of the way to Blissfield. In the end, smoking required enough active concentration to keep me from falling asleep at the wheel and going over a guardrail, or ending up lost somewhere in the back hills of Appalachia.

Bruce was back. He slid even closer across the counter, his thick forearms carpeted with curling shiny hairs.

"You ain't really changed much since back then."

It was my turn to chuckle.

"No, for real," he insisted. "You still got that young girl face."

Now he was trying to hit on me. Though it didn't happen often, sometimes, especially in the dark, a man gave it a sporting try. That is, until he got a closer look at my eyes.

"Maybe that's because nothing changes in Blissfield," I answered.

He shrugged. "I reckon that's another reason why people come back. Feels safe. Feels like home." He said that last word with another question in his eyes.

I sipped my beer. What was the point in answering? He already figured he had me figured.

"Heard 'bout your daddy," he continued, still looking directly into my face. "We was all sad about what happened. I saw your momma once, when y'all came down for a visit a long time ago. You was just a little thing—about yay-high"—he flattened his palm against the edge of the counter—"and I brought some greens from my mother's garden over to Miss Corinne's to thank her for something. I walked into the backyard and I heard the ladies talking. I looked in the window and saw this fo-*ine* woman standing by the stove. A beautiful, *chocolate* princess! I was only twelve or thirteen, but I knew if y'all moved down here, there was bound to be some trouble."

He looked briefly away, as if, considering how she died, he realized the insensitivity of his comment. "I remember your daddy, too, from way back when I was just a kid. He was the star of the football team. Quarterback. Real fast and real tricky. My father took me to the games 'cause his younger brother played tight end. He was fast, too, but not as fast as Copley—"

"That's all done and dusted," I said, lifting the bottle so high the beer arced into my mouth.

"Come on, sweetheart. Let an old man reminisce."

"You're not old and you're not reminiscing."

"What am I doing, then?"

"You're digging, and I'm telling you, there's no diamonds in that mine."

Now he laughed. "You really think there's something about your family I don't already know? Hell, that all of Blissfield don't know, inside and out? Baby, the Castles were better than the comics. Better than TV. Better than goddamn Vegas—"

"You win!" I said, faking laughter to mask my irritation.

"Everybody loved your grandmother," he continued. "No one understands how such a wonderful woman could possibly have given birth to a man—excuse me for being so blunt—like your father."

"What about his brothers?" I asked, ashamed that I was asking a stranger about shit I should have already known.

"Aw, shoot, girl—anything stupid they ever did, times *ten*, still paled in comparison to Copley. Your daddy was the smartest, coolest, strongest, and, yes, the fastest motherfucker anybody'd ever seen. But he was also one evil son of a—"

"Old news, Bruce—"

"God-doggit," he said. "You *do* remember me!"

"I never said I didn't."

"But you didn't say you did."

"Like you said, I was just a girl."

"You weren't acting like no girl then, and we both know that."

So he knew. He knew at least something about what went down fifteen years ago. Which meant that, indeed, *everyone* in this messed-up backwater of a town had heard some version of what happened between Nina and Gideon and me—

"Want another?" Now Bruce was openly appraising me with bait in his eyes. He had already brought a bottle out from the cooler behind the counter, and was preparing to pop the cap. Barry White began murmuring in the background.

"It's getting late," I said.

He sucked his teeth loudly. "Never too late for a cold beer on a hot night."

I made myself laugh. He laughed too, though neither one of us had said anything remotely funny.

"By the way," I said, raising my voice over Barry's throttle, "since you remember so much, maybe you can help me with something. I used to hang out with a brother and sister—"

"Now who would that be?" he asked, his hands growing still on the bottle.

"Nina and Gideon—Nina and Gideon Price."

He set the bottle firmly on the counter, wiped his hands on his towel, and crossed his arms over his barrel chest. "Why you asking me?"

"You said the Castles were better than the comics and TV—'"

"And you said that was back in the Stone Age."

"Do Nina and Gideon still live around here?"

"Damn, girl—you think I got time to keep up with every man, woman and child in this town?"

"It's not like we're in New York," I said.

"It's not like *I'm* looking for them."

"Wow. They steal your marbles or something?"

"If they did, it wouldn't be your problem."

"I'm just asking if they're still in town."

"Check the phone book."

Our eyes locked, and we were both surprised at the stoniness in each other's gaze. He whistled softly. "Yes ma'am—I can see you tough. Tough like your daddy. Don't got much of your grandmomma in you."

On another night I would have argued that point. That night, however, I wasn't in the mood. "Hope you're wrong," I said, fishing in my pockets.

"Don't you want this?" He gestured toward the bottle. "Might chill things out a bit."

"I'm chilled enough," I lied. Digging out a ten-spot, I set it beneath the bottle on the counter and slid off the barstool.

"Look," he said, raising his voice over the music, "I pissed you off. My bad. You never know what folks don't want to hear till it's already been said." His gaze travelled over my head to a pair of men in filthy coveralls, who were standing too close to a guy wearing a regular shirt and dark pants.

"Remember," he continued, his eyes still fixed on the men, "it's different for other folks than it is for you. Everybody done business with everybody here. Shit go back generations. Sometime it's hard to let it go." The men in the coveralls finished their conversation and moved toward the door. A moment later Whelan's was anointed with the sylvan voice of Al Green— "*spending my days, thinking about you, girl...*"

For the millionth time an image of Gideon's face sprang into my mind. Calling on every ounce of self-control the Old Man had taught me, I ignored the bottle, the bar and the bartender, and turning, I walked out into the night. The August black had grown ever heavier, mosquito-thick, and a band of fog lay low around the hedges. The sweetness of pollen-heavy blossoms hung suspended like a curtain as I passed the men, climbed into Ruby and turned the key.

Suddenly I didn't want to go back to Grandma's house. I didn't want the rooms to throw back shadows of her face and voice. I couldn't lie in her bed, fighting my feelings. Most of all, I didn't want to be up all night thinking about Gideon.

I hit the highway and hurtled down 158, not really caring if a cop decided to get involved. The windows down and the cloth roof peeled away, I felt like nothing in the world would ever get in my way. Fiddling with the radio, I caught me some Bill Withers. For some reason his voice conjured no demons from my past. I thanked the lord for sending Bill Withers to me that night.

After what seemed like a very long time I pulled back into the red dirt driveway and let the engine die, my eyes fixed on the one light in the faded yellow house.

Why the hell had I come back to Blissfield? Why had I set myself up to get the last surviving part of me destroyed—this time for good?

Slowly I climbed out of the jeep, understanding it was too late to change anything, now.

two.

Later that morning, sprawled on the center of the chenille bedspread, I worked my way through Grandma's phone book, fingering the bills, receipts, scraps of paper with names and numbers, to-do lists, and two pictures of me from when I was nothing more than a scruff of twiggy limbs and boyish frizzy hair.

Though I knew I should be looking for her will, a deed to the house, or at least the name of her mouthpiece, in all honesty I was searching for tightly folded bits of notebook paper—scraps of handwritten, cartoon-doodled messages slipped into my backpack between classes—the composed, virginal missives from Gideon. Though my head insisted this was a waste of time, my heart needed to prove that my memories weren't just opioid-induced hallucinations, made up during my long recovery from a place too dark to bear.

As I read the brittle papers, someone knocked. Gently. Almost feebly. I found my feet and made my way up the hall to the front. A wide, flowered figure filled the glass oval in the door.

"Princess?"

My heart leapt. That was Grandma's name for me and I'd never permitted anyone else to use it. I jerked the door open with the stupid hope that some monumental mistake had been made—that Corinthia Bibb Castle would be standing there, still alive.

Despite the damp heat, the beige face that met mine was powdered smooth as water on a windless day. The bluish eyes, by contrast, were cloudy as an old mirror. Strands of white strayed from beneath a straw hat, faded plastic roses clustered on one side of the brim.

"I didn't mean to frighten you," the woman said matter-of-factly, heavy arms clasping a lumpy canvas bag to her pink housedress. "I saw the foreign license plate and realized it must be you. I'm Adelaide Mitchell, your neighbor across the street. People used to say I favored your grandmother. Of course, I'm at least a couple of inches taller, and bigger-boned, too. You probably don't remember me."

"Why—why of course I remember you, Mrs. Mitchell," I responded with the answer-by-rote politeness of Grandma's well-raised girl. Though I was smiling, my hand tightened on the doorknob.

Her eyes flickered over me, then moved quickly above my shoulder, trying to see inside. "Well, I'm surprised, considering how long it's been since you lived here. I don't think I've seen you since—"

"That's true," I said quickly, a shard surfacing in my heart despite my resolve to keep my emotions on lockdown.

"You certainly do take after—"

"My grandmother."

19

"That's right, sweetheart. You know, Corinne was like a sister to me, and I miss her more than words can describe. We grew up just two years apart and even went to college at the same time. Of course, that was because I was advanced in my classes. Naturally, back in our day, girls could only be teachers or nurses. We both chose to teach, and we even roomed together down in Raleigh when we got our first jobs. It was such a wonderful time, just after the war! Teachers were very respected in those days, so all the young gentlemen—"

Perhaps reacting to what she saw in my eyes, she reached out and touched my arm. "I'm so sorry, sweetheart. I'm sure this isn't the best time. You must be completely puttered out! I just came by with some vegetables from my garden and to ask if you needed anything."

"Thanks so much," I said, "but I—"

"Don't be silly," she said, pushing the bag into my arms. "It's just some carrots and tomatoes." I accepted the gift, but braced myself more squarely in the doorframe. "I'd invite you in, Mrs. Mitchell, but I'm afraid I haven't unpacked and I don't have anything to offer—"

"Hush," she crooned, leaning forward to kiss my cheek. "Like I said—your grandmother was like a sister to me, which means you're my niece." The scent of stale Wind Song wafted around her. "How are you managing here all by yourself? That is, unless you're not here by yourself?"

"I'm doing okay, and yes, I'm alone."

"That's too bad. I thought perhaps your special someone came down with you."

"No, I—"

"And no old friends stopped by?"

Something in her tone made me pause. "Old friends?" I said.

"I thought you may still be in touch with some of the young people you used to know."

I shook my head, not trusting myself to speak.

"Well, most of the young people in our community are long gone. They go to the big city and forget all about their home." Her eyes locked with mine. "It really is a shame you missed your grandmother's memorial service. It was beautiful, and at least three hundred people attended—Caucasians, too! Of course, since your grandmother preferred to be cremated, there was no graveside—"

"I'm sorry, Mrs. Mitchell, but you've caught me at a bad time," I said, pushing back against the wave of anger that was threatening my flimsy wall of civility.

"Please, baby, call me Aunt Adie—"

"—and I'm still pretty worn out from the trip."

"Then you'll be here for a little while?"

"I'm really not sure."

She paused. "The house is coming to you, I suppose?"

"I don't—"

Her bluish eyes fixed on mine. "I hope you're not planning to sell this property to the first person that comes along. Some people may think they have a right to things they didn't earn, and your grandmother wouldn't want just *anybody* living in—"

"I haven't made any—"

"—her home. After all, it was in your family for decades, and it would be such a shame if someone who really didn't deserve—"

"—decisions. You'll have to excuse—"

"—it thought they had a claim on the property—"

"—me right now. I really am very busy."

"—and it's your duty to protect your grandmother's good name!"

"Thank you for the vegetables, Mrs. Mitchell." I stepped back and closed the door firmly. Undeterred, she raised her voice.

"Now Princess, don't you be making any decisions too fast, you hear?"

Leaning against the wood, heart pounding, I listened as she slowly made her way down the porch steps and out into the street. After a few moments my anger subsided, but something in her words grated.

What was my duty to Corinthia Bibb Castle, the woman who put me on the bus to my death, then never so much as called or wrote after I survived? Had she ignored me in her will, the way she'd ignored me in life? If so, it might only be a matter of days, even hours, before the whole town knew I was nothing but a squatter in the leftovers of my late grandmother's life.

* * * * * * *

So I got serious: I found a pair of heavy work gloves and an apron. The manager of the Piggly Wiggly met me at the rear of the store and helped me fill the jeep with empty boxes. Once back at Grandma's house, dressed to protect my arms and legs from—god forbid—deadly snake or spider bites, and with my hair wrapped like Rosie the Riveter, I started searching again, but this time, with a sense that I was working against a clock.

My grandmother's past soon became three piles: the useless, the priceless and the odd. Useless meant forty-year old grocery receipts. Priceless was the quirky costume jewelry, buttons for JFK and LBJ, and a tarnished silver cufflink engraved with the letters *JRC* and decorated with inlaid mother-of-pearl. The "odd" consisted of those things which fit into neither of the other two categories: a sheer silk, but permanently stained blouse embroidered with tiny sunflowers; a pair of kid's ballet slippers that might have once been mine and many, many, many Book of the Month Club volumes.

Then came the photographs: black and white. Sepia. Faded color. Intensely colored. Photos of folks whose names I might have learned from my grandmother, but whose faces meant nothing to me now. My grandmother, young and carefully posed beside her impeccably dressed, long-absent husband. Three boys, then two young men in uniform, and then a third, whose face I shared. The oldest two were tall, sturdy, and very pale-skinned, like their father. The third, Copley Nehemiah Castle, was a male version of his mother, with a small frame, toffee skin, freckles, and piercing husky's eyes.

Copley. My father. The male version of me.

As I stared at the photos, the fate of Grandma's two oldest sons, my uncles Paul and Jeremiah, resurfaced. Having broken her heart by joining the Army rather than going to college, this photo must have been taken shortly before they died in a freak accident that my grandmother once told me she'd never gotten over.

Thus my father was only a young teen when he suddenly became Grandma's only child. Though he should have chosen to do everything possible to ease his mother's grief, the photos revealed a young man with steely selfish eyes and a malt-soaked grin, always a grin, as if he lived inside a joke and didn't have to pay rent. There was something else, too—a weird, restless vibrancy that translated into a kind of savage beauty. It was hard to see the real Copley Castle because of all that beauty. Except for the eyes: The truth was in Copley Castle's eyes.

I discovered a yellowed envelope stuffed with photos of me, Bethany Celeste, my grandmother's restless Janus of a grandchild. I had the deep toffee skin, dancing freckles and bright, piercing eyes, but my father's meanness was absent from the face of my childself. I hadn't had the chance—though it would come soon enough—to try to murder anybody.

God knows I would soon enough try.

Working in a kind of fever, I stopped only to eat when I felt too hungry to go on, and, despite a gnawing headache, to sleep. I didn't sleep much, but when I laid down my exhaustion was threaded with a sense of mounting panic: the house was yielding up Grandma's life, but there was still no sign of a deed or a will, or any trace of Gideon or Nina.

And of course I'd looked in the phone book. For years I'd scoured the Internet and every social media site that existed. I searched their names so many times it felt like an addiction. God knows how many letters I'd written, though not one letter had ever been returned. And now, against all hope, I just prayed that I'd find a clue that might actually lead me back to them. Or lead them back to me.

Though I won't lie. It wasn't all that hard to find Gideon.

Because Gideon was with me all the time. Sometimes we were lying on the floor of the abandoned shack, his enormous hand gently kneading my belly, his lips lightly brushing mine. I could smell his clean, fleshy scent, taste his sweet breath, sense his mounting heat and careful, careful restraint. And I wanted him so badly I could scarcely breathe.

The worst part of it was how stupid it felt to dream about someone I'd lost so long ago. I mean, I'd spent every moment of the past fifteen years making it clear to anyone who'd listen that I didn't need anyone, because let's be honest: I'm not the kind of woman people fall in love with.

* * * * * * *

I got up early on the third day, and responding to something that was tugging at what was left of my heart, I climbed into Ruby and drove down 158, past miles of thick-sewn tobacco fields, to take on the memories waiting for me at Holy Redeemer Baptist Church.

Coming up on the building much too fast, I skidded in the red mud as I turned into the drive. Wrestling Ruby across the thick grooves of the dirt lot, I managed to bring her to a stop beneath the swaying branches of a rustling willow tree. In the rearview mirror I caught sight of a rickety man in loose workpants, sporting a plaid golf-cap as he emerged from a Buick so enormous it literally dwarfed my jeep. He stared a few hard moments before, unexpectedly limber, he strolled across the muddy tire-grooves and leaned in my window.

"Bless your heart, Miss Bethany," he said in a gentle voice. "Glad to see you're back. I'm so very sorry about your grandmother."

No longer surprised to be recognized by a stranger, I accepted without question that he matched my face to the Castles. "Thank you, Sir," I replied, automatically respectful.

"You remember me? Name's Saunders. Joe Saunders. Used to bring Miss Corinne vegetables from my garden when you lived there all those years ago. Took you and your Grandma shopping in Roanoke Rapids pretty frequently." He nodded his head toward my chin. "Even drove you to the doctor the day you got that scar."

Involuntarily I touched the place where I'd hit the floor after being tripped, quite deliberately, by my lab partner.

"Oh—oh my god, I mean, *goodness*, yes! I'm so sorry I didn't recognize you! I've had so much on my mind, I just—" And then I also remembered that he was the person who drove me and Grandma to the Greyhound terminal in Roanoke Rapids on that Christmas Eve, the day my long exile began.

His skin was deep brown, his face unnaturally smooth despite his advanced age, with bright gentle eyes and a hug of a smile. His silver moustache was groomed to reveal his good strong teeth, and I saw traces of white growing thick beneath the cap.

He must have read what was on my face, but instead of expressing any concern, his smile deepened, the lines on his thin face swallowing up his eyes. "I don't blame you for forgetting me," he said. "You been gone a long time."

"No—I *do* remember! You and my grandma were, well, she used to say you were 'best friends'!"

He laughed sadly and glanced away. "Yes, that's right. Always wanted to be more to Miss Corinne, but she got married once, and after her husband died she used to say she wouldn't hear of going through it a second time." His gaze returned to me.

"But how about you, Miss Bethany? Goodness knows I would have recognized you without a candle at the stroke of midnight. You're the spitting image of your grandmother, if you don't mind me saying so. It's such a blessing to have you back."

"It's really—" I started to give him a polite response, but something in his eyes seemed to ask for honesty. "Well, to tell you the truth, it's not so easy to be here."

"That's understandable. We was all very sad about what happened with your father."

"Thanks," I murmured, looking away.

He waited a beat. When I looked at him again I saw deep thought in his eyes, and he wavered a few more seconds, considering what to do, before coming to a silent decision.

"Like to see the church?" he asked, once again the perfect gentleman. "Come on in. Your grandmother would be so pleased you stopped by."

He led me into the wide, white, open-beamed room with its polished oak pews and choir stalls. Though it was mid-week, bouquets of orange gladiolas brightened the pale light streaming through the grey-stained windows. The air was close, but smelled of varnished wood and fresh paint.

"You know, everyone in your family was baptized here," he remarked, pointing to a white-tiled basin, the size of a children's pool, in the rear of the church. "This building was put up right after slavery by four families, including yours and mine. Nobody knew if the white folks was going to let it stand, considering it was on land given to our people by the Union soldiers before they moved out. Somehow, over the years, nobody seen fit to do it any harm. Lots of our churches gone up in flames, and the law never seem to catch the people who sets those fires. I guess we been lucky."

I glanced toward the pristine altar, now remembering how I waited in the pews while my grandmother, with other women of the church, prepared the church for Sunday services. I was never bored watching them; it seemed their hands worked in a shared rhythm and sometimes, when the right ladies got together, they even sang in throbbing, multipart harmonies.

"I know you'll find this hard to believe, but I also seen your grandma get baptized here when she was just a little girl."

I glanced at him quickly. He was old, but not old enough to make that statement.

"I can guess what you thinking," he said amiably. "Everybody say I don't look my age. But the fact is, my mother and your great-grandmother was friends. When I was just a little lad, your great-grandmother would drive up in her Model-T, your grandma bouncing around in the back, and the two ladies would have tea while your grandma and I played in my backyard. I had a big brown dog called Clark Gable. He loved me, and when your grandma and I got too close to the road, Clark Gable would bark until my mother came out. I usually got a switching because I was supposed to be watching your grandma, but of course it didn't hurt."

"Didn't Grandma get a switching, too?"

"Never. She was this cute, tiny little thing. She knew how to stand there, round-eyed, those Shirley Temple curls all over her head, looking like the very picture of innocence. No matter what she did, my momma blamed me! But it was alright: I would have taken all the switchings in the world for her."

"Did you know my grandfather, too?"

"Julius? I did indeed! He came from a town just across the county line, and married your grandma when she was fresh back from her first teaching job. Neither one of them was too keen on it. It was the fathers made them do it—you see, they was born around the turn of the century and had very old-fashioned ideas about girls staying close to home and taking care of their elderly parents. Besides, your grandmother's father liked Julius. Saw him as a 'gentleman farmer.' Didn't want your grandmother getting any big ideas about going away with one of those city boys she met at college, or one of us country boys with nothing to give her."

"I'm surprised you remember so——"

"How could I forget? I was courting Corrie, myself!" he laughed quietly, slipping his hands into his pockets. "I had my heart set on your grandmother since we was in diapers. Problem was, Julius had a well-stuffed mattress and I was just a local boy, glad to become a postman. It didn't much matter, however. Your grandma and I was friends for many, many years. In some ways, we was probably happier than if——"

"——You'd been married?" I said.

He laughed again, shaking his head slowly. "People in my generation wasn't interested in Hollywood ideas about marriage. You met somebody and settled down and done the best you could. We was glad to have a partner to help us get through life."

"So she never really loved him?"

"Oh, I don't know how your grandmother really felt about Julius. At first he lived with her in that house, but after she had the boys, it seemed like he lost interest in his family. Some said he went up north to pursue his business interests. Others say he was pursuing more personal concerns. Your grandmother never had much to say about it at all."

"Wasn't she sad he was gone?"

"Well, lots of couples lived apart in those days. Men found work in other cities, or joined up and went off to fight in one of the wars. She wasn't the only woman raising her children alone."

"What about my grandma's older sons? Do you remember them, too?"

"Jerry and Paul? Of course! They was nice, smart boys. Strongly resembled their father in appearance. They looked out for each other and made your grandmother very proud. It was a terrible tragedy when they died, but back then the military always used our boys to do the things white men didn't want to do."

He led me toward the pew where I'd sat between him and Grandma every Sunday, seventeen years before. "I don't know if anyone told you, but this is where she passed," he said. I stared at the smooth, shining wood, hearing echoes of the choir, the worshippers' throbbing voices, and the pastor's spirited words.

"To tell you the truth, seemed like your grandmother lost her spirit after you was gone. She spent most of her Sundays, that is, when she felt like coming to church, right here on this bench. So that's how it happened: she was singing, and then she sat down. She leaned over and I caught her in my arms. She laid there, looking up at me. She never spoke a word. I knew she was gone when her prayer book slipped out of her hands."

I thought about that. In comparison to mine and my mother's, Corinthia Bibb Castle's death had been easy.

"Mr. Saunders, I was wondering if you could tell me——"

Several car doors slammed outside. Both of us looked toward the windows. A group of elderly men and women moved cautiously over the muddy tire tracks toward the door. He excused himself and made his way to the back of the church.

I watched him with a rush of frustration. I'd been ready to ask him why my grandmother never called, responded to my letters, or made any attempt to bring me back to Blissfield after he helped her put me on that bus. I needed to know why my grandmother threw me away, like I was a greasy bag of trash.

I looked back at the pew, remembering the smell of the wood in the Sunday heat. I was suddenly awash in my grandma's perfume and the feel of her arm, pressed lovingly against mine as we shared the prayer book. I'd been safe here, seated between this man and my grandmother. It was here, on this bench, that I'd felt Nina and Gideon's presence for the very first time.

When he returned a few minutes later, I saw I'd missed my chance.

"How long you plan to be here?" he asked, his tone unexpectedly formal. I could see more old folks standing in the foyer behind us.

"No idea," I said, slightly stung by his dismissal.

He smiled again. "You been gone a good while, Princess. Give it a little time. Time usually clears things up."

"That's what people keep telling me."

"You northern folks see things a bit different from us southerners. You all have to fight to make it through the winter, but down here we know you can't make the grass grow till it's ready."

This wasn't a question, so I didn't answer.

He paused, and trouble again clouded his eyes. "You know, when you young you live in your dreams for the future. But when you old like me, you live inside your memories of the past. There was joyful times, but there was always times of sorrow. The hardest part is to learn to balance the two."

His gaze strayed to the window where, years before, a football soaring through the sky had brought me such peace.

His voice, suddenly hoarse, broke the silence. "You don't mind if I call you Princess, do you? I know it was your grandmother's name for you."

I shook my head, though I wasn't too sure I was okay with it.

"Well, Princess," he said, "it's so nice you're here. Feels like a part of your grandma just came back, when I feared I'd lost her for good." Still he lingered, as if he had more to say. "Please do come back soon. I'm the church sexton, so I'm here most every day. I got lots more stories about your grandmother to share, and I would love the chance to know you a little bit better."

With those words he ambled back down the aisle, leaving me alone. I sank down on the pew, in the exact place where my grandma took her last breath.

I wondered if my father had ever sat there as a boy. He certainly hated the idea of church as a man. There was a church just down the block from our house in Akron, and I could see the mothers and fathers and their kids going inside every Sunday morning. I wanted to go just to see how those people behaved in their dress-up clothes. Momma longed to go, too, but Daddy always came in after dawn on Sunday mornings and would fly into a rage if anyone, or anything, woke him up. Momma sometimes tried to get me dressed in absolute silence, but if I so much as whispered she was in for a good beating. All he had to do was to look at her and she'd begin to quake.

Life had been entirely different for me here in Blissfield. From the day I arrived I'd eaten a royal breakfast every Sunday morning. Grandma dressed me in tights, pastel dresses and pressed and curled my hair.

For two years I'd gone to church, usually two or three times a week.

For two years Grandma's home, and this church, had been the center of my life.

Now I sat on Grandma's pew and waited.

Somehow, there would have to be a sign of what to do next: a redbird flying beside a crow; a sunbeam hitting the cross dead in the center, or — hell, I don't know.

Without some message, I had no idea what to do. Not that minute, not that day, or in any of the uncountable, empty, directionless days to come.

II.

akron, ohio.

1982.

three.

The Akron of my childhood was a city of derelict tire factories and a downtown solitary enough to roll bowling balls down Main Street after dark. Our neighborhood, entirely Black, consisted of neat 1930's Dutch colonials built for whites enjoying good union jobs in the tire factories. Those factories, and the white people, were long gone, and few of my neighbors had work or money. Those who were retired painted their houses, grew melons and tomatoes in their backyards and waxed their cars in their driveways in the spring and early fall. The rest of us watched as if they were aliens, for our cars were wrecks, our furniture stained and broken, and we didn't have grass. We had weeds.

My father, Copley Nehemiah Castle, washed up in Akron with his best friend from childhood, Pilate Halifax, who, like my pops, was also a bar-fighter and a card shark. Friends since the schoolyard, the two stole cars, shoplifted and drank whatever they could get their hands on, until law enforcement in Blissfield—partially out of respect for my grandma—suggested they enlist rather than spend some time behind bars.

Copley and Pilate shipped off to Vietnam and served two tours, then spent almost five additional years in the Philippines. They brawled together, shared women, got arrested on the regular, and spent their time in sweat and cement lockups, watching each other's back. My father used to say they were so close, if one saw his friend in trouble, the other caused even *more* trouble just so they could experience the outcome together.

Things started to unravel after they'd been in Akron for six months. As veterans, they'd taken advantage of a job placement program that sent them to Goodyear. They could have gone to college, bought new homes on low-interest V.A. loans, or even opened their own business. Instead, despite having good union jobs, they quickly decided that getting up in the mid-afternoon to make double overtime on the night shift messed with their all-night poker games, and made it damn near impossible to prove they were the baddest motherfuckers on the Akron streets. So they shared a room, rarely paid the rent, drank their meals and lounged outdoors when they couldn't afford an actual lounge.

One afternoon they were in Perkins Woods, a lovely hillside park of soaring oak and chestnut trees, a public swimming pool and a small, sad zoo. Copley was two Miller High Lifes in, with Pilate working hard to keep up with him. Sprawled on a park bench, my father was halfhumming a Smokey Robinson tune just loud enough to be heard by passersby. He'd left his driver's cap upside-down on the bench beside him, just in case anybody had a quarter to spare.

Pilate was the first one to lay eyes on Bebe J. He whistled low through his teeth and sat up straight on the park bench, setting down his beer. Laughing, as always, Copley leaned his head back against the top rail, as if the sight of my future mother was more than he could take. This was a game they often played: one man would spot a woman; the other would show his level of appreciation for her by the intensity of his reaction. If they both agreed that she was worth the effort, the competition began.

Brenda Berniece Johnson was making her way home from her job in a small corner liquor store at the bottom of the hill on Market Street, to her mother's house, at the top of the hill on Diagonal Road. She had been on her feet all day, and getting up that hill, even beneath the gently swaying branches of a July afternoon, was enough to make her ignore the two men drinking beer and slouching on the park bench.

"Hey, beautiful," Pilate called, doing his best imitation of Melvin Franklin, his favorite Temptation.

Bebe J kept walking, her eyes on her aching feet.

"You fine enough to make a brother get a job!" Pilate remarked, glancing sideways to see what Copley thought of his game.

Head thrown back, Copley just observed, his malamute eyes fixed keenly on the prey.

"I love the way you wearing that blouse," Pilate called out, even as she passed the men without so much as a nod. She might as well have been deaf for her reaction to Pilate's' down-home jive.

Five feet further on, there was a sudden movement as Copley, who had left the bench only three times that entire day to pee in the bushes when no one was around—sprang into action and was suddenly pacing beside her, matching her step-for-step, a beer can tucked into his palm.

After a few steps she stopped walking, uneasy. She lifted her head and risked a look at this guy who was way too close. What she saw would have stopped a smarter woman cold.

For Bebe J glimpsed her future: the child that would come within a year, the mother-in-law who'd turn out to be kinder than her own mother, and the first and last man of her life, pulled from the taffy of muscle and punk-ass energy marching stepforstep beside her, along with the riff of fear in her heartbeat.

"Good evening," Copley murmured in his softest Carolina drawl. "You sure is a lovely sight. Don't know where you going, but maybe talking to me a little while will make the trip go faster."

She hesitated. First mistake.

When he lifted the beer slowly, sipped from it and then offered it to her, she smiled shyly. Second mistake.

When he dipped his head twice to the side, enticing her to drink, she let him bring the can to her lips. He held it there until he saw the very tip of her tongue, like a kitten's, touch the sour liquid.

"What's your name, baby?" He pierced her with his keen, blue-grey, prey-loving eyes.

"Brenda—Brenda Berniece," she whispered.

"Oh, you so beautiful your momma gave you *two* names!" he purred.

She blinked, and in the instant between her lashes coming together, he had her.

That is how Copley managed to get my mother's name, phone number, and to walk her to her front door the very first time he saw her. Was he serious about her, or was it just a man-versus-man contest that he simply couldn't let Pilate win?

He didn't know or care. He met up with Bebe J three more times that week. Within four weeks, he'd moved in with her. A few months later they had a place of their own.

* * * * * * *

Things were never quite right between Copley and Pilate from that day forward. Though they still ran the streets on the nights Copley wasn't making love to Brenda Berniece in her room with the paper-thin walls right next to her mother's, the bond they'd shared since playing football, picking cotton, and carrying rifles in rice paddies clear across the world, was broken.

Copley tried to pretend he was just messing around with the lush body and gentle spirit of the woman he renamed Bebe J, but even Little Stevie Wonder could see that Copley was getting primed to lose his mind if Bebe J wasn't where he wanted her to be, whenever he wanted her to be there. He had her, but it felt like *she* had *him*.

It was on one of those nights that Copley and Bebe J were wrestling underwater, Marvin Gaye crooning on the radio, that Pilate got shot in a backroom card game. He'd won it fair and square, but he made a joke about the loser's ratty conk, and the loser decided in turn to mess Pilate's hair up permanently. By the time Copley heard the news, the room had cleared and the only things left on the stripped body were Pilate's high school ring—which was too tight for his killer to pry off his finger—and his tattoos, among them one of a lovely dancing girl, who reminded him of a woman he'd tried to bring back home with him from the Philippines.

After that, Copley went a little mad.

He started drinking a lot of gin, and imagined that Pilate's killers were after him, too—which wasn't the case—but he told himself they might try to get to him by getting a hold of Bebe J. By then I was on the way, and he was keeping her close to a prisoner in the rented, run-down house that would be my first home. He was drinking his meals while she worked in the store, and by the time she got off work he was evil drunk.

It was on one of those nights, when she came home a few minutes late, that he slapped her for the first time. She took the slap with a whimper, her slender hands covering her stinging face. He stared at the tears in her bambi eyes and realized he liked them, so soon, if she made the mistake of doing anything that displeased him, he slapped her until she begged him to stop. He particularly hated her being anywhere other than work or at home, as if the thought that she was out of his control, even for a short while, was an insult to his manhood.

Fear never kept *him* off the streets, however. In fact, playing poker in stealth games all over town was turning out to be his most reliable source of income. He selected the game after asking around to make sure none of Pilate's enemies would be there, then turned up late, played swift and hard, and left before he'd won enough to sign his own death warrant.

Now he slapped Bebe J for looking in his face, or for looking away when he wanted her to look in his face. He punched her if his food wasn't hot enough, or if the coffee was too hot when she served it. He knocked her down every once in a while just to keep in practice. Sometimes he'd even get on top of her and choke her while she tried to pull his hands away from her throat. When he let her go she'd curl up on her side, coughing and struggling not to spit up whatever had risen in her throat. He'd stand over her, watching, as if measuring the ratio between the amount of pressure he applied to her neck and how long it took her to recover.

My mother spent her evenings in the front room, watching the black and white television with the sound off so she could hear him when he hit the porch steps. If he was walking heavily, he was happily drunk, and might not hit her more than once or twice before bed. If he was moving fast, however, and particularly if he took the steps two at a time, she never knew if he'd won too much and was dodging his opponents, or whether he was broke and filled with rage. Either way, the tension that had made him the greatest quarterback in the history of Blissfield, North Carolina, now made him as sensitive as a landmine set to explode at the slightest provocation.

Along with the beatings came his precise and imaginative verbal cruelty. He found fault with every part of her body, face, walk, voice, hair, smell—even her terrorized silence. He used language I didn't recognize as foul until teachers starting washing my classmates' mouths out with soap for using it. When Copley got really angry the combination of his fists and his ranting was nuclear. He could make my mother flinch by looking in her direction. He found that particularly funny and sometimes chuckled about it all day.

Of course, from my earliest days on earth I was right there, watching him hit her, day in and day out, for some imagined insult, some hesitation to fulfill his wishes, or simply for being alive. I heard everything he said to her, and about her, and I easily believed it. This was just a normal part of our family life.

My mother took most of the blows in silence, especially when I was in the room, but I heard her crying at night from behind their bedroom door. She feared his shadow, his liquor scent and his blank animal eyes, which locked on hers with furious desire. Sometimes, though I didn't understand it in my childhood, I could feel how deeply he wanted her. But it wasn't lust that drove him—it was his need to consume her. I would know that desire, too, many years later.

Bebe J never called the police, and rarely raised her voice while begging him to stop. It was the neighbors who called the cops, because they were sick of my father's yelling and screaming. The men in blue came to the door, politely inquired whether everything was alright, then announced that because it was a domestic dispute, there was nothing they could do. Sometimes one of the cops lingered on the front stoop. They knew my father—and knew exactly what he was doing—but the law protected him.

Back then, they couldn't step in. Or maybe they just wouldn't.

And anyway, my mother's skin was too brown to show most of the bruises, so she kept on going to work, cooking, cleaning, and living the nonlife of a caged woman. She never spoke about it, so I figured it didn't hurt that bad, or she'd given him good reason to hit her. Maybe she didn't measure up to what my father expected from a wife and mother. Or maybe she just didn't try hard enough to please him.

Occasionally I got a whipping, too. Mostly it was when I didn't listen when he told me to do something, or when I made a noise when his head was hurting. My whippings didn't hurt too bad, and after I cried for a while I forgot about them. I knew they were my fault and my daddy always forgave me.

So I ignored what was happening to my mother, even when it was going on in the same room where I was sitting, eating or watching TV. Part of me detached and floated free, danced to the window, or the door, or into whatever was happening on the TV. I ignored the muffled fists on flesh, or the cuffs to her face, or her muted, strangled cries. I marveled at the way his shoulders flexed when he pinned her to the floor, at the corded strength in his lower arms when he flexed his fingers after striking her, and at the ever-stony coldness of his eyes. Copley's anger was fierce, his punishments sharp, calculated and precise. I found it all kind of beautiful.

Why didn't my mother leave this man, who made her days and nights constant, anticipated misery? When I was little, I figured she stayed because underneath it all, she was okay with what was going on.

Now I think that Bebe J knew even then he'd never let her live if she tried to escape. And she knew he'd never, ever, let her take his daughter. I was the anchor that tied her to him forever. His flesh. His blood. The next generation of Castles.

Long live the Castles.

* * * * * * *

Many years later, in the glass-walled room, the Old Man with the white hair asked me to describe my earliest memory.

Talking was still pretty new to me, and memories were even newer. I hedged, not particularly eager to travel back to that war-torn country.

"She was crying," I finally said. "I was in bed and she thought I couldn't hear her."

"How do you know?"

"Because she never let herself cry in front of me."

"Why, do you think, was that?"

"I don't know."

"Do you think she wanted to protect you?"

"I don't know."

"Is it possible that she didn't want you to know what she was feeling?"

I tried not to picture my mother, alone, in pain, sobbing into the sheets or a towel. "Maybe she just figured nobody gave a shit," I said.

For a long time the room was quiet. Then the Old Man shifted and his leather chair sighed. "Perhaps," he said, "it's harder for you to express your anger or fear for the same reasons."

"It's not hard for me to express them," I said. "I just do it my father's way."

* * * * * * *

When I was five years old my daddy stole a couple of bikes, spray-painted them, and taught me how to ride so we could go on long afternoon tours of the neighborhood. He asked me what color bike I wanted, and I said 'canary yellow' (the color on the paper of one of my crayons), so that's what I got. He bought some shiny plastic strings to stick out from the handlebars, and put little orange reflectors in the spokes. He found a white seat from somewhere, and my new bike, with its chrome splashguards, silver streamers and bright sunny color, was the envy of all the girls in the neighborhood.

My daddy's favorite game on the bicycle was "I'm Lost." We'd ride a few blocks away, then he'd say he didn't know how to get home. I'd try to give him directions, but he'd always go in exactly the opposite direction from whatever I said. In other words, he'd get us *more* lost, rather than less. Sounds crazy, perhaps, but because of "I'm Lost," I had a dead-on sense of direction—well, that is until he fractured my skull.

Whenever we rode, people commented on how sweet it was for a father to be out with his daughter. It was very clear we were related; Copley loved being my escort, and often told me so. He never said I was his 'girlfriend,' but he reminded me every day I was his 'baby,' and that felt very, very right to me. I thought he was the handsomest, smartest, wisest, *baddest* daddy in the universe. He smelled of a cologne called 'Aramis,' his menthol cigarettes, and the cognac he drank from an engraved silver flask in his rear pocket. I saw the way some men, as we rode past, nodded to him with respect, and the way others turned away. If I sensed they were afraid of him, I thought their fear came along with the package. After all, my mother was scared of him, too, and she never said so much as a single word against him.

Sometimes we rode all afternoon, then stopped off at the Dairy Queen for a chocolate-dipped ice cream cone. My momma was at work while we were gone, but she'd better have some dinner on the stove when we got back. After he knocked her down twice for not having his favorite: fried okra, collard greens and ham hocks—prepared when her "man and kid crossed the threshold," she never made that mistake again.

Copley kept me and Momma in high style. He said no woman of his could be seen in public looking less than her best, so he stayed on my mother about her weight (looking back, I know she had a blessedly beautiful body), and he took her weekly to a beauty parlor run by the girlfriend of one of his buddies in the basement of their home. Copley never came into the basement while her hair was washed and combed out, but he always offered his opinion on the style of Bebe J's press n'curl. Momma never disagreed; she understood how lucky she was that her man cared how she looked.

Daddy, however, never let the hairdresser lay a hand on my head. He said, "Castle hair don't need no heat or grease on it, 'cause rainwater don't send our hair back to Africa." I didn't understand what that meant, but I saw the other women exchange looks whenever he declared it.

Secretly I *wanted* to get my hair done. I wanted to feel that hot water pour through the hose, and get my scalp massaged (this was the one moment during the entire week when my momma looked truly happy and at peace). I loved everything that went on in that basement: the smells of lavender hair ointments, acidy perms, the low growl of the dryers, and the sharp sizzle and clackety-clack of the curling irons. I loved the way Momma's hair shone when the hairdresser whipped the apron away and turned the swivel chair before my father's appraising eyes.

Because that is what womanhood was all about: pleasing your man! Sometimes I looked at my momma and couldn't understand why she always made him mad. It just didn't seem *that* hard to make him happy. Whenever I set the table, I always knew where the utensils belonged because my daddy was the knife and I was the spoon, and I loved standing right next to him. It was Momma who had to stay on the other side of the plate! She couldn't come between my daddy and me!

Daddy was also very generous. When he took us to the Wooster-Hawkins Shopping Center, he selected my shoes, slips, skirts, pants and dresses. He watched my mother try on the articles of clothing he selected, then announced what he would buy. I knew my momma had no kind of taste, because he told her how to dress for him and no one else. He liked soft knits that hugged her waist and rode on her hips. He liked a low-cut sweater, but only low enough that someone real close could see the "V." He said if any other man got near enough to see that "V," somebody was going to pay. His mouth laughed when he said it, but the laughter died long before it reached his eyes.

When I started kindergarten I felt like one of the luckiest girls in the world. Daddy had come home with a black Cadillac a few weeks before, and he drove me to school and picked me up every day, while the other kids had to walk. Momma left us a lunch waiting at home—soup and sandwiches—then I took a nap before the two of us went on our afternoon bike ride.

When the weather got cold Daddy took me to the movie matinees, or on long drives in the car. We never talked in the car because he turned the radio on and sang along with the music. He said one day we would visit Motown, where all the great singers, like the Temptations and Marvin Gaye, lived. He said Detroit was a city where a Black man could make *real* money, unlike Akron, where Black people either had to live a low-class life, working for the whites, or find a way to beat The Man at his own game.

Daddy didn't get truly mad unless he needed to. He would slap or hit Momma whenever she moved too slow, or showed him any attitude. I understood why he had to do it. She just didn't seem smart enough to understand what he wanted. *I* understood what he wanted, of course, so he almost never got mad at me. I often found her irritating, and even straight-up stupid, and didn't blame him for his reaction. A man as good as my father deserved her appreciation, and she didn't have enough sense to show it.

four.

Two times we made the drive all the way down to North Carolina, so my father could see his momma, Miss Corinthia Bibb Castle.

The first time I was too little to remember, but the second time, when I was six, I thought we were never going to get there. All that distance my momma sat in the front seat, not speaking, and I bounced around in the back, fighting carsickness and trying to occupy myself with my Barbie. Every hour or two he'd stop, take a piss by the side of the road, and drink a beer from a cooler in the trunk. My momma would take me into the bushes, where we'd crouch down and tinkle, then wipe ourselves with Kleenex. When we got back to the car, he'd let me eat a bologna sandwich, while Momma, who said she wasn't hungry, watched.

Sometimes I'd sleep, then wake up to find the world outside the car windows had changed. First it was hilly, then covered with high, sharp turns and blue rocks. Then it seemed to flatten out and redden. Finally the car grew hot and steamy, and the houses were wood-slatted, with peeling paint and metal roofs. Nobody had a garage and drainage ditches bordered the roads. The trees rose sky-high and were often webbed, as if by enormous spiders. Even the flowers were different—wild and deeply colored, exploding from everywhere.

We finally rolled into a red-dirt yard beside a house with tiger lilies overflowing from the drainage ditch. As soon as the engine died, the sound was replaced by the dry shrilling of thousands of grasshoppers, the rhythmic scratching of the cicadas, and a mad cacophony of birdsong. The red dust settled slowly around the tires and Daddy waited, his hands still resting on the steering wheel, his body facing forward as if the trip wasn't over for him. Momma didn't move, either, though she looked at him expectantly.

I peered at a low-slung house painted bright yellow, my favorite color. A porch, supported by pure white columns, ran all the way around the sides, and the wide-slatted silver roof reflected the blinding sun. An old-fashioned antenna was attached to the brick chimney, which was laced with vines, and the whole house nestled in a kaleidoscope of roses.

Suddenly a compact woman in a belted flowered housedress, her dark hair cut loose and short—I thought it looked like frizzy sound waves in the summer heat—strolled from behind the house, a basket of wet laundry in her arms. She set the basket on the ground, peering toward our Cadillac, and her face opened to a head-shaking, arms on her hips, half-bemused smile.

Mother and son regarded each other without speaking. Only then did I understand that Grandma didn't know we were coming. I wasn't sure whether my momma knew that Grandma didn't know, but she was the first one to open her door.

Grandma looked toward her and her smile broadened. "Looks like you could've let me know so I'd have something ready for you all to eat," she said, as if we just happened to stop by.

"I'm sorry, Miss Corinne," my mother said as she climbed out of the car. "Copley must of forgot to call ahead." I slipped out behind her and straightened up, breathing in the thick-scented air and, suddenly shy, leaned into my mother's hips.

The older woman's eyes, so much like my fathers', now focused on me. "*You*—little princess, come *right* over here and give your Grandma a great big hug!" Though I walked the first two steps, as I got closer something in me seemed to swell, and I forgot the hesitation I often felt when approached by grownups—particularly those who reached for me too quickly—and ran the last few steps, straight into her arms.

Grandma smelled of sundried wash, and I felt her heartbeat though the calico of her dress. "And you, Brenda Berniece—what are *you* waiting for?" Grandma said, lifting one arm from my shoulder in order to include my mother. The three of us hugged while my father remained in the driver's seat, watching.

"Son," my grandmother said over her shoulder as she led Momma and me into the house, "go and get us a melon, a loaf of bread and a couple cans of tuna, you hear? You can carry the suitcases in when you get back." I peeked over my shoulder, stunned to see Copley Castle obediently turn the key in the ignition, and without a single word of protest, pull backwards out of the drive.

I soon found myself in the kitchen with the two women, eating sugar cookies ("I made them for Social Hour, but I'll just bake up another batch before Church tomorrow"), and drinking crème soda. Grandma explained that she didn't much care for soda, but she kept some in a crate on the back porch for her best friend, Mr. Saunders. She moved about her kitchen, taking out eggs and butter, potatoes and greens, as if we stopped in for lunch every day.

Though my momma was normally quiet, she exploded with words as soon as the Cadillac was out of sight. Removing the bandana that held her curls in place, she wound her hair up off her neck and pinned it back so it would be cooler. She slipped off her shoes and joined Grandma at the sink. With hands that were steadier than I ever saw them at home, she began peeling potatoes while speaking in a quiet voice.

Momma didn't offer much detail about the things Copley was into back up north, but she spoke about how hard it was to afford our little house in Akron, how being on her feet all day in the dry cleaners was hard on her back (Copley'd made her give up the liquor store as soon as I was born), and what she was thinking about me.

"She learn real good in school," Momma said, with a nod in my direction. "She just love to read books. She want me to take her to the library all the time. Her teacher said we should move her to a Catholic school, with nuns doing the teaching. But we can't do it on the money I make, and Copley say she fine where she at."

Grandma, who was now lighting the stove, gave me a warm, approving smile. I couldn't see it then, but now I know she was measuring how much of me was Bebe J, and how much was my daddy.

I was looking at Grandma, too, waiting for my daddy to appear in her eyes. To my surprise, he wasn't there, and I whipped around to see if my momma was watching.

Momma was looking straight at me, and I saw the gentle love in her gaze. "The teacher said if she stay in public school, we should get her moved up a grade. She had to wait to start kindergarten because her birthday in January, but she already smaller than most of the other kids, and I don't know how she would do if she the youngest, too."

Grandma nodded without speaking. Momma went on. "Copley don't like her playing outside the yard. He'll let her go to a birthday party once in a while, but he won't let her go to Sunday school. He say he don't know the people at the church, but I think it would be good for her."

Grandma's shoulders stiffened just a bit at these words, and she reached over and covered my mother's hand with her own. The two women looked at each other. My mother went on talking, as if she just couldn't stop. "My momma too sick now to help out much, so Beth is with Copley every day after school. I don't get home sometimes 'til late, and then he mad if there's no dinner ready. He say I need to have food on the table every night by 6 p.m. I do my best, Miss Corinne, but sometimes—"

Momma's voice broke, and there was a sudden quiet. Grandma kept on looking at her, and finally Momma took a deep breath and let it out real slow. For a reason I can't explain, I jumped up from the table and ran over and wrapped my arms around Momma's hips. I never did this at home, even on the rare occasion when she couldn't hide her tears.

"Brenda," Grandma said in a soft voice, "go on into the front room and lie down. You need to rest from your long trip. Princess, I want you to go and lie down right beside your momma. Take a nice nap and have a beautiful dream for me. When you two wake up, supper will be ready. We'll have plenty of time to talk later on."

All I could think about was how much I wanted to explore the yard, chase my grandma's chickens around the coop behind the garage, and swing on the old tire swing hanging from a thick oak behind the house. But somehow, when Grandma said you should do something, just like my daddy, you did it.

Momma took my hand and we walked up the hall, past the pictures of the Castles that went back almost a hundred years, and into the front bedroom. The bed was made, as if ready for us to appear out of thin air. We laid down, pulled the chenille bedspread up over us, and Momma put her arm around me. The world slipped into the warmth of dusty sunlight, the sweet peonies beyond the open window, and the patiently drilling cicadas.

* * * * * * *

Who knows what else Momma told Grandma about my daddy while I played outside in the days that followed? Who knows how much Grandma figured out just by watching my momma and daddy together? All I know is that after that first night, Grandma invited me and Momma to sleep in her room with her, leaving my daddy the bedroom at the other end of the house. I was glad not to be alone in a new place, and my grandmother's enormous bed, with its tall pineapple bedposts, had the softest mattress and sweetest sundried sheets in all the world. Momma and I curled up in the big wooden bed, and Grandma slept on a smaller bed in the corner. Freshly bathed and exhausted from a day of hard, earnest playing under the huge oak in the backyard, I fell asleep each night before my head hit the pillow.

It wasn't only about the backyard, however. Grandma kept me learning new things throughout our visit.

"Come on, Princess, let me show you how to pick corn," she said one morning, as she led me to her car. No one had ever called me "Princess" before, but it was perfectly alright with me. We drove the short distance to some fields she described as "our family land," which was now being farmed by a sharecropper and his wife. We cut several heads of golden corn, and grandma showed me how to shuck it.

A different day Grandma taught me how to snap the ends off green beans. She placed a heap of the stalks on the table, and gave me a big round bowl. We sat there talking about my reading—she liked the *Madeleine* books as much as I did—and about riding my bike with my daddy, and my one or two skinned-kneed buddies from down the block. She listened mostly, asking a question now and then, but not saying much. Just like my momma, once I started talking, I couldn't seem to stop.

Then there was a day where we picked, battered and fried okra. Momma tried to get me to eat okra at home, but I wasn't too crazy about it. There, in Grandma's kitchen, things were different. She put something in the batter that made it spicy and sweet, and most of the slime seemed to be gone. Though I won't say I loved it, I did enjoy the ham and cornbread she served along with it.

She also let me help her hang up the wet clothes and take them down after they dried. Used to washing our clothes at a laundromat, I loved the thick smell of the wet cotton, and its sharp clean tang of dried sunlight. I also loved seeing the sheets and panties billowing gently in the breeze. I wondered why summer didn't feel or smell this way in Akron.

Every afternoon my mother napped—another thing that never happened in Ohio—because most days, if she wasn't at work, my father got in the Cadillac right after breakfast and didn't return until after I was in bed. Those days, Momma had to look after me, clean the house and cook. She never complained, however; she just labored in silence while I watched TV.

At Grandma's, Daddy was gone most of the time—but neither Momma nor Grandma seemed much worried about it. For some reason, I barely noticed his absence, either. I was having too much fun to miss him.

Still, when Grandma and I were alone, Daddy was the subject of many of our conversations.

"Does your daddy ever get mad at you?" Grandma asked one afternoon as we drank sweet tea at the picnic table behind the house. The air was hot and sticky, and I welcomed the sweating pitcher tinkling with big square ice cubes.

"Not really. But he get mad at Momma a whole lot."

"Princess, please say '*gets* mad at Momma.' I want you to learn to talk like a teacher."

"Momma and daddy don't talk that way."

"That may be true, but talking like a teacher will help you later in life.

"Are you a teacher, Grandma?"

"Yes I am. I've taught children of every age for over thirty years."

"*Thirty* years? Don't you get tired of them?"

"Sometimes. But I love helping them, too." She smiled. "I understand you're very, very good in school. If you study hard, you can be a teacher, too."

I thought about that. I had never given any particular thought to helping anybody, and I didn't care much for the other kids.

"When your daddy gets mad," she said in a conversational voice, "what does he do?"

"Sometimes he yell at Momma. Then sometimes he hit—" Grandma's brows went up, and I corrected myself—"he *hits* her."

"Oh dear," she said quietly. "You know, Princess, a man shouldn't hit a woman. Not for any reason."

I looked at her, amazed. "But what if she deserve it?"

"No one *ever* deserves it, Princess."

"But Daddy say—"

"I love my son, baby, but he's not right. Do you hear me?"

"Yes, ma'am," I said, responding the way I heard others speak to her as we went around town.

"No, Princess," she said. "I mean it. A man and woman should be kind to each other, and help each other out of love. Hitting someone is *never* an act of love. Hitting, slapping, pinching, or any other kind of violence is not love."

I was confused. I knew my father loved my mother. He was devoted to her. He paid for her clothes and hair and food. He protected her from other men. He always said he was a good provider.

"Has your daddy—has he ever hit you?" she asked.

"Not really," I answered, even more uncomfortable.

"Not *really*?"

"Well, I get a spanking sometimes if he get mad."

"A spanking with his hand?"

I stopped talking. I knew she was going to be upset if I told her he sometimes hit me with Momma's hairbrush, or with a wooden kitchen spoon, or—well, it was my fault because I'd broken his favorite beer glass—about the time he hit me with his belt. I had cried for a little while, but then he took me to Dairy Queen and I knew I was forgiven.

"Princess?" she said in a quieter, but more insistent voice. I shook my head. It felt weird, because I never thought about those times when I made my daddy mad. Even now, when Grandma was asking me about them, I found them kind of hard to remember.

"He spanked you with something else?" she probed. Reluctantly I nodded.

"Something in the house?"

I nodded.

"From the kitchen?"

I didn't move.

"With his belt?"

I couldn't look at her. She lowered her head, then turned her whole body away. For a few minutes the cicadas were so loud my head started to hurt. Then she turned back and opened her arms. I leaned toward her, and she pulled me close. "Honey, I'm very, very sorry. I didn't raise him to be this way."

"What way?"

She shook her head. I could feel the beating of her heart.

"It's okay, Grandma," I said. "It don't hurt that bad."

After a while she got up and went into the house. Through the open window I could hear her moving around the kitchen. Nervously, I went over to the tire swing, which hung from a branch of the enormous oak tree. I leaned the upper half of my body into it and watched my feet leave the earth as I swung. I wondered if she would tell my daddy. I wondered if he'd think Momma told. I wondered what he'd do to us both when we got back to Akron.

* * * * * * *

When Daddy came home that night, though it was very late, he found Grandma sitting in the front parlor, reading the most recent volume of the Book of the Month Club. He couldn't get to his bedroom without walking right past her, and I heard her speak to him in a calm, measured voice. Neither one of them got loud with the other, but their voices made a strange, serious duet beneath the rhythm of Momma's snores. Daddy never talked soft like that when we were home. Very carefully I got up and crept to the door.

"Copley, it's time you settled down and married that girl. She's the mother of your child and that precious baby deserves it."

"We fine just the way we are."

"Marriage is important, son."

"What would you know about that?"

"Don't be ridiculous—I was married for decades."

"Yeah, right."

The room was quiet for a few moments.

"It wouldn't hurt you all to live down here," my grandmother said. "You're not doing anything of value in Ohio, and Blissfield really is your home. You should establish yourself and your family near people who genuinely care for you."

"Ain't nothing down here for me."

"Of course there is. We have land and responsibilities to others."

"I don't got shit here," he answered with the tremble in his voice that came from a long night of drinking. I could tell how hard it was for him to stay calm.

Grandma's voice, remarkably, remained steady. "Our family has possessed this land since slavery. Our family members fought and died for it. It's important to take care of it and pass it on to the next generation."

"That's just stupid talk."

"You've got to leave something to your daughter."

"Right now I'm not worried about that."

"Well, *that* much is obvious. Honestly: what are you doing up there in Ohio, anyway? Hasn't it occurred to you that Brenda and Bethany need you?"

"I take good care a them."

"Not by doing whatever it is you're doing."

"You have no idea what I'm doing."

"I know that a man who can't tell his mother where he works certainly can't afford to drive a Cadillac."

"There's plenty a ways to make money. I don't have to work in no rubber factory to do it."

"You've got to be a man, Copley, not an overgrown child."

"What's that supposed to mean? She say something to you?"

"Brenda doesn't have to say anything. I've got eyes."

"Stay out of it, Momma. I don't need to ask or answer for nothing."

"What about that woman and child?"

"They both doing just fine."

"Then why have you got Brenda working in a dry cleaners?"

"She like working there."

"I don't believe that for a minute. Like most women, she's just doing whatever it takes to protect her baby."

"Like most women, she tell a bunch a lies. She got a house to run, a child to raise, and a husband that provides."

"She's got a man who leaves every night and does things that may stop him from making it home in the morning. No woman can live like that."

"We do alright. I paid cash money for that Cadillac."

"Copley, a car means nothing if your family's not safe. You weren't raised to value objects over your own blood."

"What in hell would I do in Blissfield? There's no work for a man here. And before you even start to think about it—I am not going to work in *nobody's* fields, even if you want to pretend they're ours!"

"There's plenty you could do. Start a business. Use your VA benefits to finish your education. Go to work fixing up this place—"

"And what about Beth? You can't believe my daughter will get a better education in that schoolhouse that date back to slavery!"

"You know very well they built a whole new wing onto the old school. It's as modern as anything you've got up in Ohio—"

"But her classmates would be living in shacks."

"I'll tell you right now that a sharecropper values education as much as a man working in an office. Maybe more."

"I'm thinking 'bout putting her in Catholic school."

"Bethany needs to be here with her people, Copley."

"Her people?" he echoed, his voice bitter. "Don't come at me with that bull-shit."

There was another long silence. If that had been Momma, he would have thrown something, or yelled, or slapped her by now. But something in Grandma tamed my daddy—tamed him *good*.

"She's a beautiful child," Grandma said softly. "She's got the best of all of us inside her."

"Don't talk like I don't know my own daughter."

"Give her a chance, Son—"

"Stay out of it, Momma."

I heard the horsehair sofa creak as Grandma stood up. "Do what's right for your family, Copley."

"I am," he argued, but he sounded oddly meek.

"We're not talking about what's right for *you*. As soon as a baby is born, the parents' main responsibility in life is to take care of their child. Do you understand? Nothing matters as much as Bethany Celeste."

"You can't tell me how to be a husband *or* a father," he snarled, his voice low and vicious. "You never knew how to be a wife and you never provided me with a father."

"I did the best I could for you," she answered, and I could hear the hurt in her words, "and you had a better life than anybody you knew in this town. You are blessed to have a woman like Brenda and a daughter as lovely as Bethany."

But the next day Grandma sat me down on the edge of her bed and began combing my hair. Momma was in the backyard hanging up clothes, and Daddy's car was gone. As she combed out my braids, Grandma spoke to me softly.

"Princess, I reckon your daddy's getting ready to pack you all up and take you on back to Ohio," she said. "When you get there, I want you to do a few things for me."

I nodded.

"You're getting older now, and I want you to look after your mother." Our eyes met in the mirror of her vanity across the room, and I realized hers were exactly the same shape and color as mine. "I'm going to tuck my phone number in your suitcase, and I want you to call me if you need me. You can call me for any reason at all: just to talk about your day, or about your friends, or about your mother and father. Alright?"

I nodded again.

"I want you to remember what I told you. No man should ever strike a woman. I know how much you love your daddy, but your daddy should never, ever hit you or your momma. Do you understand?"

I looked at the floor.

"And I want you to keep on reading those books. Read every book you can get your hands on. I don't care what the book's about: you just read it. And then you go on to the next book and the next, until you've read every book in the library. Whether you go to the same school, or to a school with nuns, always be the best student in your class. Always learn everything you can. Don't do it for your teachers, or for me, or for your father, or even for your mother. Do it for yourself. You learn for *yourself.* No one—and I mean, *no one*, should ever stop you from learning. Do you hear me, Bethany Celeste?

I smiled. "Yes, Grandma."

She bent down, kissed the crown of my head, then braided my hair into two plaits that began at the top of my forehead and circled my face like a laurel wreath.

five.

Akron seemed faded and scentless in comparison to Grandma's. For the first time I saw that the floors in our house were rough and stained, the baseboards warped and chipped, and the even the window curtains were frayed. I knew Momma washed, but our sheets were gray, and our blankets, which always smelled sour, didn't keep me warm at night.

I ate the food she put down in front of me, and went on with my daily life, but some part of my heart stayed in Blissfield. Grandma's house: the neat, clean rooms, the photographs of our family, even the heaping plates of chicken, mashed potatoes and greens—felt like a completely different kind of world. Though we were only there for a couple of weeks, the whole time we were in Blissfield I didn't see my father hit or yell at my mother. Not even once.

I figured he didn't want to wrestle with my grandma.

It didn't take him a minute to get back to it after we got back to Ohio. The first night Momma came home from her job at the dry cleaners, he slapped her for not getting his coffee fast enough after dinner. He brooded for a couple of days, ignoring me when I asked if we could go on a bike ride, then he started vanishing in the car before my bedtime and not coming home until dawn. He yelled at my mother less, but she seemed even more afraid of him than before. It felt like Blissfield had cast a spell on us, and we were all changed in some kind of way.

I didn't end up going to school with the nuns or moving up a grade. Copley refused to go over to the school to sign the papers, and my mother was scared to do it. The boys in my class, seeing I was too smart for them, started pushing me around on the playground, so I made the decision to fix it. One day when Louis Drexler came up behind me and tried to pull me down by the hood of my jacket, I whipped around and hit him in the face as hard as I could with my math book.

The teachers came running, and I quickly fell to the ground, holding my throat. When they lifted me up, I said he nearly choked me with the drawstrings on my coat. They saw the marks under my chin, and hauled him off to the principal's office with blood from his broken nose streaming down his face. Then they called my daddy, who said that if Louis ever so much as *looked* at me again, he would personally burn down his parents' house. The principal moved Louis to a different class. After that, everybody left me alone.

I never told the Old Man with the white hair this story. I figure I wasn't ready to admit that as early as the second grade Copley was already making an appearance in me. Looking back, I'm not sure if this had a whole lot to do with my daddy, or whether I was trying to follow what Grandma said about me learning as much as possible. I figured that if I let that boy get the better of me, every single day somebody would push or trip me, knock my books out of my hands, or refuse to sit with me at lunch. I would be sad, the kids would mock me, and the teachers would put me at a desk in the back of the class. Then I would be angry all the time, and do things to mess up the class. In other words, it just made more sense to take care of the situation when I had the chance.

I knew the other girls were scared to be my friend, but I also knew they were *more* scared to be my enemy. I chose one or two of the pretty ones and let them know they were okay with me, and soon everyone adopted me as their favorite student. I was learning that keeping myself safe was easiest when I inspired a blend of fear and respect in others. My daddy wasn't good at the "respect" part. Momma didn't know how to make a fly afraid of her.

But I was good at both.

* * * * * * *

That's how it went from there. I was never Class President, Student Council President, or the lead in the school play, but nobody messed with me, which is saying something when you consider that I barely crested five-foot-two and had a hell of a time getting past seventy-five pounds, even when I started eating the same shit as my classmates (barbeque chips and soda, *holla!*). My period didn't kick in till I was over fourteen, which made me a genuine freak in my neighborhood. Some of my classmates had already been pregnant by the ninth grade, and there I was, still confused about how to use tampons.

Around the time I hit fifteen my father was also beating my mother in daily, deadly earnest. I guess he figured it was high time he started beating me, too.

It was the sprouting of my tiny buds that set things in motion. Early one morning before school, as I walked from the bath to my bedroom with a towel wrapped around my body, my father, who was staggering up the stairs, growled something raw and crude in my direction. I just *knew* he was snarling at my mother—nothing new—and kept on moving. Suddenly he appeared at my door, his face bloated and eyes swollen nearly shut. I could barely understand his slurred accusation that I'd been out on the streets the night before. Me? *Out on the streets?* Why would I be outside in the snow in the middle of the night?

I was so naïve I didn't even know what he meant. I watched him with confused suspicion, uncertain why he was using his "Bebe J" tone with me. This clearly made him angrier. He moved inside my door, now shouting cognac-stinking words like "streetwalker" and "slut." I knew what those words meant, but I didn't know what in the world they had to do with me. As he backed me into a corner, howling about me walking around half naked and showing myself off to anyone who was willing to look at my skinny ass, my mother appeared in my door.

"Copley," she said carefully, "Beth's going to be late for school."

"Who gives a fuck?" he screamed. "*She* don't! Just look at her, parading herself around the house like a ten-cent ho!"

Tears leaped into my eyes. My stomach coiled up. He'd never spoken to me that way before.

"Honey," Momma said, trying to see me over his shoulder, "get your school clothes and go back into the bathroom to dress. Let me speak with your father."

I realized that my hands were fisted, and though I was terrified, I was perfectly ready to stand my ground and come right back at him. I also knew that some kind of line had been crossed, and there was no talking with him until he was completely sober.

Quickly I collected my shirt, jeans and hoodie, and swept past him back down the hall, clutching them, along with the towel, to my chest.

My mother tried to follow. He grabbed her arm at the door.

"Copley, let me get you some breakfast," she said without looking at his face.

"You helping her," he answered nastily.

"I'm trying to get her to school," she stated quietly.

"Naw, you trying to help her get away from me."

"No, baby."

"I see what going on in this house. You think if you can turn her out, she'll meet some motherfucker and leave."

"No, Copley—"

"She ain't a girl no more!"

"She—she just growing up."

"That don't mean she can disrespect me."

"She didn't mean to dis—"

That was when he hit her. It was a slap, not hard enough to leave a mark, but hard enough to hurt. He accompanied the slap with a sharp twist of her arm, and she ended up wedged between his body and the door.

"You trying to tell me my own daughter don't have to do as I say?"

My mother let out a gasping whimper, and he twisted harder.

"Is that what you saying, Bebe—that I'm not the head of this motherfucking household?"

She cried out incoherently, and I was filled with a sudden, intense rage.

"Let her go," I shouted from the bathroom door.

My father turned to stare, incredulous, at me. "What the fuck did you say?"

"Let her go! She ain't done nothing!"

"Bitch! When I get through with her, I'm a come over there and kick your ho ass, too." With that he gave my mother another hard slap, and her head slammed into the door. Throwing my clothes aside, I picked up the two-by-four we jammed into the window frame so burglars couldn't get in. Blindly, without any thought of the consequences, I sprinted the length of the hall, my arms raised.

Though I knew he saw it coming, he was so busy pinning my mother to the door that his arms weren't free to defend himself. I planted my feet, the way he'd taught me, and swung straight and hard, hitting him just behind his ear, the way Hank Aaron smashed a home run. A perfume of sweat and booze and stale cigarette rose from his shirt. The surprise in his eyes was worth the pain I knew was coming, but I didn't care. He had made the mistake of giving me just a taste of what my momma endured every single day, and it was enough to make me see who he *really* was. I suddenly understood that Grandma was right: even if he killed me, that morning I became determined that I would never, ever just stand by and let him put his hands on me again.

I was late to school that day. None of my classmates asked why I had a black eye and swollen lip. Instead, the teacher sent me down to the nurse, who also asked me to show her the bruises on my neck, back and thighs, then plied me with stale cookies and juice boxes from a little fridge beside her desk while she contacted the police. As I was sitting in the nurse's office waiting for something to happen, it occurred to me that I would never let *any* man put his hands on me. I knew how my father "loved" my mother; I heard them at it in the night. And I certainly didn't enjoy listening when he came home drunk and made love to her, or when he came home drunk and beat the hell out of her. It was all the same to me.

The nurse appeared at the door with a bored-looking cop. The two came and sat down on either side of me. The nurse asked me to explain how'd I been injured that morning. I looked at her, then over at the officer.

Telling them the truth was a risk. Sure, they might go looking for my father, but he would make up some kind of story ("My daughter tripped and fell down the steps"), and when he got home, he'd be angrier than ever. They couldn't possibly protect me and my momma from what happened inside our house. Hell, we couldn't even call the cops till *after* my father had hurt us!

I apologized to the nurse and told her I'd lied about my bruises to avoid taking a test. I'd tripped and fallen down the steps. No one ever hit me. I really was alright.

Though I saw she didn't believe me, there wasn't much she could do. The two of them went out into the hall, where I could hear their murmuring voices.

As I stared blankly at the glossy photos of white kids with backpacks and creased khakis in a magazine called *Students Today,* I knew Copley had to be stopped, and my mother wasn't strong enough to do it.

* * * * * * *

Now there was too much woman-energy in the house, and things just got crazier over the following weeks. Copley's booze-soaked rage was like a hulking beast, crouching low and menacing on my horizon. Whereas once he welcomed me home from school with a sweeping hug, now he greeted me with eyes like slits, as if I was a gold-digger looking to lift his wallet.

"You better not be wearing make-up!" he snarled one freezing afternoon as I stepped in out of the cold.

I screwed up my face. "Make-up? Not even."

"You talking back to me?"

"You accusing me of something I'm not doing!"

He came off the sofa like he had springs in his ass. I stood rooted on the spot, unwilling to let him see how frightened I was.

"Say something else," he spat, his face inches from mine.

"Like what?" I held my gaze steady.

His pupils darkened. "Girl, I'll slap your mouth off your face."

"*Then* what?"

He stared at me in disbelief. "Bitch ho! You better not forget that you only on this earth because of me. You eat because of me, you sleep because of me. You only have this roof over your head because of me."

Strictly speaking, he was wrong as watermelon in winter. By the age of ten or so I already understood that Momma was the only one really working. I knew he lost as much gambling as he won, and even when he won, the money almost never made it home.

"Can I come in?" I answered a bit too impatiently. It's cold outside."

He looked stunned that I dared to speak.

"Girl, I'll make you—" The fist came out of nowhere, catching me square in chest and knocking me breathless. I stumbled, holding my right breast, back against the doorframe. He took a step forward, slapped me hard in the face, then stood there waiting until I dropped my gaze.

In my room that evening I stared at the ugly bruise with a hand mirror. I heard him screaming at my mother downstairs, and heard him hit her once or twice. The sound was loud enough to make it all the way up the stairs, and her silence meant he'd struck her harder than usual. I waited, holding my breath, but he didn't show up at my door.

This went on for nearly a year. I didn't exactly tip-toe in his presence, but I tried to make myself scarce when he arrived. That summer was misery: I was out of school, too young to get a job, and he was laid-up most days, seething with uncontrolled rage. I cooked his food and served him in silence while he complained about everything from my appearance ("Don't eat too much! I don't want no fat bitches up in my house!"), to my clothes ("Why you got so much shit in your room? You don't got nowhere to go and I better not *ever* catch your ass out on the street at night."). The thing he hated most was to see me with a book. Just the idea that my mind might be somewhere he couldn't reach seemed to drive him crazy. It was me reading a book in bed one night that got me the beating that probably saved my life. He slapped me hard enough that my teeth cut the inside of my cheek, then cuffed me in the ribs so I couldn't breathe. Looming over me, his eyes taking in my blood-choked attempts to rise, I saw he was looking down at a woman—not his daughter. That's what scared me most of all.

I waited until he went out, then called Grandma. I fumbled with trembling fingers to find the little folded paper she'd tucked into my suitcase eight years before. I'd taken it out and placed it beneath the fake pink velvet in my jewelry box. Though I knew Copley was unlikely to ever find it—there was nothing in the box but a few broken trinkets from the Goodwill store—I was pretty certain that slipping it under the box's lining was an extra smart move.

I knew it was going to cost some money, but Grandma told me to call if I needed her, so I did it. I dialed "O" and got an operator on the line, who put the call through. After it rang a long time, Grandma answered. The operator explained that it was a "collect call," and, though I heard the worry leap into her voice, she immediately accepted the charges.

"Brenda?" She wasted no time on greetings.

"No—it's me—Bethany."

"What's wrong, Princess?"

"He been hitting me, Grandma."

"He hit you?"

"Yes." I swallowed. My mouth was still bleeding.

"And your momma?"

I knew I was taking a terrible risk, but it was too late: I'd made the call, and Grandma understood, even without me speaking.

"It—it's worse than ever," I said.

"Today?"

"Every day."

There was a long silence on the line. "Did you call the police?"

"The school did, back when he started."

"They know about it at school?" I heard something like relief in her voice.

"Yes."

"What did the teacher do?"

"She sent me to the nurse, and she called the cops, but—but I didn't tell them nothing," I said.

"Why, baby?"

"I didn't know what he would do."

It was strange: only at that moment did I realize I had never told the full truth to anyone. Teachers had asked me once or twice why my mother never came to parent-teacher conferences, and I lied and said she couldn't get off work. The truth was that she more than likely had some kind of cut on her face, or body, that she didn't want anyone to see.

The neighbors certainly knew, because Daddy shouted terrible things at Momma while he was hitting her. Come to think of it, some of my teachers lived nearby, too, and if the neighbors knew, so did they. But no one had ever come to the door and knocked, or looked in on Momma the following day, or said anything to me at school.

Grandma's voice came back on the line. "Are you alright, Bethany Celeste?"

I was surprised she called me by my full name. I thought about it. "No," I said quietly. "Not really."

"Bethany, where's your father right now?"

"Gone." I said. "He always gone at night."

"Can your mother come to the phone?"

"She downstairs, but she'll get in trouble if he find out I called you."

"I'll make sure he doesn't," my grandmother said.

"Yes, but—"

"We'll make sure he doesn't," she repeated. "Now go and get your mother. I need to speak to her."

They were on the phone a long time. I tried to listen through the door, but my mother was mostly silent, as usual. I heard her grunt quietly, in agreement, as the conversation lengthened, but she said little. When she hung up, she opened the door and looked at me. "Come with me, baby," she said. I followed her down the hall and into the bathroom. She stood behind me and we stared into the mirror.

There was no denying I was a Castle, but for the first time I genuinely feared the parts of me that were my father.

"Bethany," she said quietly, "sometime it's hard for men when they see their little girl grow into a young lady."

"I'm not a la—"

"Bethany," she said with the closest thing to sternness I'd ever heard, "please listen to me. Sometime a father love his daughter like crazy when she a little girl, because she admire him and love to be with him, and that make him feel powerful. But when the girl begin to grow up, and maybe start looking for a boyfriend, her daddy feel lost, or left out, or maybe even a little bit jealous, because he not the only man in her life no more."

"I'm not even looking at boys!"

"But soon boys is going to start looking at you. Can't you see your body is changing? Soon you'll be shaped different, and you'll be interested in going out to parties, and wearing nice clothes, and doing things with people your own age."

"But only the stupid girls at school are into that stuff."

"Sooner or later almost everybody do those things, baby. It's part of growing up."

"But that's no reason for Daddy to hit you or me!"

"You right," she said, her voice breaking. She continued to speak, but there were tears in her reflected eyes. "I don't know how to make him stop, baby. I've worried about it for years, but I don't know where we could go where he wouldn't find us. I thought I could take it, so long as he didn't hurt you."

"So what are we going to do?"

"Your grandmother has a idea," she said, "but I told her I have to talk it over with you." Turning away, she went into my bedroom and sank down on my bed. I came and sat down beside her. There were blue marks on her upper arms, her neck and the side of her face. He'd knocked some of her teeth out, so she rarely smiled anymore.

"Your grandma said she would send me enough money to get away from your father. She told me to rent a post office box, so the money won't have to come to the house."

"Where would we go, Momma?"

"I would go to my aunt in Maryland," she said softly.

"You would go to Maryland? But what about me? You're not going to leave me here with—"

"No, Bethany. Grandma want you to come down and stay with her."

"With her? But what about —"

"You could live with her and go to school. She would take care of you and give you everything you need."

"But why can't I come with you?"

"My aunt won't have room, baby. I can sleep on her couch and try to get a job. I'll earn enough money to get a place of my own, then you can come and live with me. We'll start all over again, far away from your father."

"Then you should come with me to Grandma's."

"If I do, he'll just drive down there to get us."

"What if he come looking for me?"

"He won't get past his mother," she said in a hushed voice. "And he won't try because he know she'll keep you safe. I'm sure of that, too."

"Do I have a choice?"

"He not giving you or me a choice."

I looked at her tear-washed face and understood she had, indeed, survived my father's cruelty for years in order to protect me. Now, in order to protect me, she was going to have to send me away. We sat there for a long time, both of us staring at the floor.

"Your grandmother going to need a few weeks to get the money together," my mother murmured. "So we have to wait. Please, Bethany, try not to get in your father's way. I don't want nothing bad to happen to you, because if he ever seriously hurts you, God knows, I don't know what I would do."

* * * * * * *

It took six weeks for that check to arrive.

I turned sixteen in the interim, though we hadn't celebrated. During that time my father had graduated from knocking me into a corner, to the time he lifted me off the floor and pitched me against a staircase, bruising my back, thighs, shoulders and head. The pain left me winded, but when he stood over me and aimed a kick at my ribs, my enraged fear was more intense than the pain. All that night, as I lay balled up beneath a pile of thin blankets, I tried to figure out how to kill him.

After all, in our home, 'kill-or-be-killed' had become my reality.

It was right after Presidents Day, when I trudged home though a foot of snow, my knees blue and muscles hurting, that Momma met me at the door, excitement in her eyes. She smiled a genuine smile and ushered me to the kitchen table, where a bowl of soup and a grilled cheese sandwich were waiting. Though it was very late in the day, my father was still asleep.

She raised her chin and placed her finger on her lips. When I sat down to eat, she slipped into a chair across from me. "What did you learn in school?"

"Math. I hate math."

"Did you have Geography?"

I peered at her, the spoon halfway to my mouth, and raised my brows.

"How far away is Maryland?" she whispered.

"I don't know. I mean, I think it somewhere near Washington."

"It's like North Carolina. They don't have winter there. I heard it don't even snow." Her eyes went to the stairs. There was no sound from their bedroom, above us in the front of the house.

"The semester over in two weeks, Beth. Then you have a week-long break. We should think of something special to do over the break."

I understood her, and nodded once, solemnly, in agreement. Nothing more was said.

Copley had started watching me day and night—driving up to the school just as I walked out of the building with my classmates, waving me over and insisting that I get into his hearse of a black car. Though he still went out in the evenings, he sometimes banged into our kitchen unexpectedly, only half as drunk as usual, and stood behind me as I washed the dishes. I pretended he wasn't there, answering his questions ("Who was that little shit talking to you today?") with as few words as possible, and biting my lips to keep from saying too much.

He did his best to provoke an argument: he kicked a stack of library books down the stairs, watching as I scrambled to pick them up. "Why you wasting time with that shit?" he growled, raising his chin so he could see me through swollen eyes. You need to get a job after school and contribute to this household."

Fire burned in my heart, but I thought of my escape and simply nodded in agreement.

Another evening he came after me as I washed the dishes. "Listen here, heifer—and look at me when I speak to you!" I glanced at him quickly.

"I know you been sneaking around. I seen it in your face. Your momma don't even try to stop you. She ain't no kind of mother."

The suds were warm on my hands. I put my mind on the handle of the knife submerged in the foamy water.

"And why you wearing them tight pants? Your momma got those for you? What the fuck is she thinking?"

"Momma didn't see them," I said softly. "I got them at Goodwill and I only wear them in the house."

"You a liar just like she is, and you look like a slut."

My heart sped up. "I'm sorry," I said through clenched teeth. "I'll change as soon as I finish the dishes."

"You do that. I didn't raise no sluts in this house."

I kept on washing. He thought about what he could say to push me to mouth off. I could actually hear him thinking. I picked up a heavy pan, set it carefully in the sink and grasped a scrub brush.

"Don't you leave no food on that." He was standing so close I could feel his breath on my neck. I kept on working without saying a word, then turned away from him to dry my hands. He smelled of booze and smoke and sweat, and some part of me knew he was smelling me, too.

I sensed that Momma had crept down the stairs and was in the hallway, listening. I wondered what he'd do to her if he knew she was there. Would he go after her, just to see what I'd do?

He finally turned around, drunker than I'd realized, and staggered toward the back door. I felt a slap of cold air, then silence.

The next day, while he was passed out upstairs, Momma rode the city bus with me to the Greyhound station, clutching a small duffle bag she must have packed in secret. When we got to the bus she hugged me for a long time. "Write to me at the P.O. box," she said, before pushing me onto the bus steps.

"You're not going back to the house, are you?" I asked, suddenly alarmed.

"Only to get my stuff," she said.

"You told me you're going to your Aunt in Maryland!"

"I am, baby." There were tears in her eyes. "Later on today."

"Don't go back to the house," I begged from the bus steps. "Don't!"

"I'll be alright," she said. "Give Miss Corinne my love."

She raised her hand in a half-wave, and I leapt forward, making to get off the bus. She looked over my head at something, and the driver closed the door. "Take your seat, Miss," he said. "We got to get going."

I knew, even as I watched her shrink as we pulled away, that she wasn't going anywhere. I also knew she couldn't accept what we both knew to be true: Copley Castle beat my mother to control her, because he took such deep pleasure in her pain. But Brenda Berniece Johnson chose to believe that beating her was Copley's crude and cruel form of love—the only form of love he was capable of.

heather neff.

III.

blissfield, north carolina.

2016.

six.

The Old Man with the white hair spent a long time trying to teach me to use meditation, deep breathing, and something he called "guided imagery" to help me manage difficult situations.

None of it worked.

He never understood that when life is trying to fuck you up, the last thing you want to do is let your guard down. I felt a little bit bad about how hard he tried. But then, he didn't have a street of abandoned houses to deal with. If he had, he would have understood that life is a balancing act of drawing on the past to find strength when you need it, but slapping it back down when it tries to take over. It's not that the past was more difficult than the present. It's that you need the past in order to figure the present out.

Blissfield was still playing hard and fast with me. Before dawn the next morning a sharp clanging sent me scrounging beneath a stack of books to snatch up the receiver of Grandma's heavy old rotary phone. A mature, pipe-smoker's baritone waited on the line.

"This is Richard Armitage. To whom am I speaking?"

"Bethany—Bethany Celeste Castle." I peered behind the blinds, afraid that another one of my grandmother's people might be standing in the yard. Fortunately, there was nothing to see but thinning mist in the gathering light.

"Ms. Castle, I'm your grandmother's attorney."

Two days. It had taken only two days for the news to spread that I was in town and holed up inside the yellow house.

"I realize it's early," he said, "but I assume you're quite busy and I wanted to catch you before you went out. I'd like to set up a brief meeting to discuss your grandmother's estate."

He proceeded, in brisk business-like fashion, to invite me to visit his office that afternoon. I hauled myself awake, thinking fast: though it would have been better to put him off for another day or two—just so I could finish going through my grandmother's papers—I was scared he would take some action to remove me from the house and, hell, my pockets were light and my options amounted to smoke.

I agreed on a time and he described the location of his office, though he really didn't need to. I knew exactly where it was—in a stately brick house once owned by an old spinster lady who was the last descendant of a proud slaveholding clan—or at least, that's how Grandma once described her.

So at precisely two o'clock I entered the stately brick house with Grandma's words ringing in my ears. Georgian in design, a bronze Heritage Society plaque was mounted beside the front door. When I was a small child I heard my daddy say that he'd always wanted to see how fast a slaveholder's house would burn. He said it was somebody's duty to bring an end to those slaveholding clans. I kind of agreed with him.

The front hall was dark, narrow, and smelled of gently rotting wood. A flowered runner led me past the parlor—now converted into a library replete with leather-bound legal volumes, and toward an office at the rear of the house. There was no receptionist, but as I started down the hall I was met by a surprisingly fit, silver-haired man with a cyclist's tanned legs and cradling a tiny cup of coffee.

Though he'd set up the appointment, he paused in surprise at my appearance. "Richard Armitage," he volunteered unnecessarily, looking directly into my face as he shook my hand. His white polo bore the insignia of a popular brand of running gear.

"Bethany Celeste Castle," I replied. "What a lovely house," I added, wondering if he'd catch the light sarcasm in my tone. "It looks like it's been here for at least a century!"

"That's what they say," he replied. "My wife and I purchased it a few years back from the estate of the original owners. They'd been in the house for some four generations. It was kind of a wreck, and frankly, it still needs a lot of work." He heaved a sigh as he led me down the hall. "Termites."

His office was a bright room dominated by a massive cherry wood desk. He set the coffee gingerly on a Blue Devils coaster, glanced up at me and gestured toward the cup. I shook my head and he indicated I should sit on one of the heavily upholstered armchairs facing the desk.

"I apologize for staring when we met," he said. "You bear a startling resemblance to your grandmother."

"So I'm told."

He smiled pleasantly. "You've been finding your way around town?"

"I lived in Blissfield some years ago," I said, remembering with a stab of pain that I'd once stood outside this very house with Gideon.

"Oh, yes—your grandmother did mention that." He took a seat behind the desk and appraised me again. I'd dug a dress out of my duffle bag—a navy blue, short-sleeved sheath I used to wear to retail management trainings. Though it fit me well, clothes that make it hard to move make me vaguely anxious, so although I looked like Corinthia's granddaughter, I felt Copley lurking just behind my eyes.

"Your grandmother was quite a woman," Armitage said. "Though we were two decades apart in age, I thought of her as a personal friend. I feel quite honored that she asked me to serve as her attorney."

"Oh, really?"

"When I was a child she used to come to school board meetings to discuss matters related to Booker T. My father was on the board and I remember how the room went quiet when she spoke. Later we served together on committees to raise funds for the library and a new pre-school. I greatly admired her.

"And of course," he added, "I was about the same age as her older sons. We attended different schools—" he glanced away, deftly avoiding the realities of segregation "—but I unfortunately sometimes met them on the football field." We both laughed lightly.

"Did you know my father?" I said.

"Copley? He was younger, of course, so I never knew him personally. I remember him as a gifted athlete, but if you'll excuse me for saying so, he always seemed to be into something. He had a friend, a fellow called—I believe it was Pilate—and the two of them almost took this entire county apart. Just petty crime—underage drinking and the occasional shoplifting, but they were as cool and sophisticated as city guys. They were much too much for Blissfield, so they went into the service as soon as they came of age.

"You know, your grandmother's good name kept your father out of lockup," he continued, "but even then he was already courting a long-term prison cell. He was, as we sometimes say, an angry young man, and sadly, he didn't seem to care what his actions did to his mother."

The lawyer took a sip of his coffee. I hoped he couldn't read the tangle of emotions I was trying my best to hide.

"Might I ask if you are still in contact with him?" Armitage asked.

I hesitated, weighing whether I wanted to talk about Copley, but after a few seconds I knew I'd have to eventually. "No. Why?"

"I thought he might attempt to claim the estate."

"I don't know if he's even aware that my grandmother's dead."

"Then she cut all contact with him after——?" He paused as if acknowledging the invasiveness of the question.

"No idea," I said, and though I told myself to stay cool, I heard the tension building in my voice. "To be honest, my grandmother never even contacted *me* after my father murdered us."

"Us——?"

"Yes, both my mother and me." I was suddenly oppressed by the weighted silence of this house, as if the past pressed in through every wall, making it difficult to breathe. Cars cruising down the street outside sounded like freight trains, and a bee near the window ground the air like a chainsaw.

His brows rose, then his eyes shifted as if something he hadn't understood was beginning to make sense. "I'm genuinely sorry to learn that," he said with what I perceived to be a measure of kindness.

"Now may I ask you a question, Mr. Armitage?" I said. "Why did you go ahead with my grandmother's funeral without me?"

He leaned forward with the practiced calm of someone used to guiding people toward sharing his conclusions. "The Ohio police had no current address on file for anyone with your name, so we had the coroner's office leave a message with someone whose name resembled yours. Not knowing whether we'd find you, I took it upon myself to make the arrangements for her burial. She'd left written instructions that she wished to be cremated."

"What happened to her ashes?" I asked.

"The urn is in a very nice columbarium on east Central Street."

"Central Street? Everyone in Blissfield knows we have a family cemetery."

"Well, that situation is rather complicated," he said carefully.

"Situation?"

"At the moment," Armitage said, "it is unclear who the Castle properties actually belong to."

"Other than my father—and she can't possibly have left anything to him—I'm certainly her sole beneficiary."

There was a pause. "Ms. Castle, I'm sorry, but you are, in fact, not the primary beneficiary of Corinthia Castle's estate."

"What—did she leave it to her church?"

Avoiding my eyes, Armitage rose, crossed the room and brought a thick file from a cabinet in the corner.

"Actually, she didn't," he said, returning to his desk. "There are, however, other parties with whom we need to establish contact before I can discuss the details of her will. I've begun searching for these persons, and I'll convene a conference with all of you as soon as we're able to make arrangements to meet."

"Who is it?"

"I deeply regret that I'm not at liberty to reveal this information until all the pertinent documents, including the identities of the beneficiaries, have been retrieved and certified."

"So my grandmother didn't leave *any* of her property to my father or me?"

"I'm afraid we'll all have to wait to learn that."

"I don't—you must be kidding—"

"Ms. Castle," Armitage said quietly, "having known your grandmother, I don't have to guess how difficult her passing must be for you. I'm going to ask for your patience while we work out some legal entanglements that were created some time ago. In this case, there are prior exigencies that may influence the way the entire estate is apportioned."

"Entire estate?" I said. "Aren't we just talking about the house and the farm out on the highway?"

"Yes and no. Your grandmother not only possessed the house, but the surrounding land all the way to the corner. She also served as the custodian of over fifteen hundred acres of timberland out on Route 158, and at least ten plots suitable for construction near the old high school. She allowed farmers to work much of the land, and she asked to be paid only modest amounts, mostly in food, from what I understand. She was exceedingly generous with her tenants."

"But why didn't she get what the land was worth?"

"Either she didn't feel it was right, or it just wasn't in her character."

"She never seemed to have much money," I said, remembering her frugality. "Why would she live like a poor person when she didn't have to?"

"I believe she felt that the people who worked the land needed it more than she did. And of course," he continued, "all of these properties are part of the estate. In principle, the beneficiaries will have to decide whether or not they should be sold."

"That's crazy." The words came out of my mouth like bullets, though I knew exactly nothing about farms, timberland, construction-worthy lots or taking care of a house. I didn't even know if I could bear to live in Grandma's house—that Petri dish of the past.

Armitage laid his hands flat on the file. "I wish I could answer your questions, Ms. Castle. Legally, I see no reason why you shouldn't continue to stay in the house for a few more days—that is, until the other beneficiaries have been contacted and the ownership of the house becomes clear, but you should be prepared to leave the premises immediately should the property pass to another heir. And though I cannot stop you from sorting through your grandmother's belongings, I must ask you not to take or discard anything at this time. We need to be sure her belongings are distributed exactly as she desired."

He stood and held out his hand. Like the old man in the church the day before, his tone suggested our discussion was over.

"I apologize again if you are uncomfortable with my actions concerning your grandmother's burial," he said. "Should you decide to make other arrangements, I must still ask you to refrain from placing the urn in the Castle cemetery until it has been determined that the land is actually yours."

* * * * * * *

Though I knew the lawyer had gone to some trouble not to upset me, a needle of pain pierced my left eye as I climbed into Ruby and hurtled down Main Street, stirring up a cloud of red dust and narrowly missing two Black children dragging a puppy by a rope across the town's one intersection. Within moments, a circuit board ignited in the front of my skull. At the east end of town I spotted the spiked iron fence of the white folks' cemetery and skidded to a stop in the parking lot. Armitage was right: it was neat, well-maintained, and—something I hadn't expected—now integrated. Several Black women and two white families were placing plastic flowers in various planters along the grassy paths. A Black family gathered around a mound of red earth. They looked up, surprised at the sound of my car. Understanding the local code of conduct, I gave them a sharp little nod that they politely returned.

Rows of gravestones, some in the flecked grey granite of recent years, and rounded cement markers listing to the side, stretched about two-tenths of a mile in both directions. Three enormous oaks formed an interlaced umbrella over the plots. I stood for a moment, getting my bearings. A small, white-bricked columbarium stood to the left, with dogwood trees planted in a circle around it. This was a beautiful place to be dead, but it wasn't the place for my grandmother.

Inside the columbarium the air was close, cool, damp. Shelves that resembled a sophisticated bookstore formed niches, holding urns of all shapes and sizes behind glass windows. Some of the niches also had photographs of their inhabitants; others had small budvases with plastic flowers. Brass plates bore the names of the deceased.

It didn't take me long to find her. Someone had chosen a squat brass urn encircled by a gold band. My heart sped up. This was all that remained of Corinthia Bibb Castle? My grandmother was trapped in this showcase like a football trophy? Even if she had abandoned me, I couldn't leave her to this fate. My headache surged, and without a moment's hesitation I picked up a rock, smashed the glass, removed the urn from its stand and tucked it under my arm before tramping back to Ruby.

The white ladies had turned and were staring hard in my direction as I passed.

"Hope you're having a lovely day," I said between gritted teeth. Moments later I sped away.

I brought the urn into Grandma's house and set it on the center of the dining room credenza, among the many family photographs. Backing into a doorframe, I stood before it, head ringing, and stared into nothing.

"Because you are nothing," I said out loud, hearing the raw, rough syllables absorbed by the dense silence of the house. "You—Corinthia Bibb Castle—were so much larger than life. Everybody in this town bought into the myth of you—the powerful, fearless, warrior-goddess. It looks like I might be the only one who knows you were nothing more than a shitload of secrets and lies. This is exactly what you are: a stranger in an ugly bronze pot."

Now my tears were heavy, hurtful, and dredged from the deepest part of my body. I wept right there, clutching the doorframe, making great, whooping sounds that would have been embarrassing if anyone else had heard. Or maybe I didn't really give a shit if anyone heard.

Because I loved my grandmother and trusted her.

She had lied, ignored and abandoned me.

Children may not remember everything they feel and hear and see. But they never fully recover when someone they believe in betrays their trust.

Suddenly I was hauling boxes of ancient papers from the bedroom and dumping them in the yard. Crumbling books and damp-rotted newspapers followed. Old, ragged and faded garments came next. I finally added the moth-eaten sheets and the stacks of almanacs that stood in the screened porch in the back.

Dripping with sweat, eyes burning and my brain feeling like it was ready to explode, I poured lamp oil over the pile and lit it with matches. With a loud *whoosh*, the fire leapt for the sky, and I felt a ringing sense of satisfaction as I watched the flames curl and crack. For the first time since I'd arrived, I felt like I was in control of something.

The fire burned for hours, but that's because I continued to feed it. Nearly staggering under the weight of my migraine, I threw Reader's Digests and Ladies Home Journals, sour-stained dishrags and worn-down shoes, paper plates and faded clothing into the black-fingered fire. As darkness fell the flames subsided, and moving like a machine, I brought pots of water from the kitchen and drowned the embers, smoke leaping up toward the darkening sky. Arms aching from carrying boxes, my head throbbing along with my heartbeat, I watched the colors fade and die.

Now I was safe. There was nothing left of Corinthia Bibb Castle to hurt me anymore.

* * * * * * *

Friday night was different.

Cars were strewn about Whelan's yard like Matchbox toys, some head to head, others half on the curb and half in the lot. The O'Jays' *"money money money MONEY!"* pumped loud enough to rattle the glass in the windshields, and shifting shadows of men and women posed on the hoods and trunks, with bottles, joints and other remedies to life's meanness passed casually between them.

The only light came from the rectangle of the screen door, the music swelling with every opening. There was no reason and every reason for me to be back in Whelan's. Passing through the door was like crossing into some kind of under-world, with so many people I couldn't even see the bar. Tables pushed aside, a couple of women danced rough on others, clearly flush with drink. The music was too loud to think (*"money money money MONEY!"*), the lights too low to risk flirting with a stranger. I didn't need a drink as badly as I needed not to be alone, yet I shouldered my way toward the bar, hoping that no one would recognize me, but pretty sure that somebody would.

The air felt like I was breathing wet felt, despite the rusty fan blades wobbling on the ceiling. It took me a while to get the bartender's attention. It wasn't Bruce—this dude was tall, thick-waisted and even *more* cop than Bruce (if that was possible), and looked as if, even when he was off-duty, he'd savor the chance to bust somebody's head.

A woman leaned toward him, her black dress missing its front. Unmoved, his hands went about the business of producing bottles and mixing drinks without missing the slightest movement in the rest of the room. Tonight a couple of wait-resses were working the floor, too—at least three short-skirted weave-wearing women ping-ponged between tables and the counter, trays laden with orders. Laughter hit that pitch where each table was fighting to outnoise the next, and I knew from experience that scenes like this always ended with someone bloodied, handcuffed or dead.

Hell, I knew I should leave, but the Castle in me either couldn't, or just plain wouldn't. Once I got the bartender's eye, a bottle was passed, hand-to-hand, back to me. I sent the cash forward and started making my way through the sweating flesh toward the relief of the door. I'm not tall enough to stand out, and I'd dressed in my black tee shirt and black jeans, hoping to be ignored. I figured I'd make my way to a neutral corner of the bar before the ceasefires ran out.

"You wanna dance, baby?"

As soon as I heard him, that other scar—the one beneath my chin—began to itch. Images of a different guy, years ago, leapt into my mind. I shook my head, saving the energy it would take to try and speak over the noise.

"Why not?" he said. "Come on, baby. Let's dance."

The voice—I refused to really turn around and get a look at the face—was right behind me. I knew he was about my age, maybe a bit older. Nasal. Over-weight—closer to fat—but tall, insolent, insinuating, unschooled. At that moment, as if perfectly on cue, the tin whistle introduction to Herbie Hancock's "Water-melon Man" filled the place.

Years of experience had taught me to ignore shit like this. To speak would invite conversation; even to *look* at him would increase his interest. *Just keep moving,* I told myself, taking a page out of my social survival handbook. He'll give up and go on to the next—

But he didn't. Mistaking my lack of reaction for fear, he placed his hand along my waist and ran his fingers smoothly down the melon curve of my pants, ending their journey with a squeeze.

"Hmmm," he said. "Not too bad. I never seen you here be—"

I stopped moving, but didn't turn my head. "Don't touch me," I said, loud enough that several people looked our way.

"Let me see you work that *thang*!" he answered, throwing in a couple of pelvic thrusts for the benefit of his boyz, who burst into shards of laughter. Assholes like him always traveled with "they boyz."

"Take your hands off me," I said, louder still.

Instead of letting go, he used both hands to pull me backwards against his pants, while simultaneously grinding himself against me.

My beer bottle clocked him clean on the side of his head, and when I pulled my thumb from the top, the liquid exploded over his beige safari shirt—*when did I start attracting pitiful creeps like this?*—and down the front of his pants. Too shocked to react, he sputtered, reaching for his temple and batting at his attire simultaneously. If this had been a circus, he'd have been in the center ring.

Without even looking at his face, I continued my journey toward a table at the back. Though I'd just cracked a full bottle of beer against a stranger's head and decorated him as if he'd peed himself, I found myself completely relaxed. I was just sorry I'd wasted my beer.

That was Copley, my daddy, working his magic through me, and *dayum* it felt good!

The table I wanted was, miraculously, still free, but that was due to its location behind a support beam in the darkest corner of the room. Great for drug deals and, if no one was watching, a quick bit of trim, but useless to men on the prowl. Once seated, you'd be hidden away from the milling drinkers and the two or three couples squeezed onto the square they'd cleared for dancing. It was the perfect place to sit if you were watching the door. If you were looking for someone. My only problem: would the waitresses ever show up to replace my wasted beer?

I was only steps away from my little hutch when, unfortunately, Mr. Ringling Barnum and Bailey caught up with me. I heard the voice before I turned because, stupidly, he decided to make a production of confronting me, rather than just doing whatever ugliness he thought he was going to do.

I didn't care. Copley was in control, now.

So he called me a "knotty-headed bitch," loud enough that his clown's voice carried over the music (Marvin Gaye's *Got to Give It Up!*), and all the shouting in the bar.

Once again I stopped dead in my tracks, ready to turn around and confront him right back. I truly didn't want to see him, because if he looked like his voice, he'd have a big red ball stuck on the end of his nose and Bozo-red hair framing his face. I knew I'd start laughing, which would only make matters worse.

On the other hand, if he produced some kind of weapon—including a beer bottle of his own—I needed to be ready to do whatever Copley suggested. That might include a well-aimed knee, a true "bitch" slap (since he'd identified me so correctly), or another, meaner conk upside his head. Maybe I'd even have to take out my hunting knife, which operated on a spring-blade and opened to eight full inches. I thought it over quickly: On the upside, it would feel great to watch him hit the floor. On the downside, however, the bartender might, indeed, be a cop, and I wasn't looking to get arrested.

So I turned. The dude was a pathetic sight: forty-ish, big-bellied, with slicked-back hair (didn't jherri-curls go out thirty years ago?), and, sadly, the eyes of a man who was only trying to celebrate the end of the work week.

"Hey," I said.

He looked back quizzically, not sure why I was coming across as kinda chilled.

"Hey," I said again, with all the friendliness of the gal-next-door.

"What," he replied, "you tryin' to act like we cool?"

"We cool," I answered, and made to walk away.

Of course, it was too much to hope he'd let things go. I'd made it only one more step before he reached for my arm and jerked me back toward him. I felt a kind of string tear inside of me, like when the rope that works a marionette breaks loose and the puppet goes out of control. Actually, Copley was *really* having fun, now.

I wheeled around and brought the butt of my free hand up into his lower jaw just as hard as I could. I had reckoned that his mouth slamming shut might get a corner of tongue, or trap a lip between his teeth. I really didn't care which. I just needed him to know he was not going to touch me and walk out of there unbloodied.

The explosion wasn't pretty, and certainly messed up his safari shirt for good. He fell backwards, covering his mouth, and two or three people jumped away as he smashed against a table, upsetting drinks, bottles and a woman's purse, and hit the floor hard. I was still holding my half-emptied beer in my other hand, my legs braced apart, my wrist aching from the blow. I measured the crowd to see if any of his *boyz* might want to try me out. No one volunteered.

Slowly and pathetically he got to his feet. He peered quickly in my direction, then, noting the blood pouring through his fingers, he pushed his way toward the door. The crowd closed in around him, and I was again aware of the music (James Brown, *The Big Payback*, appropriately), and the free-flowing sound of voices.

Sometimes, despite everything, I find my asshole father very useful.

I finally took my seat at the small table in the rear. I exhaled into the smoky darkness, realizing I was bathed in cold sweat. It didn't much matter. Everyone in the room was swimming in the dank, murky air. Though I could barely make out any faces, the chaos had a certain shared sweetness, as if all of us were glad to be breathing in each other's funk.

I found myself lulled into a kind of peacefulness. My grandmother had hated Whelan's; if my mother was alive, she, too, would have warned me away from it. But I had to admit that some part of me felt very much at home, right there, in this cinderblock, alcohol-drenched pit in the middle of the no-place backwater town of Blissfield.

And then.

As my eyes traveled, I saw Bozo coming back. I knew, though it was somewhere in a pocket of his clothes, that he was coming back with something intended to fuck me up *good.* Something I might not be able to walk, run, or get up off the floor from.

Hell, I knew how *that* shit went down. I wasn't interested in getting murdered again.

I rose, slowly, thinking about which part of the crowd was thinnest. How could I get to the relative safety of the counter—*could I get behind it?* —or the door—*could I make it to Ruby?* In the two or three seconds it took to clutch my bottle and grasp my knife, I was counting on my well-honed skill of sluicing myself through walls of milling people—one of the few advantages of spending many hours working in retail—to get myself somewhere safe.

He had spotted me and was now no more than ten bodies away, wedging himself through the crowd, his eyes fixed on me. I too was moving fast, loosening my muscles to roll, rather than push, myself forward. Eight steps out, I looked back to see him six bodies back, still shoving. I bent a little lower, my face coming close to a pair of aubergine breasts that were quickly replaced by a broad, muscled chest. Standing once again at my full height, I saw that Bozo had, unfortunately, gained on me, and was now merely an arm's length away. I figured he couldn't do too much, long as I stayed in the thick, but I still hoped to reach the counter before I had to cut him.

In a perfect world, Bruce would have been slinging bottles that night, but the stranger behind the bar neither knew me, nor seemed to connect me to my grandmother. Maybe he'd only heard about my father in passing. He certainly didn't have any allegiance to me, a stranger in this strange land. It was even possible that Bozo was his cousin, or one of his oldest friends.

But still, I touched the edge of the counter with the hope that being in the reflected neon light, and in the double sight of the mirror, might serve as a kind of *allee-allee-in-free,* and would stop my aggressor in his tracks. I peered into the reflection in time to see his bulk parting the crowd like a freighter parts water, and actually gritted my teeth, ready to hit the spring on my blade and go for his throat.

The last patrons seemed to peel apart and the clown stepped into the free space between the tables and me.

The dude was a mess. Visibly panting, soaked in sweat, lips bloodied and swollen, beer-drenched and defeated, he went into his pocket to withdraw my punishment. The room was roaring like waves on a stormy day. Ten-thousand balloon faces froze and stared with identical, intensely concentrated excitement.

The bartender seemed to appear from nowhere. He took a firm stance, legs apart, towering over me.

"Gerry." His voice was low, but somehow carried clearly. "Gerry, you got to chill."

The thick hand in Gerry's pants pocket was shaking.

"Gerry: don't do any stupid shit up in my place."

Bozo ignored him.

"You hear me? Don't try anything stupid in my place. Won't nobody take your side in this. Everybody saw you put your hands on her first."

"You didn't see shit," Gerry growled, his red eyes fixed on me.

"I don't need to see it to know how it went down. This woman don't have to be interested in you just because you want her to. She didn't come in here lookin' for anything but a cold drink on a hot night. Let it go."

"That bitch—"

"Go on home, Gerry. Don't make me throw you outta here."

There was a long, tense pause. The balloons bounced gently in place. Either the room had gone silent, or I just couldn't hear anything but my breathing.

"Gerry? I'm telling' you—I don't want to take you out of here in handcuffs."

"Fuck you, Brandon—" The hand moved deliberately, as if unlocking something.

"You need to think this through, Gerry. If you take anything out your pocket that I don't like, you might make the acquaintance of something I got in my pocket, too."

For a long moment the entire room watched as Gerry's eyes flitted between the bartender and me. The bartender spoke again, his voice still calm. "Is that what you want, Gerry?"

Slowly Gerry's hand emerged, empty. He rolled his shoulders. He stared at me. "Fuck you, bitch," he said with great southern charm.

Wheeling around, he moved, with an attempt at manhood-saving nonchalance, toward the door. I watched his elephantine figure depart.

"You alright?" The bartender was looking at me. His eyes were very light brown and his body was mercilessly hard beneath his black shirt. I could now see that he was strapped.

"Thanks." I also realized I could hear again. Gladys Knight was singing about the midnight train to Georgia.

"You sure?"

"Yeah," I said, my voice raspier than I expected. He looked smoothly away from me, and instinctively my eyes followed his, coming to rest on a figure leaning just inside the door.

I drew in a breath.

There's a dirty truth to the fact that the most *expected* shit always happens when you *least* expect it.

A kind of ghost had appeared in the doorway of the roadhouse. My skin registered its presence before my head caught up, a shiver racing down my arms and back despite the sweat-soaked heat.

Even with his face blurred by smoke and shifting bodies, I knew it was Gideon. The lift of his shoulders, the longlean torso, the massive hands resting casually—as if he was at home—against the frame of the doorway. The slight tick in his hip making one leg carry all his weight, while the other bent easily at the knee. His strong neck not matching his almost delicate, perfectly symmetrical face—a face fathomed by an artist making charcoal sketches on rough, loving paper. *I'd rather live in his world—*

Gideon. Beautiful, raw, gentle-souled Gideon: the only man I'd ever loved; the manchild lost to me fifteen years before—*than live without him in mine...*

Yes, I knew all along that *if* he was still in Blissfield, sooner or later he'd probably turn up at Whelan's. Of course that was the real reason I was here that night—the *only* reason.

But why would he turn up just when Bozo was fixing to make me suck the barrel of his gun—or worse?

And if I could see *him*, certainly he could see *me*. So why was he nesting in the doorway instead of moving in my direction?

Her man, his girl...all aboard!

I had taken one step when the barman grasped my elbow. "Hey!"

I glared up at him. He studied me, his expression cold, and spoke clearly. "You been in enough trouble for one night, you hear? That thing in the doorway—" he gestured toward the phantom with his chin— "Not for you."

"I don't—"

"—You hear me, Ms. Castle? Not. For. *You.*" He emphasized the word with such force that I felt his hot breath on my face. Regaining his full height, he held my gaze for a few seconds, then returned to his bottles.

Despite his words, I started for the door, only to find it empty. Embarrassed, I returned to the bar. I could feel the bartender watching me in the mirror.

"How do you know I'm a Castle?"

He pursed his lips. "Let me see," he said, taking a mock inventory. "Castle-face. Castle-body. Castle-*mean.*"

"I was just defending my—"

He moved closer, not buying it. "Bruce told me 'bout you. Said you come down here to settle up Miss Corinne's accounts, but you restless. You restless like your old man."

"You knew my fath—?"

"Honey, I'm sure my brother told you that everybody in Blissfield knew Copley Castle. He may of got his momma's face, but he ain't got her spirit. I would have made you for a Castle a full football field away. Everybody here can see what blood you walk with. The question is whether it's Miss Corinne or Mr. Copley's *spirit* lives inside you."

"I guess that depends."

"On?"

"On which one I need."

His shrewd eyes took a quick tour of the place, and like his brother (I could now see the resemblance), he began washing glasses with one hand while wiping down the counter with the other.

"Look," he said, "I know you didn't bring that shit on yourself tonight. Gerry find his stupid real fast when he been drinking. But you not up in Chicago—or wherever the hell you come from—right now. Down here, dudes don't like getting punked right out in the open. So if you come in here, either watch what you do, or learn how to deal with the consequences."

His face was smiling, but his words weren't. For a split second I thought about coming back at him with words of equal wisdom, but two things got in my way: First, he was right, and second, I had other things to think about.

I glanced at the door again, as soon as the barman's eyes caught up with his hands. It was still empty, except for the men and women heading in or going out. Had I imagined it? Had Gideon really been standing there, staring in my direction?

Of *course* he had—the barman saw me seeing him and remarked on it.

"Hey, Bruce's brother," I called toward the sink, where the barman was stacking glasses in a rack to dry.

"That's Brandon," he said without looking up.

"Yeah, Brandon, my name is—"

"Bethany," he said without a change in intonation. I was surprised we could hear each other so well over the shouting and the laughter.

"What did you mean about that 'thing' in the doorway?"

"Just that. Leave it alone."

"Because?"

"Because he off limits."

"But wasn't that Gid—"

"Look, sweetheart," he said with finality, "it would be best if you drank your beer and went on home before it get too late. I'm hoping Gerry somewhere in a motel room with someone he can afford on his shitty-ass paycheck. Problem is, if he ain't, he probably drinking even more this very minute and thinking about coming back up here, looking to make some more trouble with you."

"You kicking me out?"

"Can't run my business and take care a you at the same time. And besides, he a regular and you a tourist. If you go at him again, I might lose a reliable customer."

I couldn't argue with that, though I wanted an excuse to take a tour around the place to see if I could spot my phantom. Stupid, perhaps, but you don't wait fifteen years just to be cheated out of the reason why you were there in the first place.

"Can I get another beer?" I had spilled most of the first one, and figured it might buy me some time in case my phantom came back.

"You could—but only if you play nice and sit right here at the counter where I can keep my eye on you."

"I'm not a kid."

"But I'm a cop. You can drink if you sit."

Irritated, I stood up. "In that case—" I set down a ten-spot, "I'll be on my way."

Strangely, he reached out and grabbed my wrist. His grip was strong and very steady. "Ms. Castle," he said, his eyes as coldly direct as the midday sun in winter, "you been away a long time. Don't confuse any memories you may of brought in your suitcase with the way things really are. Understand?"

"No."

"It ain't so tough," he said, letting me go. "Just remember that some doors not yours to open."

* * * * * * *

It began to rain hard as I parked beside the yellow house. I ran from the jeep to the back door, tripped on a tree root and almost fell through the screen. Inside, I was met by the chaos of remaining boxes and emptied drawers I'd created in my frenzy several hours earlier. Dripping and beersour, I stripped off my clothes and turned the hot water on in the kitchen. Rain thrummed the roof, then swelled to solid drumming that seemed to vibrate through the house. I washed off quickly, surprised at the soot that went down the drain. I then hand-washed my clothes and hung the pants and shirt up in the screened porch to dry.

I lit a cigarette and sank down on a kitchen chair. The drumming overhead went to snare, and then softened to a cymbal shish.

Overcome with exhaustion, I couldn't stop myself from thinking. I knew that thinking was about the most dangerous thing I could do. One thing I'd learned during my years in the nuthouse was that thoughts were a labyrinth with nothing but monsters inside.

But I'd seen someone who looked like Gideon, and nothing could stop my thoughts that night.

So here's the truth: my last roommate moved out because I couldn't deal with the parade of human dildos that dropped in for regular booty calls with her—then tried to crawl into bed with me. Once she was gone I couldn't afford my rent. I came home from work one night and found what was left of my stuff strewn out on the sidewalk. I missed so much work filing small claims against my ex-roommate and the landlord that I lost my job, and with no credit and no cash for first, last and security, I ended up sleeping in Ruby.

Maybe that's what I deserved for believing that eight years managing a chain-retail teen clothing store was actually a career.

As I sat in my grandmother's kitchen, rolling an unlit cigarette between my fingers, I had four hundred and thirty-nine bucks to my name, an eleven-year old ride with 179,000 miles on the odometer, and nothing to go back to. So even though I was very likely squatting in Grandma's—no, in somebody else's house—it was still better than living in the Jeep.

I didn't know when the other heir to the Castle estate might show up. I also didn't know when it would be safe to set foot in Whelan's again.

And I had no idea how to find Gideon, my phantom love, or his phantom sister, Nina. If they wanted to be found at all.

seven.

During the many months I was mute, the Old Man had them run every test on me they could think of. They wanted to know whether being murdèred had done some permanent damage to my vocal cords or worse, to my brain. They wondered whether I was suffering from a depression deep enough to disconnect me permanently from their reality. They wanted to know which drugs they should give me, not so much because they believed the drugs would work—no, they were just interested in recording the results.

Most of them, including the Old Man, assumed I was silent because I simply couldn't cope with life anymore. They thought my spirit was broken—that I no longer had the will or the strength to get back in the game. But what none of them imagined, or *ever* understood, was that it took much more courage, willpower and strength *not* to speak. Holding in what I was feeling was much, much harder than letting it out, and since none of them had ever been to the places I'd gone, I just didn't feel that any of them were worth speaking to.

* * * * * * *

Shortly after sunup I climbed into Ruby and drove. The years had erased the directions to the place where, fifteen years before, Gideon and his sister lived with their mother and kid brother, but Blissfield wasn't large enough for me to get lost, and stay lost, past noon.

So I started on Blissfield's main streets and worked my way out. Few people were about. Maybe it was due to the blowtorch heat. Or maybe the Blissfielders knew something I didn't. I was learning that people either congregated at church or in bars, but otherwise kept to their own private territory. This was a town built on people living off the scripts of those who came before. White folks were politer than back in the day, but Blacks still knew where they did and didn't belong.

Crickets screamed from every direction; enormous webs weighed down the branches of the oaks, and cotton stalks waved wearily in the hot, damp air. I rode past neat frame houses with TV voices threading through the screens. Soon they were replaced with unkempt shacks, raised from the ground on cinder blocks, guarded by sleeping dogs chained in the yard.

I remembered that fifteen years earlier, Gideon and Nina's home was down a dirt road that ended in a thicket of bushes. The jeep took the red dirt roads as easily as it had the highway, passing children in too little clothing playing with sticks, or rocks, or with the dirt itself. They looked up at the roar of my engine, and when I waved, they waved back.

The road twisted around a copse of wide-bellied oak trees, dipping suddenly beside a grass-haired stream. Red-brown cows lounged on the other side of the water, switching their tales to a silent rhythm. They, too, peered up lazily as I drove by, their tails swaying out a welcome.

The spokes of a broken gate suddenly appeared, blocking the road like an open palm. The ruins of a farmhouse, wood bleached and sharp-toothed, lay behind it, near the fossil of a tractor. With a great deal of attention to the soft red shoulders, I backed Ruby up, pulled hard on the wheel, and got her facing in the opposite direction. Tobacco fields spread out in neat rows around me. There were no other human dwellings in sight.

The next road I took led me past a row of plywood shacks held together with rough nails and sheets of corrugated metal. Black people sat outside on plastic barrels. I looked hard as I passed, the tips of my fingers raised in greeting, and saw what might have been several generations of a family. I wondered if any one of them ever had the slightest chance of getting out.

So maybe the Gideon Price I'd met seventeen years before didn't even exist anymore. Maybe the guy I'd seen, angled like a vise in Whelan's doorway, wasn't even him. Maybe Gideon was in Fayetteville, Baltimore or even the Bronx. Maybe he had signed up and shipped out, or had found a blue collar in Detroit. Maybe he simply belonged to some other woman.

If it was him, I mean, if that guy at Whelan's really had been Gideon, why hadn't he reacted to the sight of me? Every damn person in town, even people I'd never even met, seemed to recognize me. And he couldn't have missed my close encounter with Bozo. Everyone in Whelan's definitely saw *that*.

Yet the man in the door hadn't moved. He'd been like a guardian, trapped between my present and my past, the reason I'd been banished fifteen years before, and the real reason I was now trying to stay.

Was I *seriously* thinking about staying?

At last the road curved around to the bottom of a hill outside town, passing the single story Booker T. Washington High School and its dusty school yard—and some of Grandma's property, as I'd learned the day before. I saw swaying trees, a bait store, a barbeque shack and a storefront church in what used to be a gas station. The pumps, round-topped and rusting, had certainly witnessed the Great Depression. Several parishioners were busy pulling weeds from a bed full of Rose of Sharon bushes framing a neon cross. Everything shimmered in the broiling August sun. Sweat had already soaked through my tee shirt, which I was using to mop my brow.

Finally I drove down Main Street, past the pharmacy and a hardware store, a restaurant—Marla's Kitchen—and a funeral parlor. I pulled up to the glass-fronted Piggly Wiggly and turned off the motor. Ruby shuttered as if haunted by what pretended to be a town. A few other cars were scattered throughout the small parking lot, pointing in odd directions, ignoring the yellow lines meticulously painted on the asphalt. Huge paper banners were taped to the glass windows of the store; one proclaimed in bruising red that Mondays were 'Bacon Brownie-Days,' Tuesdays were 'Bacon-Corndog Days,' Wednesdays were 'Bacon-Basket Weaving Days,' Thursdays, 'Bacon-stuffed Chicken Days,' and—

I stopped reading.

Inside, the store was cool and quiet, with twangy voices singing softly in the background. Two or three white kids in aprons and polo shirts stocked shelves, while a couple of older Black men carried groceries out to customers' cars. Everyone's eyes followed me as I filled an arm basket with a loaf of bread, a jumbo package of sliced bologna, a block of cheddar cheese, a liter of cola and the largest bag of potato chips I could find.

Fourteen of my four-hundred twenty-five remaining dollars went into a till, minded by a woman with lacquered orange-brown hair and meticulously painted shell-pink nails. She told me to "Come back soon," with the warmth of Anchorage in January, and I smiled right back, with a little Lake Erie in December.

I stood outside, remembering. The rusted bike rack was still there, though dented as if someone had plowed into it on some moonshine night. The road wandered away from the store, down the hill past the whitefolks' houses, and then to the red-dust street and my Grandma's yellow frame home. How many times had I made that journey, walking beside Gideon as he opened his heart?

It was time to go home, take a Book-of-the-Month from the boxes I'd filled from Grandma's shelves, eat some fatty, salty shit, and read myself, very slowly, to sleep.

No more calculating neighbors, procrastinating lawyers, wise-cracking barmen, drunken Bozos, chain-smoked cigarettes, or sad and lonely granddaughters. No more Nina. No more Gideon.

I just wanted to feel safe. I wanted to be loved.

Sometimes I honestly hate being a Castle.

* * * * * * *

Blissfield only had one family restaurant: Marla's Kitchen. It stood smack-dab in the center of Main Street, across from the pharmacy and hardware store. When I visited Blissfield as a small child, Black people could order food at a window on the street and take it home to eat. This wasn't legal, of course, but it was one of the time-honored traditions that the Blacks in Blissfield shrugged away. About the time I entered high school we were finally allowed to sit inside, after the old owner passed away and his daughter took over. I never believed the daughter really wanted Black folks in the place; it was just economically impossible to stay in business without us.

The place had been redecorated so recently that the main dining room still smelled of paint. Tables with brightly flowered vinyl covers were squeezed close enough together for everybody to hear everybody else's conversation, but the good people of Blissfield didn't seem to mind. After all, they'd hear each other's business from someone else tomorrow, anyway.

I had decided that, given everything that had gone down over the past couple of days, I owed myself a decent meal in a decent place. As soon as I hit the door, smiles broke out all over the room. I was shown to a tiny table in the front window by a sullen, overweight girl wearing pigtails and an apron that matched the tablecloths. Country music by some North Cackalacky artist was crooning from speakers overhead. I almost laughed, thinking that maybe I'd been put in the window to show that times really had changed, but of course, the waitress was way too young to be that cagey.

She set down the menu and told me in an oddly cadenced monotone that cabbage stuffed with meatloaf was the day's special. They also had fresh-baked peach cobbler and triple-layer chocolate cake for dessert. She asked if I wanted a beer. I ordered the lasagna and—because of the chaos at Whelan's the night before—water.

I could feel the ping-ponging of secret glances from throughout the room. Though this kind of annoyed me, I really couldn't blame them for looking. Some of them might have remembered me from my childhood. Certainly everyone already knew some version of what went down with my father.

Moreover, with my hair washed, oiled and carefully brushed away from my forehead, my face gained an adolescent quality that made me very popular with certain types of men. I was too thin and knew it—my calves and thighs were ropey and muscular, my arms sloped down from boney shoulders and my boy-breasts stood upright, even without a bra. I'd made up my eyes, put on a little lipstick, and even managed to dig the only other dress I owned out of my bag. It was a plain cotton tee-shirt dress in American red, a great color for coppery skin. I'd found my sandals, too, and worked a bit on my feet. All in all, I wasn't too ashamed to be seen. I knew I looked alright, as long as no one looked into my eyes.

When the food arrived the waitress put the bill down with my pasta, making it clear she wasn't waiting around to see if I wanted some cake or cobbler. This annoyed me, too, because having made an effort to dress and behave like a regular gal, it might have been nice to eat like one.

The lasagna, however, was too good for me to stay pissed for very long. Clearly fresh, the edges weren't hard or burned, as "recooks" often are. The tomatoes hadn't lived in a can, either. There were thin slices of eggplant and zucchini between the sheets of noodles. The sauce had a rich, red-wine flavor. The lasagna even came with a thick slice of buttered garlic bread.

I peered out of the window at Main Street Blissfield while I ate. Though it was still early (everything closed before eight), the town had a Twilight Zone quality of pickups parked and left by the curb the way cowboys tied their horses in front of saloons in the olden days. The empty stores stared back. I remembered seeing a Wal-Mart outside Roanoke Rapids—clearly the end of Main Street.

As I watched the falling darkness, a shadow passed the window. A few moments later it passed again. I knew it was the same person because I caught a glimpse of the Louis Vuitton bag—well, clearly a *fake* Louis Vuitton bag—of enormous proportions. I could have carried everything I owned in that bag. A woman had her arms looped through the handles so that it was perched like a tortoise shell on her back.

The thing was, when she passed the second time she had slowed down enough to analyze whether my eye shadow was Cover Girl or Maybelline. I tried to see her face, but she turned away just as I looked up. I just hoped she wasn't Gerry's girlfriend. I didn't particularly want to fight anybody that night.

The bell on the door twinkled and there was movement to my right. I deliberately didn't react until I felt someone looming over me. She lowered the Louis Vuitton bag and set it silently at our feet.

I looked up and my heart hurtled over a cliff.

Because I refuse to believe in miracles, and almost nothing in my life had ever gone particularly right, for a split second I actually thought my mind was playing tricks on me. But that would have been ridiculous, because the next best thing to finding Gideon standing beside me was this caricature of his sister, my beloved, beloved Nina.

Jesus, had she aged! The last time I'd seen her, when I was seventeen and she was almost nineteen, she'd had the washboard body of a boy who'd outgrown his pajamas. Stalky, unassuming, fearless, she'd stared with disconcerting directness while speaking clearly, astutely and calmly. She was the girl men didn't see as a woman, and a woman who hid by masquerading as a girl.

Now her eyes emerged from a nest of fine twigs and her hair, once goldenrod briars, was laced with white beneath her grey knit cap—a *knit cap* in a North Carolina August! Greying hair on a woman who had barely seen her thirty-fourth year! Her belly had swollen and softened and poured over the hem of her elasticized pants, which were six-inch floods. Her men's running shoes were unlaced, but her knobby ankles seemed to keep them on anyway. The rest of her was all bulky clothing and bad attitude.

I thought of trying to hug her, but her hands went to her hips and she stared down at me, her blue grey eyes cold as a scalpel in a morgue. I wiped my mouth and set my napkin on the table. Slowly I rose and faced her. She was at least eight inches taller than me, so even though I was on my feet, I still had to look up. She spoke first.

"Jesus know I heard, but I didn't believe."

"Hey, Nina," I said softly. "You looking just like yourself, fifteen years forward."

"That's some bullshit and we both know it." Her voice was rock hard and a bit louder than necessary, especially since she was standing so close I could count her eyelashes.

"Sometimes bullshit's right," I said.

"'Specially when you know you been wrong."

"If I've been wrong, nobody told *me*."

"I'm telling you, now," she said. "How'd you up and leave Blissfield like that?"

"I didn't have a choice."

"I'll never believe that."

"You forget what happened?"

"I ain't forgot nothing."

"Then you know why I had to be gone."

"Cause you wanted to be gone."

"My grandma didn't ask my opinion."

"Well, it was still your fault."

"Howso?"

"Only a fool wrestles with a rattler."

I stared at her a moment, then said, "I was trying to protect someone."

"Nobody axt you to."

"Nobody had to."

"That was right stupid."

"I can see *that's* true." Anger crept into my voice—and the volume notched up, too.

She struck her version of a hip-hop stance and crossed her arms, tilting her head skeptically. "You trying to pretend you cared about somebody back then?"

"I don't need to pretend, Nina."

"How I'm 'sposed to know that?"

"I risked my life for you."

"You did something crazy, then you disappeared."

"I wrote you a mountain of letters," I said.

"I didn't get no letters."

"I still wrote them."

"Maybe you never sent them."

"Or maybe," I said, "you never answered."

This caused her to inhale slowly, and I figured I was right. "Why didn't you write *me*, Nina?" I knew I sounded pathetic, but I couldn't hide my sharp, smothering sadness.

"How was I 'sposed to find you?"

"My grandma had the address."

"Wasn't you in hiding?"

"Not from you."

"Then from who?" she said. "Wasn't nobody coming to Ohio—wherever *that* is—to settle no scores."

"You think I was scared of something?"

"You must of been, the way you vanished. Like a alien abduction!"

"In a way, it was," I said, almost smiling. Somehow she hadn't changed very much.

Nina continued to stare down at me. A murmur rippled across the tables closest to us. "Ok, you a little bit different," she observed. "'Cept you still small."

"And older," I said.

"And meaner."

I shrugged. She was right.

"So what happened to you?" she asked.

"What *didn't* happen to me?"

"That's why you should'na gone."

"Christ, Nina—I. Did. Not. Want. To. Go!"

"You was handcuffed or something?"

"Pretty damn close."

"With a gag down your throat?"

"No voice," I said, "and no choice."

"Took you fifteen years to find yourself some choice?"

"Seems that way," I said, looking away.

"Fifteen years ain't no trip to the corner store."

"Dang, Nina," I said softly, "quit trying to pretend you don't know what went down with me."

"I heard rumors," she admitted, "but just 'cause folks say it don't mean it's true."

"Then why don't you believe *me*?"

"'Cause the old CeCe never would never of lost a fight."

"She lost one," I said.

"But you still here."

"A few days too late," I said. "I only found out a week ago that she died."

Nina knew I was telling the truth. Still, she stared down at me with hard, clear eyes. People at the neighboring tables began to twitter.

"I feel bad about that," she conceded. "Miss Corinne was a good person. Good to us and a lot a other people."

"Sit down," I said, pulling back my anger. "Let me get you something."

"If I sit down, I'll be late."

"Where're you going at this time of night?"

"Work. Some of us got to."

"Where you got to work at night?"

"Where they need people at night."

"Like the morgue?" I said.

"What morgue?"

"Looks like you got a body in that bag." I nudged the brown duffle with my toe.

For the first time she smiled, her face cracking even more deeply. To my surprise, she pulled out the chair and sat across from me, once again crossing her arms over her chest. "That's my uniform and my change a clothes," she said. "I got Bible study in the morning."

"Bible study?"

"Better than *bottle* study," she remarked with a beady glance at my water glass. Jesus! Had she heard what happened at Whelan's the night before?

"You seriously work all night, Nina?"

"Better than wasting time driving up and down the highway."

"Dang, Nina. How'd you know I—"

"Folks got eyes."

Shit, I thought. People really *were* keeping tabs on me. "Well, you're here now, Nina. Let me order a slice of peach cobbler to take with you. You loved peaches back in the day," I added gently.

"That was back in the day," she said coldly. She turned her head to stare at an elderly white couple who shrank from her gaze. I could see several other guests trying to signal the waitress, who was doing her best not to notice. I didn't blame the waitress. Even *I* wouldn't have wanted to confront the likes of Nina and me.

"OK," I said abruptly. "Let's save some time. Where is he, Nina?"

She arched an eyebrow. "Who?"

"You know who."

"Do I?"

"Come *on*!"

"Can't do that."

"Is he here in town?" I asked.

"Uh-uh." She shook her head, her crossed arms tightening. "You not getting nothing out of me."

"Why not?"

"Because you ain't earned the right to know."

"You wouldn't believe what I've been through to get here."

"We all been through a lot, Miss Bethany Celeste," she said. "I just don't want to bring no more pain down on my brother."

"I'd never do anything to hurt him."

"Assuming you ain't hurt him already."

"Fifteen years, Nina."

"That's exactly my point," she said. "Fifteen years, CeCe."

"Nina, I need to see him." My voice had risen, but frustration and loneliness were braided into the sound.

"You didn't *need* to see him for one-hundred eighty-seven months and twenty-four days."

"You *counted?*" I asked.

"Always was good at math," she answered, squaring her shoulders.

"And you're wrong," I said under my breath. "I've never stopped needing to see him—*or* you."

"Well," she answered, leaning forward in her seat, "it don't make no difference. He ain't free like he was back then—and *neither* one of us need to see you."

"Christ, Nina," I said, annoyance getting in line behind my frustration, "we didn't have any choice back then!"

"You want to believe that because it make things easier."

"Why do you say that?"

"Because," she said, "you and me was best friends when you lived here fifteen years ago, and the only thing you axt about since I found you sitting at this table in a restaurant where everybody know the cook spit in Black folks' food—" she had raised her voice theatrically, and was looking pointedly at the people seated nearby. One couple stood up, eyeing her warily, "—and the *only* thing you axt about," she continued, returning her attention to me, "is my crazy, dummy, fool-ofabrother."

"I'm already talking to *you!*"

"This conversation don't mean a thing, Ms. Bethany Celeste Castle."

"Please help me," I said in a near-whisper. "I don't know how to find him."

"Course you don't. And you *won't* find him unless he want to be found."

"You mean he knows I'm here?"

"You forgot where we at? This is Blissfield, Ms. Bethany Celeste. Ain't nobody got no secrets in Blissfield."

"But—"

"Gid don't do nothin' till he ready," she said. "That's what other people found out."

"Other people?"

"What, you think he been waitin' fifteen years for *you?*"

My face must have looked like somebody stomped on it, because somebody had. She shrugged loosely. "CeCe, I got to go, but tomorrow I might do you the favor of calling you. Give me your number. Miss Corinne took herself out the phone book years ago."

She didn't smile as she took the napkin I handed her. "If I call, Bethany Celeste Castle, I don't care what time a day or night it is—you better answer."

"Nina, I—"

"You better answer," she repeated grimly as she stood, picked up her bag, hoisted it onto her back, and marched out into the night.

IV.

blissfield, north carolina.

1999.

eight.

Though it had been the dead of winter when my mother tricked me into getting on that Greyhound in Akron, it was already spring when it sighed to a stop in front of the one-room Roanoke Rapids terminal. I climbed down, exhausted from sixteen hours of blink-eye glimpses of other peoples' lives. My sixteen-year-old mind had a hard time watching the artic Akron snow melt into the sooty grey of Pennsylvania mining-towns filled with rusting pick-ups, then ignite into florescent early-leaf green as we sliced through the newly-planted fields of Virginia. We crossed the Carolina state line and the world shouted itself alive with bowing magnolias and dainty cherry trees, and somehow, despite my sadness, I felt like I was coming home.

The humid-heavy air was a balloon about to explode, and the streets of the small city actually rustled with people. I remembered it was a Saturday, which explained why so many kids were out of school. Everything shimmered in the hungry spring sunlight.

Grandma appeared in the doorway of the terminal waiting room, her figure still tiny and her now silver-grey hair trimmed close to her scalp. She held me in her arms a long time, then laughed and held me at arm's length to look me over from head to toe. Behind her, a lean dark man, who she introduced as Mr. Saunders, reached for my duffle bag. Grandma explained that he was a deacon at the church, a good friend of the family, and would be driving us home.

The last thing I wanted was more travel time, but I had the good sense to thank them politely for coming to get me, and to thank Grandma for inviting me to visit. Both of us knew this wasn't a visit—I was going to stay with her until my mother escaped from my father—but it seemed indelicate to mention that right away. My father sometimes complained that feeding and clothing me was "sending him to the *po*-house," so I figured my grandmother would have to sacrifice to take me in. Still, she was willing to do it, and I needed to find a way to show her some genuine thanks.

As we walked to Mr. Saunders' big, old-model Buick I had the chance to take a closer look at my father's mother. We were about the same height; I would soon be an inch or two taller, but in coloring and physique we'd grown even more alike. It was a new sensation to live with a woman I really resembled, but at the same moment I realized that maybe my father had learned to be so mean in her home. What had I gotten myself into?

Grandma was taking equal measure of me. I figured she was wondering what I had learned from my father: Was I already ruined by what I had seen and heard in Akron? Was my personality a closed book, or did she still have time to cultivate the better parts of my nature?

Funny: neither of us was smiling while we made our evaluations. I guess both of us were being completely honest, and honesty, in its raw and unpainted face, is never pretty.

Suddenly she shook her head. "Lord knows, Bethany, you grew up fast. When you left a few years back, I wasn't sure when I'd see you again. I'm glad you're here, baby. I hope you like being here, too."

We hit the two-lane blacktop that rolled between miles and miles of pine-tree forests, the air so heavy you could put it in a jar and use it as a salve. When we made that final turn past the ditches already wild with flowers, I felt, for the first time, that sudden rush of safety: the "*drenching.*" It was like all my anger, distrust—all my *fight*—just drained away. The bright yellow house surrounded by round, white columns, smiled at me.

* * * * * * *

After we arrived, Mr. Saunders, Grandma and I ate breakfast in her small kitchen, though it was nearly lunchtime. I was a little ashamed of how hungry I was, but Grandma kept loading my plate with eggs scrambled with bacon, slices of grape-jelly toast and ladles of thick buttery grits. Mr. Saunders made polite conversation about someone's nephew coming back from Brooklyn to build a ranch house out on the highway, but I knew he was just covering for me. I was eating so fast I couldn't even grunt out an answer to any questions, including whether the Greyhound seats were comfortable or if I'd slept during the trip.

Grandma was very quiet as she watched me unpack. Most of my clothes were purchased for a much younger and smaller girl. She shook her head without speaking when she saw that many of my things weren't properly washed or mended.

That same afternoon she took me to a store on Blissfield's main street and bought me two dark blue skirts, white, pink and yellow tee shirts and a pack of bobbi socks with lace trimming. She also bought two pairs of blue jeans and some new sneakers with heart-stopping fluorescent yellow laces. I sat in utter silence on the way home, surrounded by boxes and bags. I was aware that my pink nylon tracksuit was worn through at the knees and elbows, and much too tight in the crotch, but I'd never even dreamed of having anything better.

The following morning Grandma sat me down on a stool in the kitchen, and using plenty of olive oil, patiently detangled and combed out my hair. The radio talked about the weather, the news from Raleigh, and played twangy country-western songs, and we listened without speaking. When I winced because she hit a particularly tough knot, she leaned forward and kissed my forehead, then began again, more gently. When she finished, I had a neat French braid. She had woven a ribbon into it that matched my outfit.

We repeated these rituals—a huge, solid breakfast, combing out my hair, and dressing me in clean, sundried clothes every day for almost a week. Grandma didn't mention me going to church or school. She just went about her day, taking care of her chores, with me, like a kitten, walking right behind her.

Still, every night I lay awake, thinking about my mother. And some mornings I woke up with a reptile in my belly, making me as evil as Copley. Those mornings

Grandma spoke to me with plain, simple words, as if she understood I was already struggling. Some days she said very little, but she never let me stay in bed: I had to get up and help her garden, clean, cook or paint. We might not say ten words the entire day, but we worked side-by-side, dripping in sweat, then sat at the table and ate bologna and mayonnaise sandwiches, oatmeal, or chicken, sweet potatoes and greens.

Two weeks into my stay she drove me across town and enrolled me in Booker T. Washington High, which turned out to be a lot like my school in Akron. Parts of the building were very old, and there wasn't a white face to be seen among the students or staff. The classrooms smelled of damp heat and hair grease, and the textbooks had been signed out by thirty years of kids. The school was noisy, but the sounds were familiar and comforting, and Copley remained buried deep inside of me.

For six weeks or so, on the days I went to school, I sat near a window and stared at the too-bright colors outside. My soul seemed to alight on the bushes and trees exploding into bloom. The hot sweet air filled my lungs to bursting, and I found it hard to focus on any particular memory, or thought, beyond the dogwood, apple, peach, and forsythia blossoms waving in the breeze.

The teachers didn't pick on me, probably out of respect for Grandma. I knew the other kids were watching carefully and wondering why I showed up—or didn't—and why no one explained anything. I couldn't think about any of that at the time, because just getting through the day couldn't have been harder if I'd been digging ditches for a living. Some days my knees and ankles hurt so badly I thought I wouldn't be able to walk. Other times I found myself crying great silent tears for no apparent reason. I could barely speak and had to work real hard to chew. On my worst days, Grandma let me sleep with her. Those nights, sleep hit me like an anvil, and I awoke with less sadness, though still saturated with thoughts of my momma.

I kept hoping for a letter, but none showed up. Twice we called the house, and both times Momma spoke very softly, as if my father was somewhere nearby, asleep or passed out—or as if she was in pain. She insisted she was fine and made me promise not to worry about anything, but I could tell by Grandma's face that she was worried, too. Once or twice I caught her looking at me thoughtfully. I knew I couldn't put anything past her, so I didn't even try. After the second call Grandma didn't mention calling again. I guess she figured it did me more harm than good.

Easter came, and Grandma had Mr. Saunders drive us back to Roanoke Rapids so we could shop. She said if she ordered me a dress from a catalogue it might not fit, and she wanted me to be "just right" for my first appearance at Holy Redeemer Baptist Church.

I didn't really know what that meant, but I got into the Buick anyway. I was surprised to see that even more wildflowers danced restlessly between the pines as we made our way back to Roanoke Rapids. I felt my soul tiptoe from petal to petal, coating me with thick pollen from their velvety stamen. With the windows down, the air smelled of pine resin and hot motor oil. The sweat beading my hairline was swept away. I felt something close to happiness.

Roanoke Rapids was still a village, compared to Akron. We passed the bus terminal and drove to the end of a long block of older storefronts. White people strolled back and forth, entering the businesses with easy purpose. There were few Black people to be seen.

Grandma took me into a dress store with old-fashioned white mannequins in the windows. Some of the plaster women had chipped noses, and their painted hair was styled the way women looked in black and white movies. Inside, the big room smelled of dampness, plastic, and dry-cleaning chemicals, but the white-haired white women who came from behind the counter greeted Grandma warmly.

They made me stand on a round, carpet-covered pedestal, and took my measurements, then brought frilly dresses out in clear, hard plastic bags. I was shown into a small, mirrored closet where I tried each dress on, then walked out to be judged by the women. Heads tipped, hands reached for under-slips, clasps, and zippers, and finally they seemed to decide, with very little discussion, which dress we'd buy.

They then measured my feet and had me try on a series of low-heeled white shoes. All the shoes were ornamented in some way, with shining buckles, flowers, or buttons on the toe. I walked back and forth, and the ladies observed how the shoes clasped my heels and whether there was space enough for my big toe. Still a bit confused, I watched Grandma open her wallet and pay cash for the two ribboned boxes she handed to me. I looked straight into her eyes and thanked her, then thanked the ladies working in the store. I could see that made her proud.

On the way home Mr. Saunders stopped at Poppy's. There was a Poppy's near our house in Akron, but I'd never been there, so I didn't know what to order. Grandma got me a cheeseburger, fries and a vanilla malted. I ate every bite and loved it.

She also took me to Miss Zelda, a mighty force of a woman in a pink plastic apron, with enormous soft arms and a warm belly that pressed against my shoulders as she washed my hair in her sink. She sat me down on a padded chair that jerked upwards when she pressed a pedal at my feet. Then she took a wide-toothed comb, separated my hair into sections, slapped a fingerful of blue grease on each section, and pulled the hot comb, with a stinging *stsssss*, from my scalp to the ends.

My father had never allowed me to get my hair done, so I was literally round-eyed as my curlynappy hair, under the unflinching coercion of the hot comb, instantly gained two or three inches in length. Other women were getting similar makeovers in neighboring chairs, their hairdressers laughing and gossiping throughout their transformations. The richly scented hair pomades couldn't vanquish the acrid odor of burned hair, lye and peroxide. But that didn't matter: the near-agony of having a glowing metal instrument stroke our tender scalps was a ritual of Black womanhood, and Grandma was determined to end my exile from our world.

* * * * * * *

On Easter Sunday, Grandma got me up early and had me sit on a stool on the back porch while she combed out my hair. She smoothed it with olive oil, then tied a light blue ribbon around one of my curls.

The dress was blue—robin's egg blue—and with my new white shoes and shining, freshly straightened hair, I felt like royalty. Grandma had a new outfit, too—she'd purchased a short-sleeved lavender dress with a matching jacket and shoes. She had a drawer full of jewelry, and she let me wear some of it. "Princess, we're going to have to pierce those ears," she noted when she realized she had no clip-on earrings for me to wear. "And it's time we got you some perfume. Maybe we'll start with a little bottle of *Charlie*. Or *Chloe*. No lady is completely dressed without her scent."

Holy Redeemer Church was a blur of pastel colors and joyous song that Easter morning. I don't remember the particulars, because I had never been to church before, and it seemed like the service, though grand, went on forever. Grandma couldn't sit with me because she was with the Women of the Church. Some of them wore white and helped out the parishioners who were overcome by the heat or by their faith. Mr. Saunders sat beside me on the front pew, where he clapped and sang, and once or twice got real quiet (I think he was praying).

Everyone in the church wore elegant hats adorned with feathers and flowers, and many carried bibles. Small children clearly knew more about what was going on than I did, because they sat absolutely still on the pews while their parents danced, shouted, and joined in with the singing. I tried to follow the service for a while, but my eyes strayed to an open stained glass window and the field beyond. Though it seemed like every Black person within eighty miles of Blissfield was in church with us that Easter Sunday, I saw someone with sun-browned skin walking back and forth, throwing a football to another person I couldn't see. My gaze settled on the ball, which rotated, as if in slow motion, as it took flight. While that ball arced back and forth across the rectangle of open window, I rested. The music, sweating bodies, and shouting people went away. I felt calm while that ball was free.

As the service ended the churchwomen surrounded me, hoping to get a closer look at Miss Corinthia's granddaughter—and Copley's offspring. I knew they were examining every detail of my appearance, and it made me feel angry and rebellious, but out of respect for Grandma I greeted each church lady as if she were my Aunt, kissed their sweaty cheeks, ignored their vinegary perfumes, and gave them my carefully rehearsed Castle smile.

Even so, I could hear them whispering about how much I looked like my daddy, Grandma, or some odd combination of both, as soon as they thought they were out of earshot. Grandma caught my eye and winked, and for the moment everything was ok.

The church doors sprang open and the pastel-rainbowed congregation poured out onto the grass beneath the mighty oak trees, where picnic tables had been covered with white tablecloths and platters and platters of food. The people set on the chicken and potato salad, cole slaw, macaroni and cheese, collard greens, cornbread, watermelon and something called *ambrosia*, iced tea and lemonade and Pepsi and water. There were coconut cakes and cobblers, pound cakes and lemon meringue, cherry and apple pies with thick crusts molded by expert fingers, and banana crème made with cinnamon and buttermilk.

I sat at a picnic table next to Grandma, beneath the outstretched branches, my plate heavy. Glancing up, I saw a reflection of myself in a car window. There I was in my robin's egg blue dress and white shoes. I wondered at this womanchild struggling out of her girl's body and into the odd new identity of an elegant young lady.

Suddenly I felt afraid. Who were these people all around me, and what were they celebrating? Why was I letting myself get "fixed up" this way? Where was my mother's daughter? Where was my mother on this Easter morning, and what was my father doing to her?

Way over, on the edge of the field beside the church, sat two boys on large rocks, watching the feast. One was taller than the other. They both wore white tee shirts, jean shorts and baseball caps. One of the boys was holding a football. Neither made a move toward the congregation. No one invited them to join in.

I watched them as I ate. The flowing sea of talk and laughter melted into a river of sound. My eyes found peace in the white tee shirts, and in the hand that palmed the football. They must have been hot, those two boys sitting on the big rocks in the sun. They must have smelled the chicken, the greens, the pie. They must have hoped someone would ask them to join in, especially on Easter Sunday.

I don't remember going around and filling the plates, but I do remember the sudden, knife-sharp stab of sunlight on my shoulders and back as I left the shelter of the trees and began to walk over the field toward the rocks. The plates were balanced on one arm, a skill I'd learned when carrying my father's food on the rare occasions he showed up to eat during daylight. I had two plastic cups of iced lemonade in my other hand.

My shoes made no sound in the grass, but the wind was loud and hot in my ears. I heard birdsong and the sudden silence of the people under the trees behind me.

The boys sat up straighter as I approached, both as attentive as hunting dogs. I kept my eyes on the plates so they wouldn't fall. When I got close to the boys, I looked up.

I heard a sudden intake of breath: my own.

One of the boys was a girl. Washboard thin, chestnut skinned and dusty-blue eyed, I noted her shorts were tethered to her hips by a frayed belt, and she seemed to be wearing boys' tennis shoes. Rough yellowish hair poked out from under the hat.

The other kid, by contrast, had the strangled look of a man imprisoned in the remnants of his boy-body. In this, he was not unlike me. He had the girl's lean face, distinct cheekbones, reddish-brown hair and bright, blue-grey eyes. The arms emerging from his sleeves were long and thick, and his neck had the same hard-muscled look. Though he didn't seem to be too tall, his hands were large enough to go all the way around the center of the football.

They watched me approach, their faces curious. When I stopped, three or four feet in front of them, they glanced at each other and looked back at me uncertainly.

"Hey," I said. "I was thinking you all might want some lunch."

Neither one of them answered.

I stood there, feeling ridiculous, but unwilling to walk back over to the churchgoers with the plates and drinks in my hands.

"It's—it's pretty good," I said. "I tried most of it myself, if you're worried about being poisoned."

For a moment there was silence, then the girl let out a rusty laugh. "You crazy," she said.

"So are you, if you don't take these plates. They're heavy and my arms are killing me."

She sprang up and took the food, handing one of the plates to the guy. I waited while she settled down again. They both looked at the heaped mounds of potato salad, cole slaw, chicken, ham, greens and cornbread. Then they looked at each other.

Something about their movements made me giggle. They were like two halves of a whole. They even moved their heads the same way.

The girl shot me a look, like she was waiting for me to say something mean.

"I'm sorry, but are you twins?" I said.

I thought she would drop her food. "Me? Twins with *that* dummy?" She jerked her finger in the boy's direction. "First of all, he way younger than me. Second of all, he don't do nothin' unless I tell him to do it. Third of all, he ain't good for nothing except football, and that don't do nothing for me."

I looked at the boy who, surprisingly, stared back at me with his steady, blue-grey eyes. He watched me like a cat protecting its prey from another cat. I found myself shifting my weight from one foot to the other.

It was hot. I knew I should get back to the church folk, under the shelter of the towering oaks. I turned to go.

"Hey," the girl said.

"Yeah?" I looked back.

"You a Castle?"

I nodded.

"Why you done this?" she asked.

"What?"

"This." She ticked her head toward her plate.

"Do I need a reason?"

"I expect so."

I lifted my face to the hot wind and the sky. Something in me felt very sad.

I walked away.

* * * * * * *

A few days later a girl named LaToya Smith decided it was time to start some shit with me in the schoolyard. I had spent my first ten weeks in Grandma's house negotiating the rude transition between Copley's prison and my Grandmother's sanctuary. Now, as the sun rose higher, the days grew longer, and Grandma's good food, routine chores, quiet evenings, and safe, warm bed helped me manage some of the grey.

No part of me wanted trouble with anybody. But once reignited, no part of me was going to back away from it.

LaToya was one of those girls who heard from her family that lighter-skinned Blacks had been chosen by some form of natural selection to rule over browner-skinned Blacks. Her press-n-curl hung about an inch below her shoulders, and she carried a pretty good copy of a Coach bag. She ruled the tenth grade class at Booker T. Washington the way I'd ruled my class back at home. Some of the girls loved-feared her, and a few loathed her but were afraid to show it, so she chose to ignore them.

With me, things were a bit more difficult.

Even in the early, ugliest days, when I sat alone by the window, not speaking, I kept my peripheral vision fixed on my surroundings. I saw how LaToya moved around me, sometimes vying for my attention—which she didn't get—and other times leading her posse, Breeana Darnay and Maybell Harris, to do little bitchy things to see how I'd react—which I ignored. Their surgical gazes, whispered talk, bursts of mean laughter and taunting comments had zero impact on my force-field. I looked at them calmly, with exquisite boredom, and responded as if they were aliens communicating via farts.

But something about that brother and sister on Easter Sunday had pierced my impenetrable wall, and I was now rather dangerously raw, my lingering sadness just barely kept at bay.

So it began in the bathroom, like so much bullshit between high school girls.

I came out of a stall just as LaToya Smith and Breeana Darnay were at the mirror, finishing up their mascara. I proceeded to the third sink, washed my hands, and without a glance at my face, prepared to go on to Algebra.

"*Daaayum*," said LaToya. "You seen that shit?"

"I seen what look like shit," Bree answered.

LaToya: "Why you think we got to have some shit like that in our school?"

Bree: "Maybe we should let it know it need to be moving on."

LaToya: "'Cause it don't seem to take a hint."

Bree: "And I think we been pretty clear."

I walked past them, then stopped at the spooled towel to dry my hands. Normally their voices were like bees droning around flowers. That morning, for reasons I can't explain, they were like dinosaurs tramping on my egg basket.

"It ain't nothin' but a ugly lil' runt," LaToya continued.

"And don't nobody want no crossbreeds in they backyard," the delightful Bree replied.

"Just look at it," LaToya suggested. "It not black or white. Just some kind of mixed-up mess."

"I know," Bree crooned. "Check out that weird hair. And freckles? *Wooow!* I guess that's the hillbilly just below the cocopuff."

I thought about it: I had given them plenty of time to look me over, get used to my presence, and respect the fact that I actually was going to stick around. Instead, they had mistaken my silence for fear.

What a terrible mistake!

My hand found the bathroom door. I decided I would give them one final chance to chill—though secretly I was praying they wouldn't.

Don't ever say dreams don't come true.

"My momma say she just like her daddy," LaToya said, her voice rising before she drew way back in her throat and spat a thick wad of saliva on the toe of my shoe. "She come from a mongrel hoodlum, so she ain't nothing but a mongrel bitch."

With Copley precision and speed I grabbed her greasy press 'n curl with my left hand and opened her face from her nose to her left ear with the plastic Cracker-Jack engagement ring on my right. I then slammed her head into the bathroom mirror and stomped, with all my weight, on her right foot. She hit the floor in a heap, blood spouting between her splayed fingers. Meanwhile, I wheeled around, ready to negotiate a Copley-style armistice with Bree, but barely got the chance: abandoning her buddy, Bree turned and headed for a stall. When she tried to locked herself in I kicked the door with all my might, enjoying the resonant *clunk* of the metal making friends with her forehead. After a moment her voice ignited in a scream of gurgling pain.

Without a word I splashed cool water on my face, dried my hands, smoothed my hair and went on down to Algebra.

The Assistant Principal, Ms. Prentice, showed up at my classroom door about fifteen minutes later. Though Ms. Prentiss was a very proper woman, I'd seen a selection of paddles hung on the wall of her office when Grandma enrolled me on my first day. Just like me, it appeared that Ms. Prentice could take care of things in her own way, if needed. I decided it might be better to avoid provoking her.

When we got to her office Grandma was already there, speaking in a pleasant voice with the secretary, whose round eyes fastened on me curiously. I wondered how I looked: five-foot three, eighty-eight pounds, clean jeans, pink sweater, neat French braid.

Next door I could see the school nurse's back as she taped up LaToya's foot. Some kind of antibiotic ointment coated the left side of her face. She was crying. I knew she was in pain. Her pain wasn't the same as mine, but it was real, nonetheless. I'd seen my father stomp on my mother's foot. She hadn't walked right for a long time afterward.

The Assistant Principal's hand guided me by my shoulder into her inner office. Grandma followed. When the door closed behind us I was left standing between two no-bullshit women.

"Bethany, what happened?" my Grandmother asked before the Ms. Prentice could speak. I saw that this irritated Ms. Prentice, but she deferred to Grandma, who'd taught at the school for forty-four years and was two decades her elder.

"They been talking stuff and laughing at me ever since I arrived," I said. "I ignored it for weeks, but today they cornered me in the bathroom, called me a—please excuse my language—a mongrel bitch, and LaToya spat on me for no reason at all. I'm really sorry about what happened. I was scared they wouldn't let me out."

My answer was more honest and complete than either woman expected. A silence fell, and held. I looked at my Grandmother, who looked back with complete understanding—and absolutely *no* pity. Ms. Prentice wavered.

"Bethany," she said haltingly, "it's always hard when a student has to change schools. It's even harder in the middle of the year and when you're coming from far away." She cleared her throat. "I assume you're aware that your grandmother taught two generations of Blissfielders. Out of respect for her, I will not only take your words as the truth, but I will defer punishment, based on how you behave until the end of the year. Do you understand?"

"Yes, Ma'am," I answered respectfully. "Thank you very much. I promise I won't let you down."

"I hope not," she answered, casting a quick, doubtful glance at my grandmother. "You can go home, now," she added.

My grandmother rose without a word. I followed her past the secretary's critical eyes and out into the heat. Once we were sitting in her car, she turned to me, a steeliness in her eyes that I recognized, but never expected to see in my grandmother.

"Princess," she said, "I've been watching you, and you've been watching me watching you. Considering all the stuff you're working through, this was bound to happen sooner or later. *However*—" she paused "—your grace period is over. You have my permission to leave class and call me wherever you feel particularly angry or sad. But there can be no more incidents like this."

"I understand, Grandma," I said, meaning it with my head, if not my heart. "I really am sorry."

She turned the key in the ignition, but let the car idle. "I know you saw a lot of bad things while you were growing up. Some of those things are alive inside of you, whether you recognize them or not. But hurting people is never acceptable, Bethany. When you feel your daddy coming on, think of the happiest things you can remember. Let happy memories be your guide. And if you've got no good memories to hang onto, we need to try to make some soon."

* * * * * *

It was time to go to my alternate plan for survival. Taking care of LaToya and Bree—I kind of regretted that their third buddy, May, hadn't been in the bathroom, 'cause I would've fixed her, too—was a good thing, and my first step toward joining, instead of only witnessing life at Booker T. Washington. But I had to figure out a way to take care of myself while staying on the right side of Ms. Prentice and my grandma. Even though Grandma didn't react like Copley, I saw a spark of his anger there, in the shadow of her eyes.

I got back to class a few days later, because Grandma kept me home for a week to chill me out. After she dropped me off I headed straight for the schoolyard to look for someone to become a member of my *own* future posse. I needed a security squad.

Unlike Akron, where my elementary school had a sloping, tree-filled playground with World War II-era swings and slides, the schoolyard at Booker T. was in the center of a red dirt schoolyard, surrounded by the building's wings. Students gathered in the schoolyard before classes and during lunch. Though socially challenging by small town standards, the Booker T. schoolyard was no threat to a former urban bully like me.

It was, on the contrary, the ideal setting for me to begin my recruitment.

As soon as Grandma drove away that morning, right there in the middle of the schoolyard I peeled off my purple cardigan to reveal the tee-shirt I had on beneath. I took off the hair-tie and opened my French braid, shaking my hair until it formed a humidity-driven, curlynappy halo around my head. I then rolled the waistband of my skirt until I was two-thirds thigh. So now, though I was still small, I was a pint-sized package of *fuck y'all*.

The entire schoolyard, filled with kids from the ninth through twelfth grades, went silent. The other students shrank back as if I had a very big weapon under the few inches of skirt that were still visible, leaving a crop circle around me. When I reached up to smooth my eyebrow a girl actually flinched. That made me smile, then laugh.

I started walking toward the school door, calculating that the others would follow me, like the kids had followed after my little choking incident with Louis Drexler in Akron. A few steps from the door, however, someone got in my way.

I found myself looking at a plank of a girl with electrocuted golden hair. Her eyes were dusty blue and her expression was oddly closed, as if she'd been partially blinded by a flash of light.

Suddenly I realized she was the girl I'd given the heaping plate of food on Easter. Now she was wearing a faded, but clean yellow dress with a ripped hem. A worn backpack hung from her bony left shoulder. She looked down at me from her full height, and her expressionless face did not smile.

I looked right back.

She tipped her head, measuring, but it wasn't my face, hair or clothes that interested her. She was seeking something else—something less obvious and, to her, more important than my appearance.

I kept on looking, too.

Behind me, somebody in the crowd called, "*dykes!*" in a voice that was loud enough to carry, but not loud enough to identify the speaker. I whipped around, hoping someone would laugh so I could get to work, but before I could take a step back into the schoolyard I felt someone brush by me.

The Plank took a stand in the middle of the space I'd just left, and struck a pose, one leg extended, fisted hands by her sides.

"OK," she said in a rough voice that carried throughout the yard. "Whoever said that is now on notice: You can fool with me, *But. You. Do. Not. Fool. With. Mz. Castle.*"

The first bell rang and the yard emptied faster than I would have believed possible. The Plank picked up the tattered backpack she'd tossed on the ground moments before. Again we came face to face. She looked down at me and stuck out her hand.

"Nina."

I paused. "Bethany."

Her blue eyes flickered. "Don't like it."

"Bethany *Celeste*?"

Again, she tipped her head. "Celeste. That'll work. But you gonna be CeCe to me."

"That's funny," I said. "My momma's name is Bebe."

She croaked out a laugh. "First come the B's, then come the C's. I guess it was meant to be. What do you think of 'Leah'? My momma named me for that stupid girl in the Bible that Jacob had to marry, even though he wanted to marry her sister."

"What?"

"When I was little they called me 'Leah,' but I looked like a dummy."

"Why?"

"Don't you know your Bible stories?"

"'Fraid not."

"Jacob wanted to marry Leah's sister Rachel, so he worked for seven years to get her father's permission. Then the father said Jacob had to marry Leah first, and work seven more years before he could get the one he *really* wanted."

"Dang," I said. "That's kind of strange."

"Sound like Jacob was a real dummy," she said.

"I'll bet Leah was mad."

"Not as mad as Rachel," she said. "Rachel had to wait fourteen years to marry a dummy who didn't even see he was getting played."

"So you changed it?"

"I just started calling myself 'Nina' and nobody noticed."

"Your momma didn't care?"

"Guess not, 'cause she call me Nina, just like everybody else. It mean 'little girl' in Spanish."

"I never really thought about changing my name," I said.

"Slaves did it all the time when they got free."

"I never knew that."

"You should give it a try. It feel good to name yourself."

"I'll bet," I said, laughing.

"I heard what you did to LaToya," Nina said. "She is messed *up*. They saying her foot is broke and she might have a scar on her face."

"Didn't mean to do all that."

"Don't matter. Ugly on the inside, ugly on the outside. Heard you got Bree, too."

We walked a few steps together. The second bell rang.

"We late," she said.

"So?" I said.

Again the harsh giggle. "You crazy."

"So?"

"So what they say about the Castles is true."

It was my turn to cock my head, though it was hard to show attitude to someone almost a foot taller and just as fearless as me. "What do they say?" I asked.

"They say y'all fall into two camps: the good and the bad."

"So what am I?"

She shrugged. "Oh, I don't know."

We were inside the building now, moving toward the classrooms.

"Why were you in that field on Easter Sunday?" I asked.

"What field?"

"The field by the church."

"Oh, I don't know."

"Don't you go to church?"

Her face closed, and her eyes filled with an emptiness I recognized from looking into mirrors. "Well," I said, closing up the silence, "I'm glad you go to school."

She laughed. We walked a few more steps.

"Don't forget," she said at her classroom door. "No matter what they tell you, my name Nina, now."

"Okay."

As I walked away I heard her voice behind me: "Thanks for the food, CeCe. Nobody ever done nothing like that for us before."

* * * * * * *

Nina was waiting for me at lunch. We sat on an oak-shaded log under a wide-armed tree and opened our paper bags. Grandma had packed me a tuna fish sandwich. Nina had butter on white bread. She looked at the tuna.

"Want some?" I asked.

"Can't eat that," she said. "Smell fleshy. Taste alive."

"It was."

She laughed croakily. "You crazy."

Around us other kids ignored their lunch bags in favor of basketball (one side of the schoolyard), and hair styling and nail polish upgrades (the other side of the schoolyard). Three or four teachers were seated together at a picnic table beneath an awning, eating out of plastic containers and laughing a little more loudly than I would have expected.

Most everybody was wearing the same simple tee shirts and shorts, so the girls competed on the basis of nails and hair. The boys didn't care about their nails—that was strictly girly nonsense—but they couldn't get enough of that "*good*," or long, curly hair, and the girls knew it.

Nina and I watched, without really watching, as the lighter-skinned girls combed and brushed each other's pageboys. Though Nina could have matched any one of them for skin tone, it was clear that no one had ever put any relaxer on her scalp. Her rough kinks were thick enough to clean an oven, yet she didn't seem to care.

"Why are you sitting here with me?" I asked, taking another bite of the tuna.

"Why not?" she said. "You somethin' new."

I laughed. "That's it?"

"Naw. I owe you for the meal. Some of it was pretty good. You cook?"

"Not now. I live with my grandmother."

"Why's that?"

"My daddy's crazier than me," I said. "Momma sent me down here to get me away from him."

She grunted in support. "I never seen my daddy up close. My momma said he moved to Texas, but I don't believe her. She just don't like him, is all. I don't really care. We do alright without him."

"What about your brother?"

"Gideon? Like I said, he a dummy. But he alright, too."

"You get along?" I asked.

"Got to."

"That's it?"

"Naw, my momma had a baby a couple years back, so I got a baby brother, too."

"You take care of him?"

"Nope," Nina said.

"You like babies?"

"No, but he alright."

"Your brother's name come from the Bible, too?"

Nina chuckled. "Gideon in the Bible was a warrior, but my brother wouldn't kill a flea if it bit him."

We ate in silence. The nail and hair side of the schoolyard was now standing in a row, practicing cheers. Their hair bounced up and down when they jumped, in perfect rhythm with their breasts.

"You like it down here?" Nina asked.

"I guess. You?"

"I never seen nowhere else. But you come from——?"

"Ohio. That's up north."

"Bet it get real cold in the winter," she said.

"Yep. Sometimes it snows so much you can hardly walk."

"You can't get out your house?"

"Sometimes."

"So you stay in bed and drink hot chocolate all day?"

I laughed. "I wish it was like that, but they almost never close school. You just have to keep going, no matter what."

Nina shook her head. "I don't know. I might prefer to stay down here, even if this *is* no-place land."

I gave her a quick sideways glance. "You thinking about leaving?"

"Yeah, but I don't know to where. Everywhere else costs too much, and I got my family here."

"Maybe they can go with you."

"My momma wouldn't, but my brother might. He figure he gonna be in the NFL one day."

"For real?" I asked.

"He ain't too big right now," she said, "but he gonna get bigger when he older."

"You live with your mother and your brother?"

"Yeah, and the baby with us sometimes."

We finished eating, and Nina began singing Al Green songs in her out-of-tune, rangy voice. I knew without knowing that with her by my side, I could lock Copley in his cage and relax for a while. She really didn't care what anybody thought about anything, and she, too, felt good just being there with me.

nine.

I seemed to settle after that.

The teachers started speaking a language I actually understood, and the home-work came easily. My tests were returned with A's, and Grandma rarely made me rewrite my essays. No one fooled with me in the bathroom, and Nina sat under the trees with me without incident. And though she was still on my mind, I worried less than before about my mother.

Grandma tried to get me to sing in the church choir, but the music director gently suggested I would make a better usher. I liked that, because those long choir robes would have driven me crazy on those furnace-hot Sundays, and ushers got to stand in the back and help the old and disabled people into and out of their seats. We could go up in the balcony during the sermons and watch everything going on below. We could sing along if we wanted to, or look out the windows without anyone noticing.

Best of all, I could watch a football soaring soundlessly back and forth in the field outside, while the rest of Black Blissfield swayed to the piano, guitar and drums down below.

When school let out Grandma had Mr. Saunders tune up a boy's bicycle that was rusting away in her shed so I could ride up and down the dirt road in front of the house. I got some spray paint and painted it lavender, for no good reason. Grandma also started teaching me how to play her old spinet, which was weirdly out of tune, but sounded like St. Peter's pearly gates to me. I could spend an entire afternoon picking out songs I heard on the radio, or polishing the porcelain figu-rines in her glass case.

Grandma passed by the parlor, bringing in the wash, and gave me a loving smile when she saw me sitting there, bathed in the sunlight streaming through the front window. I realized I was living in a house where anything I did was welcome, as long as it didn't involve hurting someone. Sometimes when I inhaled, I felt like I was breathing in freedom and breathing out safety. I wondered how my heart had managed to beat so long without them.

In the mornings Grandma got me up early, and we worked side-by-side in the yard, pulling weeds and harvesting fat red and green tomatoes, bushy carrots, and thick lumpy yams. Her greens grew in fairy-tale abandon, almost overtaking a third of the backyard, and she took bags and bags to church to give away.

At first I hated the sweat staining my chest and running down my face; hated the red dirt in my socks, tennis shoes and inside my little bra. Grandma taught me how to tie a bandana around my forehead to keep the dirt out of my hair, but nothing kept it out of my teeth and eyes. I didn't like the bugs, either, but she just shooed them away, as if they didn't matter. She worked beside me, eyes crinkled against the merciless sun, a straw hat perched on the back of her head. She had a big straw hat for me, too, but there were limits to what I was willing to do and how I would allow myself to be seen.

She talked quietly to me about all things Blissfield: the slave history of the town, her grandfather's memory of the days right after the Civil War, the times when white people would lynch a Black person just for the sport of it, and the Civil Rights days, when it was almost more dangerous to be Black than way back during slavery. Though I didn't realize it at the time, she was helping me understand my new world, and why people thought and behaved a certain way.

The old fool from across the street, Mrs. Mitchell, showed up regularly, unannounced, which she pretended was an expression of southern neighborliness. I was sure she was just spying to see what the girl who disfigured one of Blissfield's young beauties was up to, but she never found me doing anything but quietly helping my grandmother in the yard or working around the house.

I greeted her politely, like Momma taught me, and never showed her any disrespect, though I could tell Grandma didn't like her, either. She always concentrated especially hard on whatever she was doing when Mrs. Mitchell appeared, just to let her uninvited guest know she really didn't have time to socialize. Mrs. Mitchell ignored this, of course, and stood there talking about Laurel Monroe's "cheap little Japanese car," Carrie Beauregard's sister's dark-skinned baby, Shirley Abraham "always trying to steal somebody else's man"—her mouth just foamed with gossip, her eyes rolling around like the ball on a roulette wheel, trying to find something to say about us.

The problem was that there really was nothing to say. Grandma's flowerbeds were velvety tapestries, her bushes were sculptures, and she even cleared the pebbles from the red dirt of the backyard with a rake. Our wash was hung out every morning and taken in by afternoon, and any food that was put out to marinate, or to cool down, remained inside the screened porch, where it attracted no flies.

So sometimes, when she ran out of things to say, Mrs. Mitchell literally began to sing church songs that went on and on, or love songs from that distant era when she was young. She would begin by claiming "the spirit was moving her to raise her voice to the Lord," and she'd let loose. Grandma's jaw would tighten, but she'd say nothing. Even now, after years of therapy, I have no idea how she managed it.

* * * * * * *

I was beginning to wonder if the entire summer would be this way when the telephone rang one morning. I ran into the house to answer it, hoping it was my mother, but instead I heard Nina's voice on the line.

"CeCe, that you?"

"I don't know. Depends on who's asking."

She laughed. "You crazy. What you doin'?"

"Working in the yard."

"Okay. I'll be over there in a little while."

She hung up abruptly and I returned to Grandma, who looked up expectantly. Mr. Saunders had been hanging around a lot, lately.

"It's my friend," I said. "She's coming over."

Grandma smiled. "Which friend would that be?"

"Nina. She goes to my school."

Grandma's smile deepened. It hadn't occurred to me that my teachers were reporting back to her, and that she already knew Nina and I lunched on that log every day. It hadn't even occurred to me that since Nina was in my life I hadn't had any more trouble with anybody. I just felt grateful she didn't see any reason why Nina and I couldn't be friends.

Copley sure would have.

About an hour later Nina's popsicle figure pedaled up on a noisy piece of rust. She was wearing her boy's pants and a man's sleeveless t-shirt. It was clean, but a bit too large, and you could see her cupless, faded bra beneath it.

"Good morning, Miss Corinne," she said as she simultaneously dropped the bike and walked toward us. "Your roses thriving."

I peered at Nina to see if she was serious—*nobody* our age used words like *thriving*—and found her blue eyes fixed openly and easily on my grandmother.

"Why, thank you, sweetheart," Grandma said, rising to her feet. "So you and Beth are becoming good friends."

"Yes Ma'am," Nina replied, ducking her head shyly. "But if it's okay with you, I like to call her CeCe. That's my pet name for her."

Grandma laughed. "If it's okay with Bethany, then it's okay with me."

"I thought about Annie, you know—like Beth*annie,*" Nina said thoughtfully, "but she don't look like one of those."

I glanced between the two of them, only then understanding that Grandma already knew her, and knew her well. Maybe even better than was typical, even in a town as small as Blissfield.

"Would you like some sweet tea?" Grandma asked, and Nina nodded once or twice, still staring at her own, flip-flop clad feet. I felt a sudden stab of jealousy, but it was nothing like the bitter, angry jealousy Copley displayed when I showed affection to my mother. And anyway—how can anybody be jealous of their own grandmother?

"How's your momma doing these days?" Grandma continued as we followed her into the kitchen. I took three tall plastic glasses down from the shelf and filled them with ice.

"Momma out at Mr. Brown's place," Nina said. Before sitting, she washed her hands at the sink and dried them with the dishtowel. She then slid onto a kitchen chair, her thin arms like beech twigs on the table. "She cleaning the house and helping in the fields."

I sat in the chair across from her.

"She leaves early?" Grandma asked as she poured sugared tea over the ice.

"Before dawn, and mostly get home after dark. She don't like the work, but it pay pretty good."

Grandma came over with a little tray and handed each of us a brimming glass. She put a plate of Ginger Snaps in the center of the table.

"Who's taking care of the baby?"

Nina took a napkin from the holder in the center of the table, unfolded it, and set it delicately in her lap. Then, with one hand resting on her lap, just like a rich lady, she took a polite sip of her tea. "This is so refreshing!" she exclaimed. She glanced at the cookies and back over at Grandma, who nodded encouragingly.

Nina took a cookie and held it carefully, as if concerned about dropping crumbs on the table. "My baby brother stay with Auntie June during the week, and she bring him home on the weekends."

"So you're by yourself in the house all day?"

"Gideon be there with me most of the time. He play a lot of football and basketball in the yard."

"You helping your momma out, too?"

"I keep the place clean and weed the garden and such. We got beautiful greens this summer. Guess it's the weather."

Grandma smiled at me. "I think Beth's a little bored here with me."

"No, Grandma—" I began, but she reached over to touch my face. "I'd be worried about you if you weren't."

"She can come up to the school with me and get some books from the library," Nina suggested. "They open up every Wednesday afternoon for two hours. I try to get a bunch of books every week, and turn them in for new ones the next Wednesday."

"Are you reading anything right now?" Grandma asked her.

"Yes, this book about a family from Michigan that drove all the way down to Birmingham—"

"I read that back in fourth grade!" I said without thinking.

Nina's brows came together. "Don't brag, CeCe. Some of us is not a prodigy, like you."

We looked at each other, her blue eyes scouring my face. Suddenly she guffawed, "I got you, good! You really looked scared, Miss Bethany Celeste Castle!"

I felt myself color, and glanced over at Grandma, who laughed, too. "Looks like you've got a very smart friend, Princess. I absolutely think you two should head over to the library together."

We both stood up, and Nina took our glasses to the counter. She was about to wash them, but Grandma said it was okay—she'd do it herself. Nina thanked her for the tea and cookies, and told Grandma she hoped to see her again soon.

The two of us rode our old bicycles to the school and we wandered through the library, under the watchful eye of the librarian. In the end, I took out two books (the limit we were allowed each week), and Nina took out three (the librarian pretended not to notice).

As we were getting back on our bikes, our borrowed books hanging in plastic shopping bags from the handlebars, a group of older boys roared up in a pickup missing a muffler. They tumbled out of the front seat, hooting and shoving each other, and burst into laughter at the sight of our broken-down bicycles. I thought about telling them what to do with themselves, but Nina acted like they weren't even there.

The thing that impressed me most about Nina was that even when she was surrounded by boys, she didn't too much care. I'd had my period for nearly a year, and my body was starting to shift around in some interesting ways, but I still didn't understand why some girls couldn't keep their hands out of their hair whenever a boy was nearby. Nina thought those girls were beneath mention, and rarely talked about them. I, too, thought they were really stupid, but I kind of enjoyed hearing their life stories. Nina knew something interesting about every one of them.

As we slowly pedaled down the dirt roads that afternoon, she talked randomly about one girl, then the next.

"LaToya—the one you beat up good—she got a sister who ran away with a soldier. They say she was eating for two, if you know what I mean," Nina added wryly. "I saw the guy one time, when he came through on his way to Raleigh. Wasn't much to look at, but they say she got her own house over at Fort Bragg. Not bad for a girl who ain't even eighteen."

"What, she's seventeen?" I asked, incredulous.

"She nine months older than Toya. That's why Toya such a dummy. She lost her mind when her sister got out. Here she is, stuck in Blissfield, and she think she better than the rest of us 'cause she so light."

"You're kinda light, too," I said.

"Naw, I'm just a mutt. All mixed up."

"Your momma's white?" I asked, genuinely curious.

"Hell, no. Don't ever say that nowhere near our house!"

"But you got blue eyes—"

"I can't help it!"

"And your hair is yellow!"

"And I'm so glad its nappy," Nina said. "I ain't trying to put all that chemical on it, just so I can pretend I'm *halfnhalf*. I like people to know *exactly* what side of town I come from."

I peered at her, barely missing a rut in the road, and my handlebars twisted suddenly. I grabbed them and managed to avoid colliding with her or falling, and even though she laughed, for once she didn't call me "crazy."

"Why'd you say you're a mutt?" I asked when we got to the end of the road.

"You a mutt too, from all appearances," she said grimly.

"Am not. I look exactly like my father. And my grandmother, too, in case you haven't noticed."

"Yeah, I can see all that. You do look like a Castle. Everybody in Blissfield know about the Castles."

"What about the Castles?"

"I told you already. Half of 'em alright, the other half got screws missing."

"I think you mean 'a loose screw,'" I said, miffed.

"No, it's worse than loose. They gone!"

"Shut up!" I said sharply.

"Okay," she answered, bursting into laughter. "You don't like being a nut without a bolt!"

"What are you talking about?"

"How turnt up you get over nothing," she said calmly. "Anyway, that's not what I meant."

"When?"

"When I called you a mutt. See, here in the south, whiter-skin people always trying to boss the darker-skin people around. Don't tell me you never heard about the paper-bag test."

"The what?"

"If your skin darker than a paper bag, you out."

"Out of what?"

"Everything. You can't marry lighter people, or join the light-skin clubs, or go to the light-skin schools."

"That's crazy! Nobody believes that."

"Yes they do," Nina insisted.

"Well, I can't pass the paper-bag test."

"Me, neither."

"But couldn't you get in those clubs with your blonde hair and blue eyes?" I asked.

Abruptly Nina stopped riding and put both feet on the ground. Her bag of books stopped swaying, and she did that tilty thing she liked to do with her head, sort of like a bird on a branch.

"You just don't get us folks down here in Blissfield," she said, flicking the rusting bell on her handlebar with her right thumb. "Can't you just let go of that? Everybody down here mixed up—even the *white* people! Look: nobody can help being born in a certain body. So why worry about it?"

"You just said lots of folks care about stuff like that."

"*But you and I don't have to*," she declared. "All kinds of other stuff to—hey," she added suddenly, "if you follow me down this, here," —she pointed to a narrow dirt path between uncultivated rows of bushes and trees, "I'll show you something you never seen up in Ohio."

"What's down there?"

"You trust me?"

"Sure, but I don't trust snakes."

She brayed out another laugh. "You don't have to worry, I'm a charmer."

"You'd probably just try to outrun me if anything happened."

But she'd already thrown down her bike and walked off the road into the bushes. Nervously I followed. Beating up LaToya and her buddy was one thing. Meeting something slithery was something else.

Once off the road the crickets shrilled even louder. Birds scrambled into the sky at our approach. Nina pushed the bushes away and bent to avoid low tree branches. "Come on, city slicker!" she called without turning her head.

I followed, more nervous than ever. It was hard walking through the tall grass, and bushes and shrubs cut at my arms and face. "Nina—"

She ignored me. I lost sight of her heels for a moment, then caught up with her when I entered a clearing. Birds flew furiously back and forth over the empty space, as if they hadn't been disturbed in years. The ruins of a stone dwelling stood beside a well with a caved-in roof. Trees had grown up through the stones, suspending a thatch of green above the broken walls. The air seemed to calm around us, and I could hear the crickets and birds once again.

I stood stock still, feeling like we were disturbing a holy place. "Where are we?"

"Oh, I don't know. Might of been a school for Black folks. Or maybe a church. I only know it really old."

"You came here before?"

"Yeah, sometimes." She looked around. "I go everywhere. Especially when school out." She took a few steps forward and picked up a twig, swishing it back and forth through the air. "I like it when I'm all by myself. Don't nobody bother me."

"You're not by yourself now."

"In a way," she said, "I am. You a lot like me, CeCe. When I'm with you, I feel like I'm by myself and with my best friend at the same time."

I stared at her. She had turned away while speaking, and now she swayed gently back and forth as she examined her twig.

I took a step forward. I had never had a best friend, outside of my father, but I was starting to understand that my 'best friend' couldn't be the man who hurt my mother—and who had started hurting me. Confused, I reached out and touched her shoulder.

"You—you mean you like me that much?" I stammered. "You want me to be your best friend?"

She shrugged loosely, and returned to slinging her twig back and forth, making an anxious whirring in the air.

The whirring stirred my thoughts, and the blood in my heart, and even the stones that formed the foundation of my Self.

"Okay," I said. "I accept."

"You sure?" She was still looking away.

"Yep," I said. "Very, very, sure."

Her blue eyes turned on mine. She smiled. My heart smiled, too. She reached over and lightly slugged my arm.

"Come on. Let's have a look at those books."

I laughed. She laughed with me.

Yes, she was my best friend.

My first real friend.

My only forever friend.

Leah "Nina" Mirabel Price.

ten.

The Old Man in the nuthouse spent a lot of time on my father. He used to say I should "work between the space" of how I thought about Copley when I was young, and what I understood about him now. It sounded like a perfectly reasonable exercise when the Old Man suggested it, but that's because he had no idea what I was up against when I tried to get some clarity on the man.

From the time I was a kid I knew my daddy was smarter than most people. He could tell from someone's eyes what they were thinking, which, as he often repeated, was a survival skill for a card shark. He was a graceful liar, too, which he believed set him apart from most of his enemies.

For some reason, Copley never gained weight or lost his lean, powerful, compact frame. Pictures of him as a soldier reveal the same man twenty years earlier, with the exception of his hair, which faded a bit with time.

The only thing was the noise: Whenever you were around Copley you couldn't focus on anything but him. He was always talking, moving, tapping on things with his fingers or his feet. And he'd go from a normal voice to screaming, anytime at all, for no particular reason, then just as quickly start whispering.

So when I was with my father I couldn't think. I didn't realize it when I was small, or even after I grew up. I didn't really begin to understand it until I moved in with Grandma. Around her there was a blessed stillness. We could work all morning without saying a word and feel perfectly content. Even when we were speaking, I sensed the periods, commas, and spaces around words. I could breathe, smell, taste and hear details that were hidden from my life in my father's home.

For example, the textures of the lace on Grandma's tablecloth beckoned my fingers. It was delicate to the eye, but rough to the touch. I also sensed the arcing of the sun over the day, and by midsummer, I could sense the time without looking at a clock. I could instantly recognize the different flowers in her garden, merely by their scent, when they opened at dawn. And I could tell the difference between the tastes of white and brown sugar, clover and lavender honey, speckled brown and white eggs on my first mouthful of cake, bread or an omelet.

But most of all, in Grandma's presence, I could think. And once I started thinking, things I'd never thought about before leapt to the front of my mind, like a lifebuoy bursting to the surface from a deep, dark sea.

"Grandma, why's my daddy mad all the time?"

Grandma was leaning close to her old black Singer sewing machine, mending a pair of shorts I'd torn on a nail the day before. Her brows came together and she paused and leaned closer to the needle before answering.

"Do you know how to sew, Princess?"

"No. My momma can sew, but she never had the chance to show me." This was a lie; Momma always asked me to come and learn how to operate her sewing machine, but it made my father very angry when she and I did anything together.

"It's quite useful to know how to make your own clothes," Grandma said, "so I'll start teaching you tomorrow."

I waited, standing beside her and watching the denim make its way steadily toward the beating needle. She continued until the seam was done. Then, sitting up straight, she bit through the thread and turned off the machine, handing the shorts back to me. Though she was smiling, her eyes looked like somebody who was about to walk across a floor of broken glass with bare feet.

"Grandma," I began, already regretting the question, "it don't matter. We don't have to talk about it."

"*Doesn't* matter, baby. And it's fine."

She gestured toward the chair across the table and I sat down. The light made deep cuts on her face. She was wearing glasses she'd bought at the pharmacy so she could see how to thread the needle. Those glasses were the only time Grandma looked old.

"Your daddy wasn't like his brothers," she said in a voice that told me just how carefully she was choosing her words. "Jeremiah was quiet and thoughtful, and always tried to do what was right. Paul, on the other hand, liked to make people laugh. He always had something funny to say. But Copley was different. At first I thought it was because he was so many years younger than his brothers. He always struggled to keep up. Then, over time, we all gradually understood that he was, for lack of a better word, troubled."

Surprised, I leaned a little closer. "How?"

"Teachers couldn't do a thing with him. He'd fight the other boys on the playground, get real mad if he didn't win every game, and he just couldn't sit still in class. I believe the teachers were scared of him, even when he was a small boy."

I watched as she placed a cloth hood over the machine and sat back in her chair. "We all knew he was smart—he was probably the smartest of the three—but it seemed like he enjoyed using his mind to frustrate and upset everyone. Let me tell you a story."

She sighed. "Paul and Jeremiah went fishing one day. I made them take Copley along, though they didn't want to, and I even got a pole and some bait for him. While his brothers were sitting beside the pond, your daddy decided to use the stick to knock a hornet's nest down from a nearby tree. The nest was bigger than his head, and the hornets were the size of small clothespins. Just to be sure his brothers knew what he was doing, he called them by name right before he whacked the nest.

"Of course the entire colony came swarming. Hundreds and hundreds rose up from the hive, like a blood-red shadow. Paul and Jeremiah didn't think twice: they jumped into the pond and ducked their heads under. But your daddy couldn't swim. When he saw that swarm he couldn't think of anything better to do than to run.

"I was rolling out the dough for the dinner biscuits, and I heard him scream-ing from what seemed like a mile away. His voice got louder and louder as he got closer to the house. By the time he made it into the yard, he'd been stung forty or fifty times. I ran out with the broom, swatted the things away, threw a sheet over him and pulled him inside. He was already swelling up so I ran a bath, poured in an entire bottle of calamine lotion, put him in, and went to work with the tweezers. I managed to get the stingers out of his head, shoulders and arms, but his face looked like somebody set him on fire.

"The doctor came and gave him a shot that knocked him out. We had to watch over him nonstop for two whole days. I honestly thought he was going to die. Of course he pulled through, but from the way he carried on afterward, it was clear he hadn't learned anything at all."

"That's crazy," I said in a half-whisper, as if he could hear. "He never told me about that."

"I could share a whole bucketful of stories that were even worse," she said. "I always worried more about your daddy than his brothers. They got into their fair share of trouble, too—boys are always more troubled when their fathers are away—but neither Paul nor Jeremiah had your daddy's ingenuity. They stole candy from Mason's store, got caught cheating on their math tests, got in scrapes over marbles, put a dent in the fender of my new car. But they never went looking for trouble like Copley. He was a prospector of trouble, like a poor man in a gold mine."

I thought about that. I'd always known he was smarter than everybody. I'd just never, ever thought he wasn't always right, even when he was screaming crazy things at Momma and me.

"Grandma, what happened when his brothers died?"

With unexpected slowness, my normally spry Grandma stood and placed the sewing machine beneath the table.

"Honestly, baby, that was a very bad time," she said. "I tried my best to control myself in front of him, but I cried many, many nights, and your daddy saw and heard my grief. He'd lost his father and both his brothers. I've always thought that maybe that's why he has such a hard time showing love. Deep inside he may be afraid that anyone he cares about will abandon him."

"Where was his father?"

"He wasn't living with us when your daddy was small."

"But where was he?"

She paused for a moment and looked toward the door as if she thought he was just outside. "He worked in another city."

"What about your farm?"

"He preferred to work in an office."

"So my Daddy never got beat for doing bad stuff?"

She looked over at me so quickly I thought I'd said a dirty word. "I never beat your father, Princess."

"Not even a spanking?"

"*Never*," she repeated firmly.

"So—so were *you* ever scared of him?" I asked, thinking of how my mother shrank in his presence.

Again she paused. "Of course not, baby! Are you?"

I felt her probing gaze and answered as best as I could.

"He can be crazy sometimes—well, most of the time," I said. "But he didn't scare me that bad. Usually he just made me mad. Then I would fight him back, even though I knew he was going to win. I didn't care if he beat me. I just wanted to hurt him, even if it was only a little bit, the way he hurt my momma."

She was silent for a long moment. "I think you were pretty brave," she said, "though nobody should have to be afraid of their mother or father, and no parent should ever hit their child. Copley never scared me because part of him lives inside of me. The big difference between the two of us was that I learned a long time ago to control my anger, so it doesn't take control of me."

"You think he could control it?" I asked.

"If he wanted to. The thing is, your daddy likes it when folks are scared of him. It makes him feel powerful."

I thought about that. Rain began to tiptoe on the metal roof.

"What about my momma?" I asked. "Why's he so mean to her?"

"He's afraid to lose her, so he scares her into staying."

"I tried to get her to go, Grandma, but she tricked me and stayed."

"I know you're worried about her, baby, but your mother believes his behavior is the same thing as love. You can't make her see things differently. Until she changes her mind, she's going to stay there." Grandma paused. "You've got to promise me you'll never get confused like that."

"I'll try."

"No," she insisted, taking both my hands in hers. "You must never let anyone hit you. Ever. If someone hits you, even *one* time, you've got to drop everything and go. Even if you love that person very much. Understand this, Princess: when someone hits you and you stay, they believe in their heart you've given them permission to do it again. They'll apologize and promise they won't, and even beg you on their knees to stay. But you've got to leave. Do you understand?"

She had never spoken like this before. The darkness had returned to her eyes, and my heart stirred at the sight of my father in her face.

Nodding, I flinched as she squeezed my hands more tightly.

"Princess," she said, "promise me out loud."

"Okay," I said. "I promise. But—but what about my momma?"

She stared at me for a few seconds, then let my hands go. "I think that's enough talking for tonight. Isn't it about time for 'Who Wants to be a Millionaire'?"

* * * * * * *

That was the first night I had the dream. I was in a softly lit room full of women wearing thin pink or white shifts. I was still a small child. A man came into the room and said he wanted something special. Some of the other women shook their heads. Others stood and walked out. One woman, a pretty woman with skin the color of milk coffee, said something to him and they left the room together.

Then I was in another room. It was dark, and I was bringing water, or towels, or something else to them. The shadows were so heavy I could only see the woman's legs as she lay on a bed. The man was seated near her upper body, and I could make out his silhouette in the shadows. He was doing something terrible to the woman—cutting, burning, or striking her—and each time he did it, she cried out in the same low-pitched moan, and her legs bounced, like the legs of a marionette, in agony.

I fled, and the dream faded the way the television screen sometimes fades between scenes. And then I found myself entering a hospital room, where the woman lay on a bed. A white wooden box was placed over her entire face. Smaller boxes hid her arms, the trunk of her body, each thigh and each lower leg. Wires escaped from each of the boxes, tethering her to a tree of antiseptic branches. She wasn't moving. The only sound was the swishing grunt of a machine beside her weirdly dissected body.

I looked, though I could hardly bear it. I knew she had allowed the man to hurt her. She had agreed to let him do this. She had, in some completely bizarre way, welcomed her mutilation. As I stood there, watching myself watching her, I woke up.

Terribly, terribly afraid.

* * * * * * *

Years later, the Old Man with the white hair asked me if I ever dreamed about my father. I said I couldn't remember any dreams about him. I said I could barely remember what my father looked like, and I had no memory of the sound of his voice. None of this was true: I saw Copley's face in every man who made me afraid, and heard his voice constantly, but I thought that keeping him close was safer than letter him get so deep inside me that I wouldn't know what he was doing.

The Old Man looked at me. I think, now, that perhaps he wasn't actually old—it was simply that I associated white hair with the elderly. "What do you remember about your mother?" he asked. His office, flanked by large windows overlooking a garden, was full of light and it set his hair shining, flossy and angelic, in the afternoon sun.

"I knew when I was a kid that she was terrified of him," I said. "And I knew she believed she couldn't manage without him."

"Even though he was so abusive to her?"

I didn't say anything. I had only rediscovered speech a few months before, and often my thoughts were too complicated for my words.

The man waited patiently. Sometimes he waited all afternoon for me to speak. That day he was lucky: I saw a robin land heavily on a pregnant pear tree outside the window, and a thought burst from the scrawl inside my brain.

"We didn't think that way," I said.

"What way?"

"About getting hit."

"Can you explain this to me?"

My chest tightened and my breaths shortened. His head turned toward me. "Longer breaths will calm the mind," he said simply. "

Again he waited. When the fat pear buds came back into focus, I said: "We didn't think. We survived."

I knew he knew these things—that men, women and children being beaten or raped dance out of their bodies and watch, with a certain respect, the audacity and creativity of their tormentor, and that each time they look back at their flesh they're more certain their flesh has no value.

Still, he asked, so I told him.

"My mother had to love my father, because she couldn't have stood what he did to her if all she'd felt was hate."

"Then do you think she allowed herself to be abused?" he said kindly.

"I think," I said, "that my mother believed it was better than nothing, and after she'd been with him for a while, she saw herself as less than nothing."

"And why didn't you feel that way, too?"

I laughed and, once again, the sound really surprised me. "That's simple," I said. "I'm not like my mother. I'm like my father."

* * * * * * *

I saw Nina many days that summer, and she was just as ornery, and strange, and wonderful as any girl's best friend could be. We rode our bikes all over the area, stopped to buy a soda from Branston's family store (Nina knew which stores were for Black folks and which weren't), and read books lying on our backs beneath the sun-flecked thatch of our secret stone hut.

She read everything, turning the pages of each book with extraordinary speed, but I was never sure how much she was really taking in. When I asked whether she liked the book, she'd shrug. "Better than boring," she'd say. If I asked for more detail, she'd answer, "read it yourself, then we'll talk. I don't do homework for nobody but me."

Once or twice, when I followed her orders, I discovered that she had, indeed, both read and committed the books to memory. Her ability to recall the details of the texts was astounding: "Yeah, that was on page seventy-seven. That girl Sally finally realized the box had a magic globe inside. Seemed kinda stupid to me. I would have figured that out by page three."

I loved debating the value of the books with her: "*The Hound of the Baskervilles* is pretty scary," I said.

"No it's not," she answered. "Any fool out walking around in a swamp is already crazy. How could he not recognize it was a dog covered with paint?"

Or, "I kinda liked *Great Expectations*, but I thought Pip and Stella would get together."

"Why would he want her?" Nina replied. "She just a young hag in that old hag dresses!"

Another time I asked about a book I was really enjoying. "What did you think of *Jane Eyre*?"

"Oh, that one was *really* crazy," she laughed. "The rich guy don't care about his money, even though he married the nutcase so he could get at her money, and then he fell for the girl who thought she was broke but turned out to be rich, too."

"Don't tell me the end!"

"Don't worry: you could never guess the end in a million years! The thing I *did* like was Jane. When do you read a book about a scrawny, ugly, poor little thing that nobody wanted? Look like she wrote it just for me!"

"You're not ug—"

"Shut up, Ms. CeCe Castle! I don't like it when people lie."

"But you're not—"

"I like being exactly how I am," Nina said. "I don't need nobody trying to sell me some Disney!"

Nina was, to be honest, the oddest person I'd ever met. She never changed expression, never let on that she was joking, but her mind was sharp enough to shave steel, and she cut even the most difficult stories back down to fairy tales. I had never met anyone as smart as me, except my father and my grandmother. In many ways it was a relief to know that in smartness, the Castles were not alone.

August rolled around and, unexpectedly, I got a letter from my mother. We had managed snatched phone conversations when my father was out of the house, and she usually sounded okay. She said that though he was mad at first, my father accepted that if I was with my grandmother, I would have to behave myself, so he didn't blame her too much for putting me on the bus. She never said anything about what was going on between them, except that she was still working at the dry cleaners and he was out most nights.

So her letter came as a surprise. I opened it while sitting on the front porch steps, surrounded by Grandma's rose bushes. My mother had looping, rounded handwriting, as if she was one of my classmates.

> "Dear Beth,
>
> I hope you are having fun at your Grandma house. We miss you here at home. The weather has been very hot, and I picked up some more hours at work, so I am pretty tired when I get home. You father never got around to putting on the ~~screan~~ screen windows, so it is hard to sleep at night. If we open the window the room will be full of moskitos. I will be happy when fall come.
>
> I hope you are looking forward to school. Do you need new shoes? Can you still fit in your winter coat? I will try to send some more money at the end of the month, if I can.
>
> Do you want to come and visit for Xmas? I will talk to your father about it. He is very busy and when he is home is usually tired. Be good and mind Miss Corinne.
>
> I will call soon. I love you,
> Your Momma"

I folded the five-dollar bill that was tucked into the envelope, then dropped the letter and slowly crushed it with my foot. The door opened and I felt the wooden slats of the porch shift beside me.

"Is that from home?" Grandma asked.

"Yes." I nudged it with the toe of my sandal.

"From your mother?"

I gave her an affirmative grunt.

Grandma descended the porch steps and stood with her back to me, looking at the flowers exploding above the drainage ditches. Bending to brush a Japanese beetle off one of her roses, she gently rubbed the pink flesh of a blossom between her index and thumb. "No matter what she said, remember that your mother loves you."

"She loves him more."

"She loves him differently, Princess."

"But he don't love no one."

"That doesn't stop her from loving you."

"I just can't take it," I said.

"Take what?"

"He's still hitting her—"

"Well, I hope not."

"—and he's gonna kill her, Grandma. I know it and I just can't sit here and act like I don't."

There. I had finally said it out loud.

Grandma's shoulders shifted, and when she turned back to me, sadness darkened her eyes. "Let's pray that's not true, baby."

"He's going to try," I said. "If she ever does something that really upsets him, he'll—"

"Hush, child. Some things just shouldn't be said out loud."

"But Grandma, he—"

"Stop!" she said sharply. Our eyes locked, then she continued more gently, "believe me, I worry, too."

We were silent, both of us thinking about Bebe J.

"Princess," Grandma said quietly, "you'll never get too many letters from your mother. Let's iron that one out and keep it somewhere safe."

"He's a bad man—"

"Princess."

"He is!" I said.

"Bethany—"

"And she's letting him—"

"Baby, you don't have to worry about your father and mother."

"But what if—what if I'm like him, too?"

"Hush, baby—"

"No, Grandma. I feel him sometimes, like a great big animal inside me—" I threw my arms out, "—and I got to let him out or he'll tear me apart."

"Oh no, sweetheart," she said, "Just remember, when you feel bad, you'll always have a home here."

"But—"

"You'll always be safe here."

"I—"

"You'll always be loved here."

"Grandma —"

"Princess, you *will*."

We stared at each other another hard minute. Though she was doing everything in her power to reassure me, that haunting trace of Copley paced just behind her eyes.

"Princess," Grandma said in her too-bright, give-the-girl-something-else-to-think-about voice, "I've been thinking about getting the spare room painted. Make a nice bedroom for you. What do you think?"

I looked in her direction and couldn't see her, because my father felt much too close to push away.

"What do you think, Princess?" she said again. "Purple or pink?"

eleven.

The first day of school Nina rode up on her nutty bike, and I joined her on mine. We waved goodbye to Grandma and made the three-mile trip down the red-earthed road, the cicadas screaming so loud we couldn't speak. School buses rumbled past and the schoolyard was an ant farm.

I didn't pay much attention to the teachers, who delivered the First Day Speech at the beginning of each class, signed out books, told us to read Chapter One and answer the questions on page eleven. My boredom was hideous and real. I wanted nothing more than to get to Nina and to sit on our log under the trees. I wondered if her experience in the eleventh grade was as deadly as mine at the beginning of the tenth. How did Grandma *do* this for forty-plus years?

The bell rang and I watched people falling all over each other to get outside. It was so hot it might as well have been July, and folks were willing to fight for even a sliver of shade. I could see from the top of the steps that a bunch of young girls, probably ninth graders, had taken up residence on our log, and a familiar simmering began in my chest: I would need to take care of *that* immediately, even if it meant, proverbially speaking, some sorrow, tears and blood.

Stalking down the stairs into the sunlight, I didn't expect the unfamiliar voice that called my name. I looked around to see a tall boy with blue-grey eyes standing a few steps away, holding something in his hand.

"CeCe, I got this for you."

For one extraordinarily bizarre moment I thought he might be about to offer me a ring or some other proof of his undying affection, but then I realized that was stupider than me thinking my father might become a Buddhist.

I must have looked confused, because he came a couple of steps closer. He was now a head and a half bigger than me, and he was at least twice as thick, but still Hermes slender—as if he could run like the wind and even fly, if that's what you needed—and despite being kind of a stranger, he seemed incredibly familiar.

"Nina's class right next to mine," he said, "and she gave me this note. Here—"

He held out the piece of paper, but I was still too busy staring at him to take it.

His red t-shirt had taut, weird ripples across the chest, and his arm had a ripe bulge above the elbow. His neck was corded, tanned, and his face, which was so different from his sister's, was somehow still the same. Though his waist was lean, his thighs were rounded like a horse's, with muscled, clean calves.

I remembered with sudden unease how Nina and her brother seemed to be twins, though it was more than that: they were like kindred beings split apart from one honeyed body, moving at the same out-of-synch time, inhabiting identical, but disjointed space, but with yin/yang kinds of energy. Nina was all things clunky, rusty and ornery, and Nina's brother was inherently peaceful, as if his quiet strength was in perfect synch with his sleek athletic frame. She was all angles. He was all grace.

Something literally stood up and sat down again inside me. I could not, even if I'd wanted to, remove my eyes from his face. His hand was still outstretched, but I had turned into one of those plaster mannequins in Grandma's old-lady dress store.

He tilted his head—a typical Nina gesture—and laughed hoarsely.

"Okay. I'll just read it to you." The paper crackled (*so* Nina). The words that followed were lost on me, because I was awash in the cinder-sandy voice, like someone had torn up his throat and replaced it with grit.

He finished reading and waited for my reaction. I vaguely remembered that a few seconds before I'd been mad about something, but I couldn't say what. I'd been on my way across the schoolyard, but it seemed completely pointless, now. I wished I could talk to my best friend, because something had just happened that left me thoroughly confused. The only problem was that I wasn't sure what it was.

I needed someone to slap the shit out of me!

He continued to stare back, then, as if he didn't know what else to do, he shrugged.

"Okay," he repeated, an odd smile on his face, and pocketing the note, he backed up a few steps before turning to walk away. It was only then that I noticed he'd been palming a football with his other hand the entire time.

"Hold up—Gideon—wait!"

He glanced back, then pivoted on his heel and shot an imaginary lay-up.

"What—what did Nina want?"

"Nothing. Anyway, here she come, now." He was looking over my shoulder. I almost immediately felt her playfully slug my arm.

"I got held behind by that zombie, Mr. Morton!" she said. "Already giving me some dookee on the first day of class! Lord, I hate Geometry. Must of been thought up by some crazy people, all those corners and lines going everywhere. Just give me some numbers. At least they make sense. Anyway, why do we have to go through this, year after year after year?"

I listened to her complain while we walked around to the back of the school, where there was undiscovered shade behind the enormous trash bins. We sat down to eat, but I couldn't focus on what she was saying, or what we were eating.

After six months of being her best friend, I had only for the first time really seen what I should have *already* seen that distant Easter Sunday.

Gideon Price. *Lord*—Gideon Price. Nina Price's younger brother.

* * * * * * *

I had Biology that afternoon, and my lab partner was London Richardson, the Principal's son. The Hair and Nails clan found him incredibly attractive, which was clearly tied to his later prospects in life, because to me he resembled a *burtle*. By that, I mean to say that he was hulking and overweight like a bear, with miniscule, bespeckled eyes and a hooked nose, like a turtle.

The problem was that London thought himself a ladies' man because of the unearned attention he got from lint-brains like LaToya, Breanna, and their ilk. When the teacher, a sly-looking old coot named Mrs. Barnes called London Richardson's name right after mine, I looked up and saw the mean twinkle in her eye. I figured word had spread around the school that I was razor-smart and rattlesnake-mean, and she wanted to see how I would get along with the Principal's son. I'd have to be crazy to act up with the boy who reported directly to The Man, so pairing us as lab partners was the quickest way to get me to (a) settle down or, (b) get kicked out for good.

Either way, it must have seemed like a lot of fun to her.

London lumbered to the lab table and sank down beside me. Mrs. Barnes was busy designating other partners, so we looked each other over critically. I sat stock still as he examined my hair, breasts and face.

I didn't like him examining my hair, breasts and face.

"You look like you about twelve years old," he said, confirming my suspicion that he was an idiot.

"And you look like you should be wearing a helmet."

"I ain't no cop."

"No," I said, "but some bubble wrap might protect your golf-ball brain."

"Whatever," he mumbled and, unable to figure out what to answer, he said exactly what I'd expect from a moron: "I heard you come from someplace nobody ever heard of."

"Unlike Blissfield, the Manhattan of North Carolina."

His beady eyes were still fixed on my teeny breasts. "Bet they chased you out of wherever you came from."

"Sure did," I answered, "soon as they saw what happens when somebody fucks with me."

"Yeah, I heard what you did to LaToya and Bree."

"And you know what? It was actually *much* worse than whatever they told you." With those words I smiled. Well, my eyes didn't smile (*classic* Copley).

"Damn," he said again, under his breath. "A true Castle."

"No," I whispered, "my grandmother is the true Castle. I'm the dangerously flawed version."

"Damn," he said again. "I got to put up with this a whole year?"

"I don't know," I answered, equally quietly. "I guess we could fix it so you'd be out of school for a while."

He didn't give me any trouble for the rest of class, because he saw real fast that the work was easy for me, and he knew a hostile lab partner who could do the work was better than a flirty lab partner who couldn't.

* * * * * * *

The rest kinda fell into a rhythm, as well. Nina and I rode our bikes to and from school together, talking about whatever was happening in the schoolyard, the classrooms, and the bathrooms of the high school, and every day I waited for any and every possibility to get a glimpse of her brother.

Even a glimpse.

Because from that first day of school I hadn't stopped thinking about Gideon.

I couldn't tell Nina about it; I knew something about it wasn't quite right. Part of me found it stupid and confusing, another part of me felt ashamed, and yet I also felt like a lush that couldn't wait to sip from a bottle of sweet Gideon wine.

Sometimes I got lucky—although he was only a freshman, Gideon had been named the starting quarterback on the football team. After classes Nina and I often rode our bikes over to the football field, about a block from the school, to drop off some change or food for her brother. Usually he was running drills or listening while the coach gave them instructions. I'd chill by the bikes while she bounded over the pile of backpacks, jackets and water bottles, and set the item beside his things. My eyes bounced between her popsicle-stick figure and his smooth, comic-hero form, nowhere near as thick as the others, but far more graceful, especially when they were horsing around.

Though he seemed awkward in normal life, Gideon was always completely at ease on the field, which made zero sense to me. Football was about helmet-crushing crunches of broken bones, players running the gauntlet of other players, and weird pileups that rearrange faces. Gideon, however, was the antelope that pauses beside the pond and stares languidly at the lions before leaping into the underbrush. While all was chaos around him, he paused calmly, the ball tucked protectively beneath his arm, then took off, his spinning legs propelling him like a missile.

"Why's Gideon just sitting there?" I asked one day after Nina jogged back to me. Her brother was sitting alone on the bleachers while the rest of the team warmed up.

"He don't like that number they gave him. He wanted the number of that guy who play in New York."

"Which guy?"

"I don't know," she said with exasperation. "Who cares?"

"He does."

"I been telling you he a dummy." She laughed. I didn't. She looked at me. "Why you askin' about Gideon? He don't think about nothing but football and basketball."

"He eats, right?"

"Okay. He might think about eating every once in a while. You know what? You a dummy, too."

We both laughed and started to walk away. I couldn't stop myself from peeking back over my shoulder at the players.

"Hey—I saw that." Nina eyed me critically. "Who you looking at?"

"Nobody."

"Don't try it, knucklehead."

"Shut up."

"*You* shut up," she said. "I see everything, even when I'm not looking."

We mounted our bikes and pedaled up the road toward town. The weather was cooler now, and the locusts were less insistent. Nina didn't speak.

"Dog, Nina—you mad just because I looked back at the field?"

"You was looking at my knucklehead brother."

"I'm not trying to look at your brother."

"I told you I seen it!" she said.

"You didn't see anything."

"I saw enough."

"What difference would it make?"

"That would be incest," she declared.

"What?"

"I'm your best friend. He my brother. That's incest."

"I'm not trying to *marry* him!"

"Still."

"Now you're the one being crazy."

"Maybe, but still."

We rode along in silence. I saw that a few of the trees had leaves dappled with oranges and yellows. A fat white duck, squawking like it had heard something hilarious, swooped past; it was so heavy I hoped there was a pond nearby.

"Ever seen a duck land on the water?" I asked. Our legs moved up and down in rhythm.

"Of course I have."

"Don't you think it's funny how they skid to a stop?"

She paused before answering, and I realized how angry she really was.

"Nina, don't be a *gump*," I said.

"What's that?"

"Somebody who's stuck up and goofy."

"That would be *you*," she said.

"Because I looked at Gideon?"

"Because you won't admit it."

"Okay," I said. "I looked at Gideon. Alright?"

"Why'd you do it?"

"Why *not* do it? I didn't break any laws—"

"I told you, he like a brother to you!"

"Lord, Nina—*that's* why I wouldn't admit it. You're taking this way too serious!"

"You wouldn't of lied if it wasn't serious."

"Nina," I sighed, "I looked at your brother. It's not my fault. He's an eye-magnet."

"What's that mean?" she said. We had pulled up on the street in front of Grandma's house.

"He looks good. Is that news to you?"

She cast me a sulky sideways glance.

"Come *on*, Nina," I said. "That doesn't mean you're not my best friend. I don't like him better than you."

She sighed and her face relaxed a bit. "All my life it's the same. Momma prefer Gideon, teachers prefer Gideon, my cousins prefer Gideon, even *I* prefer Gideon."

"What does that even mean?"

"He prettier and nicer than me."

"Prettier?" I said.

"I don't know," she answered quietly. "It's like I got all the boy stuff and he got all the girl stuff. I'm smart and he dumb. He so pretty he can get away with everything. At home I got to work and he just hang around, doing nothing but shooting hoops and throwing that damn football."

"So that's why you're mad? Because he gets away with stuff?"

"I guess." She looked at the ground, troubled.

"Nina, you're my best friend. You said so yourself! Don't be mad at me. Please!"

Suddenly she laughed. "It's okay, CeCe. I'm used to it, really. I guess things just turn out the way they have to, you know?"

She turned her bike around. "You want to do something later?"

"No, I got to go to church with Grandma. Choir practice—and they won't even let me sing."

"Why not?" she asked.

"I sound like a frog!"

"Hush, CeCe. I can teach you how to sing!"

"Right. And I can teach you how to fly."

"You crazy," she said.

"You, too."

She smiled and pedaled off, the treads of her tires making snake-skin patterns in the damp red dirt.

V.

blissfield, north carolina.

2016.

twelve.

So there I was: a thirty-two year-old, homeless Molotov cocktail squatting in a dead woman's house, ten seconds from broke and on a mission to find the last two people on earth who, I prayed, might still care that I was alive.

And then, for no good reason except the bitch-slap of fate, it was Nina—a million years older as she passed Blissfield's one and only restaurant, hauling a coffin-sized, fake Louis Vuitton bag—and by plain dumb luck—who found *me.*

After staging a reunion with the warmth of a subzero freezer, she'd ended our little chat abruptly: *"CeCe, I got to go, but tomorrow I might do you the favor of calling you. Give me your number. Miss Corinne took herself out the phone book years ago."*

I'd scrambled for a pen, and finally someone at the next table—surely hoping to speed Nina's departure—handed one to me. I wrote my number carefully on a napkin and handed it to her. Rather than looking pleased, a threat was in her face as she departed: *"If I call, Bethany Celeste Castle, I don't care what time a the day or night it is—you better answer."*

"Nina, I—"

"You better answer..."

I sat up most of that night smoking Camels and thinking about Akron, my father, and what it was like, seventeen years before, when I first arrived in Blissfield. I thought a lot about the Nina I used to know. About how weird it is that folks never get older in your memory. How you go on loving the person they used to be, and how unprepared you are for the way life beats them into somebody new. Hell, if anybody should have been an expert on that, it was me.

I wished I could fish the Old Man up—without returning to the nuthouse—and get his take on what was going on around me. I knew he'd tell me to chill. To accept things the way they are. To make peace with the way things had changed.

But I also knew that you can't make peace with hunger and thirst, and the years without Nina and Gideon had nearly starved me.

In that hollow ash black border between nighttime and dawn, something hit the bedroom window with the force of a stone. I started up, heart beating wildly, and actually shouted out loud.

The only reply was the sweet questioning of the birds, whose song formed a descant to the cicadas. I threw off the sheets and walked to the door, which was locked tight, as it had been when I'd fallen asleep, alone, the night before. Outside, the porch creaked under my weight as I made my way barefoot along the uneven slats, avoiding rusty nails, deep splinters and invitations for a nasty fall.

There was no sign of a pre-dawn visitor. Instead, I found the broken body of a crow that had mistaken the reflection of the blooming light on the ancient glass of my bedroom window for a pathway to the sky.

Suddenly, after days of no calls, the sound of my cell phone was startling. Running back into the house, I tripped on the doorsill and just missed crashing headlong into the credenza.

"So you really there," Nina said in her unnaturally loud voice.

"I told you I'd be here."

"No. I told *you* to be there."

"What difference does it make?" I said.

"You really axin' me that?"

"Dang, Nina! Why'd you call if you're still so mad?"

"Got to get it out the way."

"For what?"

"For whatever got to happen next."

"That will be precisely nothing, the way we're going."

"What way is that?"

"Nina," I said, "I was glad to see you in the restaurant last night, but I don't feel like fighting. About anything. Do you understand?"

"This ain't fighting," she said.

"It's not exactly Sunday dinner."

"So it's Saturday night with you getting beat at poker."

"I'm not playing games," I snapped.

"Nobody said this a game," she said. "In fact, you the one pulling the vanishing act, then showing up fifteen years later, like some kind of Houdini."

"I wish I did know some magic," I said.

"Look like magic to me."

"Unemployed, broke and homeless doesn't feel so magical."

The phone went silent. Somewhere, in the quiet distance of the line, I thought I heard a door open and close and, a few seconds later, an engine's angry roar.

"Nina—you still there?"

"You didn't hear me hang up. And about that," she added crisply: "Tell me again why you just *had* to go away."

"Christ, Nina—you were there!"

"So?"

"You know why I had to go."

"I thought you didn't have no choice."

"And I didn't."

"You should of come back."

"I should've done a lot of things."

Again the phone went silent. I thought she might have hung up, but for her heavy breathing.

"Nina? You there?"

"Where else would I be?" she said. "I'm still waiting on a bunch of answers."

I sighed. "I'm sorry, Nina. I'm sorry about everything that happened that day. I'm sorry I left and couldn't come back. I'm sorrier than you'll ever know. I don't know what else I can say."

"I don't expect nothing else."

"Then why'd you bother to call?"

"Just making sure you wasn't no haint."

"A *haint*?"

"A evil spirit in CeCe's shape."

"Be serious, Nina."

Unexpectedly, she laughed. "I see you lost your sense of humor up there in Ohio."

"I see you went crazy right here in Blissfield."

She laughed again. "You right: I always *was* the crazy one. That's what happen when you stay in this town."

"It also happens when you leave," I said.

"Well, you back down here now," she said, and I thought I heard a faint glimmer of hope in her words.

"I never really left, Nina. At least, not inside."

"Don't be stupid," she said, the coldness returning.

"Where are you?" I asked. "I'm coming to get you."

"For what?"

"For breakfast."

"I got to go to bed."

"It's seven in the morning!"

"I just got off work."

"Well, you're not in bed yet."

"I need to do a hour of Bible study, then get some shut-eye before church."

"Then tell me when I can visit."

"Nina—"

"You think just because you here, nobody else got a life?"

"Fifteen years, Nina."

"Bills to pay, CeCe."

"Okay," I said, "let me drive you to work."

"Told you last night I walk."

"Let me drive you to church."

"Don't need a ride there, neither."

"I want to see you," I said.

"No you don't."

"I need to see you."

"Be honest, CeCe.," she said. "You and I both know this ain't about me."

"It is, too."

"No, it's not."

A long silence held the line. Then I spoke. "Yes it is, Nina."

"It's about him.," she said. "Don't lie."

"Nina—"

"Don't lie, CeCe."

"You were my first," I said. "My first, and in truth, the only one I've ever had."

"What?"

"Friend," I said simply. Though I never would have expected it, I felt a wetness in my left eye and reached up to brush it away.

Again I heard her breathing. "You don't know where I'm at, CeCe."

"Just tell me when and where."

"But you can't come here."

"Why is that?" I said.

"Because I ain't ready."

"Stop talking that way. Wherever it is, I've seen worse."

"Why you assume it's bad?" she said. "I could be living in a mansion."

"I don't care, Nina. When and where?"

Silence. For a moment I thought she'd hung up. She'd blocked her number from appearing on my caller ID, so I couldn't call her back.

Then she spoke. "Above the pharmacy."

"Which pharmacy?"

"There ain't but one pharmacy in Blissfield."

"You mean on Main Street?"

"Of course, dummy."

"Time?"

"Seven."

"Can I take you to dinner?" I said.

"I eat at work."

"Maybe tonight you could do something different."

"I got to be there by eight."

"So I'll pick you up earlier."

"I told you I got church."

Now I was silent. I knew Nina. I knew she was making this difficult to punish me. She was right to punish me.

"I'm sorry, Nina," I said.

"You back to that?"

"I'm sorry. Do you hear? *I am sorry.*"

No sound issued from her end of the line.

"Nina," I said, "I know you think I forgot you. I know you think I went away to something better. I know you think I could have come sooner. But one thing I learned from my doctors was that you can never do anything one second before you're ready."

"What doctors?"

"I can't tell you unless you give me the chance."

"Okay," she said very quietly. "Come over at six."

"Five."

"Five-thirty."

"You gonna let me in?"

"We'll see," she said, hanging up.

* * * * * * *

The pharmacy was across the street and down the block from Marla's Kitchen. Except for the hardware store, it was the only other building on Main Street that wasn't vacant. As I parked I remembered going into the pharmacy with Grandma years before. The pharmacist, a big pink man whose mouth frothed when he talked, had probably been trying out homemade blends of the stuff he was selling.

I was surprised to find the door to the upstairs flat, located around the corner from the pharmacy entrance, unlocked. The enormous Louis Vuitton bag—well, the *fake* Louis Vuitton bag—was lying in a heap at the bottom of a flight of very narrow, very steep dark stairs. The sight of those stairs welcomed me back to the street of abandoned houses—one of my memories once dulled by opioids, but now sharp and mean enough to make me hesitate. I thought about shouting up to Nina and inventing some story to get her to come downstairs, or just telling her I was sick and would come back another day. Then I heard her voice echoing down the stairwell.

"Taking measurements for new wallpaper? Stop acting crazy and hurry up or you'll make me late for work!" She was standing in the half shadow, looking down from the top.

One step at a time, I clutched the railings while the stairwell pitched and spun with my climb.

"How old is this motherfucking house?" I complained, reminding myself, as the Old Man always said, to breathe.

"Long as it wasn't built by no slaves, who cares?" she said, hands on her hips and tapping her foot impatiently. "Why you acting like this the Kilimanjaro?"

Awash in sweat, I reached the top. She stood there in an old-fashioned calico housedress, something I might have found in Grandma's closet. Her hair, uncovered, was still a briar patch. She wore no makeup, and her blue eyes were piercing.

I'd purchased a box of Whitman's Chocolates at the Piggly Wiggly down the street. It was the same gift I'd brought that Christmas Eve, fifteen years before. She accepted the box, turned it over to the picture of the sweets inside, and smiled.

"Never thought this day would come," she declared. We were standing in a narrow entrance hall.

"It hasn't come yet," I said. "You gonna let me inside?"

She turned and led me into a living area that spanned the width of the pharmacy below. A tan leather loveseat and matching recliner looked new, and she had a coffee table loaded with paperbacks. The cream-hued walls drew in light from the small lace-curtained windows, and everything smelled of the vanilla candles placed on the sills. The room faced the street and, beneath the gospel choir rolling on the radio, I could hear the low swish of the occasional passing car.

"This is real nice, Nina."

She set the chocolates on the stack of books. "You sound like you surprised."

"Hell—it's a lot more than I got."

She looked at me skeptically.

"Damn, Nina," I said, "Ohio's not Hollywood! I don't know any rich people, and that would include me!"

She laughed again, gazing down at me from an advantage of at least eight inches. The top of my head came only to her collarbone, which was prominent beneath her housedress. Without the bulky clothes I could see that with the exception of her belly, she was still much too thin, and purple shadows bloomed beneath her eyes.

"You okay?" I said softly.

"Are *you*?" she replied, the surliness back.

"No," I answered plainly, "I'm not."

"So that's why you came back."

"You know why I came back."

"Would of made more sense to come before it happened."

"I couldn't come until it happened."

"You done it before."

"Back then folks wanted me here."

"What folks?"

"My—my grandma. Your brother. *You*." I couldn't believe how hard it was to say this out loud.

"How you know we didn't want you to come back?" she said quietly.

"Well damn, Nina, nobody helped."

"You expect us to buy the gas?"

"No, but somebody could have answered at least one of my letters."

"What letters?" she demanded, still staring down at me. "I already told you I never got no letters. Next you'll be saying you sent lottery tickets, too!"

I felt myself stiffen. "You think I'm making it up? I wrote you hundreds of times over the years."

"Blissfield ain't that big," she said. "You tryin' to tell me each and every one a those letters got lost?"

"I didn't have your address, so I wrote to you everywhere I could think of—even General Delivery at the post office."

"Whatever." Her face closed the way, I'm sure, my own face closed whenever someone talked about my father. She stared at the floor, her head slightly tilted, then spoke again suddenly. "Time for breakfast."

"It's five-thirty in the evening."

"So?"

"So make yourself some dinner," I said.

"But then I'll miss my morning protein."

"You can eat bacon and eggs for dinner."

"Then what would I eat for breakfast?"

"I don't know—hominy and okra?"

I hoped she'd remember that Grandma tried to get us to eat a hominy and okra casserole a long time ago, but her face remained dour.

"Whatever," she repeated. "You never said if you wanted to eat."

I shrugged. "You never really asked, but don't go to any trouble for me."

"I got to eat," she said, "so you might as well, too."

The kitchen was through a narrow hallway, and I followed her. A half-moon table stood beside a two-burner gas stove and a small humming fridge. Though ancient, the cabinets were freshly painted and curtains of dancing daisies hung at the window, which looked out over a dirt yard where a black pickup truck—probably the pharmacist's—was parked. A narrow passage led to three more doors: her bedroom, bath, and maybe a closet. Everything was impeccably clean.

"Coffee?" she asked.

"Sure."

She poured me a cup from an ancient percolator without asking if I take it black. I couldn't tell if it was the same percolator she'd used in the little house in the thicket.

"You been here long?" I asked, sipping the brew. It was thick and good.

"Yes," she answered without elaborating.

"You like it?"

"What?" She was pulling cartons from the fridge and the cabinets.

"Are-you-happy-here?" I asked, emphasizing every word. She closed the door of the fridge and glanced at me suspiciously.

"I spose."

"You suppose?"

"It's a place to live," she said as she crossed the room, "not a boyfriend."

"Expensive?" I asked.

"Naw."

"Landlord cool?"

"He alright."

"Close to work?"

"Three blocks."

"Like your job?"

"Hell, no."

"Pay okay?"

"You serious?"

"Where's Gideon?" I dropped the question and watched as she twisted around from the stove to peer at me, her eyes narrowed to slits.

"Forget it, CeCe."

"Why?" I asked.

"You don't get to know."

"Nina—"

"No, CeCe. He'll find you if and when he want to."

"Then he's in town?"

"He don't have to be in Blissfield to find you. Word travels. How you think I knew you was here?"

"Did you tell him?"

"Didn't have to."

"But you have to tell me," I said.

"Tell you what, exactly?"

"How I can find him."

"He don't want to be found."

"How do you know?"

"I should know my own brother."

"Nina, please—"

"No, CeCe."

"Why not?"

"He don't want you to know."

"But you know where he is."

"I only know where he not."

"Such as?"

"Church. At work. In this room."

She turned back to the stove, where I smelled melting lard, which took me straight back to Grandma's kitchen, followed by the hiss of frying eggs. She lifted, on the edge of a knife, several strips of bacon from the package and added them to the pan. The kitchen was filled with the South. With Corinthia Castle's Blissfield. With home.

"You stayin' this time?" she asked for the second time, her back to me.

"Who gives a shit?" I asked.

She laughed.

"Find that funny?" I asked, incensed.

"You remind me of Stella."

"Who?"

"That girl always following the old rich lady around in *Great Expectations*," she said. "Figured she'd get the house and the cash if she played her cards right."

"I'm not here for the house or the cash, even though that's what everybody thinks."

"Everybody who?" she said, prodding at the sizzling bacon with the knife.

"My grandmother's lawyer," I said. "And her neighbor. And even the old man out at her church."

"Why do they matter?"

"They don't. But *you* do."

"And?"

"You think that's why I'm here, too."

She pitched me a cool look. "Where you staying?"

"In her house," I said.

"Where you cooking and sleeping and eating?"

"Alright," I said, "I get your point—but the Hilton was all booked out."

She laughed again. Her laugh was a little rusty, like she didn't use it much. "That don't matter," she said firmly. "The important thing is to tell the truth, Ms. Bethany Celeste Castle. That's something you don't like to do."

"You can't say that. You haven't seen me in fifteen years—"

"—But I known you for seventeen and you—"

"—Used to be my sister!" I said hotly.

She again looked over her shoulder, her eyes cold. "*Used* to be?"

"I figured that was the case when I never heard from you."

"I already told you I never heard from *you*."

"You never got one single letter?" I said.

"Are you back to that?"

"Not a single one?"

"Who cares?"

"*I* care!"

"That's all about *you*—not me!"

"Were you living in Blissfield?" I asked.

"Where else I'm gonna live?"

"Then it doesn't make sense."

"You never made any sense," she said.

"It's just not possible."

"Why would I lie, CeCe?"

"Shit, Nina," I said. "Everybody lies."

"I don't lie. I never lie. That's one of my problems."

"Your problem is I always know when you're not telling the truth!" I said.

She shook her head. "Okay. I'll tell you this: I went to see Miss Corinne after you left. I axt her could I write to you. She said no. Said your momma had moved and she didn't have your address. I should just wait 'til I got a letter."

"She knew where I was," I said. "She had my address."

"I figured she did. I also figured she didn't want me to contact you. That she sent you back because of what happened with DeAndre. And maybe she finally decided we just wasn't good enough, like everybody else in this town always said."

"Maybe Grandma was scared DeAndre would be able to find me if you had my address."

"Oh," Nina said, turning back to her food. "Never thought of that."

I watched for a while as she coaxed the sizzling bacon around the eggs in the pan.

"What happened after I left that afternoon?" I asked quietly.

"Why you want to talk about that?" she replied without turning her head.

"Because that's why I had to go and couldn't come back," I said.

"You said something happened in Ohio."

"A lot of shit happened in Ohio. But I wouldn't have *been* in Ohio if not for DeAndre."

"You want to talk about Ohio?" Nina asked.

"Not really."

"Well," she said evenly, "I don't want to talk about DeAndre. Some things just need to stay in the past."

"Nina: tell me why Gideon doesn't want to be found."

"I can't," she said.

"Nina—"

"That's for him to tell you. He'll turn up if and when he ready."

"I think I saw him," I said softly. "In Whelan's the other night."

"So?"

"Please help me. Please."

Nina set the fork on the edge of the pan and turned off the heat. Looking hard at me for a moment, she took a single step forward. "You still want me to be your sister?"

"Never stopped wanting it."

"You want to be part of our craziness?"

"Believe me," I said, "I *know* crazy. I'll be alright."

Shaking her head, she crossed the small kitchen and took two flowered plates from a cabinet. Returning to the stove, she turned the bacon over one more time before expertly dividing the food between us.

"Ketchup?" she said.

"No, thanks."

"Tabasco?"

"Why not?" I said, thinking of Bruce, the bartender in Whelan's.

She brought the plates to the table with a smoothness unlike the clumsy Nina of our youth, suggesting she'd served food at some point since my departure.

"Let me toast some bread," she said, eyeing her plate.

"Not for me. I'm really okay."

"Well, I like my toast and butter. And orange marmalade," she added, turning to an ancient toaster tethered to the wall by a thick black cord. I waited as she stuck two slices of white bread into the toaster and returned to the table.

"You gonna eat that before it's cold?" she asked me.

"I'll eat when you sit down."

"Why you got to be so complicated?"

"That's what CeCe stands for: Constantly Complicated."

She gave a quick, coughing laugh, then peered at me thoughtfully. "You different, but the same. What happened to you, CeCe?"

"What didn't happen?"

"You gonna tell the truth?"

"Depends."

"On?"

"If you got time to sew up the broken stitches."

She put her hollow gaze on me and I knew she knew what I meant. We let it go at that.

The toast popped up and she brought it to the table, along with a stick of butter, still wrapped in wax paper, her marmalade and the tabasco.

We began to eat.

I watched as Nina, long fingers carefully grasping the utensils, cut her bacon into small pieces and mixed them into her eggs. She doused the steaming mix with hot sauce, then loaded it onto a slice of toast. She sliced off a corner of the bread, took a small forkful and chewed daintily. Her gaze focused on me. "Go on," she said, wiping her mouth with her napkin. "Explain."

I swallowed and set down my fork. "What?"

Her blue eyes narrowed. She swallowed, too. "What you got against ketchup."

Something tore in my carefully bandaged heart and I really laughed. She laughed, too. I loved her so much at that moment my whole body ached.

"I know," she said abruptly, looking into my eyes. "Me, too."

We finished our breakfast in silence, looking at each other between bites. When she put her fork down, I quickly stood, gathered our plates and beat her to the sink.

"What do you think you doing?" she asked, genuinely piqued.

"Painting the ceiling," I said, turning on the water.

"That's not even funny."

"Okay—I'm washing the dishes."

"No you not!"

"In that case," I said, "I'm giving you time to get ready."

"You a guest!"

"I'm family."

"You don't do no work in my house!"

"Nina," I said, "listen to me: I want you to go and get dressed. Then you're going to bring your comb and brush and sit down at this table. I am going to untangle that weed lot you're trying to call a hairstyle, so you won't continue to frighten your patients to death."

Something in my voice moved her, because she stopped in her tracks, her hands on her hips. Then she smiled.

"Nobody ever been able to do nothing with this hair," she said quietly. "I'll let you try. But if you hurt me, CeCe, you're going to regret it."

"Not as much as I'll regret not trying," I answered.

She came out of her bedroom a little while later, in another homeless costume, with the stretch pants showcasing her socks, and her softening middle forming a lardy muffintop over the elastic.

"Why in hell are you wearing those clothes?" I asked.

"What's wrong with them?"

"You got a job. Why do you dress like you don't?"

"You don't exactly look like Ralph Lauren dropped by."

"At least my clothes fit," I said.

"These fit me just fine."

"Nina: your pants are too big and too short and your blouse does nothing for your—"

"I don't care, CeCe. I never cared."

"I know, but *damn*, girl!"

Once again, she considered me. Then, once again, she laughed. "You talking like you my stylist."

"I'm talking like I'm your friend."

"I don't have friends."

The statement was calm, factual, honest. My heart lurched. Then I remembered that the women I'd worked with the past eight years—the women from my Ohio life—all vanished when I was down and out.

"Me, either," I confessed. "I guess you broke the mold, Nina."

"What mold?"

"When I was seventeen years old I tried to kill a man to protect you. How could any other friend match up to that?"

This time she didn't laugh. She sat down on her chair and placed a wide-toothed comb in front of me. "Good luck," she said. "And don't take too long. I got to be at work in a half hour.

thirteen.

I spent a restless night, rendered even shorter by the phone call at dawn. I hoped it was Nina, but instead a woman's nasal voice responded, telling me she was placing a call to Ms. Bethany Celeste Castle on behalf of Attorney Richard Armitage.

I fought back the strong urge to deny any knowledge of Ms. Castle's whereabouts, then accepted the call.

"Ms. Castle, I hope I haven't reached you at a bad time," Armitage said. "I wanted to be sure to speak with you before you went out for the day."

"Well, thank you," I said, noting that it was only six fifty-five in the morning. "Do you pay your staff overtime for working before sunrise?"

"I often have to be in court by eight, so I get started early. Please excuse me if I woke you."

"What can I do for you?"

"I'm hoping you'll be able to meet with me later today. I've contacted the other parties in your grandmother's will and asked them to come in, too."

"I see."

"I should warn you in advance that nothing will be permanently decided during this meeting. There's quite a bit to be discussed, so please understand that we will more than likely need to meet several times before everything's settled. Perhaps around two-thirty?"

"Roger that," I said, wondering why talking to him made me behave, in Nina's words, like a dummy.

He hung up and I returned to bed, where I sat looking through the window at the weed-choked rosebushes outside.

That afternoon—perhaps out of pure fatigue at feeling like I had to represent my grandmother—I ignored the retail management outfit and just went as me. Yes, the knees were shredded, but I felt good in those jeans, and I was even happier in my Goodyear tee-shirt, emblazoned with a retro image of the blimp. My hair, wild and kinky, rose to embrace the late summer humidity. Face scrubbed clean, nails sanded short, bare feet in a pair of flat sandals, my heart felt more at peace than it had at any moment since my arrival.

A woman—either a secretary or the lawyer's wife—met me at the door when I entered the house. She didn't exactly smile, but I figured if you start work at seven, you're not particularly friendly to anybody by two. I can't for the life of me tell you what she looked like, though I know I looked right at her. I followed her honeysuckle perfume into Armitage's inner office, with its heavy furniture and knick-knack-crowded bookshelves.

"Nice to see you again, Ms. Castle," Armitage began, standing quickly. He was in a shirt and tie that day, suggesting he might indeed have come from court.

I was unaware that there was anything like a court in Blissfield. "I understand you paid a visit to the cemetery," he said in a slightly sing-song voice, as if he were scolding a child.

"I retrieved my grandmother's urn and brought it back to her home," I said evenly.

"So I understand. There will be a charge for your damage to the glass of the columbarium."

"Naturally," I assured him, knowing they'd have to put me to work in the tobacco fields before I'd ever pay it. "Are we ready to begin?"

"You're somewhat early," he said, placing his hands on a large file on his desk. "Might I offer you some coffee, or perhaps iced tea?"

"No, thank you." I paused. "You said there was a great deal to discuss."

"So I did. While we're waiting for the others to arrive, I suppose I could get started with just a few foundational facts. In our last conversation, Ms. Castle, I explained that your grandmother's estate is far larger than the house you're currently inhabiting. She left some explanation about her wishes concerning the house, but the rest of the estate must be divided according to the directives of a superseding document."

"Another will?" I said.

"A will that details the entirety of the estate, with the exception of the house your grandmother resided in."

"You're suggesting that my grandmother had no control over her own land?"

"Actually, she was herself something closer to a tenant on the land."

"That's difficult to believe."

"It was a difficult situation for her, too."

The phone on his desk buzzed. He answered it and made an affirmative noise.

"Once again," he said to me, "I apologize for the delay in contacting the other parties involved. I experienced some difficulty in carrying out this task—"

The door opened behind me. I looked over my shoulder and gasped.

A man stood uncertainly in the threshold. He was tall, lean and weathered, with a face browned by the sun, and intense blue-grey eyes. His gaze moved across the office, coming to rest first on the lawyer, and then, with a passing glance, on me.

"Mr. Price, please come in. Is Ms. Price with you, also?"

Because I couldn't speak, I watched in silence as Gideon's bowlegged gait moved slowly into the room. My eyes leapt to his face, which seemed shadowed in contrast to his pure white button-down shirt, the cuffs rolled at the forearm. A pair of dark, well-washed work pants hung loosely on his frame. His hair was shaved close to his scalp and his open shirt teased the tip of a faded cobalt tattoo. It was clear he'd never been in the lawyer's office before.

Armitage rose and shook his hand.

Gideon didn't speak to me, but instead lowered himself heavily into the chair beside mine. Inches from mine. Close-enough-for-me-to-touch-him-without-moving-my-hand, next to mine. But his gaze was fly-papered to the lawyer.

"I don't know whether you met Ms. Castle when she was a resident in our area some years ago," Armitage said. "Might I introduce you?"

Gideon didn't turn his head. His lips moved as he spoke to the lawyer, but I could barely hear him over the door slamming in my chest. The lawyer's brows drew together.

"Ms. Castle, are you all right? Can I get you a glass of water?"

I realized I'd gripped the edges of my chair. I couldn't look away from Gideon.

"Ms. Castle?" Armitage repeated, a crescendo of alarm in his voice.

"Gideon," I said. I don't know whether I whispered it or screamed it, but he ignored me as if I wasn't there. "Gideon: *What are you*—"

"Ms. Castle—?"

"—doing here?" my voice had hit the register of a dog whistle.

"Ms. Castle," Armitage said firmly, "Mr. Price is here by my invitation. He is, by virtue of his ancestry, one of the legal heirs to the agricultural properties tended throughout her life by Corinthia Castle."

At that moment my brain chose to go on vacation rather than explode. A kind of static started behind my eyes and drowned out all other sound, including my banging heart.

Gideon finally looked at me, a soup of contempt, muted rage and raw impatience in his eyes.

Ignoring the lawyer, the office, the *zchhhhhh* in my head, I leaned toward him. His scent of warm skin and sweet Palmolive soap instantly steadied me.

"Gideon, I've been looking for you everywhere—"

"Ms. Castle?" I heard the lawyer's voice somewhere in the distance.

"Everywhere," I repeated. "Do you hear me?"

"Ms. Castle—please try to calm down."

"Nina wouldn't tell me where you are. Why the hell are you avoiding—"

"*Ms. Castle!*" Armitage actually shouted my name. Gideon stared at me, his eyes a mirror of the Akron skies in winter.

"I see that you have indeed met Mr. Price," the lawyer said, then added cautiously, "do you think we might proceed?"

I fell back in my chair, clenching my trembling hands in my lap. My right leg began to bounce uncontrollably. I forced myself to look at the floor.

"We have," Richard Armitage stated, "an unusual and somewhat difficult situation—certainly one that we couldn't have foreseen. While your grandmother was aware of encumbrances to her full possession of the Castle estate, she never, to the best of my knowledge, made any attempt to legally overturn them. Therefore, I am relatively certain that neither one of you could have possibly been aware of this situation. Am I correct?"

Gideon nodded, his eyes again fixed on the lawyer.

"I have no idea what you're talking about," I said.

"I also suspect," Armitage said as if he hadn't heard me, "that neither one of you particularly counted on inheriting any part of this property."

Again Gideon nodded, his face grave.

The lawyer looked at me for a long moment, then accepting that I had no intention of replying, continued to speak.

"Both of you are the members of families that, by bloodline, should make financial decisions concerning the estate. If you're willing, I'd like to discuss the process of settling the estate. With any luck we should be able to clear probate within the next six months."

"*Wait*—" I said, looking up at the lawyer. I knew my voice was shaking, but I couldn't control it. "I still don't understand what you mean by '*bloodline*'."

Armitage once again flattened the papers on his desk. "I am referring to family members that are designated as heirs to the Castle holdings."

"There are only two Castles left," I said. "One is in solitary in a supermax. The other is right here in front of you."

"Let me explain, Ms. Castle. I said that this is a meeting of family members who are heirs to the estate, not a meeting for Castle family members."

That stung like one of Copley's slaps. I couldn't believe that even *this* man knew more about my family than I did, thanks to Grandma.

"Why," I said, "should I believe anything you tell me?"

"At the risk of being impolite," Armitage said, "I must insist that it doesn't matter who tells you. These documents will determine the future of the estate, whether you like it, believe it, approve of it or not. The bottom line, Ms. Castle, is that you can delay things, but you can't stop them. The heirs named in these pages are eventually going to acquire what's theirs. The decision is whether you're willing to comply with the law and accept the legal parameters of this document."

"I didn't come here for this," I said in a remarkably quiet voice.

"For what?" Armitage asked, bemused.

"I did not come to Blissfield for the will, the house, the land or any of my grandmother's belongings. I only came back to find *you*," I said, peering directly at Gideon.

Armitage leaned back in his chair. "Ms. Castle," he said wearily, "I have no idea what's going on between you and the Prices, but my responsibility is to see that the directives in these documents are carried out as required by law."

"Why can't you," I said, "and everyone else in Blissfield understand that I don't give a—"

"Excuse me." Gideon's voice—deeper, but still rough as asphalt—quietly pierced the tension in the room. "Could you give us a few minutes? I need to speak to Ms. Castle."

The lawyer looked from one of us to the other and nodded.

Gideon stood. Without another word he led me out of the office and down the hall toward the front of the house. The static had returned to my head. The odors of damp wood, of sun on old bricks, of peonies exploding with perfume—were completely lost on me.

I was walking behind Gideon.

Gideon!

He turned to face me at the white picket fence. We were standing in the exact spot where seventeen years before—me on my bike, and Gideon, a skateboard beneath his right foot and a football tucked under his arm—we'd tried to solve the riddle of first love.

He had reached his full height at some point after my departure, because Gideon Price now stood well over six feet tall. He retained his quarterback silhouette, with rounded shoulders, thick thighs and a tapered waist. He was a big man, though not deliberately menacing, as some large men can be.

The menace was there, however, contained in the blue-grey eyes that had once been filled with a guilelessness that drew girls, including me, like magnets attract steel shavings.

Something different now waited in his eyes.

In the light of the afternoon sun I could also see how he'd aged. Deep sprigs of wrinkles adorned his eyes and wreathed his lips. A furrow had opened between his brows and though clean-shaven, a wash of beard lined his chin. He had a scar, an ugly scar, along his left cheekbone. It wasn't the scar of a fall. It was the kiss of a knife. He was barely thirty, but looked much, much older.

"Gideon, I don't understand," I said, speaking first.

He looked down at me, his face guarded. "What don't you understand?"

"I've been looking for you everywhere. Not just for the past week—hell, for the past fifteen years!"

"—And now you found me."

I opened my mouth to reply, but no words came out. I had rehearsed our reunion thousands and thousands of times. Never had I imagined it might go down like this.

"Why are you acting like this, Gideon?"

"Like what?"

"Like you don't know me."

"I don't know you."

"Like nothing ever happened between us."

"Nothing did."

"How can you say that?"

"It's the truth."

"But we—we were *together*," I said desperately.

"We was kids hanging out after school."

"We were more than that."

"In your mind, maybe, but not in mine."

"You can't be serious."

"Do you see me smiling?"

"I cared about you. Damn, Gideon—I *still* care."

"I cared about you, too—the way kids care about each other."

"Neither one of us was a child," I said. "We'd seen too much for that."

"That's all over with."

"Not for me."

"Jesus," he murmured, his voice tight with fury. "You roll up after all this time and immediately start looking for a stage and a spotlight. Maybe you forgot the shit you caused the last time you was here. Or maybe they ran you out of wherever you came from for the same reasons."

"Don't say that," I pleaded. "You know I was only trying to help Nina."

"You made it worse for all of us."

"That motherfucker DeAndre deserved it, and if I'd had a gun I would have blown his brains out."

"Sorry you missed your chance."

"That's for damn sure," I replied, stung. "*You* clearly weren't man enough to do it."

The words escaped my lips so quickly that I barely had time to prepare myself for the rage I saw in his eyes. I knew that rage. I'd seen it in the mirror too many times.

I took a step backwards, even as he measured my ripped jeans and faded tee-shirt. His eyes went to my unstyled hair, then took in my furious, despairing face. When our eyes met he blinked lazily, coldly, and looked away.

"Wait—" I said, "I'm so sorry—" Desperately I stepped forward.

He again raised his hands, open palmed, and turned back toward the street. Speechless, I had no choice but to watch as he climbed into a black pickup and drove away.

fourteen.

The last traces of Copley drained out of me as I sat in my grandmother's kitchen, trying to jigsaw together how I'd gone to a lawyer about Corinthia Castle's will and come away understanding that first, she'd somehow left her property to Gideon and Nina instead of me or my father, and second, that I might as well be dog shit in Gideon and Nina's eyes.

Was this a vicious joke Armitage and his ilk were playing on the still-pathetic Prices? Was this Grandma's final way of punishing me for what I'd done fifteen years before? Or had Nina and Gideon known, even back when we were kids, that the house I slept in actually belonged to them? Was all this because of another one of Blissfield's fucked up "rules"—the "rules" I'd never truly understood?

My mind wandered back to the things Nina and my grandmother taught me about color and caste in Blissfield so many years ago.

"So what's wrong with *her*?" I'd asked Nina one day during lunch, when a girl from my English class strolled up and asked if she could borrow my copy of *The Great Gatsby*. I'd read it over the summer, so I handed the book over and she promised to return it later on.

"She stink," Nina said from where she was lying in the shade, her head propped up on her lunchbox, a copy of Toni Morrison's *Sula* folded open on her chest.

"She's alright."

"I knew her older brother. Kicked his butt back in fifth grade —"

"Nina, just because you fought with him years ago doesn't mean you got to hate on her now."

"I don't hate on her. But you don't need to get too close to her."

"She only asked to borrow my book."

"That's how it starts. They make up some fake reason to come over, and—"

"You're being silly."

"Am not. I know how people around here think," she said.

"How's that?"

"They pretend to be your friend so they can figure out your weak spots. Then, when you least expect it, they pounce!"

"But why, Nina?"

"Because everybody been here forever, and none of them ever gonna leave. *All* of us know everything there is to know about everybody's momma and daddy, grandmomma and granddaddy, uncles, aunties, cousins, *excetera, cetera, cetera.*"

"So what?"

"You just don't get it. There's *rules*," she declared.

"What rules?"

"Rules about who can do what with who. Why certain people can't run together. Can't date or get married. Can't really even be friends." She looked at me.
"According to the rules, you shouldn't be sitting here with me."

"You're right, Nina. I don't get it."

"Of course, not! You a Castle."

"I don't get that, either!"

Nina sat up, clearly exasperated. "You ever axt your Grandma to tell you your
family story?"

"Yes, and she told me, too."

"How far back she go?"

"What do you mean?"

"She tell you about her parents? Grandparents?"

"A little."

"Then go home today and ax her. Ax her to tell you everything."

"Why? You think she's hiding something?"

"Not hiding. Just not *not* hiding."

"Nina, you're being crazy."

"Nope. *You* crazy if you don't want to know the truth."

I sat there looking at her. She leaned up and looked right back. There was
something clear and decisive in her gaze, almost as if she felt sorry for me.

"Why are you looking at me like that?" I said.

"Like what?

"You know like what."

She tilted her head. "CeCe, my momma work like a slave to feed me and my
brothers. Our house so little, once we got a table and a couple of chairs in there
we just gave up on any other furniture. If I make it through high school I'll be
lucky, 'cause it might keep me from bending over in the fields for the next fifty
years. This is what my life is. I know it. I'm not even mad about it.

"But you different," she said. "You got your grandma, and she going to make
sure you never clean nobody's house or work in the dirt, unless that's what *you*
choose. I know something happened with your momma and your daddy, but I
also know you can stay here, or you can leave, and if you want you can keep on in
school until you Somebody. That's up to you."

She leaned closer. "Some things is lies, and some things is true. You should
listen to what I say, because I may be poor and ugly, but I am *not* stupid."

"Nina, you're not ugly—"

"But I *am* poor, and poor girls don't get to lie to themselves."

Strangely, tears came into my eyes and I felt a pingpong ball get stuck in my
throat. A few months earlier I would have cussed her out, maybe even smacked
her, then walked away. Instead, I reached down, pulled up a couple handfuls of
grass and looked away, praying that tears wouldn't start pouring down my face.

Why the hell was I crying? What was happening to me?

Suddenly I felt Nina's hand on my arm.

"Hey, little sister," she said in a new voice, "hold up. I wasn't trying to hurt
you."

I couldn't answer. Another new development.

"Look," she said, now wrapping her arm around my shoulder and pulling me close. "I know you sick of me. I see you looking over at LaToya and Bree and them, wondering what it would be like to worry about relaxing your hair and becoming a cheerleader. But hell, CeCe, I'm going to tell you the honest truth: you cute and you a Castle. They might let you in because you look good, but none a them would ever stand up for you in a fight. Not a single stupid one a them."

I spoke for the first time. "I don't want to fight, Nina. I just want to breathe."

"Me, too," she said softly. "Been wanting that my whole life."

The bell rang. "So long," she said, getting to her feet. "Don't wait for me after school. I'm gonna go and see my dummy Algebra teacher."

So that afternoon I asked Grandma. We were in the car, on the way home from the Piggly Wiggly with our groceries in the back. Grandma's great big car, a grey Buick—it seemed like all the old people drove cars that could have run over a dinosaur—stuttered and shook while we waited at Blissfield's only stoplight, across from the pharmacy.

She glanced at me, and I saw that odd shadow of my father in her eyes.

"People been talking?" she asked, sounding remarkably like Nina.

"Yes and no," I answered, which was both evasive and true.

"That's okay," she said. "You have a right to know."

"Know what?"

"The truth about whatever they've been telling you."

Still, she waited until later that evening, when the corn, beets and crab cakes were cooked, served and eaten. She asked me to set the dining room table, so instead of sitting at the kitchen table beside the stove, we ate our meal at the mahogany table in the formal dining room, next to the huge cherry wood credenza.

I sat a bit uneasily beside her, the table cleared of dishes that now soaked in the kitchen sink. She hadn't said much during the meal, and I didn't know whether she was trying to figure out what to say, or trying to keep herself from turning mean. I felt like it could go either way.

Grandma peered at me a little sideways, as if we were playing cards and she was guessing the strength of my hand. Or maybe I, too, was thinking with Copley's brain.

"You know, Princess," she said, "you've grown a lot since you've been here. I wonder if your mother would even recognize you."

"Shoot," I said. "Everybody I know says I look more and more like you and my daddy every day."

She laughed, acknowledging the truth of that statement. Then she leaned a little closer to me. "Sweetheart, there really are no secrets here in Blissfield." (Nina: *one*; me: *zero*). "I always knew that sooner or later someone would come at you with some sort of meanness, but to be honest, it's time you learned the family history, anyway."

She reached over to the credenza and handed me a tarnished, silver-framed photograph of an old white man who was dressed in a neat dark suit and leaning on a cane.

"Princess, this is Lionel Bibb, my grandfather."

I realized with a start that though my eyes had fallen on the photograph many times, I'd figured the guy was some old white friend of the family. His features were distinctly European and his eyes must have been a very light blue, because in the picture they appeared to be almost silver.

"So my great-grandfather was white?"

"No, Princess, he wasn't."

"But he looks—"

"His looks didn't matter. Though his father was his master, his mother was a slave, so he was born enslaved."

I must have seemed confused, because she leaned forward and placed her palm gently on the side of my face. "Baby, slavery had nothing to do with skin color. If your mother was a slave at the time of your birth, you inherited her slavery. Think of the problems it would have caused if the master's slave offspring could have claimed the right to inherit his property."

"Right," I said. "The slave owners wouldn't have gone for that."

"And because Blacks weren't included in white family histories, we memorized and passed our ancestry down as stories, from one generation to the next. This is why everyone knows everyone else's story. For Black people, this was the way we kept our history from vanishing."

"He looks kinda mean," I remarked, returning the photograph to the credenza.

"Actually, he was a leader in the community. Many of the poor farmers came to him for help with writing letters and understanding legal documents."

"So why does everybody act so weird about the Castles? It seems like everybody had a master lurking somewhere in their family tree."

"Well, some of the talk is tied to my husband's father, Samuel Redmond. After he purchased his farm, he decided to give himself a new name. He placed a high value on land and property, so he chose to call himself 'Castle.'"

"What's the problem with that?"

"Some folks thought he was arrogant—almost as if he was trying to say he was better than other people. I personally suspect he changed his name to avoid any claims on his property by any of his half-brothers and sisters—descendants of slaves by different mothers—which was seen as rather selfish on his part."

"So is *that* the secret?"

"Sweetheart," she said, looking away, "every family has lots of secrets. Whenever people like to gossip, they'll find something to gossip about."

She stood, so I did, too, and I followed her back to the kitchen. I began washing the dishes while she set the kettle on the stove for her beloved Black Rose tea. She scattered some animal crackers on a saucer and set them in the center of the kitchen table.

Encouraged by her willingness to talk about our family, I thought I'd take another stab at finding out what I *really* wanted to know.

"So what really happened to my grandpa?" I asked without turning around, but I could feel her pause to look at me.

"Your grandfather?"

"Your husband," I said. "The guy who went away."

She made her tea, added milk, and then poured a glass of milk for me. "Sit down, Beth."

"But I'm not finished wash——"

"That's okay."

I was aware of my elbows sticking to the vinyl tablecloth, which was imprinted with dancing kettles and slices of pie.

"Baby," she began, "a family history is a complicated thing. Our story brings together two families, the Castles and the Bibbs. My husband's family lived about seven miles up Route 158, just across the county line. My family, the Bibbs, were settled here in Blissfield."

Grandma sighed. "There's so much to tell about our ancestors I'd never finish in one night. But I will tell you this: things were different, back when I was your age. Many years, well, over half a century ago—family meant everything. Your mother and father, their parents, and the people who came before them—those people defined who you were. You lived exactly the way your family wanted. Wore your hair in a way that pleased them. Went to the same church and studied in the same classrooms. You named your children after your grandparents and told them stories about everyone in the family so the young would know who they were.

"Well," she said, "part of those traditions was that your parents decided who you would marry. Parents arranged marriages so the landowning families could retain control over their property when whites tried to raise taxes, or find other ways to take it away. It also protected girls from getting ruined by some breath-and-britches fellow."

"Breath-and-britches?" I said.

"Your generation calls them 'players.'"

I laughed, and pleased that she'd used the term correctly, she winked at me and took a sip of her tea before continuing.

"My grandfather, Lionel Bibb, and my grandmother, whose name was Martha Moore, were born enslaved. They worked very hard and raised a family of eight children here in Blissfield, but only one of their sons, my father, Everett Bibb, chose to make his life here——"

"What happened to all the others?"

"They scattered all over the country. The boys went to war, then settled in New York and Philadelphia, and the girls got married and moved away with their husbands. My father married my mother, Cecile Johnson, a local girl who'd had the chance to go to a normal school——"

"—They had *abnormal* schools?" I cut in.

"No," she said, laughing, "a normal school was a college that trained teachers."

"So was their marriage arranged, too?"

Grandma looked surprised. "I honestly don't know. I expect, however, that she would have been considered an excellent catch because of her education."

"Did she teach in Blissfield?"

"She taught in a one-room schoolhouse, which was the only school Black children were allowed to attend. Most of the farmers were so poor that their kids had to help out in the fields all day, so my mother rarely had more than a handful of students, from the first through the eighth grade, in the same room."

"The same *room?*" I echoed.

"Yes. They sat on benches, without books or paper, and stayed warm by the heat of a wood-burning stove."

"Dang! Did they actually learn anything?"

"They learned as much as they could, and far more than some white people wanted. Back in those days, preventing Black people from going to school was the best way to keep us powerless."

I nodded, though I was having a hard time picturing it. Grandma went on talking.

"Around the time I was born my father's closest friend was Samuel Redmond Castle. His son Julius was about my age, and our fathers believed we'd make a good couple. I never gave it much thought when I was a girl, and when my mother insisted, over my father's objections, that I go to college and follow in her footsteps as a teacher, I was sure my father would let go of the idea that I would marry his friend's son. I was shocked when he announced at my graduation that I had a suitor. I finished college just after World War Two ended, and the idea of my father choosing my husband seemed ridiculously out of date. I refused on the spot to so much as discuss it."

Grandma stopped speaking and stared into her teacup as if, instead of searching for the future, she might find a simple way to explain the past. Enthralled, I completely ignored the cookies at my elbow.

"So," she went on without looking up, "I took a job in Raleigh and began my life as a teacher. I was home on a visit during the summer vacation when one afternoon my father walked into the yard, accompanied by Sam Castle and a tall young man in a perfect, pearl grey suit. I hadn't seen Julius in years, and it took me a few moments to recognize him. There I was, dressed in overalls, on my knees, picking beetles off the tomatoes. I got up, covered with dirt. My mother insisted I wear a sunhat whenever I gardened, but I hated hats back then, so I'd taken it off. My hair was a mess, and my face was quite brown from the sun. I remember the disappointment in my father's eyes. He'd probably convinced them I was some kind of countess, but to them I must have looked like a common sharecropper."

"That was a pretty smart way to get rid of him," I said, laughing.

Grandma smiled and shook her head. "Actually, I walked over, took off my work gloves, and we shook hands, but Julius was clearly unimpressed, and my father could see it. Father's disappointment led to rage, and later, when we were alone, he made it very clear that if the young man proposed, I was to accept."

"But why, Grandma?"

"Because women got paid very low wages in those days, and most people believed that a woman's real role was to marry and become a mother."

"That's crazy! We're as strong and smart as guys!" I said.

"True, but our fathers believed that the marriage would make both the Castles and the Bibbs much wealthier."

"So, was he handsome?"

"Julius? By the standards of the time he was considered quite handsome. He looked like he was white, which wasn't to my taste, but many considered him a very desirable man. He was also very intelligent, very elegant, and very quiet. Too quiet for me. I was used to boys who competed for a girl's attention, not a man who believed that no woman was good enough for him."

We laughed, then Grandma leaned back with a sigh.

"Julius and I were married about a month later. I won't tell you how many tears I spilled, trying to get my father to change his mind. It was pointless, of course. My parents believed that the harder I fought, the happier I'd be once I settled down and accepted married life."

"Did you have a big wedding?" I asked.

"The biggest wedding Black Blissfield had ever seen," Grandma said. "My father had the entire first floor of his house painted and decorated, and it seemed like he invited every Black person in the county. He hired six men and women to clean, cook and prepare the farm for the reception. My dress was made by a seamstress in Greensboro, because I was too short to wear a mail order bridal gown, and Blacks couldn't try on the dresses in the shops in those days."

"Really?"

"Princess, there's still a lot to fix in our world, but life is much, much less difficult now than it was for Black people in the past."

"So, did you get married at your father's house?" I asked.

"We said our vows in the tiny church my grandfather built with the help of the other newly freed slaves just after Emancipation. The church was only large enough to hold our families, so the guests were invited to join us at the reception."

"Did he give you a diamond ring?" I asked, noting that she wore no jewelry.

"I preferred a simple gold band," Grandma said. "Even that seemed odd to Julius. He never understood how anyone could be satisfied with, as he described it, 'less than the best.'"

I thought about that while Grandma selected a unicorn and bear, dunked them in her tea, then slid the plate of animal crackers toward me. Normally I loved animal crackers, but I was too busy imagining my grandmother on her wedding day to eat.

"Did you go on a honeymoon?" I asked.

"Oh, no. We never even discussed it. Julius and I moved into this house, which our parents purchased for us. It was only intended to be our first home. We were supposed to take over one of our parents' houses, which were quite large, when they passed away. I gave birth to my boys, went on teaching, and my husband oversaw the family properties."

"So," I said, "what was he like?"

"He was a stately man. Impeccably dressed. He rarely raised his voice, and he was very good with numbers. His mother fawned on him, so he valued elegant things—silver brushes and combs, monogrammed cufflinks, expensive watches. He shaved very carefully and always wore bay rum cologne."

Grandma smiled. "Julius was raised with money, and liked having his shirts made by a tailor up in Virginia Beach, so he'd travel there once or twice every year.

I thought all this was ridiculous for life in Blissfield, but that was one thing he refused to give up when his father forced him to marry me."

"I don't see why he had to be forced!" I said.

"Well, anyone would feel that way if their parents tied their inheritance to a wedding."

"His inheritance was tied to marrying you?"

"You can see how much things have changed," she said.

"But you're so pretty, Grandma!"

"Ideas about beauty change, too, Princess. In my day, men preferred women with very fair skin. I was too brown and much too skinny to please."

"That's crazy!"

"Not really," Grandma explained. "Remember that in the past most babies were born at home with the help of a midwife, and some women died in childbirth. None of the local hospitals accepted Black patients, so giving birth was often quite dangerous. People generally believed that women with wide hips and larger breasts had a better chance of surviving the birth and nursing their babies to health afterward."

"Oh. I never thought of that." I paused. "Did my grandfather want you to work?"

"Not particularly. His parents strongly disapproved—especially his mother, who said I was a poor wife for wanting to be away from home during the day. But I liked having my own money, and something of my own to think about, so I never gave it up."

"Did you teach in one room, too?" I asked.

"No, after the war they built Booker T. Washington Elementary and Junior High School. Later they added the wing that now serves as the high school. I taught children from kindergarten to graduation."

"Wow," I said. "I can't believe you never got tired of it!"

She fished through the animal crackers until she found the lion. "Princess, there were children in my classes whose clothes had been sewn by hand from burlap potato sacks. Children who were so poor they never held a book outside of school, and no one else in their family could read or write. No one. They barely had enough to eat, drank water collected in rain barrels and had no indoor toilets. School was the only place they could go to be warm, or really safe from the men who owned the land their parents worked—especially the girl children. Teaching was very important to our community and I loved every minute of it."

"But wasn't your husband proud of you?" I asked.

"Well," she said, again staring into her cup, "Julius' values were different from mine. He wanted a different kind of life. I think—well, I think he felt his life was passing him by here in Blissfield. After a few years he announced he was going to Washington to work. He sent us money, came to visit on the holidays, but he never moved back."

"You never went to see him in Washington?"

"No, baby."

"Why not?"

"It seemed so far away. Back then the trip was expensive and it took almost twelve hours with the train."

"You didn't have a car?" I asked.

"Yes, but the south was very different in those days. We didn't have the high-ways, so you had to drive on two-lane mountain roads to get anywhere. It wouldn't have been safe for a woman, even with a car full of boys, to drive up north alone."

"Were you mad at him for leaving?" I asked quietly.

Grandma looked away. "Sometimes."

"Why didn't you get divorced?"

"People didn't get divorced too often in those days, baby. Many couples, sometimes because of their jobs, lived far apart. I was too busy to think much about it. I had my hands full with the boys, my teaching, and lots of church activities, too. Remember: I grew up in Blissfield, and my parents and friends were here. Julius was from another town and had no particular ties to this community."

"Didn't he miss his kids?" I said.

"Yes, but he was never the type of man to throw a football or take them fishing. He believed that sending us more money than we needed was exactly what a father should do."

We were quiet for a while. She was thinking hard about something, her eyes fixed blindly on her teacup.

"When did he die?" I asked quietly.

"Oh, a long time ago," she said without emotion. "The death certificate said it was liver disease. That probably means he drank himself to death, but I don't really know. He was only forty-two."

"How did my daddy feel about it?"

Grandma stood up, went to the sink, and picked up where I left off with the dishes.

"Sometimes it was hard, but Princess, many, many families were missing fathers in those days. The war took lots of sons and fathers, and others moved north to look for better opportunities. We weren't the only family without a man around."

She glanced over at me. "It's long over with, baby. Sometimes I feel like it was somebody else's life. Almost as if once he was gone, my real life began."

"Is that why you never got married again?"

"I suppose. But then, I had three boys. There were more than enough men in this house."

"But—but your oldest sons died."

She paused, looking out of the window and into the night. "Yes, Jeremiah and Paul joined the service as soon as they finished high school. They wanted to see the world. It nearly broke my heart—I hoped they'd go on to college—but I understood they'd been in Blissfield all their lives, and they were restless. They left together, and died together in an accident with a truck full of explosives."

Grandma paused for a long moment. "It's a terrible thing, Princess, the death of one's child. And to lose two sons, suddenly, like that: I cannot begin to describe how pointless life seemed."

"But you still had my daddy." I said.

"Of course I still had Copley."

I got up and joined her with a dishtowel at the sink. "Grandma, are you sorry you ever got married?" I asked in a low voice.

"No," she said, thoughtfully. "It hasn't always been easy, but having you here makes up for all the pain."

"My father met my mother in a park," I said quietly. "Momma was coming home from work and he was sitting on a park bench. She told me he swept her off her feet."

"Your mother is a wonderful person," Grandma said gently.

"Then why does he hit her?"

"Some men use violence to feel powerful."

"But he beats her all the time."

"Princess—"

"Every single day," I said, hearing my own voice rise. "She doesn't even fight back. She doesn't do anything to cause it. He just slaps her and kicks her and hits her and hits her and hits her, and I—I never did anything to stop it!"

"Honey, you were just a child!"

"But I saw him do it, Grandma! I saw him every day and I just acted like it didn't matter."

"Princess—"

"He hurt her. He hurt her all the time and I don't want to be like him—"

"But you're not like him!"

"Yes I am, Grandma—whenever I get mad *I'm just like he is!*"

My voice broke as my eyes flooded with tears. I was surprised I was crying. I'd never cried while I watched my father beating my mother.

Grandma had me in her arms in an instant. I buried my face in her shoulder and sobbed while she stroked my back.

I cried for a long, long time.

Now, seventeen years and a million lifetimes later, I stood at the same window looking out into the darkness, and understood that I had never stopped crying.

VI.

blissfield, north carolina.

1999.

fifteen.

Nina didn't pick me up from school the next morning, and waiting for her almost made me late. I was hurt when I parked my bike at the other end of the rack from hers and made my way into the building, though I was determined not to let it show.

Instead, I nearly bumped into her brother, who was standing at a locker near my homeroom door.

He didn't speak. He didn't have to.

My heart sped up and pummeled my chest. His hair, which he'd grown into a thick, round Afro, was picked out and perfectly shaped, as if someone had spent some serious time on it. He was wearing a knit shirt that laced up the front. The laces were open, and I glimpsed part of his hard, sun-nut chest.

Our eyes met and held as I walked around him and into my classroom. LaToya was watching the door, her eyes fixed over my shoulder. I knew what she was looking at. I didn't like it.

I started to sit down when I realized I didn't have my book. That's what happened after a shot of Gideon: I was definitely stoned!

I went up to the teacher, who was writing on the board, and asked to go to my locker. She nodded curtly—I wondered what I'd done to piss her off—but decided I had better things to think about. If I moved fast, he might still be somewhere nearby.

Sure enough, Gideon had turned away and was ambling down the hall just as Nina emerged from the bathroom, about ten feet away. She looked at me, then looked down the hall to him, then looked back at me, fresh hurt in her eyes. It only took me a second to see that one side of her face was oddly swollen.

"Ni—" I began, but she pivoted hard and whipped away, the momentum of her body launching her straight into the *burtle*, London Richardson—my moronic lab partner—who was coming from his father's office. No teacher was going to say anything to the Principal's son about anything, any time, for any offence, and he knew it.

London wasn't much taller than Nina—she really was lanky, except for her rickety gait—but the principal's son was a cinderblock wall. She hit him hard, bounced off, and he shoved her into the lockers.

"You stepped on my shoe," he said in his moronic voice, turning his foot back and forth. Two seniors, who just happened to be cheerleaders, came out of the counselor's office, saw Nina trapped between the *burtle* and the lockers, and laughed gleefully.

"Sorry," Nina said, rubbing her shoulder. "Now move. I got to go."

The *burtle* saw his chance to score some points with the cheerleaders, whose faces were hot with pleasure. His pop bottle eyes bounced from the girls, to me, then back to Nina.

"So, Thistlehead," he said to Nina in a maliciously loud voice, "you ever figure out who your daddy is? I heard your momma ain't real sure herself."

"You can talk about me, but don't you talk about my momma," Nina answered as her books banged to the floor.

"Shut up, ho-baby!" London said. He shoved her again, deliberately, and began to walk away. Nina fell back against the lockers. Two or three other tardy students looked over, round-eyed, and scurried off, suddenly eager to take that first hour Geometry quiz.

Nina took three pitched steps, like she was getting ready to perform a long jump, and launched herself on him from behind, wrapping her arms around his neck, her legs grappling to get hold of his thick, bulging waist. She looked like a spider. He yelled something real loud, his voice echoing up and down the near-empty hall. His words began with an "F" and ended with a description of her private parts.

All the classrooms emptied at once. Teachers came hurtling out of doorways. Curious faces crowded up behind them.

London pitched backwards, slamming Nina as hard as he could against the handle of a broom closet door. She gave a choking cry and let go, twisting to grasp her back as she fell to the floor. The *burtle* rolled his fatty shoulders, turning to glare down at her triumphantly.

"You stupid, pissed-colored, nappy-headed cu—"

I didn't hear him finish because a wasp had begun to whine shrilly in my head. Something moved, clean and fast, and then the wasp was on the *burtle*, and he was holding one of his eyes and moaning oddly as he knelt on the hard, red-smeared floor, a few feet from my friend.

Teachers were actually screaming now, as were the lint-brains, who had clustered close enough to see him, but not close enough to get their clothes ruined by his blood.

I hardly knew where the blood was coming from, but it was staining my shoes, and I experienced the delirious satisfaction of bank robbers driving away with a duffle full of Benjamins.

Nobody touched me. Nobody got close. My chest was rising and falling, and I felt myself smile. Somewhere in the crowd I saw Gideon shouldering his way toward his sister.

Then there was another movement. A hand slid into mine, and Nina was there beside me. Her head was tilted. She wasn't looking at the *burtle*. Her gaze was fixed on me. "Oh, CeCe," she murmured, and strangely, I heard her voice clearly over the moans, screams, cries, and the dancing of my own rampaging heart.

The rest of the afternoon blurred. The Principal was there with Ms. Prentice. Grandma was there. London was there, a big wad of white stuff taped over his eye. One teacher, then another. Two or three kids. I couldn't understand a single word they said and, frankly, I didn't give so much as a shit. My left hand hurt, or more precisely, my wrist hurt, but otherwise I felt perfectly fine. Nina had been placed in a room alone, and I had the impression that no one was particularly concerned about her, even though she was the one who'd been attacked.

It wasn't until much later, after dark, that I found myself lying in Grandma's bed, a cold cloth on my forehead, the light low, and Grandma sitting on the edge of the mattress beside me. She didn't speak, but her eyes probed and measured and probed some more, like a judge before delivering the verdict.

I spoke in a rhythmic monotone I barely recognized. "It happened real fast, Grandma. I didn't even have time to think it through. He was hurting her, so I did what I had to do."

"I understand," she said.

"Nina's my friend."

Grandma smoothed the sheets over me. "I'm glad."

"There's rules, Grandma."

"Rules?"

"Yeah, the paper bag and your momma and if you don't got no daddy..."

"No daddy?" she said.

It was quiet. Too quiet. No crickets, no dogs, no birds, no planes. Not even any rain.

"Am I dead?" I said vaguely.

"Why *no*! Why do you think—"

"It's so quiet."

"Sometimes it gets quiet right before a storm."

"It's gonna rain?"

"Yes, baby. It's also going to thunder. Are you frightened of thunder?"

"Not if you're here."

"Bet you're hungry."

I shook my head.

"Alright," she said. "Then try to get some sleep. I'll check on you in a little while, and if the rain on the roof wakes you up, I'll come and sit with you."

I listened to her footsteps as she pulled the door and walked down the hall toward the kitchen.

It wasn't until later that I heard her talking to someone in a low voice.

"No, no, but still, I'm worried. You know how they are. Even though she was only defending her friend, the school wants her out. It took some real—" her voice became muffled, followed by a long pause.

"No she didn't, but I'm not sure she realizes exactly what she did. When I talked to her she was just a little, well, *vacant*."

I listened harder.

"No, no I don't want to do that. I still think she's better off here." Another pause. "No, I don't think that's necessary, either. She's been doing so well. I hope this won't—I know, I know. But I'm convinced this girl is good for her."

I must have drifted off, because the next thing I remember was the sun slicing the wall between the slats of the blinds.

What had Grandma meant by 'vacant'?

* * * * * * *

We didn't talk about why I was home with her that week. We worked in the yard, painted the kitchen and took the car to get the oil changed. Grandma was Grandma: calm, busy, patient with me. I went through the motions beside her, but the only things I was thinking about were Nina and Gideon.

One morning we drove about five miles up the highway, the frilly columns of tobacco looking like braided cornrows on somebody's head, until we came to a wide, clear yard with the ruins of a well in the center.

"This was where I grew up," Grandma said as we climbed from the car. "My daddy's house was there, in that empty space. It was a big, whitewashed house with a porch all the way around, and a bay window in the front. From upstairs you could see for miles across the fields."

"Was it beautiful, like in a movie?"

"It was simpler than the white people's houses. Everyone knew it was unwise to rise above your station. But it was a grand place for a Black family. My father was very proud of it."

She walked with me around the entire clearing, carrying a large stick in case we met a snake.

"My daddy had stables in the back," she said, pointing toward a grove of maple trees. "Always kept two or three horses for the plow, or sometimes to ride."

"Could you ride?"

"Of course," she said. "I used to love it. One horse, named Midnight, was my favorite. His coat was so black it shone blue in the sun. I used to bring him apples every night after dinner, and brush him and make sure he was covered with a blanket in the winter. He lived a good long time."

"When did you get a car?"

"We always had cars, but we didn't have very far to drive in those days. We went to church on Sundays, and sometimes to visit people in another town, but we didn't need to go to the supermarket. Most of the food we ate came straight from these fields."

"Did you have chickens?" I asked.

"Of course—and cows and pigs. But I didn't like it when it was time to kill one for Sunday dinner, so I'd run out into the fields and disappear, so no one could make me help out in the kitchen."

"Who did you play with, way out here in the country?"

"There were lots of kids around. People worked on the farm and helped out in the barn. Some of the people were sharecroppers who lived in the area, and others were migrant farmers, who traveled around the region with the seasons. Their kids were always the most pitiful, because they rarely went to school. I used to sit with them in the shade of that big old tree—" she pointed to a wide-canopied oak on the edge of the clearing "—and read stories to them. That's how I decided I wanted to be a teacher."

"Was your friend, Mr. Saunders, around?"

"Sometimes. Mr. Saunders' grandmother was friendly with my mother, so the two of us would run around in the yard whenever they visited."

"I'll bet you had to wear dresses all the time," I said.

"I didn't, but my mother's generation did. I dressed a lot like you when I was a little girl, because my father liked to see me riding and helping my mother in the garden. Of course, he never wanted me doing any serious labor. He believed that was for the men."

"So, what was your mother like?"

"She was somewhat stern because she took her work so seriously, but she was very kind to the people who helped out on the farm."

We walked to the edge of the clearing, and Grandma led the way down a path that looked like it had once been maintained with gravel. Now wild grasses leapt up on either side, strewn with cornflowers and sweet freesia and grinning daisies.

We found ourselves standing before a listing metal fence. Inside the gate I could see neat rows of grey headstones, some mossy and nearly blank with age, others etched with names easily read, even from a distance.

The hot wind swished like cymbals as birds chattered in the trees. There was no other sound, even from the road. I thought it was one of the most peaceful places I'd ever been.

"Could I be buried here one day?" I asked, surprising myself.

"As long as we still own the land."

"Do we have to sell it?"

She brushed some vines away from one of the older stones. "I hope not."

"You want to be buried here?"

"I certainly hope to be. There's my father and mother's tombstone over there. And—" I heard the hitch in her voice "—that stone is a memorial to Paul and Jeremiah."

We stood a few moments longer.

"Let's get back," she said suddenly. "I invited Mr. Saunders over for lunch, and we need to pick up a few things from the store."

About halfway through the week the doorbell rang and I heard her welcome someone. I'd been happily ironing a basket full of blouses and sheets, a task I really loved. In some other families this might have been seen as some sort of punishment, but Grandma knew very well I took solace in the textures of the cloth, the urgent hiss of the iron and the vinegary smell of detergent, starch and sunlight.

"Look who's here," she said brightly, and I found Nina standing in the door behind her.

"Hey," I said. The swelling was gone, and her face looked exactly like it was supposed to.

She drew her reluctant gaze to me. "CeCe, they say you not coming back."

"Sure I am." I put the iron down.

"But they making a case to expel you."

This was the first I'd heard of that. I looked quickly at Grandma, who shook her head, and then, in a calm voice, reminded me that I was an Honors student and anybody who wanted to get rid of me had to get rid of her, first.

Nina laughed delightedly and I felt myself smile. Grandma had been hovering in the doorway, but now she moved off. I walked toward Nina. When we were face to face, a long moment passed. Then, awkwardly, we hugged. Her body felt like I was hugging a sawhorse.

"You should hear what they saying," she began when we were seated on different ends of the bed, the stack of folded, ironed linen between us. "London had to go to the hospital."

"I didn't mean to hurt him that bad."

"I'm glad you did it. He had it coming for the past ten years."

"Then I'm glad I did it."

We both laughed. We said nothing for a long while.

"CeCe," she said quietly, "what about Gideon?"

"What about him?"

"You know what I mean."

"Okay, I know what you mean," I said. "Why are you asking?"

"Cause it's okay with me."

"What's okay with you?"

"You liking Gideon," she said. "It's okay with me."

"That's silly."

"No, it's not. I had to think it over, is all."

"But Gideon doesn't like me."

"My dummy brother like football. That's about it."

We both laughed.

"What changed you mind?" I asked carefully.

"You tried to help me. I figure you can like Gideon and still be my friend."

"You're the dummy. I would've told you that."

She rolled her eyes. "I just take things as they are, and go from there."

She fished in her pocket, bringing out a small square package. "I brought you something."

"A toad?" I asked.

What?" her eyes widened.

"Is it a bug or something?"

"Why would I do that?"

"Because you act like a witch and make me do crazy things."

"What?" She repeated, pretending to be shocked. "Beating London up wasn't crazy."

"I hope not, cause he sure enough got it."

"Yup—by a little thing like you!"

"In front of the whole school!"

We high-fived and burst into unfettered laughter that could be heard, I'm sure, all the way to Mrs. Mitchell's.

"You sure crazy," Nina said.

"Not as crazy as you."

"That's not what London's saying."

"All he's saying is '*owww*.'"

We laughed some more.

"You wrong about Gideon," she said suddenly. "He do like you. I know my brother."

My heart sped up. "How do you know?"

"He hanging around all the time with that stupid football."

"Hanging around?"

"Where he think you gonna be. He never, ever, came to my side of the school before."

"Could be somebody else," I said.

"Like who?"

"A cheerleader?"

"No," she said. "He a dummy, but he not stupid. Those girls been ignoring us since kindergarten." She drew in her lips appraisingly. "I guess he got to like somebody. Better you than one of them sawdust heads. If *they* try to talk to him I'd have to—" she raised one fisted hand and glanced furtively toward the bedroom door. "I'd never let the likes of them get to my brother."

"Nina, I'm not trying to *get* to him," I said. "I just like looking at him. He's cute."

"Oh, no!"

"Yes he is!"

"No, CeCe. He strange looking. You seen his eyes? They like some kind of cat in the woods."

"No, Nina. His eyes are, well, I mean I think—"

"You think he *beautiful?*" She spoke in a falsetto, again rolling her eyes.

"I just like looking at him."

"That won't last."

"Yes, it will," I said, "but I promise you, I'll never do anything more than look."

"You gonna break that promise."

"No I won't," I said.

"Yes you will, CeCe. Better not say something that'll make you a liar."

I was silent, then. The conversation had once again swung into seriousness. Nina was the most complicated person I knew. Well, next to my father.

"I just want you to be careful," she observed. "Some things ain't easy."

"Okay," I said. "Okay."

Her eyes wandered off for a moment, into that place only Nina could go. I wanted to know what she was thinking, but then again, I was scared to ask. Did she want me to ask? I couldn't tell.

Her yellow hair now seemed longer, and had been combed out and neatly plaited, like mine, into a French braid. I thought she might have been wearing a little bit of make-up.

But then she looked back and smiled, clearly happy just to be there with me. I felt something pour out of me, a different kind of drenching. And I wasn't remorseful, frightened, or angry anymore. Nina was my best friend, and I loved her, I had her permission to enjoy looking at her brother.

* * * * * * *

I had forgotten about Robin Hood and William Tell and Harriet Tubman.

When I went back to school the following week, I expected to be treated like I'd escaped from Sing Sing, but instead, it was like I'd been stealing from the rich, shooting apples off a kid's head, and leading a bunch of grateful slaves to the Promised Land. I'd had no idea how much everybody, including the teachers, really hated London Richardson and his father. When Nina and I rode our bikes into the schoolyard some kids walking nearby said, "Alright, Wonder Woman?" I looked over at Nina, trying to figure out who they were talking to.

The incident repeated itself throughout the day, and by evening my confusion had turned into embarrassed pleasure. People grinned at me as I walked through the corridors between classes. Teachers gave me a sharp little nod when I entered the classroom. My classmates grew silent as I took my seat.

The only person who didn't seem in the least impressed was Gideon, who was leaning against the lockers, ball in hand, when I got to my homeroom. He said "Hey," but it was more to Nina than to me. If he'd had a hat on, he might have touched the brim politely, like those guys in the movies, but he made no move to talk. I caught an instant of his eyes, which warmed me like the heat from a pan when the gas has just been extinguished, but out of respect for my best friend, I just kept it moving, step by step by step.

It was funny: I'd been trying to get some respect by being *nice*. What a pathetic waste of time!

Now, when LaToya and those other girls hovered, Nina and I exchanged glances, and I let her decide whether we'd bother to respond. They deferred to Nina in every case, speaking to me only if she smiled and nodded in my direction. It was funny how my kicking the *burtle's* butt on her behalf had conferred a great deal of fame on Nina, too. In a sense, I'd taken care of everyone's problems with one well-aimed fist.

I knew it wouldn't last, and of course, it didn't. About three weeks into our joint fame—and just as the hot days were giving way to dreary, pissy, nonstop autumn rain—football season got going in earnest, and everyone's attention went to the players and the lintbrain cheerleaders.

God, I hate cheerleaders!

The squad consisted of four seniors, two juniors and two sophomores (LaToya and Bree, of course), all short and busty, with thickly muscled legs and miniscule waists. All of them had asses big enough that their pleated uniforms rode almost parallel to the floor, like flattened cupcake papers. Beneath the skirts their matching panties winked at the boys as they bounced along the corridors with matching pompoms on their shoelaces and hair.

If I'd been the center of attention only days before, I was absolutely invisible, now. Small, boobless, and with no kind of butt to speak of, I might as well have been a nine-year old boy in comparison to these Amazons. Though my hair was longer—which mattered a lot back in those days—I didn't whip it around, or adorn it with flashy ribbons, and Grandma made me stay pretty low-key with make-up. I saw in a minute that during cheerleading season I was on the clearance rack.

Suddenly they were everywhere: making the morning intercom announcements, selling popcorn outside the gymnasium during lunch hour, and leading the school chants during the pre-game assemblies.

The football players, big and gangly and dumb as sheep, filed into the screaming assemblies in their jerseys and jeans, and stood in the center of the gym like gladiators in the Coliseum waiting for Caesar to show. They ranged in color and build from espresso to toffee, rhino to gazelle, showing exactly *zero* interest in the chaos they were inspiring, their minds clearly focused on that evening's game. Nina explained with some pride that we actually had one of the best teams in the state. For these players, football was the fantasy path to avoid a future in the fields, the military, or in prison.

The cheerleaders ran onto the court, suddenly separating us from the players, their springing ponytails and bouncing boobs blocking my view of Gideon with maddening, rhythmic precision. Gideon, who despite his freshman status had been selected as starting quarterback, had been led to the center of the gymnasium, and now stood on the school seal, smiling blandly. From time to time a cheerleader (which one, I can't say—they were literally interchangeable) danced back and grasped his arm, as if participating in some weird pre-sacrificial ritual. Finally LaToya, probably emboldened by his patience, leapt toward him. Almost by instinct, he caught her and she ended up cradled in his arms.

Completely unfazed, Gideon smiled goofily. Beside me, Nina stiffened.

"She been teasing him for years," she stated beneath the auditorium's appreciative roar. "Everybody know she don't want nobody with nothing to give her."

"Want me to fix her?" I asked, already planning it.

"Naw. You won't get away with *that* again."

We laughed dryly. Two more cheerleaders were now threading their way along the line of players, doing a fake little can-can, panties flashing and boobs sledgehammering. Though every other male in the gym—including the coaches—was sweating, Gideon's eyes wandered to the bleachers as if seeking someone.

"You going to the game?" I shouted above the roar.

"Yeah. My momma might be there, too."

"Really?" I said. I had never seen Nina's momma, and I was curious.

"I don't know. She don't want to leave my baby brother at home, but she don't want to bring him, either."

"Why not?"

Nina shrugged and returned her attention to Gideon, whose eyes seemed to find us. He smiled self-consciously.

"What's her name, your momma?" I asked.

"Minerva, but they call her Minnie."

"That's pretty."

"I guess. Better than 'Leah.'"

"You already fixed that."

"Yeah, but 'Nina' mean 'little girl,' and that just don't fit me no more."

"Stop complaining. It's international and that makes it special."

"It short because it for short people," she said.

"It's easy to remember."

"That's because it silly."

"But *nobody* can remember my name," I said. "That's a whole lot sillier."

"Yeah, but you can change Bethany Celeste to Beth, BeBe—like your Momma—Ceelee *or* CeCe. Then there's Annie, or Lizzie or Betty, too."

"Yeah, but that's just too much. I want a clean, simple name, like yours."

"Uhhh. You always want what you can't get. Anyway, I'm tired a talking about it." We both watched the bouncing body parts.

"She don't come home," Nina said suddenly.

I looked up. "Who? Your momma?"

Nina kept her gaze on the cheerleaders. "She somewhere and I don't know where. Sometime I come home from school and there enough money to get some food. The man who own the house say he her friend, so he don't bother me about money. Or maybe she paying him on her own. I don't know."

I was silent, unsure what to say.

Nina kept talking. "She just went away after my brother was born—the baby. Seem like she just didn't want to be bothered. My aunt said she would keep him during the week. Sometime my mother go over there and get him on the weekend. They know if they leave him with me, the police will come and take him away. I don't know how the police would know, but somebody would tell for sure."

"Are you taking care of everything else all by yourself?" I said in a whisper that somehow carried above the roar.

"Gideon help."

"Who takes care of Gideon?"

"We take care of each other."

"Aren't you scared?"

"Waste of time to be scared," she said.

At least two hundred students, a number of the teachers, and a couple of administrators were shouting the school song at the top of their lungs. The cheerleaders were now sprinkling silver and violet confetti on the players. Gideon looked hideously embarrassed.

I shook my head. Nina glanced at me and shrugged. I looked away and caught a glimpse of someone partially hidden at the edge of the bleachers. It was the *burtle*, a pirate patch over his left eye, staring nervously up at me. I grinned, waved, and he vanished.

That night Grandma insisted I wear a new school hoodie she'd purchased for me. She drove me back to school and instructed me to wait for her when the game was over. I was not, under any circumstances, to try to walk home alone.

Nina was waiting for me beside the girl's john. She had on a denim jacket over a worn purple tee-shirt, but didn't seem to notice my brand new clothing. Together we made our way to the bleachers. It looked like her mother hadn't come.

I had never been to a football game before, and aside from the obvious pleasure of eating a lot of salty, greasy food, and screaming until their throats were raw, I couldn't understand what everybody was so excited about. It was impossible to understand the rules; the players stood around most of the time; although it was nearly too dark to see them, the cheerleaders never stopped blocking the crowd's sightline with their miserably stupid jumping and chanting.

The only thing I really got was this: the lean, small-waisted dude who ran breathtakingly fast and never took one unnecessary step was Gideon. Each time the players lined up the one in the middle threw the ball to another player who threw it to another until eventually it ended up in the able hands of Gideon, who was already halfway down the field. He then smoked the opposing players, blowing a zigzag to the animal howls of the crowd. When he got to the so-called "end-zone," he set the ball down as if it was a stuffed turkey on Thanksgiving Thursday.

It was only after the third touchdown that I really began to grasp the beauty of the thing. My father had watched football many afternoons and evenings over the course of my life, behind the closed door of our small living room, after my mother and I received the promise of a serious ass-whupping if he was disturbed. I'd been taught early in life that football wasn't for me.

But now it was.

Though the screaming hurt my throat and the cold night air bit my fingers, I began loving the abandon shared by everyone in the crowd. I knew nothing about the other team, which floundered early and never regained their rhythm against our thundering purple steeds. By the end of the game we were exhausted, triumphant, damp, cold, united.

Nina took me by the arm, and we made our way carefully down the bleachers amidst the hundreds of other singing and chanting students and staff. The air had turned cold, the night pouring around us like black ink, and mist exploded from our mouths along with our words. We sang the stupid school song along with the others, and it was the happiest I'd been since arriving in Blissfield.

As we reached the bottom of the bleachers Nina suddenly stopped, causing two or three people behind us to bang into each other. She was staring at a woman who was wrapped in a thin raincoat and moving her weight rhythmically from one leg to the other, as if dancing to some unheard melody.

The woman seemed young, and neither thin nor fat. She was shorter than I would have expected, and much lighter-skinned than her son and daughter. Her hair, fine and straight, was pulled into a thick, loose ponytail at the nape of her neck. There was an odd tension in her rocking, and she neither turned her head nor changed expression despite the noise and movement of the crowd.

Before I could see much more in the darkness, Nina pulled me hard to the side, guiding me back into the gap beneath the bleachers. I complained like a horse whose master had suddenly jerked hard on the reins, but she didn't change course. Tripping over the soda and beer bottles, potato chips bags and napkins beneath the wooden slats, I did what I could to keep up.

"What—Nina, hey—was that your mother?"

She didn't slow down until we emerged in the fresh night air, and even then, she kept on walking.

"Hey—wait!" I insisted, succeeding in yanking my arm away as we cleared the building. Car doors were opening and slamming all around us, and bursts of laughter exploded in the darkness.

"Why are we rushing?" I asked her.

"It's time to go home."

"But don't you want to wait for your mo—"

"Who said that was my mother?"

"You said she was coming, Nina."

"I said she *might* come."

"Was that her?"

"I don't know."

"Sure you do!"

"Why do you care?"

"I want to meet her!"

"Why?"

"Because you're my best friend and she's your mother!"

I could see Nina's bright eyes glittering in the darkness. Her stare was empty, haunted, sad. "Come on," she said, again taking my arm. "I'm ready to go."

"But—"

"We need to go!"

We didn't have to go far. Grandma was already waiting in her gigantic Buick, the motor throbbing louder than the other cars. The beams flickered as we drew close.

"Get in. We'll take you home," I said.

"Got to wait for Gid."

"You sure?"

"Yes."

"Do you have your bikes?"

"Yes."

"We can put the bikes in the trunk," I said. "Go get him."

She shook her head.

"Nina, are you alright?" I asked.

She nodded, but it was clear her joy was gone. I tried a couple more times to convince her to come with us, but the little light that had shone so brightly a few minutes before was now replaced with stony Nina, the Nina I knew all too well.

As soon as the car door closed, I spoke: "Grandma, something's wrong with Nina."

"What happened?" Grandma asked, peering through the window at the stick figure retreating into the darkness.

"I don't know. She just closed up all of a sudden and wouldn't talk anymore."

"Did she say anything?"

"No, but she's really not okay."

Grandma's hands were on the steering wheel, but instead of pulling away she sat in rapt concentration, looking thoughtfully at my friend. Nina was forced to stop as the crowd emptied the field, pouring around her as if she were made of wood.

Finally, Grandma put the car into gear and guided us through the gauntlet of vehicles parked along the dirt road.

"You think she'll be alright?" I said as she shrank into the night.

"I hope so, baby."

"It may have something to do with her momma. I think I saw her at the game tonight."

"She sit with you and Nina?" Grandma asked.

"No, but a lady was standing down at the bottom of the bleachers, and suddenly Nina was acting all strange."

"Strange?"

"I don't know—she stopped talking and just walked away."

"Princess, what seems strange to you might seem like survival to her."

"What do you mean?" I asked, still searching for her figure in the darkness.

Grandma was silent until we came to a stop in front of the pharmacy to let Blissfield's only stoplight change color. The car roared as we pulled forward again.

"Princess," she began, "it's like those days when you lived with your father and mother. Remember how much fighting went on in the house?"

"It was my daddy, mostly. Momma never said anything."

"That's how your mother survived, honey."

"You think somebody's hurting Nina?"

"I don't know, baby, and I try to ignore the gossip."

"But we've got to help—"

"We *are* helping, baby. Nina's got you. I'll bet that matters a whole lot to her."

"But, still—"

"I promise you," she said firmly. "You're helping."

I fell silent, thinking about my friend.

"You know, Princess," Grandma said as we approached our street, "you were different when you lived with your parents, too."

"I was?"

"Sure. It took you a while to figure out how to fit in when you came here."

"That's cause everybody's real tame in Blissfield," I said.

Grandma laughed.

"But what does that have to do with Nina?" I asked.

"Maybe living with Nina's mother is something like living with your father. Maybe at home Nina has to be one way, but with you she can be her true self."

"What about her brother? I mean, does he have to do that, too?"

"Probably," Grandma said.

"But then how do I know who they really are?"

"What does your heart tell you?"

I thought about it. Though on the surface the question seemed simple, the answer was deeper and more difficult than I expected.

"I never really had friends before," I said in a hesitant voice. "But when I met them—I don't know, it seemed more like I was meeting myself."

This time Grandma didn't laugh. We pulled into our yard. "Tell me something," Grandma said. "What makes you feel like that?"

"It's like—like we're pieces of a puzzle, but we're still trying to figure out how we fit together."

"I see," Grandma said.

"I hope she's alright," I repeated, picturing her standing alone in the darkness.

"I hope so, too," Grandma said. "I really, really do."

sixteen.

I didn't expect Gideon to be waiting the next Saturday afternoon when I came out of the Piggly Wiggly with a dumb-looking bag of bananas. Grandma had planned on making banana bread for church, but I'd offered to do it for her. I'd discovered I kind of liked baking.

I guess he saw my lavender bike there in the rack. I don't think he'd been following me or anything. Knowing Gideon, it wasn't even so much as a real decision that brought him there. He wasn't deliberate enough for that.

I looked particularly goofy, in that tattered and way too-tight stupid track jacket I'd worn on the long bus trip from Ohio. I hadn't done much with my hair that morning, and I didn't have on any mascara, either.

He was doing his usual Gideon pose, somewhere between a cowboy and a little kid. He was jeanned up, with a plain white tee shadowed by red dust. Leaning against the bike rack, he flipped through a magazine he'd pulled out of a bin. A battered skateboard lay upside-down at his feet.

I laughed when I saw him: "*House Heaven?*" I asked.

He laughed, too. His voice was a rough rasp, like someone who needed to cough. "It's okay."

"If you're decorating."

"Or wasting time." He tossed it back into the bin.

"You waiting on Nina? I didn't see her in the store."

He shook his head.

"Football practice?" I said.

"Not on Saturday."

"Your—your mother?"

He grunted and shook his head again.

"Then who?" I asked.

"Who what?"

"Who you waiting on?"

"Why I got to be waiting on somebody?" He smiled, his face a dandelion in a field of green.

"Lord," I said, grasping my handlebars. "Too complicated for me."

He laughed again. He was much easier than his sister.

We looked at each other shyly, then quickly looked away. My heart was slamming in my chest. Again. I lifted the handlebars and righted the bike, hooking my dumb-looking bag of bananas on the curved metal. He picked up the skateboard.

I set off, walking the bike beside the curb. He followed, grinding along the pebbly sidewalk, just a couple of feet behind me.

"Where you headed?" I asked, looking over my shoulder with my it's-all-the-same-to-me attitude. He was, after all, the quarterback and fantasy of every girl in the school. Stupid, but true.

Blue-grey eyes glanced at me. He shrugged.

"No, seriously," I said. "Where you headed?"

"Oh, I don't know." Typical Nina / Gideon answer.

"I mean, are we going in the same direction?"

"Maybe. Probly."

Though I hadn't seen it at first, I now noticed he also had his football tucked under one arm. Well, *duh*.

I crossed the street. He followed. I stopped at the curb. He stopped, too.

I looked full into his face for the first time. He looked back, smiled, then seemed to color. We stood there an awkward moment.

Come on, I thought. Stop being stupid and start being *yourself*! "You got that new Math teacher, Mr. Davis?" I said, not believing I'd just brought up his *math class*!

"I guess."

"You guess?"

"I don't know the guy's name."

"Real interesting class, obviously."

He chuckled at my sarcasm, his voice low. He was looking at the ground, his left leg pushing the skateboard back and forth.

"You like Ms. Renfrew?" I said with increasing desperation, having noted that he had the petite, bright-eyed teacher for Social Studies. All the guys followed her butt with their eyes as she walked down the hall.

"How you know she my teacher?" Gideon said, eyes rounded.

"I saw you go into her room one day," I lied, unwilling to admit that I'd roamed the halls enough to know exactly where he was from first-hour homeroom to the last period of every school day.

"She alright," he said softly, "but kinda boring."

"It gets worse," I assured him, placing my hand on his arm. "Wait till you have to take—"

He reacted instantly, his face reflecting his confusion at my touch. I withdrew my hand and we spoke at the same time.

"I'm sorry—I didn't mean to—"

"It's okay. I just—I just wasn't expecting—"

Suddenly I giggled. He looked at me and burst into nervous laughter, too. We stood there, laughing at nothing, looking at the ground, then each other, then at the ground again.

"Wow," he said.

"Right?" I said.

Our eyes met and held for what felt like an eternity.

Then he dropped his gaze. Nervously he passed the football from one hand to the other. I found myself staring at his great big hands. He stopped, looked down and stared at them, too.

"Your hands." I barely heard myself speak.

He looked up, questioning.

I raised my hand, and after a moment he raised his own, then gingerly pressed his palm against mine. Our fingers folded, lacing us together.

The flesh understands what the mind cannot. From that moment I realized I would want, no, *need*, to fold myself into his flesh and become one with him. Not only at that moment, but until the end of our time on earth.

We stood like that without speaking.

A horn honked on the street beside us. Our hands dropped.

"I've got to go," I said, trembling as I put myself on my bicycle, because the very touch of him had drained me dry.

"CeCe," he called tentatively, uneasily.

"Yes, Gideon?" I planted my feet on the ground and looked over my shoulder.

"It's okay," he murmured.

"What?"

"No, it's alright."

"What." I didn't even have the energy to make it a question.

He stared at me, silent.

"You sure?" I asked softly.

He only nodded, then put his weight on the skateboard and pushed off.

I glanced back as I pedaled away, a cloud of dust behind me. I was so shaky I could barely stay on the bike. He coasted to the curb, his head up, the ball beneath his arm.

He was looking at me, too.

* * * * * * *

And everything probably would have been alright, except that Gideon turned up on Monday, dogging his sister's heels when she picked me up for school. He had his own rusty bicycle, but it had a black banana seat and tall, souped-up handlebars like a Harley, and reflector discs in nearly every spoke of the wheels. If not for the handlebars, I would have thought he'd knocked a kid down and stolen it, but clearly someone had put some time and energy into rebuilding it.

So there they were—the two of them outside Grandma's house, Gideon a few feet behind Nina, who looked thoroughly and completely exasperated.

"Look what the cat dragged in," she muttered, tilting her head in his direction when I came around the house with my bike.

He nodded once, shyly, and looked away.

"Come on, Nina—it's not so bad," I said in an undertone.

"Oh, CeCe," she said. "You have no idea."

Nina went on complaining as we rode and he kept up in silence, like our Secret Service escort. I glanced at him once, and he smiled at me, and I snapped my head around, glad Nina missed it. We parted at the bike rack because his homeroom was in another wing. As Nina and I walked to the door, she turned and looked at me.

"What'd you do to him?"

"Huh?"

"I know something happened," she said.

"I have no idea—"

"CeCe, friends don't lie to friends."

I sighed. "I ran into him at the Pig—"

"I *knew* it!" She stomped her foot.

"He just showed up! I didn't plan to—"

"You didn't have to," she said. "I *warned* you he was getting swoll up about you!"

"Swoll up? I don't even know what that means!"

"No, *he* don't know what that means! CeCe, you got to be cool. I told you it's okay to look at him. But that's it."

"I haven't done anything else!"

"Yes you have!"

The bell rang and the last of the Monday morning stragglers ran past us.

"What," I said, looking her straight in the face, "could I possibly have done?"

"Did you hug him?"

"No," I said.

"Kiss him?"

"*No!*"

"Anything worse?"

"Nina, we were standing in the middle of the street."

"But you did something to him, didn't you? Somehow? Someway?"

I shook my head. "It was nothing."

"What was nothing?"

"We compared palms."

"You what?"

"I put my hand up and he put his hand up. That's it."

"But you touched him," she said.

"No—as a matter of fact, he touched *me!*"

For a split second her eyes flattened out and I thought I might have to fight her. Then, shaking her head, she started up the stairs.

"Nina, wait—"

"CeCe," she said over her shoulder, "I warned you he a dummy. I meant it. Dummies act like dummies. I love him," she added as she vanished through the door, "but he a dummy."

I made my way to Home Room. The teacher, whose name was Evans, was midway through roll call, which always seemed an incredible waste of time (why not just put an attendance sheet at the door and let us sign when we came in?). He raised his head from his list and glared at me. The room tittered. I was aware of fluorescent buzzing and the oily smell of linoleum.

"Nice of you to join us, Ms. Castle."

Without speaking, I sat down.

"Do you plan to make a practice of walking in whenever you feel like it?"

I reached into my backpack and produced my copy of *Jane Eyre*. Rochester had just stopped Jane in the hallway as she was tying her shoe. She'd fled the drawing room after being ridiculed by Blanche Ingram's horrible mother.

"—Or do you think the bells don't pertain to you?" Mr. Evans said.

Something white fell out of my backpack, and—

"I'm waiting for an answer," the teacher continued.

It was a letter. A folded up little fist of a letter!

"Ms. Castle, ignoring me is not going to make me go away. Your flaunting of your family connections is ridiculous. You're expected to adhere to the rules like every other student, no matter who you are!"

I knew Mr. Evans was growing angrier, perhaps by the second. I felt the other students' stares. A few weeks before, hell, a few *days* before, I would have taken the bait and climbed over the desks to get at him.

But when I looked up, all I could see was those blue-grey eyes.

"Ms. Castle, you're—"

The bell rang, signaling the end of Home Room. The room exhaled as if someone had let go of a balloon. Everyone jack-in-the-boxed out of their chairs and moved like a herd toward the door. As I reached for my backpack, the letter glued to my fist, someone grasped my arm. I looked up into the bloated and ugly face of the eggplant-shaped, razor-bumped, shining-Qball-headed Mr. Evans.

"Don't show me any attitude," he snarled. "I'd be very happy to let you sit out a few more days in your grandmother's house."

Shit, I thought regretfully, it looked like I was going to have to fight him, anyway. But then I remembered that Nina was my friend, and her brother liked comparing his hand to mine, *a letter had fallen out of my backpack,* and Grandma wouldn't want me to fight anyone—even this moron.

"I'm sorry Sir," I said in a clear, polite voice. "It won't happen again."

He knew he wasn't supposed to touch me. I knew he wanted me to mouth off so he'd have an excuse to drag me, in front of the entire school, to the principal's office. I could see it there, in his nasty yellow face.

"May I go now, Sir?"

He paused, weighing how to react. I had done nothing to provoke or justify further punishment. The few kids lingering near the door were staring. They heard my words. They saw his hands, clamped on my arm, too close to my little boy chest.

I could literally feel his disappointment. He looked at the door and growled, "Get to class!"

The others scattered. His gaze returned to me. "Don't you ever disrespect me again," he said, shoving my arm away.

I rose and pushed *Jane Eyre* deep into my backpack. Ignoring his stare, I felt like I was floating as I moved toward the door.

Out in the hall the usual clanging of slamming lockers, squealing girls' raucous laughter, falling books, hiphop verses and intercom announcements vanished, as if someone had zipped it all into a vacuum. I heard echoes of *"CeCe"* in that tweeded voice, and barely saw anything of the world around me.

I was weightless.

Warm air.

 Riding on still, warm water.

Was it possible that Gideon actually wrote me a—

A sudden sharp pressure struck my shin. My backpack sailed from my arms as I flew, now literally weightless, and crashed, face first, onto the terrazzo floor of the corridor. The pain in my knees, breasts and elbows hardly matched the sickening *crunch* of my chin striking stone. Streaks of white, an explosion of blood, and pain stampeded from my legs to my head and back.

Students at their lockers twisted around to observe me, some literally jumping up on each other's shoulders to see. Several teachers who had come to their doorways to usher in their students simultaneously moved in my direction.

But I only was aware of my reaction—faster and meaner than I would have believed possible, as every cell, every fiber of Copley Castle ignited in me, and despite the pain, the spurting hot liquid and my enraged tears, I scrambled to my feet and launched myself with bulleted precision toward the *burtle,* who had pulled his leg back from my sprawled figure to grin at the delighted, chortling LaToya and Bree.

Time shifted into slow motion as I sprang for his throat. Faces melted into the weirdly distorted masks of George Bellows' boxers—paintings we'd learned about in art class—and the bystanders' roar crested to a tsunami of vicarious pleasure.

I knew London Richardson had tripped me deliberately. Viciously. Publicly—in revenge for my nearly blinding him. But I had done my penance for that. Now, despite my promise to Grandma that I wouldn't fight anymore—I would have to hurt him again, and even worse. I'd have to hurt him the way my Daddy hurt my mother.

I got one hand on the center of his throat, near his goofily prominent Adam's apple. Though he was much larger than me, his clumsy stupid arrogant face still registered surprise as I punk-punched him, using the butt of my hand to slam his chin upwards and causing him to bite through his tongue. It was a move I'd use again, at Whelan's many years later, in homage to the *burtle*. At that moment our bodies flew together into the lockers, not unlike the way Nina had fallen when he pushed her a few weeks before.

I distinctly remember the pleasure of hearing his scream of agony before I was lifted, bodily, off his struggling form. My shins, knees, head, and hands hurt like hell, but I was still fighting as Ms. Renfrew, the Social Studies teacher, and Mr. Powers, the football coach, wrestled me bodily into a classroom and ordered a stunned freshman to get the school nurse right away.

I heard a sudden hush in the hallway outside the classroom. The soundlessness was so great that I tried to climb back out of my seat and go see what was going on. Ms. Renfrew, who dabbed my split chin with a quickly blooming scarlet tissue and scalded the wound with hand sanitizer from her desk, ordered me to sit back down. I tried to get up, but was again pushed firmly back into the seat.

There was a commotion just outside the classroom door. Within moments, I could see why.

Among the adults who'd been standing in the classroom doorways that morning was Lincoln Perry Richardson, the Booker T. Washington High School Principal—and London Richardson's father. Though he was rarely seen outside his office, he happened to have been speaking with a teacher at the moment I was tripped by his son. By the time the teachers hauled me off the stupid fool, the Principal was at his son's side. Through the open door of the classroom I saw him lift his hand high, lean back, and slap London so hard that even *I* flinched.

Ms. Renfrew wrapped an arm around my waist and I hobbled down to the nurse's office, my blouse shining with blood. Though the halls were clear, I could hear my name murmured from the rows of restless students in every room we passed.

The nurse left me alone, my trembling fingers pressing a thick wad of gauze against my wound, and went to call Grandma. Both of my knees were raw, one elbow was bloody and my chin was split open clear across the bottom of my face. It hurt so bad I couldn't speak. I remember staring at a calendar on the opposite wall festooned with pictures of blue-eyed kittens. That's the thing about cats: I like them when they grow into sleek, smart, independent creatures. But the little ones, with their goofy round-eyed faces, staring stupidly at anything that moves, really creep me out.

Still, I couldn't find enough clarity beyond the pain to focus on anything else.

It wasn't long before I was aware of movement in the door. Gideon stood there, his big hands hanging loose and lonely at his sides. His worn shirt, with a mismatched button or two, was open at the neck and the rolled-up sleeves revealed his muscled, suntanned forearms. His jeans were just a bit too short, and even though there were thin patches at the knees, they, too, were clean.

"I heard," he whispered.

"Jacked up," I muttered.

"Not as bad as London," he answered. I didn't want to, but I heard myself laugh.

"Gonna need dentures?" he teased.

"Shut up." I laughed again.

"I'll get you a walker."

"What*ever*."

"Or maybe I could just carry you," he said softly.

I looked up into his eyes and something poured through me. He took a few steps forward and, after a second's pause, knelt by my side.

"Let me see."

Carefully I peeled back the gauze and he inspected my chin.

"I'll tell you what, Raggedy Bethany: why don't you just let me be your bodyguard?"

"I can take care of myself."

"Liar," he whispered. "Let me look after you, okay?"

"First," I said thickly, "I gotta take care of that asshole."

"His daddy did it for you, so take it easy, alright? Promise me." He reached into his pocket and brought something out. It was his letter, now speckled with blood. "You dropped this while you was trying to kill London."

"I'm sorry."

"It's okay." Gently he closed my fingers over it. His rusty voice tickled the small of my back, and I twisted a little in my chair.

Footsteps approached.

"Gotta go," he said quietly. "I'll bring your bike home after practice."

Grandma crossed the room with an expression that could have melted steel. She hugged me, then inspected my chin, knees and elbows. The bleeding had slowed, but the pain throbbed like church bells in my bones.

"You're going to need stitches," she announced.

"What—no, Grandma! *Please*—!"

"Thank goodness Mr. Saunders was helping me at the house. He's going to drive so I can look after you. Don't worry: I'll get the doctor here in Blissfield to do it."

"But I'll get blood on Mr. Saunders' seats!" I protested.

"Hush, Princess! He doesn't care about that."

She stepped out of the office and several doors opened and closed. The bell rang and the halls swelled with the familiar between-classes roar. I tried to focus on the kittens while I waited, but now Gideon's big open smile and his secret letter were getting in the way.

I wondered when Nina would find out what happened. Then it occurred to me that I might be in big trouble for jumping on the *burtle*. The warning they'd given me about fighting was severe: any more violence and I would pay with expulsion. For all I knew, they were writing up the papers while I sat there staring at those idiot kittens.

The noise in the hall faded; the next classes had started. Grandma returned and helped me to my feet. When I began to speak she raised a finger to her lips.

"We'll talk outside, baby."

I don't remember much about the doctor's office, but Gideon was right: when we got home I looked like an old, much-mended rag doll. Dr. Hayes had stitched my chin while Grandma watched with a grim smile. He'd put ointment on my knees, elbows, and on a scratch on my forehead I hadn't noticed earlier. He'd also given me a little green pill to "calm me down."

Grandma sent me straight to bed, a cold compress on my forehead, though we were scarcely past midday. When she returned an hour later with a steaming bowl of soup, oyster crackers and a slice of her banana crème pie, she sat beside me.

"I understand that boy did this to you in front of half the school," she said. "He must be genuinely crazy." She picked up the spoon and dipped it into the soup. "Eat, baby."

"I'm not hungry."

"Eat some anyway. Your body's had a shock, and this is good for you."

I took a sip of the soup to oblige her. I couldn't taste anything.

"Is it too hot?"

I shook my head. She forced me to eat a few more spoonfuls, then let me lie back on the pillows. The doctor's pill seemed to have taken effect, and now I just wanted to talk, talk, talk.

"Grandma, do you have a best friend?" I asked.

"Yes, Princess."

"Is it that lady across the street?"

"Mrs. Mitchell?" She lowered her voice conspiratorially. "Never in a million years. I guess if I had to choose, it would be Mr. Saunders. Why do you ask?"

"I don't know. Best friends are so complicated." I then told her about Nina's reaction when she saw me looking at her brother. "Nina says everyone likes Gideon better than her, and she doesn't want me to prefer him, too."

"You don't, do you?"

"Nina's my friend. With Gideon it's different."

"Howso?"

"When I look at Gideon I can't think of anything else," I said. "I can't even get his face out of my mind. And when he looks at me my heart kind of leaps off my ribs and lands in my belly!" I laughed, picturing his eyes, and a lightness flowed through me.

She looked at me carefully. "You know, baby, sometimes we feel that way about people. But we can't forget the places we need to go and the things we have to do."

"I know, Grandma, I know. But it feels better to think about him than to think about the *burtle*."

"The what?"

"That's what I call the guy that tripped me. He looks like a bear with a turtle's face."

Grandma burst into laughter—a great, pealing sound that brightened the room. "I didn't know you had a special word for him!"

"He's my lab partner," I said. "He's not that smart, but all the lint brains like him because of his father. He's the closest thing to a celebrity we've got."

"Lint brains?"

"LaToya and her buddy, Bree. They're cheerleaders and think because they have yellow skin they're better than everybody, but they got nothing but lint inside their heads."

"I see," she said. She thought for a moment, then moved the tray to the floor. "Remember, Princess, I always got teased for having a boy's body, and no one wanted to date a girl who didn't look like a girl."

"But you're so beautiful!"

"Thank you," she said quietly, "but skin color was also very important to people in my day, and I was too dark for some. I never thought that way, but there were those who confused a person's character with their appearance" (me: *zero*—Nina: *one-hundred!*).

Grandma learned forward and brushed my hair away from my face. "Princess, you have to remember that it's okay to be Gideon's friend, but you're way too young for anything else."

I giggled. "I already know about the birds and the bees, Grandma, and I don't like babies," I said, my voice a bit louder than I intended. "I'm going to go to college and get my business degree and work in a bank."

"Is that what you want to do?"

"I want to have money, so I'll never have to worry about anything," I said, picturing my mother. "I'm getting a big car and a great big old house and you and Momma can come and live with me."

Grandma suddenly pulled me into her arms. Gently, without speaking, she rocked me back and forth. I felt the anger and pain of the morning loosen in my flesh. But I didn't feel them leave, perhaps because they had nowhere to go.

* * * * * * *

It wasn't until the next morning, when Grandma brought back the clothes I'd been wearing the day before, now washed clean of blood and sun-dried, that I remembered Gideon's letter. I sat straight up in bed, my heart slamming, and stared at the jeans folded neatly beneath the blouse that had been splattered with scarlet.

Grandma glanced over at me, then set the clothes at the foot of the bed. "I noticed there was something in the pocket of your jeans last night," she remarked with a mild smile. "You were fast asleep, so I put it right there." Without another word she made her way back down the hall to the kitchen.

The letter was folded into a tight little rectangle of lined notebook paper. You would have thought it was a winning lottery ticket from the way I opened it. Smoothing it out carefully on my knees, I felt a lurch at the extraordinarily neat and careful penmanship.

> Dear CeCe,
> How are you? I hope your day is going good. Did you do okay on Mr. Greens test? Nina said his test are very hard and he dont grade too fare. I know you can take care of him if you have to! (smile). I think your a very good student so it wont be a problem for you. Are you coming to the game friday night? I hope we can win against Chowan because they usually beat us. If coach will let me play my game I know I can make a few touchdowns. I will make a touchdown for you! WISH ME LUCK, OKAY?
> Have a good day.
> Your friend Gideon Price

I climbed out of bed, found my backpack, and tore a blank sheet out of one of my notebooks. Then I had second thoughts and went looking for white typing paper—after all, lined notebook paper was so *ordinary*! After walking in circles around the room, I followed Grandma down to the kitchen.

As it turned out, she was just lifting a tray heaped with scrambled eggs, toast and grits.

"Oh, baby, you're up!"

"Um—yes, Grandma." I eyed the food. It smelled wonderful, and in truth, I was starving, but at that moment I had a far more important mission.

"Sit down," she said, turning back to the fridge, where I knew she would take out a bottle of orange juice and a carton of milk.

"Okay, but, well, could I eat a little later?"

"Aren't you hungry?"

"Yes, but, I wanted to do some homework before breakfast."

"Homework? That's good, but the doctor told me to keep you home today. You can do your homework later."

"I—well, I was thinking that maybe I could write a letter to Momma, if you have some stationery."

She paused, looking at me with a half-smile. "Well, I'm glad you decided to write your...mother. I have some real pretty writing paper you can use. But first," she said, lifting her chin and placing one hand on her hip, "I'll need to see you eat some of this food."

The paper really was pretty: soft yellow, which I now understood was Grandma's favorite color, with a border of tiny forget-me-nots, and edges scalloped like a doily. I knew that having made up the lie, I'd have to write my mother a letter that Grandma could see me leave for the mailman before I could get to my true purpose.

I wrote my mother quickly, telling her that my classes were going well and the weather was better than Ohio. I told her I was learning to sew, bake and I liked going to football games. Then I stopped, because I wanted to save my best writing for my next letter.

But when it came time to write to Gideon, I suddenly didn't know what to say. It felt like putting my thoughts on paper opened me up to anyone who might read it. And I had worked very hard to convince everyone at Booker T. Washington that I was a samurai-warrior princess with a very sharp sword. How could I convince Gideon that I wasn't dangerous, while reminding him that if he ever hurt me, I wouldn't hesitate to deal with him like I'd dealt with the *burtle*?

I sat in my room in absolute silence for so long that Grandma appeared in the door, concerned.

"Princess?"

I looked up, startled. She came in and sat at the foot of the bed, her eyes traveling from the blank page to my troubled face. Once again I was surprised by how much she understood just by looking at me. She reached out and touched the hand that lay, useless, on her stationery. "Don't know what to write?"

I shook my head, embarrassed.

"Well," she said, "it makes most people happy just to get a letter. It lets them know you're thinking about them. They like to hear what's on your mind, what your days are like, and that you're okay. A letter is just another way of showing you care."

With that, she stood and lovingly brushed my hair away from my face. I sensed how much she'd always wanted a daughter, and how having me close fulfilled something she'd never openly admitted to anyone before.

She left the room and I wrote to Gideon, without difficulty, and the letter was just as she suggested: easy, warm, and full of my thoughts about our classes, the weather, and the coming football game.

seventeen.

So I started to negotiate between Gideon's calm and Copley's meanness.

I listened to my grandma and tried to live as she wanted me to, but it wasn't easy. The *burtle* vanished from our high school (the gossip said his daddy shipped him off to a military academy!), and the lint brains had seen that I was still ready and willing to fight for my life, even when I was hurt and humiliated. They also saw that some of the teachers had come to my aid, even if only out of respect for my grandmother.

Using my recovery as an excuse to live a life of shadows, I often told my teachers I needed the restroom, then slipped into the high school corridors and roamed by Gideon's classes so I could steal a quick peek inside. I'd see him leaning back at his desk with his legs thrown forward, a pen sticking out of his mouth, his gaze fixed on something beyond the window. Though his notebook was open, his arms were often crossed as if he was conserving his energy for football practice that afternoon, or for whatever else he was thinking about.

I walked past Nina's classes, too. She was usually in the rear of the room, her head raised attentively, but held at that strange tilted angle that signaled both disapproval and disbelief in whatever she was hearing. Just seeing her made me feel stronger, because she was the person I trusted most in the world besides Grandma.

I loved our strange friendship. Nina and I still rode our bikes to school together every day, with Gideon bringing up the rear. She and I ate lunch together and rode home, side by side. We rarely saw Gideon after school because he stayed behind for football practice. During lunch he hung around with the guys, throwing the football and casting sneaky glances at his sister and me. Gideon and I didn't talk and we were never alone. But somehow his letters always found their way into my backpack.

I thought of him all day and much of the night. I wrote his name in my notebooks again and again and again, backwards and forwards and in different scripts. I drew cartoon pictures of him—big Afro-wearing faces with innocent doe's eyes, a tiny nose and a slip of a smile. I wrote poems to him on scrap paper, then burned them with a lighter I'd found on the street one day, dreaming that the ashes would be carried by the wind to his front door.

And every letter he slipped to me was answered with my own missive, left exactly where he'd put mine. He wrote to me about his classes, his teachers, football practice, and his homework. I wrote to him about my classes, the teachers, books and homework. We always signed our letters "your friend," followed by a tiny symbol. Mine was two intertwined "C's." His was, yes, a football.

I was almost never hungry after I'd been close to him, even if I was in his presence for only a few moments. I'd arrive home to one of Grandma's famous dinners—greens, sweet potatoes, baked fish or chicken, biscuits, fresh lemon-ade—and daydream as she and Mr. Saunders looked thoughtfully at my untouched plate. Grandma mentioned it once or twice, and then, when I couldn't answer, in true Grandma fashion, she just left it alone.

And then there was the problem of my not being able to sleep, yet not waking up tired, grouchy, or sick. This was the best not sleeping I'd ever heard of. I laid in bed and thought about his face, eyes, hands, arms, curved muscled thighs, brownish-gold halo of hair, and that rough 'n ready voice.

How could I *possibly* sleep?

I was peaceful inside, and Grandma could see it. The rhythms of my daily life were simple and productive; my grades were so good I was on the Honor Roll, and I was the favorite of most of the teachers who were willing to like me. Even—grudgingly—that hateful Mr. Evans.

If the kids didn't like me, they didn't show it. Nobody mocked or teased me. Everybody left me alone, except for that knucklehead, Gideon.

Because something, I think, was happening to Gideon, too. Nina told me in so many ways: "He not a dummy anymore. Now he just plain stupid."

We were riding home together after what had been a good day. I'd helped Nina with a report she had to write, and she'd gotten a good grade on it.

"What did he do *now*?" I asked, looking away from her as if I didn't care.

"He don't pay attention. Ever. You be talking to him, and he sitting right there, and sometime he even nod. Then you ax him about it a few minutes later, and he got absolutely no clue."

"Maybe he's just thinking about the game," I said.

"Yeah, maybe, but I don't think so."

"Well, what do you think he's thinking about?"

"CeCe, he axt me to braid his hair and oil his scalp last night. That's crazy. Gideon never used to care about how he look. He could wear the same clothes—he would even go into my things and take my shirts. Now, all of a sudden, he want special clothes. He even axt my momma to pierce his ear."

"Your momma?"

"Yeah. She home right now."

"That's great!"

"Oh, I don't know," Nina said. "She come home, my little brother get all excited, then she leave."

"Your little brother's there, too?" I said.

"Yeah, but when my momma around, I got to put him in bed with me to calm him down, and he keep axing for her after she gone. It's a mess, really."

"But you must be glad to see her—"

"—About as glad as you," she said. "I notice you don't seem to be making plans to rush back up to your momma when school's out."

Our eyes met. I opened my mouth, then closed it, and we pedaled on.

* * * * * * *

Gideon bolted out of his classroom and jogged lightly down the hall after me just before classes ended a few days later, catching up with me by the girls' bathroom. He looked at me quickly, then his eyes fell to a little note, written on notebook paper, that he removed from his pocket. When I took the paper our hands touched.

"For you," he said quietly. Lord, I could smell the Palmolive warmth of him.

"Oh," I murmured, "I mean, thank you."

"CeCe, could I——?"

We were standing awkwardly, hands still pressed together. Slowly his fingers closed over mine. And then his body was touching me. I breathed in his clean, hard scent of soap and a trace of lemony men's cologne. The skin on his face was smooth and unblemished, and I lifted my face as his full-lipped mouth met mine.

I had never been kissed. Never knew what happens when lips as soft as a breast press against your own, and you taste the warm earthblood flavor of a man's mouth. We were so close his firm chest grazed my nipples through my shirt and my skin ignited, all my senses ablaze.

It was my first kiss, but I already knew what his lips confirmed that afternoon. I'd known it the first I saw him. *We were done.*

Gideon was my alpha and omega. He was the conspiracy of how I thought, dreamed, and everything I was willing to do to protect us.

Because I had to protect us. I just had to.

Nina knew, as she always did, without either one of us saying a word. "CeCe. Look at me."

It was the very same day as The Kiss. We pedaled slowly home through a misty rain, listening to the thuds and whistles of football practice growing fainter behind us.

Startled from my bliss, I reacted just a moment too slowly. She hauled off and slugged my arm, nearly knocking me off my bike.

"Jesus!" I cried, rubbing my arm. "What's wrong with you?"

"What's wrong with *you*?" she said. "I been telling you about what that idiot Biology teacher done to my lab report, just because he don't like purple ink."

"I heard you, Nina."

"You might've heard, but you wasn't listening. What was you doing with my brother down at the end of the hall?"

"Whoa——how do you——?"

"Abilene Smith seen you come out that corner together and she told Bette Johnson who, of course, announced it to the whole school while I was getting my stuff out my locker."

"I didn't go down there looking for him," I said. "It was just a coincidence."

"But what was you and Gideon *doing*?"

"Well let's see: we were standing in the hall of a school with at least three hundred nosey-ass students. What the hell *could* we have been doing?"

She slid me an annoyed, sideways glance. "Gideon not a boy anymore, CeCe. Last year I wouldn't have worried too much about you and him, but now it's different."

"What's different?"

"He always *was* quiet, but now he too quiet. Staring out the window instead of watching TV. Laying on the floor and looking at the ceiling instead of throwing his stupid football back and forth all afternoon. Dang! He even offered to wash the dishes last night!"

"So what's wrong with any of that?" I said.

"It like he sick!" Nina said. "Like somebody just took him over!"

"What—you think I got a little voodoo doll with grey eyes or something?"

"No, CeCe, I'm not joking! He not behaving like Gid!"

I sighed and tried to peddle through the red mud while rubbing my injured arm. "Look, Nina—I would never do anything to hurt your brother—"

"Maybe not on purpose! But you don't know how powerful these things can get."

"What things?" I asked.

"Love."

She had said it in a flat tone of voice, as if voicing the word might make it more dangerous and powerful. And she was right: the moment Nina actually described the tension between her brother and me as *love,* the bond actually hardened, like liquid metal cooling into steel.

"Do you think," I whispered, "he loves me?"

"You love him, don't you?"

I didn't answer for a long moment. I knew she was asking me for a real answer, an honest answer—not some stupid, 'I have a crush on your brother' answer—so I thought about it a while before answering.

"I—I think so," I said.

"You *think* so?"

"Okay. I know so."

"Listen, dummy: you better *not* just be messing with Gideon. Do you understand? You may be faster and meaner than me, but I will go down in the dust kicking your butt if you try to play him for a fool!"

"But—"

"CeCe, you just don't get it. LaToya and Bree and them fall in love once a week, with whatever boy happen to be wearing some aftershave and a new pair of kicks. You can't treat my brother that way. *Do. You. Hear. Me?*"

Of course, there's nothing like speaking the King's English to a pigeon. I had no way of hearing, or understanding anything that Nina was saying. Her brother had kissed me because he *had* to: Gideon and I were put on this earth to find each other, and I had survived everything Copley did to my momma and me, just so Bebe J would put me on the Greyhound bus to love.

So what was Nina even talking about?

* * * * * * *

For the next few days I thought about it.

At dinner Grandma asked why I was so quiet and I looked up from my greens and black-eyed peas, surprised to find her still sitting across the table. Later that week, Grandma peered at me with interest when I ignored the singers on American Idol. She walked by the bedroom two or three times each evening, noting that I wasn't asleep, though the lights were out and the room was perfectly quiet.

I wasn't sick. I was still thinking about what Nina said to me.

And it was Nina's words that sent me out behind the school after lunch one day, where I wandered into the cinderblock enclosure built to hide the huge steel garbage dumpsters from view.

The afternoon was an Indian summer chaos of scarlet leaves and corn-tinted sun. I hadn't intended to skip. In fact, I went into the girl's bathroom to wash my face after sitting under the trees with Nina, while Gideon sprinted back and forth in the dusty parking lot, intercepting passes thrown by his friends. Neither one of us looked at the other as we chewed, our eyes fixed on his graceful, muscular form.

"I hate *Ethan Frome*," Nina intoned, "even more than that phony Stella."

"Stella?"

"From *Great Expectations*. I tell you, CeCe, *Ethan Frome* is so much worse. I don't know if I can stand it. And did you read that one about the lady who went crazy because of her wallpaper?"

"Yeah, that was pretty stupid, but not as bad as *A Rose for Emily*. That old lady was sleeping with the corpse of her dead husband every night!"

"Musta stank," Nina agreed.

And that story about the chopped-up heart beneath the floor—"

"Edgar Allen Poe," Nina said, her eyes still fixed on Gideon. "I kinda liked the one where the giant blade was about to cut the guy in half. It was like a TV show."

"And you say *I'm* crazy?"

She looked back at me and laughed. Immediately her face soured. "I know you not crazy," she said softly. "I just hope you *real*."

The football soared the length of the lot and Gideon leapt into the air, missed it, and came down laughing as it bounced crazily and landed on top of a teacher's car.

I took a fat, yellow-flecked apple from my lunch bag, then noticed that Grandma had packed a second one, too. Without thinking I held it out to Nina.

"What's that?" she asked.

"I got two."

"I got my own food."

"So?" I said, "eat it anyway."

"I don't want your lunch."

"I don't want to take it home."

"Why'd you bring it?"

"Grandma packed it."

"She intended it for you, CeCe."

"Maybe, but *I* don't intend it for me."

"So you think I want your leftovers?" she asked.

"Nina, just eat it, alright?"

She snatched the apple up and examined it critically.

"Is it beneath your standards?" I said with irritation.

"Clearly it's beneath yours."

"Dang, Nina!" I said, "you're my *friend*. I offered you my extra apple. I didn't ask you to sell me your firstborn son, or to give me the contents of your bank account, or to clean my room every day for the next twenty years!"

She broke into goofy laughter. "First of all, I am *never* having a son. Ever. Boys too much trouble. Second, I don't even *have* a bank account. Third, you have to clean your own room, cause I'm too busy cleaning everybody else's."

Even though I laughed at her comment, I felt bad. I turned to look at her at the same moment she looked at me.

"It's okay, CeCe," she said. "I know you my friend."

I think it was those words that sent me to the bathroom to wash my face. Or rather, to wash away my tears. Because when we stood up after lunch, the apple was lying there in the grass.

I sat in a stall with the door locked while the lint brains reapplied their after-lunch makeup and talked about as many other girls as they could—including me and Nina—as if all the other girls at Booker T. Washington had four legs and barked.

A few months earlier I would have announced my presence with my fist. But that afternoon, when I was sure I was alone, I came out and stood in front of the mirror, looking at myself.

Despite Grandma's concerted effort to make up for sixteen years of haphazard nutrition, I could still pass for a late middle-schooler. I had filled out a little on top, and now required a real bra, with actual cups. But my waist and belly and hips were still girlish, and I was so small I could play hopscotch with a straight face. All I could see in the mirror was a skinny, hard-eyed tomboy who was hopelessly drowning in a pastel-eyed manchild who'd kissed her in secret and changed her world.

The late bell rang and the halls gradually fell silent. I slipped out of the bathroom, walked down the corridor and out to the back of the school and the privacy of the cinderblock wall. I had never skipped before, but I figured I could always tell Grandma I'd had a terrible headache. I did get them sometimes. And I was doing just fine in Geography, any—

I heard a noise and looked up. Gideon was standing behind me, a troubled expression on his face. He was not, for once, holding a football. Instead, his hands were in the pockets of his sun-bleached jeans, and his army surplus tee-shirt, gently frayed at the collar, was the exact color of his eyes.

"You okay?" he said. "I saw you come out the bathroom and head this way."

"Don't you have class right now?"

"Auto shop. Don't matter if I miss it. Mr. Ingersoll's the assistant football coach, and he don't care what I do, long as I show up for practice."

"Oh."

I looked around for somewhere to sit. The dumpster, nearly the size of a garage, was placed on a cement block that had cracked under its weight. We were invisible both to the school and the street, and I realized, with sudden trepidation, that he might try to kiss me again. I wasn't sure I could handle that.

"Gideon—did anyone see you come out?"

"Did anyone see *you,* CeCe?" He moved a step closer.

"I hope not. If they catch us——"

"They won't," he said. "Lots of kids come back here to drink, get high, or do other stuff——"

His eyes flickered down to mine, and I was suddenly aghast at how much he seemed to tower over me.

"CeCe," he rasped, reaching for my hand, "I was wondering if——if you would go out with me."

"Where?" I asked stupidly.

"Where what?"

"Where do you want to go? I have to ask Grandma."

For a moment he looked confused. "No, CeCe——I mean——I mean I want you to be my lady."

For the entire six months since Easter Sunday, the day I first laid eyes on Gideon, I had thought of little else but this moment. Yet now that he was standing so so *so* close, I felt clunky and childlike. Many of the girls in my grade were pretty, poised, and feminine. I was a gladiator. A freak. Why was Gideon here with *me?*

Now he reached for my waist and his big hands pulled me close. I could feel his fingers though my cotton blouse, gently stroking my back. Heart hammering, I stiffened in his arms.

He leaned forward to kiss me, then paused, his lips hovering near mine. His scent filled me up and I pushed back, holding him at a distance.

"Something wrong?" he asked.

"I don't know," I said, awash in shyness.

"You scared? Ain't nobody here but us." Still, he hesitated, his lips lingering near mine. I smelled his warm, sweet breath. "CeCe, it's okay," he said.

"What if somebo——"

"*Shhhhhhhh,*" he whispered.

Gideon's lips touched my neck. Surprised, I heard myself sigh as he brushed the center of my mouth, capturing first my lower lip, then my upper lip, between his. He did it again, as if his lips were birds seeking a leaf on which to land. Then, unexpectedly, my lips sought his, and we were *kissing.*

His tongue was full and soft, yet even as he offered it he pulled away, returning his lips to my neck. Every cell in my body leapt off a cliff.

My hands found their way to his back, then moved up to his shoulders and his face, and he pressed me gently against the wall.

I vanished into him, released all the *fearconcernworrymemorytroublesorrow-sadness* I carried, even in the deepest parts of my soul.

For the first time in my entire life I felt the desire—no, the *need,* to cease to exist. He responded by pressing against me, his hands moving to my hips, pulling me even closer into him.

"You like to dance?" he murmured as he returned to my lips.

"I've never done it before."

"Want me to teach you?"

Everything vanished except for his flesh and mine. So *this* was the reason I was born—

Carefully he pulled away and stood tall, the blue-grey eyes now smoky and hooded. His chest rose and fell, and I sensed his heart racing beneath his shirt.

"Did I—did I do something wrong?" I whispered.

He shook his head, swallowed, and let his hands hover in the air before raising them diplomatically to my shoulders.

"We can't do this, CeCe. Not like this. Not here and not now."

I knew he was right, but I wanted it so badly I wouldn't have cared if a SWAT team arrived with spotlights and attack dogs.

Gideon sank down suddenly, his back against the wall. He studied the ground as if unable to meet my eyes. "I never done nothing like this before," he confessed.

"What—skip class?"

"Naw. I mean—I mean I never been out here with a girl."

"Oh! Me neither—I mean, I've never been here with a girl *or* a boy!"

I was muttering like a fool, but he didn't seem to notice. Instead, he roped his arms around his knees. "It's like all I think about is, well..." his voice faded off.

I laughed shakily and stared down at his head. He looked up.

"You ever want to go back where you came from, CeCe?"

"Me? Well, I missed my momma at first, but now I like being here."

"Because of Nina?"

"Because—because of Nina and—and you."

Now he laughed, too, as if surprised. "We never met nobody like you before. I mean, people come down here to see they folks, but after a couple a days they can't wait to take off."

"I'm not going anywhere," I said.

"Sure?"

"Sure."

With a soft grunt he stood up. "We—we going out now, right CeCe?"

I nodded, aware that I was trembling.

"Then is it okay if I kiss you one more time?"

I nodded again and his lips hovered, lingered, then touched mine with the softness of the wind on a petal.

After a while we stopped, looked at each other, and I felt a drunken giggle rise up in my throat, and it infected him, too. He rolled away from me, took my hand, and we leaned side-by-side against the wall, laughing like fools in front of a firing squad. I was drunk (though I'd never tried alcohol), and crazily, stupidly, ridiculously high.

"Who taught you how to do this?" I said, still laughing.

He shrugged, shaking his head. "I think *you* did."

"Did *not*!"

"Uh-*huh*!"

"Seriously, Gideon—how many girlfriends—?"

"Exactly none," he said firmly. He looked down at me. "I been thinking about you for a while."

We both laughed again.

"You okay?" he whispered hoarsely.

I nodded.

"Nothing broken, CeCe?"

I shook my head, then nodded, unable to describe how much it hurt every inch of my body not to beg him to go on.

"Are you happy?" he whispered.

"Uh-huh," I whispered back.

"Then you really *are* going out with me?"

"A thousand times yes," I answered. He grinned and I felt ten feet tall just for making him happy, too. "You think we're gonna get in trouble for skipping?" I said.

"Nobody paying attention to us," he said.

"Nina is."

He was quiet for a moment. He glanced around guiltily and sighed. "My sister been looking out for me since we was in diapers. Even when we was real little, she made sure I didn't eat glass, drink pond water or get bit by a dog. She just don't know how to let go."

"Nina's my best friend," I said. "I don't want to make her mad."

"Me, neither," he said, shaking his head. "She dangerous when she mad." Once again we both laughed, without malice.

"My sister love you," he said, adding softly, "and so do I."

"Jesus on a bicycle," I replied. "I love you and Nina too, Mr. Gideon Price."

He leaned in and kissed me until the bottom of my soul opened up to let him inside.

"So what's this?" he reached around, feeling my butt through my jeans. I pulled the lovely gold-flecked apple from my pocket. I held it up to him, and he considered it for a moment before taking it from my hand.

"Okay, baby," he said, glancing down at my jeans, "you got a serpent hanging out down there?"

'No, of course not!"

"And no other sins to speak of?"

"Not yet," I said, looking into his eyes.

"Then I'm ready to risk it all for you," he announced, taking a bite.

He gave it back to me. "You have to eat some, too."

I didn't understand, as my teeth broke the skin of the fruit, that we were, indeed, setting events in motion that would exile us both from our families, from Blissfield, and—yes, from each other.

Because at that moment we were deliriously happy, blood young and completely in love. No one—not even the devil himself—could have chased us out of our fragile and youthful Eden.

* * * * * * *

He was talking.

Nina watched, but did not interrupt, as we rode together to school.

"Keelo think he a better player than me, just because he bigger, but he can't run for shit." Gideon's ruminations on the coming Friday night's game were a source of real irritation to his sister, who wanted to talk to me about *Macbeth*.

She turned her head to me. "Coach told him he ain't hardly built to run the ball, but he don't want to hear nothing about it," she said in an undertone. Then she looked at her brother. "You better watch out, or Keelo might trip you and break your leg," she said loudly, rolling her eyes.

"He have to catch me, first," Gideon answered, satisfaction in his voice. "I don't know why Coach always have to let stupid people on the team. If we had less dummies, we would win more games."

"You only lost once," I said, smiling at him. Nina grunted beside me.

"That was one too many," Gideon said. "I could've scored it if Repo Henderson had bothered to pass me the ball."

"Let it go," Nina said. "I don't want to listen to that story again."

"Maybe CeCe want to hear it."

"No she don't. She just want to hear you. CeCe would listen if you farted all the way to school."

"Shut up, Nina," I said, laughing despite myself.

"Well, one thing for sure. Gid ain't talked as much in his entire life as he has on this bicycle ride," she added drily.

"That's 'cause nobody can get a word in with you going on about that stuff you read," Gideon said. "They already forcing you to read it. Why you got to talk about it, too?"

"Some of it just crazy," she said, glancing back at her brother. "I like to get a second opinion."

"You just like listening to yourself," Gideon said.

"Never bothered you before."

"Don't bother me now, except that maybe I got something to talk about, too."

"Come on, you guys," I said, "there's time enough for everybody to talk."

"Look at you, trying to be a referee," Nina said. "I know you think he cute, but soon he gonna think he *smart*, too."

"He *is*!" I cried.

"CeCe, you couldn't see the real Gideon, even if you was trying."

"Then what am I seeing? A *hologram*?" I said.

"No, you seeing Loverboy Gideon. You got to see him when he don't want to help you cook the dinner or clean up afterwards."

"Well, she should see you first thing in the morning!" Gideon said, laughter in his voice. "You look like Boo Radley!"

"Listen to my brother," Nina said, shaking her head. "He just want you to know he made it through *one* whole book in his life."

"Shut up, Nina," Gideon answered. "You can read all them books, but you so clumsy you can't even walk in a straight line."

"Yeah, I know—they make us go to all those classes, then the real hero in the school is the one who can run with a football," she responded with a shrug. "Look like all of 'em a bunch of dummies!"

The three of us laughed as we rode into the schoolyard. Gideon left us for his friends, who were, of course, throwing a football. But not before he came over, wrapped his arms around me and lifted me off the ground.

"Don't let those teachers see you treating her like a puppy," Nina remarked irritably. "Ms. Corinne'll come up here and get you."

Gideon didn't dare kiss me in front of the entire schoolyard, but his weird hug was declaration enough to the assembly. Girls stopped primping and the football hit the ground. A couple of teachers stopped in their progress to the school building. What was *that*? The quarterback and the tomboy? The sexiest boy on the planet with that little Castle knot of a girl? Or was it that someone actually wasn't afraid to *like* a Castle?

* * * * * * *

On Saturday he met me at the Piggly Wiggly and skateboarded beside me as I walked my bike home.

Still talking.

"See, NFL players make a million dollars. But so do the guys in the NBA. The only thing is that basketball players have to play from the fall almost till summer. Football season shorter."

"Okay," I said, waiting to hear how he planned to make it onto a professional basketball team.

"Coach said if I work on my arm, I could play baseball, too."

I thought about the coach, a red-faced, red-necked, yellow-skinned man, who taught auto-mechanics during the day. Though he was very good at leading our teams to victories over the other schools scattered throughout the tobacco fields, his gestational belly and stubby arms suggested that he, himself, only excelled at using a fork.

Gideon, however, couldn't see this, and it really didn't matter to me, because it was simply fascinating to hear how his mind worked.

"Now, Benny can't do much yet, but he already throw real good."

"Benny?"

"My little brother."

"Oh," I said, looking into Gideon's face. "Nina never told me his name."

"That's because she hate it. Momma wanted to call him that. Nina insist on 'Ben.'"

"Is it short for Benjamin?"

"No, Benedictine."

"Well, you could call him Dick."

Gideon burst into laughter. "Nobody want to be called that."

"Well, what about Tino?"

"Yeah, well, I guess he cried less when we called him Benny, so Benny kinda stuck."

"Did he cry a lot when he was little?"

"I don't know. You just don't hear it after a while."

"Nina said he stays with your auntie during the week."

"Yeah. She his daddy's sister."

"Is she nice?"

"When she feel like it," Gideon answered. I could tell he didn't want to talk about it.

"Do you ever babysit?'"

"They won't let me. Nina and Momma say a boy don't know nothing about little kids."

"Except you used to be one."

"CeCe, you already know you can't tell Nina nothin.'" He laughed again. "The thing is, even when Nina know she not right, she got to keep on going. I think she just want to keep going, and the only way is to convince herself she always right."

This insight rather surprised me. "Why does she always have to be right?" I asked.

"Guess she scared not to be."

"Do you think she's scared?"

'Yeah, she scared," he answered. "We all scared. Don't nobody want to live like we live, especially when our momma not there."

"You scared of ghosts?"

"No, CeCe. That's just silliness. We get scared because sometimes people come looking for Momma, and they might not believe she not home."

"People?" I said.

"Yeah," he said, a distant look blooming in his eyes. "But we don't let them in. They leave a lot sooner now, because I got big last summer. Back when I was little—" he whistled through his teeth and shook his head.

"What happened, Gideon?"

"Things," he said, his eyes fixed on the pavement.

"Things like bad things?"

"All kind a things."

"Like you had to protect Nina-things?" I asked.

"I don't know if she would've gave me the chance," he said quietly. "You know Nina. She don't get mad as fast as you, but when you push her, she can get pretty freaky."

"*Freaky*?"

"She learned that from our momma," Gideon said. "When we was little, sometimes Momma had to get people out the house."

"Men?"

"Sometimes," he said, looking at his feet. "So she showed my sister how to fight."

"Like boxing lessons?" I said.

"No, CeCe. Not like that. Sometimes people wouldn't go, or they got mad and tried to hurt my momma. She would either have to stand there and take it, or she would have to stand up for herself."

"How?"

"With whatever she could reach," Gideon said. "Momma can be real creative if she pushed."

"Nina saw her?"

"I seen her, too."

I hesitated, and found myself watching a pebble bounce off the toe of my shoe and land in a patch of late-blooming cornflowers. "Did—did these people ever hit your Momma?" I asked.

"Yeah. One guy came after her real bad. They say he used to live with her. Nina think he may even be her daddy."

"Nina doesn't know her daddy?"

Gideon shrugged. "He just a guy."

"Is he your father, too?"

He shrugged again. "I axt, but Momma said she don't give a damn."

"Then you don't know your father, either?"

"I know I don't want to know him," Gideon said.

"But he must care about you if he keeps coming back—"

"CeCe, some men think they own a woman. Every time the guy come to the house, he say my momma belong to him. He try to tell her she'll always be his woman. That make her really mad, then they start up."

"She fights him?"

Gideon laughed quietly. "You better believe it."

"And you?"

"Do I fight him? No. Momma told me I'm too big for that. She said the guy could shoot me or stab me and say I threatened him."

"So you have to watch that guy hit your mom?" I asked.

He didn't answer. We walked an entire block in silence, the stately old plantation houses staring down at us.

"Don't feel bad," I said in a low voice. "I know how you feel."

His troubled eyes fastened on mine, so I kept talking. "I've seen my momma get hit, too. Plenty of times."

"By who?" Gideon asked. "Your daddy?"

"Yeah. He beats on her all the time. He acts like hitting her is the best part of his day. The thing is," I said, "I really didn't care till I got big. That's when he started coming after me."

"Hell, CeCe, you never been big."

"I mean big enough to understand."

"Your momma fight back?" Gideon asked.

"No. But that doesn't stop him. Seems like the more he hurts her, the more he enjoys it."

"She won't leave him?"

I shook my head, remembering the scene at the bus stop. "Grandma tried to get her to go." I said. "Even sent her some money. And I begged her, but..." my voice trailed off.

"That's why your momma sent you down here?"

I nodded.

"And that why you always ready to fight?" Gideon asked.

I didn't answer.

"You know," he said thoughtfully, "when you see people fighting for they life, it seem like a natural way to live. I guess you learn how to hit before somebody hit you."

"*You* don't hit people," I said.

He looked away, something like guilt in his eyes. Suddenly he stopped walking, and I did, too. He grasped my hand, threading his enormous fingers through mine.

"I got to get us out," he said hoarsely. "I got to get out and take Nina and Benny with me."

"What about your momma?"

"I don't know," he replied, "and I don't know if I care. We alone, anyway."

"You're ready to leave your momma?" I asked.

"She left us a long time ago," he answered. "If we can't make her choose any different, maybe we got to choose to save ourself."

Now I saw that his silence, his distance, even the football tucked beneath his arm were all lifebuoys.

"If I don't go, something gonna happen," he continued. "I can't just stand by and let it happen." He smiled faintly at my expression. "Now I guess you don't want to go out with me no more."

"Why do you think that?"

"Everybody in Blissfield know about my momma, so nobody want to go anywhere near us. People won't even let their kids be friends with us."

"I don't care what people think, Gideon. Even Grandma couldn't keep me from being with you."

We had inadvertently stopped in front of the Armitage House, with its plush lawn and white picket fence. I didn't know who lived there, and didn't care.

"Gideon, will you tell me what happens—I mean, when they come to the house looking for your momma?"

"I leave and take Benny with me."

"Where do you go?"

"Outside. Down the road."

"What if it's nighttime?" I asked.

"It usually is."

"And Nina?"

"I don't know," he said, looking away. "Sometimes she stand in the door so they can't get inside. She think if she stay there they may give up and go."

"Does that work?"

"Nina got hit once when she was little. I was real little, but I remember," Gideon said. "She fell against a table and her head started to bleed. When my momma came home, she thought Nina was dead and started screaming so loud, the people down the road called the police. They took Nina to the hospital in Roanoke Rapids, and she was alright, and after that Momma got straight for a while."

"Got straight?" I echoed.

"Yeah, for a minute."

"You mean, she—"

Gideon looked directly at me, and his eyes were suddenly filled with anger. "You come from Ohio, CeCe, not from some cotton field. Don't you know what 'getting straight' means?"

"I—I know what it means in my father's world," I stammered. "I just didn't know people down here—"

"You think we all hicks who drink corn liquor made in a still?"

"Gideon, that's not what I meant. I just didn't know you could buy that shit here. Everything seems so much—I don't know—safer and cleaner and *better*!"

I could hear how stupid I sounded, but I was only being honest. He was still holding my hand, but he was avoiding my gaze.

"I'm sorry, Gideon."

He looked back, his eyes wary.

"And," I added, "I don't care. Jesus—you and Nina don't dog me, even though everybody here seems to know a bunch of shit about my father that I don't even know."

His expression softened. "It's messed up to carry a weight that ain't even yours. People here in Blissfield got long memories. Even if Nina and me was perfect, they would still look for fault in us because of my momma."

"I wouldn't."

"I know." His hand squeezed mine. We stood looking at each other.

"When you go, take me with you," I said. "No matter what, I'm never going back to Ohio, and I couldn't live here without the two of you."

He brought my hand up and pressed his lips against the inside of my palm. "When we go," he said, "I promise you coming with us too."

* * * * * * *

During the eighty days I lived with Jesse Brantley, the cop in Ohio who tried to keep me safe, I often thought about that moment. Though it was only a few short months after the afternoon that Gideon made that promise to me, my life had changed so much I might have been living in a different century.

I was back in Akron, trapped in the scentless darkness of the arctic winter, and every person I loved had been stripped from my life. The cop and I were sitting on his sofa with the television on, the sound turned down, pretending to watch the Cavs getting whipped by the Lakers. I had already figured out that when Jesse seemed real interested in the television, he was actually intensely focused on me.

"Your team's got zero chance," I said, irritated that the game was keeping me from getting some sleep. Though I didn't sleep much, and I never slept well, I needed rest during the few hours I wasn't at work, and the sofa, after all, did double duty as my bed.

"You can't always be on the side of the winners," Jesse said without turning his head.

"I don't see any point in wasting time on losers."

He responded with silence, which said very clearly that he practiced what he preached by spending time with me. He was cradling a mug of lavender and passionflower tea, a blend he drank in the evening, and his long legs rested on the low table in front of him. He obviously wasn't in a hurry to bring the evening to a close.

I got up and wandered to a window, where snow hurled itself against the pane. I'd forgotten what winter was like while I lived in North Carolina. At that moment, looking out into the snow-flecked, pitch blackness, it was hard to believe that Blissfield even existed.

The silence persisted. It got to me, that silence.

"Hey," Jesse said. "You okay?"

I ignored the question.

"You thinking about that guy down south again?"

As I watched the snow melting to teardrops on the glass, I was, in fact, thinking about Gideon's promise on that distant afternoon. Behind me, Jesse grunted as he got to his feet and walked over to the kitchen counter. His reflection filled the kettle with water and turned on the stove. He produced a tin and spooned a measure of powder into a mug. I saw him lean against the sink, waiting for the water to boil.

When he joined me at the window, the smell of chocolate filling the room, I deliberately turned away.

"Celeste," he said, his voice soft despite the tone of authority he always struggled to keep at bay, "try this."

"I don't want—"

"It's from Mexico," he said. "It's pure dark chocolate. They—"

"I said I don't—"

"—grind up cocoa beans and add nut—"

"I *told* you—"

"Hush, baby," he said, and I heard an echo of Gideon in his voice— "don't fight so hard."

I faced him and saw that he was both impressed and annoyed by my resistance. I took the mug from his outstretched hands, glared at him for a moment, then slowly brought it to my lips.

He was right: the bittersweet chocolate in that vacant, cold, silent night felt like an echo of Gideon's face, his voice, his touch.

For a few moments he watched me, his eyes perfectly blank. "Feeling better?"

I knew it was pointless to lie, so I tipped my head in the shadow of a nod.

He actually laughed. "You," he said, "need to be careful. If you get any tougher I'd be scared of you."

"And you'd be right," I said, turning back to the window.

"I really hope that's not true."

"Be honest, Detective," I said to our reflection. "The fact that I'm tough is why you're interested in me."

"Howso?"

"I know you're using me to get to my father. That's why I'm here," I said, gesturing vaguely around the echoing room. "The longer he can't find me, the more desperate he'll be to control me. If you keep me close, you figure that sooner or later he'll show up."

"It's not that simple, Celeste. I want you to be okay, too."

I looked at Jesse's reflection in the glass. No matter what he said, I knew that *okay* was over for me. During those heady months in Blissfield I'd been unable to see the truth for all the thinly-lacquered lies. I never dreamed of a life without Gideon and Nina. Most of all, I couldn't have imagined how loving too much would wound and exile me from those I most loved.

* * * * * * *

Though I felt really guilty about it, I didn't tell Grandma what I had learned from Gideon in front of the Armitage residence that day. I sat in bed that night, my attempts to write him a letter blocked by my imaginings of their tiny house, the phantom woman who hid in the shadows of the bleachers and the men who came looking for her at midnight.

I wondered if she was as beautiful as her son and daughter. I wondered how she thought her children could survive, alone like that, with nobody else around. Then, suddenly I understood why Nina dressed like a boy, and refused to fix her hair, or style herself to be pretty. I knew that looking pretty was about the most dangerous thing she could do. I wondered what she'd already survived, and how she found the strength to keep on going in spite of it.

The football season ended with our team messing up in the semi-finals. Though everyone in the school was let down—Gideon especially—it was the farthest in post-season competition the team had progressed in over thirty years, and the fact that Gideon had three more years to play went a long way to calm the coach—as well as the lint brains, who still didn't let him out of their sight.

It now rained every day, putting an end to lunch with Nina beneath the trees, and meetings with Gideon behind the school. The students moved indoors during lunch, the boys going to the gym to play basketball, and the girls sitting in the stands to watch. Naturally the cheerleaders took their places on the side of the court, pretending to practice their cheers. Nina and I climbed to the top of the bleachers and watched the entire gym as we ate, commenting drily on the universe below.

"CeCe," Nina said one afternoon, "my English teacher axt me if I want to go to college."

"Really?" I twisted around to face her. "Where does she think you should go?"

"Some school in Raleigh. Can't do it, though."

"Why not?"

"What do you think would happen to Gid and my baby brother? They can't hardly make toast, much less live on their own."

"Gideon's almost grown," I said. "Couldn't he raise your brother?"

"Gid's only fifteen, CeCe."

"He looks older."

"He look like *steak* to you."

"That's crazy." I said.

"Nothing crazy about it," Nina said. "My auntie already don't like taking care of my baby brother, so it's going to be me. And I can't leave until Gid's old enough to take care of himself."

"But maybe you should talk to somebody. My Grandma, for instance."

"What can she do?"

" I don't know, but she went to college and—"

"That don't make you better, CeCe!"

"I know, Nina. What I'm trying to say is—"

"Not everybody can go away to school."

"Nina, if you don't want to go, that's okay. But you don't have to be so mean about it."

"You missed the point, CeCe. I *do* want to go. I want to go real bad. But you can't just get up and leave when people need you."

"Listen—"

"No, *you* listen! People need me, CeCe. I can't just vanish. Other folks done that already."

I knew she was referring to their mother, so I closed my mouth. I didn't want her to guess that Gideon had told me the truth about their family.

"Well, what if you go to college and take your brothers with you?" I asked.

"I'm not their guardian. The State will come and take Benny away."

"You'll be eighteen soon, and—"

"CeCe, I know you want to help, but you just pissing me off right now. Why don't you give me a break and just concentrate on staring at Gideon?"

She had never spoken to me that way before, and for an instant Copley stirred in my chest. But then I noticed the tears in her eyes. I reached over and touched her hand. She jerked it away and wiped her face. Without looking at her, I touched it again.

"Quit it! You want everybody to think we in love?"

"I do love you."

"Not like that."

"I don't care what people think."

"Then you a dummy."

"You're a dummy, too."

She cleared her throat. "I know," she said. "I know."

* * * * * * *

One bright Saturday morning Grandma took me out on a country road about eight miles outside of town, put the Buick into neutral and looked me in the eyes.

"Scoot over, Princess. It's time you learned to drive."

"Wait—*what?*"

"I need you to be able to run errands for me, and besides—you've been keeping up with your homework and helping me around the house. I think you've earned this privi—"

I nearly leapt across the seat before she could finish her sentence. Chuckling, she got out, walked around and calmly slipped into the passenger seat.

"Alright. It's like riding a bike, except that you have keep your foot on the correct pedal at all times. Right pedal: go. Left pedal: stop. Is that clear?"

I put her through a whiplash-worthy excursion all the way into the next county, with occasional near-misses of tractors and old women walking on the side of the road. To her credit, she said little and only grabbed the steering wheel twice.

I had never in my life felt as powerful as I did behind the wheel of that car. I couldn't believe the way that sedan floated over potholes, sending clouds of red dirt in our wake. The engine was ferocious enough to make the cows pause in their eternal chewing and curiously look our way. Smaller cars and trucks seemed to avoid me, as if they knew I was a new driver, and I managed to get us all the way home without incident.

Grandma and I went driving every weekend that winter. The winter had turned out to be a joke, with everybody complaining about the rain and having no idea what snow or ice even looked like. Grandma drove me to school when it was raining hard; I don't know how Nina and Gideon got there. She told me to let them know she would pick them up in the morning, but when I mentioned it to Nina her face closed. "We'll be alright. Rain never hurt nobody."

I didn't have to look for Gideon anymore; he found me every morning, after every class, glanced repeatedly into the bleachers where his sister and I were sitting during lunch, and managed to meet me in a deserted hall before I went out to Grandma's car when school was out, another letter tucked carefully into my backpack.

I lived for our brief, intense moments. His eyes were a drug to me; at times they were wildly innocent, as if what he felt when we kissed never failed to surprise him. Other times his expression was sly and feline, with hints of a big cat whose belly was full of something recently alive. On those occasions I glanced around fast, unsure whether one of the lint brains had just lifted her cheerleader skirt for him, but he was always alone, always quiet, always completely focused on my feelings.

He brought me tiny gifts: little whistles he'd whittled from soft wood, or a bracelet he'd found in the Salvation Army store. He once gave me a tarnished silver ring and told me it was a placeholder for the real thing, and when we were pressed together my flesh wanted him with such ferocity I literally ached.

His letters were just as sweet as ever, with simple thoughts about his future career as a football star, the house he planned to build us, and the college tuition he would set aside for Nina. My answers were just the same, with lots of discussion about whether we'd have a Lassie dog or a golden retriever, and what rides we'd go on at Disneyworld.

We also now talked openly about our families.

"I don't remember," Gideon answered when I asked how long his mother had been, as my father would say, 'on the pipe.' We were sitting on a ledge outside the small Blissfield library, where I'd told Grandma I was going to do homework. Though everyone in the town thought it was cold, the mild, 63-degree winter day seemed perfect for a long bike ride to me.

"Seem like forever," Gideon said. He'd stuck a pick in his hair, and now he pulled it out and ran the long teeth through his quietly crackling afro.

"She started way back before Benny. She don't do much when she using. I mean, she come in and lay down right away. Sometimes, when she can't get herself together, her friend get mad and start slapping her around."

"Why?"

"He want her to get up and go to work. He paying for our house and all—"

"He pays for your house?"

"Actually—" Gideon dropped his comb and bent low to pick it up "—I think the house is his."

"Who is he, exactly?" I asked.

"I don't know. He been around as long as I can remember. Momma think he take care of us, but Nina say he'd kill my momma before he'd help her get clean."

"Does she want to get clean?"

"I don't know," he said, shrugging and looking away.

"I can't remember my father *not* beating my mother," I said.

"That's what so messed up about being a kid," Gideon agreed. "You think all the crazy shit they do is normal." He looked back at me. "CeCe—I promise, no matter what, I will never hit you."

"You don't even have to say that, Gideon."

"Yes I do, baby, and I want you to believe me."

"Okay, I believe you," I said to reassure him, though I never intended to give *any* man the chance to treat me the way my father treated my mother.

He took my hand and looked thoughtfully at our enlaced fingers. "What if Miss Corinne decide to send you back?"

"She won't," I said. "She likes having me here with her."

"I don't know, CeCe. People down here strange. When things get too crazy they like to disappear—or make other people disappear."

"Soon we'll be grown, Gideon. Then we can do whatever we want."

"You think so?" he said, peering into my face.

In the months to come I would remember him that way: eyes staring wide into a future we both hoped for, but knew better than to believe in.

eighteen.

And then, suddenly, it was Christmas. I only saw Nina once over the entire break, and didn't see Gideon at all. Grandma told me to invite Nina to dinner, but she flatly refused.

"You won't even come over for dessert?"

"CeCe, we don't have no TV Christmas."

"Grandma wants you to come," I said.

"I know, but I don't know what my momma might do."

"What do you mean?"

"She might show up here," Nina said, "and she might not be right when she come. I got to hang around in case she bring one of her friends with her."

"That's why you should be here, instead."

"CeCe, we have a momma. Even if she cry half the time, or if she can't hardly find her way home, she still our momma."

"I wasn't trying to say—"

"Yes you was. If you was home in Ohio, would you leave your momma on Christmas?"

The schools, stores and public offices were closed for an entire week, but the library opened after about five days. Nina called and told me she'd meet me there. When she showed up, I was surprised to find her alone.

"Don't keep looking over my shoulder," she scolded. "He home with Benny. He gave me this card for you, though."

I tucked the envelope into my purse, then pulled out the two ribboned gifts I'd prepared for them. One held a bracelet with a little silver charm in the shape of a book. Grandma told me I could buy it with the money I'd made by doing chores around the house. The other box contained a book called *Great Quarterbacks in American Sports History*, which Grandma and I found in the Wal-Mart in Roanoke Rapids. I also gave them a big box of Whitman's chocolates.

"I don't have nothing for you!" Nina exclaimed, reddening.

"I don't want anything, big sister."

Her eyes fixed on mine. "You really see me as your sister?"

"The only one I got."

"Sisters give each other stuff," she said.

"Sisters also fight when one of them won't listen."

"If you my younger sister, you got to listen to me."

"I do listen to you."

Reluctantly she smiled. "One day you might regret that."

"I can't wait," I said as we hugged, the top of my head barely reaching her shoulder.

blissfield.

Grandma let me take my driving test on my seventeenth birthday. She said my great report card and good behavior had earned me this privilege. I could now run errands for her, so I often met Gideon at the Piggly Wiggly, and we could be seen together all over Blissfield. Sometimes we drove to remote places, where we could neither be seen nor found. Our favorite place was the old ruined cabin where I'd read books with Nina during the summer. I'd pull off the road and down the grassy drive, then we'd both clamber out and race each other to the well.

The first time the day was windy and cool by local standards, though it felt like Akron in early May to me. Bouncing winds whipped the last of the fallen leaves back and forth, and the winter sun was a tickle against my skin instead of a slap. Birds skittered in furious circles, as if playing hide-and-seek in the trees. When I called out to Gideon my voice floated away like a silk scarf on the breeze.

"Who do you think lived here?"

"Who knows?" he said, bending down to pick up a stone. "Look like it been empty a while."

I slipped my hand into his. "You want to go?"

His glance answered my question.

We might have lost ourselves that day, except that some part of Gideon resisted. When I was pressed against him, no part of my mind or body wanted anything less than to be wholly and completely his, but Gideon showed me a different side when we were truly alone.

That day we ended up back in the car, with nothing between our aching bodies but a thin layer of cotton. My hands were full of him, my mouth crushed against his, and I was ready, when he carefully and gently pulled back.

"What—what's wrong?"

He grunted, reached down and began rearranging himself.

"Wait—Gideon —"

"CeCe—" his voice was so low it was nearly a rattle.

"Did I do something wrong?"

"Wrong?" he rasped. "Oh lord, no!"

"Then why—?"

"Because we need to stop," he said. The word *stop* had a flat finality. We both sat up and the world, which had been swimming in a warm bath only moments before, clicked sharply back into focus.

"What the hell, Gideon?" I realized that my tee-shirt was pulled up to my neck, along with my bra. My own jeans were open in the front and pulled low, my damp panties wrested aside.

Gideon wouldn't look at me.

"What did I do?" I asked again, frustrated anger just below the question.

"You didn't do nothing," he said, buttoning his shirt. "I just don't want it to be like this."

"I don't under—"

"You deserve better than this."

"But Gideon—"

"No, CeCe. This is just wrong."

"I don't get it. When we're at school, we—"

"When we're at school we just messing around," he said.

"*I'm* not messing around."

"You know what I'm saying."

"No I don't!" I said.

"I want to give you more than this," he said softly.

"I'm not some stupid princess."

"You're *my* princess," he said, "whether you like it or not."

"I don't want to be anybody's princess."

"It's better than being somebody's trash."

"Are you saying I'm trash?" I asked.

"No, CeCe—I'm saying I won't treat you like trash."

"But we love each other, Gideon!"

"A man who love a woman don't treat her this way." He was staring out of the window, his gaze focused absently on the ruined hut. When I touched him, I discovered he was trembling. It was only then that I saw the wetness on his face.

"What is it?" I said, my anger draining.

He wiped at his cheek with his enormous fingers. "This is what she does," he said. "With men. All kinds of men. Any kind of man. In cars and alleys and motels out on the highway."

I moved away from him, out of breath as if I'd been punched. Words crowded my brain, but for once I couldn't decide which should be let out. Slowly I reached out and took his hand. It was cold.

"I love you Gideon, and—" I stopped. He continued to stare out of the window. A leaf, loosened from a branch, floated toward the windshield and posed there, flattened by the wind. Somehow my own mother—my beautiful, gentle mother—came into my mind, followed by the immediate image of my father, standing over her, shouting, his hand raised above her face.

"Gideon, we can't make them do what we want, even though we want to."

"I know," he said, "but I won't be one of those men."

"You're not!"

"I don't know, CeCe. I don't know."

"I do," I insisted, now moving close to him. He wrapped his arms around me and kissed my forehead, his eyes moving back to the window.

We stayed there a long time, watching the leaves dance on the gusts, the sun flickering through the naked branches, the only sound our quiet, mated breathing.

* * * * * * *

And the days tumbled around us and away from us, with Nina close and Gideon closer, yet always at a distance, and we managed to balance the routines of school and our personal lives. Gideon and I still hid in our corner of the building, still met in town, and often drove out to the ruin. But the animal insistence of our touch was replaced by something less flustered and desperate. Our certainty about each other was firmly set in place. The lint brains ignored us, and though she saw it, Nina rarely spoke about her brother to me.

Grandma must have known, too, because she seemed to know everything. She had helped me escape my father's madness and come into my new self. She knew, because she'd already seen the bond between Gideon and me, and tried, in the best way she could, to temper it: *you have to remember that it's okay to be Gideon's friend, but you're much too young for anything else...*"

But she also saw that my friendship with Nina kept me steady, and my love for Gideon gave me peace. And no matter what the rest of Blissfield thought about Miss Corinne's granddaughter and the children of this scarlet woman, Grandma never did a thing to stop us from being together.

Easter was on us so fast I could hardly believe it. The world had exploded into flowers and singing bees and new golden-green leaves, and the scents of honeysuckle and hyacinth hung heavy in the air. I asked Nina if she wanted Grandma to help her make a dress for church, and after she finished laughing, she said she might just give it some thought.

Then I put the same question to Grandma.

"Princess," she said as she bustled around the kitchen making our supper, "you know I'll help your friend if she needs it. But not everyone in Blissfield thinks the way I do. I'll pick your friends up and drive them to the church door in my own vehicle—remembering that Jesus made a particular plea to his own men to allow children to come into his grace—but I can't promise you that Nina and Gideon will be as well-received by others in the congregation."

"What their mother does isn't their fault."

Grandma glanced around sharply, surprised. "What have you heard about their mother?"

Now I was afraid to speak. If Grandma had been ignoring their mother's acts in order to give me permission to see them, perhaps speaking openly about their family might close that door.

I hesitated. "I don't really know, Grandma."

"Bethany," she said, "there are times when it's okay to tell stories, but other times the truth is important. I don't care what anyone in this town thinks about Nina's family, but I do care that your friends might not be safe. If you know something's wrong in their home, your silence isn't protecting them."

"I think they're okay, or at least, most of the time," I said.

"But when they're not okay, who looks after Nina and her brother?" Grandma moved next to me and set a heaping spoonful of lumpy mashed potatoes on my plate. I stared at the food.

"I think Nina would tell me if anything really bad was going on."

"By the time you hear about it," Grandma said, "it might be too late."

"That's probably why their Aunt took their little brother. Why doesn't she take them in, too?"

"I believe that Nina, Gideon, and their baby brother all have different fathers. Their aunt may be related to the baby, but she probably has no blood ties to them."

"She could still take them in!" I said.

"Maybe she just can't afford to."

I looked into Grandma's face and saw my own worried reflection. "Gideon and Nina would never do anything bad. They don't steal, they don't cheat, they don't even use bad words!"

"I'm proud of you for making them your friends. I was very, very proud of you last year when you walked away from our congregation and offered our food to Gideon and Nina. I have been deeply moved by how willing you are to take them into your life. It's important to care for other people."

"Do *you* know the truth about their mother?" I asked.

"I know she was an intensely beautiful young woman—perhaps one of the most beautiful I've ever seen."

"What did she look like?"

"Gideon," my grandmother said. "Exactly like Gideon."

"So what happened to her?"

"I don't really know," Grandma said. "When Miranda Price arrived in Bliss-field—"

"—Arrived? You mean she wasn't born here?"

"No. In fact, Miranda, well, people called her 'Minnie,' just appeared one day. She was young—so young that she enrolled in one of the high school equivalency programs and I taught her for a few weeks. She seemed restless—maybe even angry—and had trouble making friends. Then she was gone. Other than a rare glimpse of her on the street, I haven't had a good look at her in nearly twenty years."

"So what about Nina and Gideon?" I asked.

"People talked about each of her children when they were born, but no one knew the true identity of their fathers," Grandma said. "By the time they were school aged, people said Miranda was involved with drugs. Most of us were too old-fashioned to really understand what that meant. Certainly there are no facilities in town to help someone with an addiction."

Grandma pushed a lump of butter into her potatoes with her knife, and we both watched it melt. "You know, baby, it's hard for any woman to make ends meet when she's alone, and particularly, if she has no education. Usually, it's just a matter of time before women like Miranda get caught up in something they can't handle. In Miranda's case, a man suddenly showed up—no one really knew him before, either—and soon that man had her out at night, working the streets. You know what that means, don't you?"

I nodded without meeting Grandma's eyes."

"I don't make a practice of listening to gossip," Grandma continued, "but I've been told that she spends a lot of time at a motel out on the highway. Some say this man is the father of one or more of her children. Others say he's in and out of her life—and her house—and this is why I often worry about them, and particularly Nina."

"But their mother doesn't really live there."

"Perhaps, but drug dealers have been known to go after other family members when a debt hasn't been paid."

I thought about what Gideon said about the men who came to the house. About his sense of duty toward his sister. About how Nina tried to protect their mother.

"You *do* know something, don't you?" Grandma was looking at me.

I struggled to meet her eyes.

"It's okay," she said. "I won't ask you to betray their confidence. Just remember two things, Bethany: first of all, if anything happens—*anything* at all—please make sure both Nina and Gideon know they can come to me."

I nodded.

"Secondly, I want you to promise me you'll stay away from their house."

Surprised, I promised without hesitation. I knew Nina and Gideon preferred I didn't see their home. I didn't care how they lived, but in the year I'd known them, neither one had ever asked me to visit.

We sat for a while without talking.

"Grandma," I said, "what's going to happen?"

"To who, baby?"

"To them. To us. I mean, are we going to be alright?"

She smiled across the table at me. "Yes, baby. In the end, everybody's going to be just fine."

* * * * * * *

Nina's Easter dress was made of soft yellow seersucker, with eyelet lace trim around the short sleeves and collar. Nina had learned to sew in her Home Ed class, and she and I made it almost without help on Grandma's old Singer. Nina was so excited she tried it on again and again, even when we'd done nothing more than clip a few hanging threads from the hem. Grandma, sitting with a magazine on the other side of the dining room table, smiled at our non-stop banter.

"Are you sure," Nina asked, "I don't look like I'm ten?"

"Ten? *Whatever.* I saw a model on *Glamour* magazine wearing a dress just like this."

Nina brayed out a laugh. "I don't look like no model, CeCe."

"You do in that dress."

"You still crazy. Is everybody in Ohio crazy as you?"

"You have to come to Ohio one time and see."

"Ohio? No! Too cold for me," she said.

"It's not cold in the summer!"

"Your idea of cold not the same as mine."

"You could survive it for a couple of weeks!" I said.

"Weeks? *Weeks?* I don't know what I'd do in Ohio for two minutes at a time, and you talking about weeks?"

"Okay, then: days. A couple of days."

"I don't know," she repeated, and to my surprise, I saw her wink at Grandma. "I might come back crazy as you!"

"It's not like the flu, Nina!"

"Could be."

"Well, if you catch it, at least there'll be two of us," I said.

She burst into laughter, and after a second, so did I. Grandma laughed, too, then went back to her magazine.

Nina gathered up her new dress and put it into the bag from the fabric store. When she looked at Grandma there was sheer and unadulterated love in her eyes. I saw Grandma blink, as if unprepared for my friend's joy.

"Sweetheart," she said softly, "does your brother have something to wear on Sunday, or do you think we should take him shopping?"

"No, Miss Corinne," Nina said as she turned toward the door. "I told my mother we was going to church, and she bought Gideon something to put on. She said it would probably be too hot for him to wear a suit jacket, so she didn't need to get one right now."

Stunned, I peered at Grandma, who smiled. "Tell your mother hello for me. I hope she's doing well."

"Yes, Miss Corinne," Nina said obediently.

I followed Nina to the front door.

"Did you really tell your momma you're going to church with us?"

"Of course," she said. "I tell my momma everything."

"But I thought she was—"

"You just don't understand. Just because she messed up don't mean she don't care about us."

I thought about the last time I'd heard from my mother. It had been months, and when she stopped calling I'd hardly noticed.

"You're right," I said, suddenly awash with guilt. "Nobody loves you the same as your mother."

* * * * * * *

I'd never felt more nervous in my entire life than I did while watching for Nina and Gideon to arrive at our house on Easter morning. As always, Nina insisted they'd come to us rather than let us drive over to their house to pick them up. Grandma seemed calm, but I saw her look at her watch once or twice as the sun rose higher in the sky. Mr. Saunders was already there, in a crisp tan suit with a white carnation in his lapel.

The week before we'd made our regular trip to Grandma's favorite dress store in Roanoke Rapids, with Mr. Saunders telling funny stories about Grandma when she was young.

"Your grandmother learned to drive on her daddy's tractor," he said. "She would wait till he left for town, then she'd climb up on the tractor and drive it up and down the road. The problem was that the thing was so big, she couldn't keep it going straight. The boys would be playing in the cornfields and look up to see her zigzagging through her daddy's fields like she was crazy. Then she'd start yelling at us to come and help her stand the corn stalks back up before he got back."

Mr. Saunders and I laughed, but Grandma shook her head. "Hush, Joe! Don't tell her that nonsense!"

"You just wait, Bethany," he said. "On the way home I'll tell you about the time your grandma lost the spelling bee. She was nine years old and she tried to burn the school down!"

"Burn the school down?" I echoed, round-eyed.

Grandma peered at her companion. "Joseph Ezekial Saunders! You should be ashamed to make up such stories and tell them to my granddaughter! She'll believe I was some kind of urchin when I was little."

"You was," he said, laughing again.

We got to the store, but to my surprise, the crusty old mannequins were gone. It seemed that the owner had finally retired and turned over the store to her niece. I could see that Grandma was unprepared for the faceless silver mannequins in the window and the short, shimmering dresses on their bodies. All the shoes had four or five-inch heels, and the selection of flowered, ribboned and netted ladies' hats was gone.

Still, Grandma cast around and pulled out five or six dresses for me to try on. Though I could have made a fuss, her invitation to Nina and Gideon made me want to please her, so I chose a boring, ivory A-line dress (I'd learned that term while helping Nina sew), with appliques of pale lavender flowers (they'd match Gideon's tie!).

I'd outgrown last year's shoes, but we had to find another shoe store before selecting a pair of low-heeled sandals (Grandma said I could only wear sandals to church if I agreed to wear stockings, no matter how hot the morning).

But I didn't care.

So on Easter, when I heard the creaky clank of the Price bicycles coming down the road, I struggled not to jump up and down like a child. They pulled into our yard and let their bikes drop next to our garage. I tore out of the house, all semblance of being a "young lady" forgotten, and stopped in surprise.

Nina's tall and lanky form vanished inside of her buttery yellow dress. Some-one had combed out her hair and actually pressed it. Relieved of the fuzz, her golden pageboy hung down to her shoulders. She had on a pair of flat white shoes with a little bow at the toe—they might actually have been bedroom slippers—but instead of looking like my beloved walking plank, she was a graceful, joyful sprite.

I actually counted to three inside my head before turning to look at Gideon.

It was a good thing, too. Gideon's shirt was so white it hurt my eyes. His hair, with at least three inches trimmed from his afro, was neatly rounded. He was wear-ing a pair of slacks that might have been a bit too large in the waist, and a tad short—he seemed to be taller each time I saw him—but no one who looked at him would make it all the way to his feet, anyway.

Together, they were almost ridiculously handsome, and I had a flash of fear that when they got to church they might find themselves so welcome by the con-gregation they'd forget about me.

I heard Grandma and Mr. Saunders come out of the house behind us. There was a beat before Grandma spoke.

"Happy Easter, children. You certainly look like the Lord blessed you today."

"Thank you, Miss Corinne," Nina said. "My dress did turn out pretty good."

"And you, Gideon, will be a very fine escort for your sister. I'm glad you could come."

"Thank you, Miss Corinne," he echoed shyly.

We piled into the car, with Nina sitting between us in the back seat, and Mr. Saunders cruised down the highway, church songs playing all the way to Holy Redeemer. The day was god-kissed, as if He really was directing things from up in the sky somewhere, and I was so excited to be with Nina and Gideon that I forgot all about church.

That is, until we'd parked and got out of the car. I'd heard the expression 'run the gauntlet' since I was a kid, but I didn't know what it meant until, with Grandma in front of us and Mr. Saunders bringing up the rear, the five of us made our way into the building. Plenty of people were congregating in the parking lot: stout women in wide straw hats brimming with what appeared to be bouquets of fake flowers and held together with lace and ribbons; men in pin stripes and brightly colored suits with stickpins and carnations in the lapels, cufflinks twinkling and buckles shining on their pointy, two-toned shoes.

But they all went silent as we marched, like a family of geese, toward the church. Mr. Saunders carried our contribution to the Easter picnic, containers with at least two-hundred deviled eggs, and a woman in a questionably scarlet dress stepped forward and, keeping her gaze fixed on Nina and Gideon, took it out of his hands without greeting him.

If the Prices knew they were being ogled, they ignored it. Watching their feet, they walked right behind Grandma, into the church and down the main aisle to the front pews. Grandma and the churchwomen had spent hours the day before decorating the altar with white lilies draped in purple ribbons. The choir was in purple, too, and soon, when the service began, I noted that many people were in shades of white, pink and lavender.

The church was sardined. We were very quickly swallowed up by the massive, swaying crowd, and it seemed that no one paid any particular attention to us at all. We sang—Gideon had a very nice voice, and prayed with the rest of the churchgoers, with Grandma glancing our way from time to time. Nina faced straight ahead, not daring to peruse the faces of the other worshippers. Gideon seemed obsessed by the contents of the prayer book. I'd never seen anyone stare so hard at those prayers. Maybe he was looking for something to help with his family. Maybe he was praying for the two of us. Maybe he, too, was simply avoiding the others' faces. I would never know, because we never went to church together again.

The service seemed long, but I expected that. What I hadn't expected was the way Grandma's friends came forward and stared at my friends while pretending to greet her. Many openly assessed Nina's dress, shoes, Gideon's hair and pure white shirt. They spent considerably less time on me, as if they knew Grandma wouldn't allow me out of the house unless I was absolutely perfect.

Gideon and Nina and I made our way to the social hall and offered to help the ladies set up the picnic tables outside. One or two looked up, smiling, their faces freezing at the sight of my companions. I wondered what they thought they saw: two fallen angels masquerading as kids? Two fallen kids trying to "infiltrate" their church? Or were Gideon and Nina seen as something threatening to their own personal faith?

Grandma appeared from the kitchen. "You all can go straight outside to the tables," she said in a relaxed voice. "We'll be right behind you."

Gideon stared at his feet, but Nina straightened her back as she led us out into the enormous tent pitched behind the church. Groups of women were gathered around the buffet, laying out platters and casseroles. The men standing nearby talked boisterously about blue devils and huskies, and I saw Gideon incline his head instinctively in their direction.

Though I could usually think of nothing but Gideon when in his presence, that afternoon I felt like I needed police protection. People stopped speaking in mid-conversation as we passed. The silence that followed us felt deafening, and even moreso, because these were people I had come to know over the past year. Many spoke warmly to me each Sunday morning, asked about my grades and complimented me on my growing hair. Glancing from left to right, I was hurt and dismayed by the contempt in their eyes.

We retreated to the far edge of the tent, where no one else was sitting, set up three folding chairs, and sat down out of view. No one spoke. Reaching out, I took Nina and Gideon's hands and held them tightly. Tears flooded my eyes, but neither of them reacted in any way. They must have been used to being rejected. I guess they kind of expected it.

That made it so much worse, because I invited them. I'd helped Nina pick out the fabric, then sew her pretty dress. I encouraged her to attend, believing that the church people would welcome them, even if no one else did. I thought the people would respect Jesus' teaching that children should be suffered to come to him. I believed Grandma's friends, the women who worked with her in the church every single week, who'd sung in the choir with her for decades, would forgive Nina and Gideon for their mother's fall from grace.

The noise in the tent was soon deafening. The congregation descended on the food like a swarm of ants on a carcass and began to pick the animal clean. The minister got up and said a long and rambling prayer. His voice was already hoarse from shouting during the service, so the prayer seemed, as Nina might say, really crazy to me. But as soon as he finished, the roar of voicesutensilsnapkinslaughter just took over.

Suddenly I looked up. Grandma was standing there with Mr. Saunders. Though it flashed into my mind that I should let go of Nina and Gideon's hands, I didn't.

"What are you three doing?" Grandma said brightly. "If you don't get moving, all the food will be gone."

"Thank you, Miss Corinne," Nina said stiffly, "but I'm really not hungry."

Gideon grumbled something similar. When I looked up, however, I knew Grandma saw the tears in my eyes.

"This won't do," she said brusquely. "And I have a secret to tell you." She leaned down, and I again thought about how much I resembled her.

"Bethany told me you both love baked chicken and sweet potato pie, so I kept a whole container of my extra-special chicken, baked with mushrooms and crème, in the back of the refrigerator in the church. And I happen to have made a sweet potato pie just for the five of us. Since I'm only going to eat a little bit, there's probably enough for everybody else to have seconds."

Nina's hand tightened in mine. The three of us stole quick glances at each other.

"Now," Grandma said, "Mr. Saunders is going to walk back over with the three of you, and the next time I see you, you'd better have some great big heaping plates of food, with enough extra to take home for dinner tonight. I'm going back to the kitchen to get our chicken and pie. And Mr. Saunders—" he nodded in her direction—"would you be so good as to bring me a glass of that fresh lemonade?"

Soon the five of us were having our own private picnic, sitting in a circle on the wooden folding chairs, our backs to the others. Gradually we began to talk, then to laugh. Even Gideon said a thing or two, though he left most of the talking to Nina. Nina, of course, talked passionately about what she was reading in class, *For Whom the Bell Tolls*, which she kinda liked, and Grandma listened, smiling.

Mr. Saunders, who rarely had anything to say, just nodded in a friendly way and kept his gaze on Grandma, rising to refill her glass even before she could ask.

And I felt something that made me want to laugh and cry at the same time. This was the closest thing to a *real* family I'd ever known. I had a grandma who loved me and would do anything for me. A man who would do anything for her. And I had my best friend, who was also my sister, and her brother, who was also the boy I loved, sitting by my side.

And we were all there to protect each other.

nineteen.

And then it was summer, and try as hard as I might, Gideon would not go all the way with me. We spent many afternoons at the ruin, as if it was our secret castle.

"I'm going on eighteen," I'd complain, my lips swollen and body literally throbbing, "and I'm still a virgin!"

He laughed. "When you turn eighteen they can arrest you for being here with me."

"You'll be sixteen in a couple more months."

He laughed again. "Dang, CeCe," he said, pulling his clothes together, "we really shouldn't start something we can't finish."

"Why can't we finish it?"

"Because," he said.

"Because what?"

"Because it ain't right."

"But no one's gonna know."

"We're gonna know," he said.

"But we love each other."

"That," he said as he got to his feet, "is exactly the point."

He held out a hand so I could stand, too. Facing him, I waited patiently as he rearranged my clothes, checked my zippers and buttons, and pulled twigs and leaves from my hair. The wind had tossed mounds of leaves against the stone walls, and we saw them as part of our "enchanted forest."

As he turned to go I caught and held his arm.

"You're never going to make love with me, are you?"

Face turned away, he shook his head. "Some people would say I'm crazy," he admitted in a low voice. "But I'm not gonna turn you into a——a——" he stumbled over the word.

"I'm not a whore, Gideon Price!"

"You would be, CeCe. And I won't treat you that way."

"*Seriously?*"

"And you can't treat yourself that way."

"But——"

"CeCe, you see how everyone in this town act toward us, don't you? You understand no one want to give me a job—not even cleaning up or taking out the trash. Nina can't babysit nobody's kids. She can't even stand at a cash register. Everybody know that my mother don't stay with us—hell, Social Services be out at the house all the time—but they act like Nina and me stink of all the men my momma meet at that motel on the Interstate. They act like we can do something to stop her."

He kicked a small stone that lay at his feet. "Lord, CeCe—it's bad enough that they know I'm with you. You already been wrote off as trash, just for being seen with my sister. The teachers scared of Miss Corinne, so they don't fool with you too much at school. But do you think they'll ever give Nina an award, even though everybody know she the smartest person in her grade? Do you think anybody will help her get a scholarship, so she has a chance to get out?"

"No," Gideon said, "they gonna make sure she stay right here, so they can watch her fight to feed me and my brother. And for all we know, Momma might swing by and drop off another kid anytime. That's what happen with Benedictine. She know Nina can't stand by and let a little kid be hungry." He paused, looking down at me.

"So do you understand why you got to stay clean, CeCe? If anything happen, *anything* at all, at least your grandmother will stand by you. Any doctor can prove that you're not in too deep with the Prices."

"I would never let a doctor—"

"That's the *only* thing I can give you," he insisted. "It's the best way I can love you."

* * * * * * *

Sitting on our porch one day, Nina thrust a stick repeatedly into a mound of ants that had appeared at the bottom of the steps. I sat beside her, ignoring the insistent pressure of the wooden slats against the bottom of my thighs.

"You and Gid getting married?" she asked, out of the blue.

"To who?"

"To each other, crazy."

"If he asked me," I said.

"What would you say?"

"I'd say *hell, yes!*"

"Even though?"

"There's no even though, Nina."

"You sure?"

"Of course I'm sure!"

"He can't give you nothing," she said.

"I don't want anything but him and you."

"We would have to leave."

"Maybe."

"This place crazy."

"That's true," I said, "but still."

"You just saying that 'cause you got Miss Corinne," Nina said, accurately reading my mind. "It would be different if you was here on your own."

"Nothing could make it any different, Nina. Nothing."

There was a long silence. I couldn't tell if she was thinking about my words or thinking about what to say next.

"He love you, CeCe. Really. This is not a game or a joke."

"You think I'm kidding?" I asked.

"I think you don't know what you doing."

I stared down at my feet, which were bare despite the ant nest. Grandma had asked me to be careful not to step on anything, whether insect, animal or person, that might hurt me. But I was going on eighteen, it was summer and I was in love.

"You know I love him," I said very quietly, "but Nina, I love you, too."

She lowered her head, and her stick was still. "Yeah, I know you do."

"When I'm with him, I'm also with you. Nothing's going to happen unless you're right there beside us."

"That's silly."

"No, it's not. I've been thinking about it for months and months. This isn't like some stupid movie or TV show. I would give up anything to be with you and your brother. Anything. I don't care how hard it is, or where we have to go, or how we have to live."

"So what's gonna happen to us, CeCe?"

"You're gonna graduate and get a real job."

"Where?"

"I don't know. Maybe Raleigh," I said. "Maybe Gideon and Benedictine can come live with you. Then I'll graduate and follow you. When Gideon finishes we'll be a big old family."

"And you and Gid gonna settle down?"

"We could take turns watching Benedictine while we go to college classes."

"How we gonna pay for things?"

"If all three of us get a job," I said, "we can afford our own place."

"Furniture?" she asked.

"Goodwill."

"Clothes?"

"Goodwill."

"Goodwill for everything?"

"We don't need much," I said.

"Just clothes and food?"

"A tee-shirt or two and some jeans. Some rice and potatoes."

"Dang, CeCe, that's not enough."

"It's enough," I said.

"You ever try living on rice and potatoes?"

"Come on, Nina. Try to think positive."

"I'm thinking real life," she said.

"Real *bad* life."

"Real *necessary* life."

"You ever heard of a 'daydream'?" I said.

"You ever heard of a nightmare?"

"Everybody started out with nothing, Nina. We just have to try."

"I been trying," she said. "My whole life."

"And you got to keep on trying."

"You think I'm not?"

We sat like that for a time. A bee wandered by, then dove into a scarlet rose.

"CeCe," she said softly, "you think there somebody in the world for me?"

"Of course there is."

"But he have to be crazy."

"I'm crazy, and you're my best friend. I know that sooner or later you're gonna meet your best guy friend. And then he'll be in love with you, too."

* * * * * *

To me, Nina and Gideon Price were two of the most beautiful human beings on the planet. I just couldn't understand why nobody else seemed to see it. Then a thought began to form in my mind—a kind of grudging curiosity. I think the idea first came to me at church, when I saw how the people treated them. It didn't make sense that they saw the two people sitting next to me so differently from how I saw them. It was as if they saw aliens with two heads, while I was seeing Gideon and Nina. I began to worry that someone was making a mistake.

I knew that could happen because people made mistakes all the time. Beneath the surface, I was actually *very* different from the person Grandma saw when she looked at me. The *real* Bethany lurked, paced and prowled real close to the nice girl who went to school every day and always minded her teachers. It took only the slightest provocation, the tiniest spark, to send me careening right back into the spitting, clawing, deadly Bethany imported from Ohio. And I wondered whether in their natural habitat, Nina and Gideon became someone different, too.

I began to bug both Gideon and Nina about taking me home to the house they lived in at night. The house they never wanted anyone to see. I asked where the house was. How far away. What street it was on. If they had neighbors.

They both gave me plain, simple, empty answers: the house was 'over that way.' It was about ten or fifteen minutes away. The street was a dirt road. They didn't like their neighbors.

So, with nothing solid to set in the concrete of my mind, the question hung out there, like that unreachable itch between your shoulder blades.

The answer came sooner than I expected. Nina was at our house one day, looking through a new haul of library books, when Grandma's phone rang. I answered, and to my surprise, someone asked for my friend. She listened without speaking and hung up, her face grim.

"That was my aunt. She bringing Benedictine back to the house. I got to go."

"She called you *here*?"

"Where else would I be?"

"She has Grandma's number?"

"Everybody in Blissfield know Miss Corinne, silly." She began packing up the books, her face set.

"You okay?" I asked.

"Not really. She been doing that a lot, lately. Like, now that he bigger, she don't want to feed him, so she dump him on me when he get hungry."

"Do you have food enough for him?"

"We get by, CeCe." She sighed and stood up resolutely.

"Wait—why don't we go get him and bring him here for dinner?"

"Here?"

"Sure. I can make something—like macaroni and cheese. He likes macaroni, doesn't he? I know Grandma won't mind."

"That's nice, but I got to cook for Gideon when his football practice over."

"Nina, I'll make macaroni for all of us. Then Grandma won't have to cook for me."

"You sure?" She raised an eyebrow skeptically.

"Let me go ask her!"

I found Grandma in her room, painting her nails and listening to *Judge Judy*. I asked if I could take the car to pick up Nina's baby brother, stop by the store, and make macaroni and cheese for Nina and her brothers that evening.

Grandma's keen eyes took me in, but then she reached for her pocketbook. "Just be sure you make enough macaroni for me, too," she said, handing me a five-dollar bill and the car keys.

Soon I was guiding her monster car out of the red driveway and along the road. I was keenly aware of the drainage ditches on either side of the street, and the small rocks flying up from under the wheels.

Nina didn't offer much in the way of directions as we made our way off the main highway and into a labyrinth of narrow dirt roads, some so rarely used that they were overgrown with grass. Keeping my eyes fixed ahead of me, I had little chance to really look at anything else.

I could feel Nina regretting her decision long before we rolled to a stop. Her silence was heavy and deep, like still water, and I was unprepared for what was in her face when she suddenly turned to look at me.

"Let's go back," she said in a low voice.

"What? Why, Nina?"

"I don't want to do this."

"Do what? Pick up your brother or eat macaroni?"

"You know what I mean, CeCe!"

"I'm your friend, Nina!"

"That's why!"

"What's why?"

"That's why I don't want to do this!" she said.

"You won't let me make dinner for you?"

"I won't let you come to the house."

"What house? I don't even see it!"

Involuntarily she followed my gaze. Nothing was visible but a thicket of overgrown bushes and trees.

"There nothing to see," she said.

"Okay. So what's the problem?"

"I told you," she said stonily. "I don't want you to come to my house."

Her voice had grown hard and ragged, and my heart lurched with sadness and shame. I had pushed her into this to satisfy my curiosity, and to push it any farther would take away what was left of her pride.

"Okay," I said softly. "I'll wait for you here."

She clambered out of the car, slamming the door behind her. She had to take tall steps to make it through the uncut crass, and she was moving with the angry determination of someone who hated doing what she had to do.

I waited.

The crickets were so loud I thought my head might explode. The ruins of what must have been a shack nested on the opposite side of the road, a dogwood exploding though the missing planks of its walls. An abandoned well stood near the car, and I thought about a stupid Japanese horror movie I'd seen a couple of years earlier. It was always the worst when the ghosts came out in broad daylight. In fact—

The car door opened and Nina instructed someone to get in beside me. A little boy, his butter-caramel skin brightened to a golden sheen by the summer sun, crawled onto the front seat and sat down. Clad in an oversize navy tee-shirt and black basketball shorts, he immediately reached for the radio and heat dials, giggling wildly, and Nina, who had squeezed in beside him, grabbed his little hands.

"Ben—Benny, you listen! You can wreck the car by touching the wrong thing while CeCe driving."

"Who CeCe?" the child asked, swiveling his head as if he'd only just noticed my presence.

"This her car, Benny. You got to show it some respect, like you gonna respect her and her grandmother. You hear me?"

The child turned his face to me and I saw he had Gideon's eyes.

"Hi," I said, a bit nervously.

He didn't answer, but his smile was glorious, unchecked and unconcerned.

"Let's go," Nina said.

I turned the car around by maneuvering it back and forth very carefully, mindful that glass shards, nails, and even metal, lurked in the tall grass. Nina kept up a steady stream of warnings, as if talking fast enough might make Benedictine behave.

At the Piggly Wiggly the little boy ran up and down the aisles, behaving as if the store was his own private NASCAR track. Nina called after him to no avail, and the sight of her anxious face seemed to spur him into overdrive.

I snatched several boxes of elbow macaroni, a package of Velveeta, and made it to the checkout before anything flew off the shelves. Nina appeared with her brother in her arms, kicking madly. As we drove toward the high school I began to understand that Benedictine wasn't like other kids: he didn't seem to cool down or run out of gas. He was tuned to a different frequency, or spoke a different language, or worse, he was a guy in a silent film, moving faster than people in the regular world.

Nina didn't meet my eyes at any point, from the time we left her house until Gideon turned up, walking away from the high school with his sports bag over his shoulder.

He twisted around at the sound of the car, perhaps thinking of trying to hitch a ride, and his face brightened as he recognized us. I slowed down carefully, pulling to a stop alongside him.

He got into the back seat, grinning, and Benedictine scrambled from the front and dove straight into his arms. They play-wrestled all the way to Grandma's, with grunts and squeals and guffaws and fake cries of pain between flying arms and legs and elbows and knees.

As we rolled into the drive Grandma appeared behind the house in her favorite apron, a mixing spoon in her hand.

"Hi, kids," she said warmly. "I need some help out back."

Gideon was holding his baby brother around the waist, the small boy's legs pinwheeling through his giggles.

"Coming, Miss Corinne," Gideon replied respectfully, carrying his load slowly toward the picnic table and tire swing under the trees. A silver barrel was set on the table.

"I have a surprise," Grandma said.

Nina and I went into the house and straight to the kitchen. Through the window we could see Grandma showing the two boys how to churn the great big drum, which turned out to be an ice-cream maker.

I filled Grandma's largest pot with water, salted it, and set it on the stove. With the heat turned up, I set to cubing the Velveeta with Nina's help. She wasn't talking, and her gaze remained low. I knew she was very unhappy.

Outside there was laughter. I saw her look nervously toward the window. Grandma was encouraging Gideon and Benedictine, whose hands were side-by-side on the handle of the barrel, turning it faster. All three were laughing—Benedictine madly and gloriously, Gideon easily, and Grandma nostalgically. She had never laughed that way with me.

The water boiled. I poured in the macaroni and tossed in two teaspoons of cooking oil. Nina stood awkwardly beside the table, her gaze shifting between the stove and the merriment under the trees. It was almost as if she didn't know which was more real.

"Hey, big sis," I said, just loud enough to be heard over the fizzing water. "You alright?"

"I don't know."

"What is it?"

She shrugged.

"Nina," I repeated, "what is it?"

She looked back toward the trees. "CeCe, my auntie don't want him back."

"Why?" My question came out as a whisper.

"She said he out of control. Tearing up her place. And she don't like his daddy, either. She don't want him coming around."

"But that's her bro—"

"She said she don't want him or Benny in her house no more."

I stared at Nina. "So what's going to happen?"

She shrugged again. If I hadn't been there, she might have started to cry, but I knew she'd try not to cry in front of me.

"What about preschool? Like, Head Start or something?"

She shrugged yet again, blankly. I looked toward Grandma, who was now sitting beneath the tree, watching Gideon churn as Benedictine ran wildly across the backyard, jumping up and down every few feet.

"Nina, if he doesn't have a sitter—"

"I have to take care of him," she said.

"But you have school."

"He can't stay in the house by hisself."

"There must be someone who'd look after him."

"You think?" she chuckled bitterly.

"What about a neighbor?"

She shook her head.

"Other family?"

"No."

"Your mother?"

She shot me a haunted look.

"Maybe Grandma can help you find somebody," I said.

"You seen how they acted at the church, right?"

"But everybody can't be like those stupid people."

"They been that way our whole life."

"But this is different, Nina. He's a little kid."

"Gid and I was little kids, too."

"But—"

"We raised ourself, CeCe. My momma showed up every once in a while, then went away again. I like it better that way. If she stay longer, things get...." Her voice trailed off.

We were silent. Benedictine was leaning on the swing, swaying back and forth and shrieking wildly.

I saw Grandma rise and walk toward the house, automatically stepping over the thick roots of the tree. She was still smiling privately, as if remembering something that gave her pleasure. The screen door squeaked, then slammed behind her. She appeared in the kitchen door.

"Looks like somebody lost their winning lottery ticket," she remarked, glancing between Nina and me.

"Something like that," I said, returning to the pasta. I dug in the back of a cabinet and brought out the colander. Without being asked, Nina joined me at the stove, lifted the heavy pot, and together we drained the pasta water.

Grandma watched, arms crossed.

I dumped the macaroni back into the pot and added the cheese. Grandma went to the fridge and handed me the milk carton, then watched as I stirred milk into the melted cheese.

"Smells good," she remarked. "Need a little butter?"

I nodded, keeping my eyes on the food. Nina was standing beside me, her face tilted oddly, sadly.

"Nina," Grandma said gently, "help me get some plates and bowls. Looks like the dinner is about ready, and I know your brother is tired of churning the ice cream."

Glad for something to do, Nina helped Grandma set the picnic table while Gideon chased Benedictine around the yard. I poured a pitcher of water—all the ice had gone into the ice cream maker—and then brought out the pot. We sat together, with Ben between Nina and Gideon, and Grandma and me across the table. Grandma said grace, and I ladled out the mac.

For a long time no one spoke, but we ate a lot. *A lot*. Benedictine polished off several bowls. His sister and brother both looked like they were going to die of shame at the way he tore into his food. Maybe this was the first food he'd had that day. That *week*?

Grandma started a conversation about the prospects for the football team in the fall, and Gideon answered in short, polite sentences. Nina still wasn't talking, even after her second bowl of hand-made banana-pecan ice cream, and though Grandma didn't visibly react, I knew from the concern in her eyes that she was very aware of my friend's silence.

Benedictine ran non-stop until dark, when Grandma piled all of us into her car and drove to the beginning (or end) of their street. Nina reluctantly accepted a big bowl of leftover macaroni. We watched the trio disappear into the darkness, even as the noises of the night swallowed them whole.

Neither of us spoke all the way home. But that night, after I'd washed the dishes, bathed and climbed into bed, Grandma came into my room.

"So, what was going on tonight?" she asked without preamble, sinking down at the end of my mattress.

"I don't know," I said, avoiding her gaze.

"You sure?"

When I didn't answer, she ran her hand back and forth across the chenille spread, and I knew she was feeling the soft nubs of thread beneath her fingers.

"Princess, I know you're trying to respect Nina's confidence, but if you don't tell me there's nothing I can do to help."

I wavered. If Grandma learned about Nina leaving school to care for Benedictine, she might call the police and they might take Benedictine away. But they might take Gideon away, too. And then Nina might also be sent somewhere, because she couldn't possibly live there all alone.

"Those kids really are brave," Grandma remarked lightly. "I hope someone is looking out for them."

Still, I didn't speak. She waited, observing the indecision in my face.

What does betrayal look like? I wondered. Who, at that moment, deserved my allegiance more?

Of course she saw that, too.

She shifted. "You know, all those years when I was a teacher, I learned a whole lot about people. Even though I was working with children every day, I learned even more about their parents. You see, some children were very poor, but they were also very loved. Other children had plenty to eat, but when they went home at night, they saw violence and cruelty. Then there were the kids who had nothing. Nobody was looking after them, and they had nobody to serve as their guide. I think those kids were the saddest, because they were looking at everybody else, and just picking and choosing who, and how, to be. Who to follow. Who not to follow. And they were in mighty need of love."

She smoothed my quilt and tucked it carefully around my shoulders. "Princess, I don't know what you're not telling me about those three children, but I *do* know when I see kids who really need help. So ask yourself this: how are you helping them tonight?"

Her voice wasn't mean, but it was serious. She stood and went to the door. She turned off the light and closed the door behind her.

* * * * * * *

I couldn't sleep for most of that night. Things were changing so fast I couldn't keep up, and I didn't know what to do.

If Nina really was going to watch Benedictine during the day, the boy's father would be coming to the house. Maybe even when Gideon wasn't there. Though it was hard to think about, I knew it was wrong, and I knew she wasn't safe. I knew Nina would go to her grave trying to protect her little brother. But who would protect her?

This troubling thought is what made me get up with the sun, dress, ask Grandma for the car keys, and drive, just as the day climbed up into the sky, across town and back down the dirt path and into the dense overgrowth.

The car made a shuddering, clicking noise as I turned off the motor, and then all was silent. Around me stood the ruins of the other shacks. I got out of the car and closed the door softly. Treading up the grassy, overgrown path, I made my way toward the shrubs where Nina had vanished the afternoon before.

A narrow footpath opened behind the shrubs and I followed it over a knoll and down a short incline. The thicket opened to reveal a small frame hut, raised on cinderblocks, and no larger than a single unpainted room. It had no porch; a cracked cinderblock beneath the door served as a step. The one window was missing a pane. A square of cardboard covered with aluminum foil was duck-taped in its place. The walls were raw, wind and sun-blistered, and the roof, consisting of peeling sheets of asphalt, was sunken in some places.

I stood at the top of the rise, knowing that Nina had never intended for me to see this. Knowing that she would be hurt and enraged if I came there, uninvited and unannounced. Knowing that I had violated their privacy.

And I had no idea what Gideon might feel.

What was the right thing to do? Why had I even come?

I had just turned to go when I heard the door open behind me.

"CeCe! CeCe—don't go."

Nina was standing in the open doorway in a tattered sweatshirt and a pair of Gideon's sweatpants. The pants hung off her bony frame like a scarecrow. Her hair was brushed back and covered by an oily bandana.

Slowly I faced her.

"I knew you was coming," she said. "Saw it in your face last night. It's okay. You can come inside."

Awash with guilt, I walked down the short slope and stepped on the cinder block placed in front of the door. She moved back and I was inside.

The room smelled of cooking oil, camphor, warm bodies and Palmolive soap. A half-moon table with two chairs stood against one wall, and two mattresses lay on the floor. Remarkably, the back of the room had a small sink, a humming, waist-tall fridge and a two-burner electric stove. A curtain separated the final corner from the rest of the room. I suspected a toilet—or bucket—might be back there.

Gideon was on one of the mattresses, curled beneath a blanket with Benedictine, who was sleeping soundly. Gideon turned over and sat up sleepily at the sound of my arrival.

"Oh, wow, CeCe—"

"It's alright, Gid. I invited her in," Nina said.

He reached for the pair of shorts at the foot of the bed and leaned back to thrust his legs into them.

"Nina, I'm so sorry," I began, but she raised her hands and shrugged.

"Sooner or later," she said. "What difference do it make?"

"I was worried about you."

"I know. You want some coffee?"

"Coffee? Grandma doesn't let me drink co—"

My words fell between us like stones. I realized how childish I sounded. How adult she had to be. How vastly different our lives were.

"Well," I stammered, "I guess if you have some, I could drink some this morning."

She paused, taking measure of me, even as I understood that she very likely had nothing else to offer.

"Sit down," she said, nodding toward the table.

We were speaking in regular voices, so I figured they weren't afraid of waking Benedictine. Gideon climbed to his feet and stepped outside, closing the door firmly behind him. I didn't ask where he was going. One glance at the curtain in the corner told me that there was no privacy for certain things.

Nina set a small teapot on a burner and took a carton of milk from the fridge. When she opened it I could see cheese and butter, some greens and eggs and a loaf of bread inside. I also saw the bowl of leftover macaroni.

She kept her back turned and didn't speak. I could hardly raise my eyes from the table's chipped surface. Outside birds chorused furiously. A plane roared high overhead. A Stephen King paperback lay on the floor beside the chair.

Gideon returned, leaving the door open behind him. Shirtless, hair flat on one side, eyes a little crusty, his hot earthy smell made me breathe a little faster.

I couldn't tell if he was angry or not. In this small space he seemed enormous, his rounded shoulders and slim waist almost comical, especially in contrast to his sister's rickety frame. He looked down at me, face empty of all emotion.

"I was up all night," I said in explanation.

Gideon cast a quick glance at his brother, whose undisturbed breathing continued.

"I want to help," I said.

Nina grunted softly from her place at the stove.

"Do you want me to talk to Grandma?" I asked hesitantly.

"About what?"

"About—about helping you."

"What can she do?" Nina asked, turning around to face me.

"I don't know. Maybe she could babysit."

Gideon and Nina glanced at each other. Then he shook his head. "No, CeCe, she might try for a coupla days, but it wouldn't be right."

"Why not?"

"Well, he—I mean, our momma—" Gideon stammered.

"I know what you're about to say," I argued, "but Grandma and I don't care!"

"The rest of Blissfield do," Nina said, walking over to the table. "You see, it's one thing for Miss Corinne to have us over to sit in the yard. It something entirely different if she lets us in the house."

"But you come over all the time, Nina."

"*I* come over," Nina said, again glancing at Gideon. "But boys is different. When I come in, Blissfield calls it charity. When boys come in, they think, well, they see it as dirty."

"*Dirty?*"

"They believe she exposing you to our momma," Nina said with a soft hitch in her voice.

"But Grandma knows about me and Gideon!" I argued. "She never said I shouldn't—"

"CeCe," Nina said quietly, "nobody in Blissfield ever been as kind to us as Miss Corinne. Nobody. But there's limits to what even she can do. And besides—you saw Ben yesterday. I'm about the only person who can make him mind."

"But your aunt—"

"She gave up, CeCe. When he was a baby she could put him in a playpen and leave him there. Now he can climb out and she was just yelling at him and hitting him all day."

I glanced over at the sleeping child, whose deep exhaustion seemed almost unnatural.

"So what are you planning to do?" I asked.

"We have two choices," she said. Behind her a sudden hissing announced that the coffee had boiled and would soon be ready to drink. The aroma filled the room and I suddenly very much wanted a cup. She turned off the heat and filled three plastic cups with the black liquid, then poured milk into each.

"Sorry," she said as she turned back to the table. "No sugar."

She sat across from me, and Gideon leaned in the doorway, cradling his cup in his hands and blowing on it.

"Well," Nina went on, "either I stay home this year and try to finish next year, when Ben is big enough for kindergarten, or Gid stay home during the day this year so I can finish, and he take night classes in the trade program at the high school."

"Night classes?" I repeated dumbly.

"I could learn auto mechanics," he said.

I looked at him speechlessly. He stared into his cup as if he could read his fortune.

"You're thinking about leaving school?" I asked.

"No, just transferring to night school."

"I could help you with your homework—"

The sister and brother again exchanged looks. "No, CeCe," he said patiently. "That wouldn't make any difference."

"But what about football?"

"Football don't matter," he said unconvincingly.

"But you're the quarterback."

"Look: even if we won every game between now and my senior year, let's get real. I'm never getting recruited. Scouts don't come to Booker T. Washington High School in Blissfield, North Carolina."

"But what if they did?"

"I still have three more years before I graduate. If I do night school, I can probably get a job in a garage somewhere by next summer. If Nina working, too, maybe we can afford to move somewhere different."

"But if you leave school now you'll never go to college!" I said.

Both of them laughed as if they'd heard something incredibly silly. "CeCe," Gideon said softly, "that may happen one day, but it won't be for a while."

"If you don't go to college you'll be stuck here," I said.

"We can't worry about that right now, either," Nina said. "Right now we got to make sure Ben's okay. I *already* need to get a job on the weekend. That boy can really eat."

Nina and Gideon were talking about things I had never seriously thought about: feeding and clothing and caring for another person. Finding someplace to live. Working to pay for a roof, water, heat, electricity.

I sipped the bitter coffee and looked around the small room, now seeing that there was order, even in that small space. I'd noticed the clothesline strung up between the trees outside. Neat stacks of folded clothing were placed beside the mattresses. In the kitchen the dishes sat on a small cabinet, with a couple of pots and a frying pan placed neatly on a shelf overlooking the cooking area.

"What if I got a job, too?" I asked tentatively. "I could help out with the bills."

They exchanged glances. "Miss Corinne would never let you do that," Nina said.

"I could do whatever I want with my money."

"Your grandma will take those car keys and make sure you never see us again!" Nina said. "The only thing she's interested in is you graduating high school and going to college. And anyway—you a Castle—"

"So?"

"So nobody going to give you a job."

"Then what can I do to help you?" I said, my voice cracking, my eyes filling with tears. "Don't you understand? I love you. I love *both* of you."

Tears came into Nina's eyes, too. "We know. We love you, too."

"You can't go away! You can't leave me! I can't make it without—" my voice faded at the look on their faces.

"Yes, you can," Nina said gruffly. "Because you got to. Just like we got to take care of Benny right now."

Nina got up and moved like an old woman toward the coffee pot. Gideon shifted restlessly in the door. I glanced from my sister to her brother, my heart swelling.

I would again never feel as powerless in my life. Even when I watched my father killing my mother.

twenty.

The world was empty without Nina and Gideon. Or without Nina and Gideon as I knew them.

Gideon produced a note from his mother giving him permission to leave the regular high school, much to the chagrin of the principal, the coaches, the cheerleaders and many of the students, to attend the night school program in auto mechanics. Nina got a job on the custodial staff, taking care of the grounds before school, during her lunch hour and the last period of the day. Our lunches beneath the trees watching Gideon and his friends, were over. In fact, though I saw Nina in the halls, I almost never saw Gideon during the week.

And the weekends were worse.

On Saturdays Gideon worked as a stock boy at the Piggly Wiggly, and on Sundays Nina washed dishes at Joe's Catfish Shack, a white family's restaurant on the edge of town (no one Black would hire her). I went to the grocery store to steal a couple of minutes with Gideon behind the dumpsters, where we kissed and shared cigarettes—Gideon had suddenly begun to smoke, while I only faked it. Nina barely smiled when I passed her in the mornings, as she weeded and picked up trash, or swept the entrance to the school at the close of day. Though I offered to stay and help her, she brushed me aside with an absent nod.

"I don't have time, CeCe. I got to get home so Gideon won't be late to his class."

"I don't mind—"

"CeCe, if they see us talking, I could lose my job!"

"Nina—"

"Look," she said coldly, "I got to buy food and stuff or those people from the government might step in and take my brother."

"But you're eighteen—"

"That don't matter to them."

"Maybe your aunt—"

"No, CeCe. Ben won't mind nobody but Gid and me. He different from other kids—you seen it—and if they take him away I don't know where he might end up." Her shoulders drooped. "I know he crazy, but he my brother and I got to look out for him."

Over the following weeks Gideon morphed so fast that sometimes I wondered if he was the same boy who'd thrown the football back and forth, day after lazy day. Now he was training in a garage beside older students, veterans, ex-cons, and guys who were sent by the state when their unemployment benefits ran out. He talked less, smoked more, and began to cuss whenever he spoke. Though he was barely sixteen, he gained the rough swagger of a man, and I could hardly believe it when he looked beyond me one day, his gaze fastened on the rolling hips of a lushly-built woman pushing a shopping cart across the parking lot.

"She got magnets on her ass or something?" I asked.

He flicked the butt of his cigarette into the tall grass.

"Hey," I said, waving my hand up and down in front of his face, "want to catch a ride with her?"

His troubling gaze returned to mine and softened. "Sorry, baby. Just tired, I guess."

"Tired of what?"

He didn't answer. Our football team was floundering without him, and I wondered how it felt to be cut off from all the guys who once considered him their hero.

"Look," I said, "why don't you come over after work tonight?"

"It'll be dark already, and it's way too cold to sit outside."

"Grandma won't mind it you come in."

"You better ax her, first."

"Okay, then. I'll get the car and we can go somewhere. Want to see a movie? Get something to eat?"

"Don't got dough for that."

"I've got enough."

"No, CeCe."

"Then we can just drive."

He shook his head and removed another Marlboro from his pack. "Nina and I been thinking that if we could put some cash aside, maybe we can pay somebody to look after Ben and I can come back to regular class. It might not be till the winter, but at least—" he paused, drew hard on his cigarette and snapped his lighter shut.

"You don't like the auto mechanic thing?" I asked softly.

"It's alright. I mean, it'll get me a job and I don't have to stay here to do it. But—" He looked at his scuffed gym shoes. "But I wouldn't mind being back with—with you."

I reached for him then. He smelled of cigarette, of cold, of the sausage kept in storage in the back of the store. He didn't smell of Gideon.

"I'm still with you," I said emphatically. "I am always with you. I will never, ever leave you."

He smiled down at me, wrapped his arms around my back and kissed my forehead. But he didn't respond.

"Gideon, do you hear me? Do you feel me here, holding you?"

He held me closer, and I smelled his unfamiliar smell.

He didn't respond.

* * * * * * *

I waited, looking for him everywhere, imagining I might glance up and he'd be outside the house on his bicycle, ready to ride with me to school. Or he might turn up at lunch, the ball floating lazily through the air. Or I might just hear his voice outside my classroom when I made my way outside one day.

But it didn't happen. And Nina, who was sent indoors to clean the auditorium and administration offices over the lunch hour, was nowhere to be found. She called Grandma's house sometimes, but her conversation was simple and empty, as it had been when we first met, as if she was devolving from the person who loved to talk about books, dumb teachers, and the crazy lint brains.

With Nina gone, I found myself alone in a way I'd never been before. I hadn't realized how close we really were. How much she understood me without my having to explain. How accepting she was of my "craziness," and how she never, ever questioned me about my past, or showed any jealousy toward my privileges, or held me to my promises about the future.

Grandma asked me what happened, and I told her that Nina had a job and Gideon wanted to learn to be an auto-mechanic. She didn't answer. I figured it was just a matter of time before someone at church told her the truth, because it was nearly impossible that someone didn't know what was going on in the tiny house in the woods. Grandma watched me, as always, and gently offered to teach me to quilt, but without Nina to help with the project I really wasn't interested.

I did fine in school, and Grandma mentioned that it was time for me to start thinking about college. Though one part of my heart felt a lurch of happiness at the idea that I might soon be living on a campus, entirely on my own, another part of my heart knew that leaving for college would also mean I was breaking the promise I'd made over and over again to the brother and sister I loved.

My mother occasionally sent a short, bland letter that only mentioned my father in passing, and in fact, I started to believe that Copley had faded from my body like old bruises. Though the places I'd been hurt were still vaguely tender to the touch, all visible signs of the injuries were long gone.

I could hardly imagine Akron now. My memories were like old Polaroids, fading with time. My mother's love, too, had been supplanted by Grandma's, which, though no stronger, seemed firmer and more protective. My mother had taken the punches intended for me; Grandma stopped the punches from even being thrown.

Now that I was alone, I found myself thinking about my past more often. School in Akron wasn't real different from school in Blissfield, and I lived around Black people in both communities. I didn't miss the winter, and realized how much I really hated the snow. I came to understand that I loved digging in the earth beside Grandma. I could no more picture myself returning to the north than I could picture a future without Gideon and Nina, even if—at that moment—life had forced us apart. I was certain that Blissfield was my future, and that certainty kept me peaceful and allowed me to accept the circumstances of our separation. LaToya's sister had done it—run away with a guy from the Army—so even if I had to convince Gideon to elope, there was no doubt in my mind, even for a moment, that one day soon I would be Bethany Castle Price.

* * * * * * *

The day after Thanksgiving Mr. Saunders drove Grandma and me to Roanoke Rapids to get me a winter coat. The weather had just started to turn really ugly, with cold rain replacing the showers that made the earth smell deep, sensual and alive. When I slipped my arms into the jacket I'd worn the year before, Grandma's brows went up.

"That's over and done with, Princess."

"But it's my favorite!"

"You're not getting any taller," Grandma observed, setting down the cup of tea she'd been drinking, "but you're certainly getting more grownuppity."

"Grownuppity? What's that supposed to mean?"

"Too big for her britches," she laughed, "but too young to do anything about it."

"I wouldn't mind getting a job," I said, Nina and Gideon entering my mind.

For a moment she seemed to consider the idea, then she shook her head slowly. "Here in Blissfield there's nothing much you could do, Princess. We don't have many stores, and most restaurants use their own family members as waitresses. I don't want you in anybody's kitchen, or taking care of anyone else's children. Too much can go wrong for a young woman in another woman's house. No, Bethany. For now, you're doing exactly what you should be doing: going to school and behaving yourself."

Now that the old ladies had given up Grandma's boutique, the store in Roanoke Rapids had sexier and more stylish clothing than before. We walked through the displays, with Grandma looking critically at the thin, short jackets that were in style that winter, before suggesting that we shop around before making a decision. We drove through the small city, passing a number of restaurants and churches, before coming to a strip mall in the last block of the shopping district. Goodwill had taken over what appeared to be a sprawling former supermarket next to a brand new dress store, and the parking lot was brimming with cars.

As we approached the doors to the store, I glanced in the window of the Goodwill and felt my heart move over in my chest: there was Nina, her back turned, sorting through a loaded rack. She was wearing men's clothing, as she had when we first met, her unstyled hair simply stuffed beneath a baseball cap. I told Grandma I'd catch up with her in a minute, then took off to find out how Nina happened to be there.

The Goodwill smelled of stale bodies, damp wool and mold. Crowds of people filled the aisles, digging through the racks and racks of donated clothing. Nina had moved on from the men's to the children's clothing by the time I made my way through the throng and came up behind her.

"Hey, Nina," I began, reaching for her arm.

She turned abruptly, eyes round, and took an involuntary step backwards, nearly upsetting the heavily laden rack. Several women reacted with annoyance, grabbing the rack to keep it from tipping over.

"What's up?" I asked, surprised at her response.

Her eyes registered shock at finding me there, but something else was in her face. Though I wouldn't have believed it possible, what I saw was fear.

"What you doing here?" she asked coldly.

"I saw you through the window and came in to say hi."

Her eyes leapt to the window and swept the parking lot. "Did you drive here?"

"No. I'm with Grandma and Mr. Saunders."

"Oh," she said. "You better go find them."

"I don't have to. They're next store waiting for me."

"Well, don't make them wait."

I stared at her. Her face, which once shone with pleasure at the sight of me, remained closed, as if I was a stranger.

"What's going on?" I asked quietly. Around us women were working their way along the rack. One nudged Nina, and she took another step backward.

"I'm real busy," she said.

"So busy you can't speak?"

"Hi," she said, turning away.

"That's the best you can do?" I said.

"What do you want, CeCe?"

"Well, I didn't *want* anything," I answered, stung. "It's just that we never talk anymore and—"

"You see I'm busy," she said, "but you want to start some craziness right here in the middle of this store? Why you got to act like a dummy?"

"I'm not—I mean, I only wanted to—" my words vanished and I stood like a fool, tears in my eyes. Not wanting her to see me cry, I turned away. "Go fuck yourself, Nina," I said, making for the door.

I had only taken two or three steps when I felt a familiar surge in my chest. Copley had been buried for so many months that at first I was frightened by how powerfully he surfaced in me. Then, finding a kind of steadying joy in the rush of clarity brought on by my anger, I turned back to face her—or rather, to face her down.

She had moved on to the next rack, and I noticed for the first time that she had a plastic shopping basket brimming with clothing at her feet. As she made her way down the aisle she was pushing it with one foot so she could use both hands to better comb through the clothing.

"I want to know what I'm supposed to have done to you," I said in my clear, low, Copley voice when I came up beside her.

She spun around, recognizing Copley, too. I had forgotten that back in the early days she'd seen me take on the lint brains and the *burtle,* and she knew *exactly* what Copley could, and was perfectly willing to do.

"CeCe," she said softly, "I don't want no trouble."

I felt a riff of joy at the fear in her words. "Then don't treat me like shit."

"I'm not, CeCe. I'm just—I can't—I don't want no trouble today."

"I thought I was your best friend," I said coldly.

"You are, but right now I—"

If I hadn't been so angry, so hurt, I would have heard the plea in her voice. "You *what?*" I said quietly. Too quietly. Even I was surprised at how low and tense my voice had become.

"I've got to get this done real fast—"

"I'm not stopping you."

"I *said* hi, CeCe. Let me call you when I get home." Her eyes left mine and shot back and forth, scanning the room.

"That's all you got to say to me?"

"Can't you just listen? This ain't about you!"

"Then what the fuck is it about?" I heard my voice, but I didn't recognize it.

At that very instant she seemed to shrink before my eyes. I felt a shadow fall over her, and I turned in time to see the man walk up on her, too close to her, and stand just a hairbreadth away.

He wasn't tall—I'm sure Gideon was taller—but he was thick, and packed, and all things mean. About the color of a white man who needed a bath very badly, his skin had a transparency that made it possible to see the reddened bones beneath his flesh. The eyes he turned on Nina were an empty silvery blue; his lips were heavy, and his face was dominated by his large-pored nose. The straight, thinning hair above his shirt collar was a yellowing grey.

"You standing over here talking shit?" he said to her. The voice was deep, and although I could hear every syllable, I doubted anyone else on the aisle had made out a thing.

She lowered her eyes. "I just ran into this girl from school."

"So fucking what?"

Nina glanced at me involuntarily, and the man's eyes followed her gaze.

The stamp of his features marked Benedictine's face, and for a terrible moment I thought I saw Gideon in him, too. His impatience with Nina translated to a lack of any particular relationship, except that he needed her to take care of the child no one else wanted. Planting his feet and crossing his swollen arms, he watched as she shakily went back to sorting through the clothes.

I could see his gaze taking in her roughly brushed hair, uncertain hands and cowed silence. And then his head rolled sideways and he was looking at me.

Or rather, he was looking at Copley.

"Yeah?" he grunted.

I didn't speak.

"Do I know you?" he said.

At that instant the image of a swine entered my mind, and I envisioned his thick head on a pig's body. I did nothing to hide my contempt.

As if reading my mind, he said very casually, "you need to take your little dyke ass away from here before I teach you something about men you don't want to know."

Nina's hands froze on a boy's Detroit Lions tee-shirt. She didn't turn her head, but instead kept her gaze fixed blindly on the clothing rack.

"Nina," I said calmly, "if you want, you can come home with us."

The man's eyes ricocheted to Nina and back to me. "Who the fuck is you?"

"Nina," I repeated, "there's plenty of space in our car."

"What, you think you in charge here?"

It was as if someone had placed noise-cancelling headphones on me: every sound in the Goodwill went away, though I could clearly see that loads of people were talking, laughing and moving noisily about the racks.

"From what I can see," I answered, "Nina's not your slave and I'm pretty sure she's not your daughter, so she can come home with whoever she wants."

The man could not believe what he was hearing. Wavering between a level of rage to match my own, and the sense that he'd look stupid to take on a womanchild only half his size, his eyes measured every inch of me anew.

I stared right back, hands fisted, heart slamming. I was coiled and straining not to release myself. All it would have taken was one rude word or a simple obscene gesture to set Copley in motion.

Nina, still turned away, reminded me of a doe on the side of the road, afraid that to move was to meet death on the grill of a very large, very fast semi.

And then I felt a cool stirring and found Mr. Saunders standing beside me. His tall, lean frame loomed over all of us. Even more, the stillness he carried with him broke up the scene, far more than words or weapons would have been capable of.

"Bethany," he said in his rarely-heard, gently measured voice, "your Grandma was getting worried. You come on with me now."

Inclining his head politely before the stranger, he gave Nina a slow glance.

"Why, hello Miss Nina. Haven't seen you since summer. If you need a ride, we're right next door, alright?"

He nodded politely to the man while slipping his arm around my shoulders and gently drawing me away. I thought about making a few more comments, just to prove to the pork that I wasn't afraid.

I peered up into Mr. Saunders' face as he escorted me out the door. He was looking down, concern in his eyes.

"You know I have to tell your grandmother," he said gently.

"I didn't do anything."

"You certainly was thinking about it."

"Thinking isn't a crime, Mr. Saunders."

"Maybe not, but acting on it could of landed you right in jail."

"I don't know what you mean," I said.

"Sweetheart, you may be able to lie with your mouth, but what you're thinking is written plain as day in your eyes."

He opened the door to the store next to Goodwill. Far fewer people were in the store, and Grandma was standing beside an underwear display, gently feeling the cups of the bras for under-wiring, which she didn't approve of.

She looked up. "What took you so long? I thought you were just planning to say hello."

I didn't answer, but caught the looked that passed between her and Mr. Saunders.

"Seriously?" I said, still feeling some Copley in my blood. "Are you two communicating telepathically now?"

"Nina," Mr. Saunders said diplomatically, "wasn't alone."

"I see," Grandma replied, still looking at him. Neither spoke for a few seconds. Then she smiled at me. "I saw a real pretty red coat over there. Why don't you have a look and tell me what you think?"

I stalked across the store, my head still roaring, and found myself standing before a rack of bright, knee-length, military-style coats—similar to the white coat made popular by the Princess in England. The brassy buttons literally glowed in the sunlight, and without even thinking about it I knew the square cut and epaulets would look great on my boyish frame. The color would suit me too—Grandma knew me so well!—but part of my heart just refused to be seduced.

A few feet away my closest friend—my *sister*—was being terrorized by a man she feared so much she could barely speak. And this man was going to take her back to the house. He could enter that house any time of day or night. When Gideon wasn't there. When she was alone with Benny.

My mouth was dry and my hands began to shake. I couldn't just stand here trying on new coats as if I didn't know what was going on. Grandma couldn't ask me to do that. I had done it for fifteen years in my father's house. I had let my father hurt my mother every day and done nothing. But I couldn't continue to do that now because I loved Nina and Gideon.

"Bethany?" Grandma's voice was gentle. She was standing beside me, her face filled with concern. I knew Mr. Saunders had filled her in. "Come on outside for a few seconds, okay?"

I followed her outside and we stood in front of the store, with me staring blindly into the rainy parking lot. I didn't dare to so much as glance at the Goodwill lest I lose control and run back inside.

"That man is the little boy's father," Grandma said, her tone even.

"That's obvious," I said.

Ignoring my rudeness, she touched my arm. "He's also the man who keeps Nina and Gideon's mother—well, who keeps Minerva away from home."

"You know who he is?" I asked.

"Everyone knows, baby. This began long before you arrived."

I looked at her and appreciated the fact that she looked right back. "Who is he, Grandma?"

"Oh, I don't know if his name really matters. Just understand that their momma got involved with him a long time ago and has never gotten away. No one really knows why. Sometimes women believe they love the man who hurts them, even though everyone else in the world can see how wrong it is."

With her eyes holding mine, I understood very clearly what she was trying to say. She wanted me to forgive myself, both for the things I didn't do in Akron and might not be able to do in Blissfield.

My anger flooded out of me like water from a punctured bag. I felt a sudden void. I didn't know what emotion should replace my rage.

Grandma drew me close. "Now baby, I know you want to be friends with Nina and Gideon for a long, long time. The best way to do that is for you to go on to college. You'll need a degree in order to get a job that really pays."

"Grandma, I never said I wanted to quit school—"

"Sometimes we do things because we think we're helping others rather than ourselves. But in the case of school, I have to ask you to be selfish. Whatever you do, Princess, please promise me you'll stay in school as long as you can."

"Oh, Grandma—"

She pulled back and looked me in the face. "I mean it, Bethany—stay in school. Go to college. Make something of yourself so you won't spend your life at the mercy of people like the folks in Blissfield."

There. She'd said it. For the first time she'd admitted that the town she lived in, the town where she was born and had spent all of her life, was a dead end in the heart of empty. Life in Blissfield wasn't just a prison sentence for Nina and Gideon.

It was death row.

* * * * * * *

That December Grandma occasionally let me take her car to pick Nina and Benny up and drive around town. I'd take Nina to the store for a few groceries, or to a park so Benny could run himself out. Nina talked of nothing but how hard it was to keep him under control in their small house, how much he ate and how much she missed everything about the old days—even the lint brains. Gideon also seemed further removed from me than ever. The weather had changed, so trips out to the stone cabin were impossible, and even worse, one day when we were standing behind the Piggly Wiggly, sheltering from a cold wind, he admitted that his auto mechanics classes weren't going well.

"They won't let me do nothin'," he said, drawing deep on his cigarette. I watched with some concern as he lit one cigarette after another, his eyes distant as he smoked.

"The instructor say the older guys need the training more than me, because they got families and what-not. He don't believe somebody my age should be in the course."

"Can't you tell anyone? I mean, the principal or somebody—"

"It's a different principal at night. From what I can see, he the instructor buddy. Look like they go hunting and fishing together on the weekends. They don't want to hear nothin' from me."

"But what'll happen if you don't finish the program?"

"They don't give a fuck."

"But you have to—"

"CeCe—" he turned on me, his voice rough, "you just don't get it. Nobody give a fuck about nobody. No matter what you try to tell yourself, it just don't work like that."

"I care about you—"

"Because you want me to be with you," he said matter-of-factly. "If you didn't want me you wouldn't be standing here right now."

"What's wrong with me wanting you?"

"You just don't see it," he said, stomping out his cigarette. "You don't see who I really am. You just see who you *want* me to be."

"What are you talking about?"

"I'm not a toy you can take out and use to get your kicks," he said.

"My *what?*"

"You think I look good. You think other girls want me. You think I need you because Nina and me don't got shit. But none of that got squat to do with anything."

"What the fuck are you even talking about?" I said.

"Everybody see Gideon the football star, Gideon the blue-eyed boy, Gideon the guy with the great body. But don't nobody give a shit about nothing else."

"*I* do!"

"Do you? Do you *really?*" He was staring down at me with such ferocity that for a moment I was afraid.

"Believe it or not," he continued, his voice a bit calmer, "it really gets old. Sometime I want someone to understand that, that—" his words came to a dead stop. The manager of the store, a big-faced rednecked who looked like the place was named after him was standing beside the dumpsters, his butcher's apron bright with blood.

"Don't have enough work to do?" he asked, his eyes vised on Gideon.

"Yessir," Gideon said, automatically moving toward the rear of the store.

"What chu doing out here, anyway? Is this where you bring your girls? I thought places like this were reserved for your *momma.*"

My heart stopped and bile rose to my throat. What made tears come to my eyes, however, was that Gideon lowered his head and walked within inches of the man, not speaking. I watched his back as he made his way to the door, shoulders rounded, not looking back.

The manager eyed me. "And what's your name, little honey?"

For a moment I didn't answer. Then I, too, turned to walk away.

"I asked you what 'chor name is," the swine said, raising his voice.

I took several more steps, making my way around the store to the parking lot and Grandma's car.

"Listen here," he called after me, "if you want to suck somebody's dick, do it somewhere else. I run a clean establishment."

I stopped in my tracks, my head swimming. Strangely, it was sadness, not rage, that directed my response.

"You asked me my name," I said as I turned and walked back to face him. "It's Castle. My family's been here since the time this land belonged to the Indians. No matter what sick shit is going through your inbred hillbilly brain, I promise you I would rather slit my own throat than dishonor my family's name by doing anything immoral behind your fucked-up, low-class cracker store."

His mouth opened and shut, working furiously. I knew it wasn't so much that I'd called him a hillbilly and a cracker, but rather that I'd identified myself as a Castle. Being a Castle meant, for the purposes of this particular meeting, that I was untouchable.

As I walked with almost supernatural calm to the car, I thought about the bridges I was burning, particularly for Grandma. But at that moment I hated the whole world. It was as if all of Blissfield was conspiring against us, yet I was the only one fighting back.

* * * * * * *

Gideon's words drove me home. He'd lost weight, muscle and the quiet vibrancy that once commanded and held my gaze. Though he'd never talked much—Nina was the family spokesperson—he'd always been gently alert to whatever we had to say. Now he was distant, different, prickly, secretive. I felt he'd entered a domain of men who exist in rough-hewn worlds, where physical labor is often painful, underappreciated and poorly paid. These men made up for their barbed-wired lives with deliberately vulgar behavior, particularly towards women.

At the house, Grandma was moving around the kitchen with her sense of automatic purpose: something was on her mind, and she was trying to figure out the best way to deal with it. "Princess," she began, a hitch in her voice, "there's a letter for you on the table in the hall."

I looked at her. She didn't raise her head or meet my eyes. Instead, she cleared her throat.

I went into the hall and saw the envelope. It had already been opened, so I turned it over and saw that my mother had addressed it to her.

Inside I found a thick packet of papers, with an additional envelope inside. The inside envelope, still sealed, was for me.

For a moment I wondered whether Grandma had simply forgotten to move her letter to a private place. Then I realized it was the contents of her letter that had cast a pall over her that evening. She'd left it there on purpose. She intended for me to read it.

I sank into a chair, my hands suddenly clumsy and damp.

Dear Corinne,

I hope you are feeling good and that the winter has not been to harsh for you down there. This been the hardest winter I can remember here in Ohio. Almost every day we get more snow and it is hard for me to keep the heat on. I am working extra hours to cover the bills, but I really can not afford the house. I know it is time to give ~~the~~ it up, but I keep thinking that when Copley and Bethany get back we will be a family again. At least it is very warm at work.

I want to thank you for the money you sent to us. Being able to afford a good lawyer has been very helpful in Copley case. I was scared the lawyer from the court would not do a good job and things would end up so much worse. I hope that these months will give Copley time to think about everything and maybe he will take a chance on us moving down to N.C.

I am honestly really scared of the people he like to spend time with. I am very glad you was able to let Beth live with you so she wouldnt have to be around those men. The only thing is that sence she been gone he spent so much more time with them, and often they were in the house when I come home from work. I think some time it is a blessing he got sent away, so maybe they ~~can~~ will move on.

Copley is due for his parol hearing in 2 months and I don't mind telling you I am worried. He somehow got it in his mind it was my fault when the police come to our house that night and he did not forgive me when I tried to explain. He said his new lawyer came from you, and that I would have been happy if he been sent away for a much longer time. Of course that is not true but he seem to believe it.

You know I have tried for almost twenty years to be a good wife to Copley. But after he left I joined a church not far from the house, and I been going to conseling with the pastor. He a good man and when I told him all the things I been through, he said if Copley don't find the Lord and change his ways something truly terrible likly to happen. If he would consider moving closer to you I think he might do better. But I just don't know how to make him.

Thank you for writing to me all this time and giving me the strength to bare the difficult days. I know you have saved my girl. If she is more like you then she will have a much better life.

Please ask Bethany to write to me, as I cannot afford to call these days. I hope to hear from you soon.

Love,
    Brenda Berniece

Now my hands were shaking. I set Grandma's letter down and picked up the envelope addressed to me. Inside was a single page.

Dear Beth,

Your grandma say you doing well in your classes and you have made 2 very nice friends. I am happy for you. I know you must like living there because your to busy to write, but I hope you think of me some time. Your daddy miss you a lot and say hello. Please write to me when you can.

    Love,
    Your Mom

I laid the letters side by side on the table. Hearing a noise, I realized Grandma had come out of the kitchen and was standing beside me, a dishtowel in one hand, her apron in the other.

"Come on in and get something to eat, Princess."

"But—"

"It'll be easier to talk after you've had some supper."

She'd made sweet potatoes, greens and ham, and we ate in silence without my looking up. I felt her gaze on me, not exactly measuring, but wondering. Surely she knew how I was feeling—she always seemed to know that—so she must have been waiting for my reaction.

She reached across the table and touched my hand. "You okay?"

"I really don't know," I said.

She got up and poured hot water into two cups, then added hot chocolate mix into both. She brought the cups to the table.

"Why did you let me read Momma's letter to you?" I asked, an edge I couldn't control entering my voice.

"I thought you should know the truth."

"Daddy's in jail," I said.

"Prison, Princess."

"What's the difference?"

"One is local. The other is more serious."

"So where is he?"

"In Cleveland, from what I understand."

"That's not far from Ak——"

"No," she said, "but it's a federal prison. That means his crime merited a different level of punishment."

"How long?"

"He's been gone fourteen months. His sentence was two years, but it appears they may release him sooner."

"What did he do?"

"Possession of drugs with the intent to sell them," she said. "It seems he was running an operation out of the house. When the officers arrived he tried to fight his way out. It's a good thing the police came when your mother wasn't there or she might be in prison, too."

"How did the police find out?" I asked.

"They'd been watching your father for a while. It seems he had huge gambling debts and had been coming up with money, though he didn't have a job."

"Grandma, my momma said that when he gets out, she wants him to move down here."

"Yes, she thinks it might help him."

"But he doesn't want to, does he?"

"Oh, I don't know, baby. Your father hasn't called or written to me since your mother put you on that bus."

"I don't want him here," I said. "He'll do something bad to me."

"No!" she responded, so abruptly we were both surprised. She leaned forward and grasped both my arms at the wrist. "Your father won't——"

"Then why did he hit me?"

"Because he's afraid."

"Of what?"

"Of you growing up and seeing him as a failed husband, father, and to be honest, as a failed man."

Grandma was looking at me, her expression laser-focused. "Bethany, your father—my son—is damaged. I've known it for years—practically since he was born. I've worried and worried about him, and about your momma, because I've always known he would hurt anyone who loved him. And god knows, your momma loves him."

"Is it because his daddy left?" I asked.

"It could have been because he was born on a Wednesday," Grandma said. "I've told you before and I'll tell you again: Copley was angry from the start, and it took every ounce of strength in my body to keep him alive to manhood. When he left for the Army I figured my work was done because he'd either die, like his brothers, or come out on the other side of it, ready to be a man."

"But he didn't, Grandma."

"I know that, child. What I don't know is when evil stops being a choice and simply becomes who a man is."

"You're saying he can't stop himself from hitting us?"

"I'm saying your mother should have left him when you were a baby."

"You wanted my momma to leave my daddy?"

"What I want," she said, looking away, "is for your mother to stop pretending his violence is a form of love."

"But—"

"That's what men like Copley try to make their victims believe," Grandma said, her eyes again fixed on mine. "Teaching children to confuse violence with love is like mixing milk with poison. Every time your anger turns you into your father, that poison surfaces. Watching him abuse your mother day after day, year after year, made you think that violence is the only way to deal with your anger. But that only makes it inevitable that you'll abuse people, too."

"Some people who deserve it!" I said hotly.

"But how do you choose, Princess? Even if you feel that strangers have hurt or threatened you, what would happen if you got really mad at your husband or child?"

"I would never hit anyone I love!" I said.

"Are you sure?"

The question was simple enough, and I opened my mouth to answer, then suddenly remembered the times when I'd been so angry it really didn't matter who I hurt. *Even Nina.*

"It's terrible," she said quietly, "when the feeling of power you get from causing pain becomes a drug you can't live without."

A wind suddenly rattled the windows. We sat there with me staring at the checkered tablecloth. She sipped her chocolate, her eyes on me.

"You know something?" she asked very softly. "You are much, much stronger than you realize."

I looked up.

"Princess, when you came here you didn't know anybody. Not even me. You had no friends, and you'd left your family, your school, and the place where you were born. But you survived. You've made friends, learned the local customs, done your schoolwork and—" she paused an instant "—you've made me very proud."

"But I've also kicked some—"

"Yes, at times you've acted out of anger," she said, "but it's always because you were trying to defend people you care about. In other words, you haven't used your anger to gain power over anyone."

I thought about that for a moment. "So you're not mad about—"

"I'm not happy that you resorted to violence. And I want you to think about what violence brings. Look at your own father, sitting in prison, and your mother, who's terrified of him. And then look at you, far from home because of his actions."

"But if I hadn't come here," I protested, "I'd never have met Nina and Gideon!"

"I know you love them, Bethany. And that's what gives me hope for you."

"Hope?"

"Yes," she said. "I pray every day you'll find a way to manage the poison your father put in you, and make your life about love."

"But sometimes you *have* to act—"

"Baby, I have never hit anyone in my life, yet it's safe to say that people respect me and care about me here in Blissfield."

I shook my head. "I can't be that way, Grandma. I just can't."

"Why not?"

"Because, I don't know, maybe I got too much of my daddy and not enough of you. I can't let anybody treat me the way Daddy treats Momma. Or the way that man in the Goodwill was treating Nina. The way Toya and Bree were trying to treat me. Or the way London was trying to treat anybody he could. I just can't."

She nodded slowly. "Okay, baby."

"And I will never," I said, "ever be like my momma."

She nodded, her eyes still fixed on me.

"But I won't hit anybody I love. I promise," I declared, "and I do *not* want my father or my mother, under any circumstances, coming down here."

twenty-one.

So this is how it happened.

Nina telephoned on the morning before Christmas because, as she explained, no one was watching and she could finally call. I'd put up a small tree with Grandma's help, using ornaments that had been around since before my father's time. Celebrating the holiday seemed like a joke because I hadn't heard from Nina or Gideon since school closed days earlier.

"CeCe, where you been?"

The question was off, her voice was off, and I could hardly believe that after days of silence she spoke as if *I* was the one who'd disappeared.

"You know where I've been every hour of every day," I answered.

"Don't be like that."

"Like what?"

"Like a dummy who don't know how things are."

"I *don't* know how things are," I said. "I never see you or your brother."

"Why you saying you don't see Gid?"

"You know he doesn't come to school anymore, Nina."

"He come to school later, but he do come."

"He comes after I'm at home. And when I go up to the store he stands there pretending he's someplace else."

She was quiet for a beat. "Well, you don't see me pretending."

"You don't even speak to me when you see me," I said.

"I can't talk when I'm 'sposed to be working."

"You can say hello."

"CeCe, I can't say nothing."

"Why?"

"Because if I do I won't be able to stand it," she said quietly. "How would you like to spend every free minute sweeping up behind the people who treat you worse than the dirt you sweeping?"

"You don't have to sweep up after me."

"I do, too—after all of them and after you, too."

"I don't treat you like dirt, Nina."

"No, but you keep trying not to understand."

"At least you're making money—" I said.

"CeCe, this ain't my money. I got to feed us and put some heat in the house."

"Still."

"Still nothing," she said. "You want to play like you grown. Like you in love with Gideon. But CeCe, for you this is a game. For us, this is real life."

"That's not fair, Nina. I can't see you. I can't even call you. I don't care if you bring Benedictine with you. Just come over."

"I can't, CeCe. Things is different, now."

"Because of that man?"

Another pause. A longer pause. "You need to forget about him, CeCe. Do you hear me?"

"Why?"

"Because he don't mean a thing to you."

"He's the reason why you never call me," I said.

"*You* the reason I never call you."

"What's that supposed to mean?"

"You so evil all the time!" she said.

"I miss you!"

"That don't make no sense. If you miss me, why you act like such a dummy when I call?"

"'Cause I don't know how else to be," I said.

"In that case, I better not call. I don't know what you might do."

"Nin—"

"No, CeCe. I seen you when you get mad. You don't think about nobody. You start barking and biting and scratching, then somebody get hurt."

"I'm not gonna hurt you," I said.

"But you *do* hurt me, CeCe. When you act crazy somebody got to pay."

"Are you talking about that man at the Goodwill?"

"Forget about him," she repeated.

"Did that man do something to you?"

"Leave him out of this," she said warily. "I called to wish you a happy Christmas. I'm not talking about nothing else."

"How's Benedictine?"

"Benny okay. He a dummy, but he okay."

"Since you called, would you like to have dinner with us tomorrow?"

"On Christmas? No, CeCe, I told you last year that's a day for your family."

"You're my family, Nina!"

"Oh, heck, CeCe. Stop saying that."

"It's true," I insisted. "You used to believe it."

"Quit talking so much."

"Why'd you call if you don't want me to talk?" I said.

"Just quit talking crazy."

"Nothing I said is crazy."

"You should hear yourself," she said. "You trying as hard as you can not to see things the way they are."

Now it was my turn to pause. When I'd heard her voice, I thought for one wild, fleeting moment she was calling to say her aunt had relented and agreed to take Ben back, and she and Gideon would quit their jobs and become regular students after Christmas break.

"Okay, Nina," I said, defeated. "Merry Christmas."

"I also called because I miss you, too."

The tears that hit my eyes made me angry. I knew she couldn't see them, and I didn't want her to know, so I laughed. I didn't want it to sound mean, but I knew it did.

"I'm going," she said abruptly.

"No, wait—"

"I got to go, CeCe."

"I wasn't laughing at you. Seriously."

"And I got to go. Seriously."

I was wiping my face, holding my voice steady with miraculous effort. "Can I—could I come over there?"

"No," she said with such finality that my sadness began to shift, and a flicker of anger came into my words.

"Since when are you too important to see me?"

"CeCe, you know better than that. It's just that sometimes Ben's father come by. He won't want to find nobody at the house."

"Then let me bring you guys over here."

"I'll call you some other time," she said.

"Wait—don't you hang up, Nina Price!"

"I'll talk to you soon," she said, and the phone died.

I sat at the dining room table listening to the dial tone until the phone started to bleep. I hated the sound, but I couldn't put the receiver down.

Between the brother and sister, it was Nina who understood and could explain things best. I knew she still cared about me. The grown-up part of me, the part Grandma was working so hard to bring out, *did* understand. But that aching, gnawing, needy, childish part of me just couldn't let it go.

I wanted to see them both. I wanted to feel the heat and tension that knotted up my insides when I was close to Gideon. I wanted to make Nina smile and laugh with me.

I'd bought a box of Whitman's chocolates for Nina, a Barry Saunders tee-shirt for Gideon and a book with pictures of farm animals for Benny. Grandma's keys were in her purse on the kitchen counter. She was in the bath. I didn't bother to ask her if I could use the car, or to leave a note telling her where I was going. I stuffed the gifts into a plastic bag and bounded out the door.

The rain had made the dirt roads slick, and the shoulders were soft with overgrowth and mud. I had to slow the Buick to crawling pace to get all the way to the clearing near the little wooden house. I pulled off the main road and turned the car around, facing the road, and got out and looked at the tires to make sure they wouldn't get stuck. I'd seen Mr. Saunders do this plenty of times in the church parking lot, so I knew it was a smart move.

Setting off down the narrow path, which was slippery and more overgrown than ever, I stopped at the top of the rise and listened. I thought I could hear a radio, so I figured someone was at home.

Smoke was coming from the chimney of the little house, and the door was propped slightly open. The curtains were drawn, however. It was still early, so though it seemed too soon for Benny to be taking a nap, it was perfectly possible that he wasn't up yet.

I stepped on the cinder block and grasped the door handle, pushing it open a couple more inches. "Nina? You there?" I called out in a stage whisper. I heard rustling, a quick step and the door opened.

Nina stood there in faded pajama bottoms, her tattered sweatshirt and some slippers. Her hair hadn't been combed for what looked like days, and her face actually seemed unwashed. I had hoped for a smile or a hug, but my presence was met with something more like terrified despair. "Shit," she whispered.

"Damn, girl!" I said. "What's going on with you?"

She looked over my shoulder quickly, but remained standing in the doorway. "CeCe, I was afraid if I called you might try something like this. I already told you not to come. You *cannot* be here right now. Do you understand?"

"I'm not gonna do anything crazy," I said. "Let me in for a minute. I've got some stuff for you."

"Gid's at work. Why don't you go over to the store?"

"Why? Is somebody else here?"

"No, but you need to go."

"Is it that man from the Goodwill?" I said. "You want me to get help? The police—"

"No one is going to help us, CeCe. You already know that. Please go. I'll call you tomorrow. I promise."

Her face was so tense that I felt ashamed. "Okay," I said. "Okay. I'm sorry."

I turned, heart thumping, and took a couple of steps up the path when she called my name, her voice strained.

"What?"

She motioned to me to come back, so I returned to the house.

"I hear his car," she said, her voice low. "Look—go around to the back. Wait out there until he leave. When he go it'll be safe. I'll try and get rid of him real fast, okay?"

I slipped and slid my way around to the back of the house, where the grass was much higher. A septic tank about ten feet away was tilting oddly, clearly needing work. I could also see the phone and electric wires strung through the trees in the direction of the street.

Afraid of snakes, I avoided the taller grass. The house was built up on cinderblocks, with a crawlspace of about two feet. Bending down, I could see the legs of the man as he worked his way cautiously down the slippery path and approached the door. He didn't have to knock. Nina met him before he could set foot inside. Though her voice was low, it carried as if I was standing just beside her.

"Hey, DeAndre. Ben's sleep right now and I don't want to wake him up."

"He sick?" the man said.

"He didn't sleep much last night," Nina said softly. "I'm just trying to let him rest."

"I want to see him."

"Let him sleep a little while longer. I told him Santa Claus is coming, and he want to stay up and wait."

"Where you get money for that?" he asked.

"Gid got him something at work."

"What?"

"Not much," Nina said. "A little truck and some coloring books."

The man's legs grew still, as if considering. "Let me get a drink of water."

"Just wait there and I'll get it."

"You trying to stop me from coming in?" he said.

"He's sleep, DeAndre."

"You got somebody else in there?"

"No!" she said quickly.

"I don't want no bullshit around my son, you hear?"

"That's crazy talk."

The legs shortened as he stepped up on the cinderblock in front of the door. "Who you calling crazy?"

"I'm just saying that nobody here but Ben and me," she murmured.

"Whose car is parked out there by the road?"

"What car?" Nina asked. "I ain't left out of here all day, so I ain't seen no car."

The legs turned as he looked toward the rise, gauging whether she was telling the truth.

"You don't got nobody in there?"

"Do I look like I got company?"

The legs turned back, the voice becoming lower, as it had in the Goodwill. "You listen to me—if you lying, you in trouble."

"I ain't lying."

"You like your momma. She lie all the time," he said.

"I told you—"

"Don't lie to me, bitch!"

Nina was silenced, just like my mother was silenced when Copley's voice hit a certain pitch.

I knew she stepped back because his legs suddenly vanished.

I bent so low I could have climbed beneath the house, if not for the dirt and the spiders. I wanted to be sure, however, that if he looked out the back he wouldn't see me there, listening.

I could hear their footsteps as the man marched heavily across the floor, which creaked beneath his weight. Nina said nothing, and I had the impression she was still standing by the door. He came to the back, where I was crouched down, and suddenly the back window opened.

"It smell like shit in here," he said.

"Sometimes Ben don't make it to the toilet," Nina said.

"He still wet the bed?"

"Not all the time."

"What the fuck is wrong with him?" DeAndre said.

"Nothing."

"Don't give me that shit. He too old for diapers."

"He don't wear diapers."

"Then why do this place smell like shit?"

"We—we don't have too much space for our stuff," Nina said quietly.

"The house was fine when I lived here."

"I know."

"And you don't have to pay shit."

"Thank you, DeAndre," she said.

He paused. I could almost hear it creeping into his head. "You really want to thank me?" he asked.

"I said thank you."

"I ain't sure I got that."

"Thank you," she repeated, and I heard the trembling in her words. He heard it, too, because when he spoke again, he spread a saccharine sweetness over his anger.

"Why don't you come over here and show me how thankful you are?" The floor creaked in the direction of one of the mattresses.

"I can't."

"Come here," he said.

Nina didn't move. Whether it was because of Ben, or me, I didn't know.

"I ain't going to tell you again," the man said, his words so slow and distinct that I might have been sitting right beside him.

"DeAndre," she said softly, "I can't."

"Don't give me that."

"Please," she said, and I almost lost the next words, "let me be."

"You don't have to—" he paused, grunted, moved around "—just come here and take care a this."

"Gideon will be here in a minute," she said desperately.

"Don't lie to me."

"Please, DeAndre."

"Bring your skinny ass over here and—"

"No, De—"

I struck the side of the house with the butt of my palm as hard as I could. The sound echoed loud enough to still the birds, and all movement ceased.

"What the fuck is that?" DeAndre said.

"I—I don't know," Nina said as she walked to the door and stepped outside. Her spindly legs descended the cinderblock and she moved away from the house toward the rise.

Quickly, almost instinctively, I ran into the trees and made my way as quietly as possible in a slow circle around the house, coming out between Nina and the street.

Then, with strides as natural as I could make them, I made my way down the muddy path toward the house.

Nina was standing anxiously at the top of the little hill in her pajamas and sweatshirt, her face carefully emptied of all emotion, her weight shifting from one leg to the other.

Her shame and terror were obvious, and I felt Copley coming alive inside of me. My smile probably looked natural to anyone who didn't know I was a Castle. But to anybody who did, it should have served as a warning.

"Hey, Nina!" I said with mock-genuine brightness. I was almost stoned on my own boldness as I approached the house.

"Christmas Eve!" I raised my plastic bag and shook it gently.

Nina literally whipped around, an expression of desperate disappointment on her face. "What are you doing?"

I looked over her shoulder toward the front door. A shadow loomed, just inside. I wondered why he didn't come out into the yard.

"Hey, I got something in my bag for everybody!" I announced. "Why're you still in your pj's? It's time to go."

"I—I—" She was pitiful.

The shadow shifted toward the window with the cardboard pane.

"Look," she said, "this isn't a good—"

"I know I'm early," I said, "but Grandma fixed lunch and she's waiting for us."

"Oh," she said, now tilting her head with an expression of desperation that, because she was facing my direction, the man couldn't see.

"Let me help you get Benny dressed!" Inside of me, Copley was applauding.

"Ben's still sleep and I don't want to wake him up."

"He can take a nap at Grandma's," I said.

I don't know whether I was counting on the man not wanting to be caught alone inside the house with her, or whether I thought he'd had enough sport with her for that day. At that moment, Copley was directing me and I was just going along for the ride.

"Look," Nina said, avoiding my name, "maybe we can get together tomorrow."

"But I brought these gifts over so you'll have them when you wake up on Christmas morning."

Nina glanced over her shoulder for the first time. "I—"

"Come on! Let's go!" I was now commanding her, too.

Nothing moved inside the house. "I can't today," she said, her voice sounding like she'd just got life in prison.

"Sure you can," I insisted warmly.

"CeCe—" her face broke my heart, "—I'm telling you I can't."

"*Pleeeease?*" My voice, by contrast, grew more strident with each exchange.

The sound in the door got my attention before I actually saw him. Nina spun around, too, and we simultaneously inhaled as he emerged from the shadows.

He'd been close enough to touch me in the Goodwill. In fact, he'd used his pit bull bulk as a threat until Mr. Saunders showed up—yet I was still surprised at how grotesque he was. Nina seemed surprised, too, as if his appearance was some kind of apparition.

He was dressed in a pink shirt with black embroidery on the collar and lapels. The shirt was tight across his barrel chest and soft belly. I figured he'd shown up in the same fake leather jacket he was wearing in the store, but he'd already begun to undress. The shirt was untucked and hung down over his hips, along with his open belt. His worn jeans were faded and somewhat threadbare at the knees, which I didn't quite get. Since he was living off their mother, why didn't he look better? No pimp in my father's world would ever appear in public like this.

But then, he still resembled an unwashed white man, his marble-blue eyes empty, cold, his red cheekbones visible through his skin.

He leaned in the open doorway and casually lit a cigarette. "*You* again, bitch?" he called to me in greeting.

"Come on, Nina," I said. "Wake Ben up and let's go."

Nina, who was now standing almost directly between the man and me, lowered her gaze and stared at the muddy earth.

"Do you want me to get him?" I asked.

She shook her head.

"You need to get lost," the man said evenly.

"Fuck you," I answered, my eyes fixed on Nina.

She didn't speak.

Irritated, I walked up to her and looked her hard in her face. She turned her head, avoiding my gaze. So I pushed by her, stepped up the cinder block, and came face to face with the man.

"Wait, CeCe—" I heard her call.

But once again, the sound of birdsong, the wind in the trees and even the radio playing softly in the background—all of it vanished. The low buzzing in my ears helped me focus only on my mission: to get Nina and her brother out of that house.

To my surprise, the man laughed a kind of chocking growl, and leaned back so I could pass him. I took several steps into the room and was met with the odor of unwashed clothes, wet towels and grease. Notebooks and papers were scattered around the floor, and the sheets were torn off the mattresses, as if someone had either been upset, or in a monumental hurry. The boy was an unnaturally still lump of flesh beneath a blanket. I bent to shake him and looked up.

DeAndre filled the doorway, blocking my way.

"You was in a big hurry to get here," he observed, still pulling hard on his cigarette. "Now you in a hurry to leave?"

"Move," I said.

"Excuse me?"

"Move," I repeated, taking a step toward the door.

"Naw, baby," he said, walking closer to me. "Let's talk."

He was nearly three times my size and, I already knew, easily as mean as Copley. Maybe meaner. I had seen that Nina was deathly afraid to cross him, and now she remained outside, a good ten feet from the house. I didn't even know if she'd turned to look in our direction.

"Get the fuck out of my way," I said calmly, feeling my father take control.

DeAndre threw his cigarette butt outside the door. "A minute ago you was standing outside, running your mouth like a Porsche take a racetrack. Now you rushing to go. I figure that since you here, we should get to know each other."

"Move, you fat fuck," Copley said through me.

He laughed again. "You mighty fresh for a little bitty thing. Guess that why Nina like you. She ain't got one ounce a backbone. You should give her lessons."

"Don't make me fuck you up," Copley said, my voice dangerously low.

"*Ooooh*," DeAndre purred. "You scary!" His eyes roved lazily over my body and back up to my face. "How old is you, anyway?"

I then saw that Nina had come up to the house and was standing a few feet from the step. Her arms were wrapped tightly around her chest, and she was rocking back and forth, looking sideways, her head tilted as if it was about to fall off.

"She too young, DeAndre," she said in a near-whisper.

"Too young? She up in here, ain't she?"

"She lookin' for Ben, that's all."

"What she want with my son?"

"She our friend," Nina said softly.

"She not *my* friend," he said. "She come up on me like a little bitch in that store, and now she standin' here in *my* house, though I know *I* didn't invite her in."

"She just come over to wish us a happy Christmas," Nina murmured, again looking at the ground.

"She ain't wished *me* no happy Christmas," DeAndre said. "I heard her call me a fuck. That *is* what you said, correct?" He turned back to me, still blocking the doorway.

My rage was growing but I knew I couldn't take him in that small space. I had to get outside before I could do anything at all.

"Please," Nina said, looking up at him for the first time. "Just let her go."

"Give me one reason why I shouldn't get me a little holiday treat first," DeAndre said lazily.

"Please," Nina repeated.

He turned around slowly, shifting his lizard gaze to my friend. "You gonna take her place?"

My heart began to pound so hard I thought it would explode. I looked back and forth, careful not to move my face, and saw Gideon's baseball bat lying on the floor beside his mattress. I would need to get to the bat before he realized what I was doing—but I'd also need to take Nina and Ben with me after I'd done it. And that was the problem: would Nina leave if I opened up this motherfucker's skull?

Of course not. I knew it, he knew it, and even *she* knew it.

"Nobody gonna take nobody's place," I said quietly. "Move out of my way. Nina, Ben and I are going to leave."

He looked back at me and his expression folded inward as he wondered whether I was out of my mind. He was used to terrifying Nina and cowing Gideon. He didn't have the slightest idea what planet I'd come from.

Slowly, as if I was picking daisies, I took three steps across the room, bent down and lifted the bat. He watched, still trying to understand if what he was seeing was real.

By the time he'd figured he wasn't hallucinating, I was standing the bat's length away, my weapon raised firmly behind my left shoulder, where I could swing fast, without the force necessarily becoming deadly.

"What the fuck?" he said ironically, trying to laugh.

"Move," I said for the last time, Copley so close to the surface of my skin that you might have seen *his* face instead of mine if you'd turned on a bright light.

Nina let out a wail. She knew I'd do it if provoked, and she knew that if I began, nothing would stop me.

The air inside the house shimmered. Whether it was the cold outside, or the heat inside, or my enraged contempt—something softened and gilded the air with a marigold glaze. I could smell him: cheap cologne, sweat, stale clothing, unwashed polyester. The pink shirt and watermelon belly, the grey skin and colorless eyes. The stringy greying hair.

His blue eyes rolled like marbles in his porcine face. He was starting to comprehend that my vicious willingness, or maybe *eagerness*, to cause him pain was perfectly balanced against my lack of body weight.

Now his laugh was more interested.

But I wasn't laughing. Not at all. I ached to feel the thrust of that bat as it took the air, and had already steeled myself for the *feel* of it as it met his sagging flesh.

Something in his posture changed. It wasn't that he was afraid. No, he didn't really believe I'd do it. But he *did* understand I was capable of trying, and perhaps with some luck I might just do him some serious disservice. Or maybe he didn't want something to happen that might get the cops involved. So he thought it might be best to haul ass out of the doorway.

He climbed down the cinderblock and stopped in the dirt, a few feet to the left of my friend. I was disappointed, because once summoned, Copley didn't like to back down.

The light in the little house seemed to double once he was gone, and before lowering the bat, I took another good, adrenaline-fueled look around.

The place really was a mess, just like Nina was a mess, with their private belongings everywhere and nothing clean.

The boy was sleeping like he was dead, and I looked at Nina, who was still shifting her weight between her legs and staring into the distance, while keeping that swine in her peripheral vision.

I strode to the doorway and stepped carefully down the cinderblock and out into the front yard. Bloated with rage, DeAndre was waiting, adjacent to the door, his pants now buckled and his hands fisted. By daylight he was exponentially uglier than he'd been under the fluorescence of Goodwill and the darkness of the house. It was hard to believe that nature had created anything quite like this, and I was now certain that he was neither Nina nor Gideon's father.

He took me in with such hatred I was actually flattered.

Bat in hand, I walked toward Nina. "Get Ben," I said, taking her arm.

"No, CeCe, I can't!"

"You going to start that shit again?" I said.

"I can't go with you."

"You can go if you want."

"No, CeCe. I really can't."

It came to me in a rush that maybe she really couldn't leave. That what he intended to do to her might be better than what her life might be like if he didn't.

241

That she could never earn enough sweeping up at the school, and Gideon could never earn enough, cleaning up at the Piggly Wiggly, to pay for a house, heat, lights, and for food.

I looked into her once-bright eyes and saw sadness and surrender. I saw that she believed there was no alternative to what she was living. And I saw that she feared I was about to fuck it all up.

"Please," I said.

She shook her head, tears in her eyes. Absurdly, tears also burst from mine.

"What's wrong with Ben, Nina?"

"The lady coming from the government office. She say he can't live here because we don't take good enough care of him. I gave him one of momma's pills so he won't act so crazy when she come back."

"Why won't he wake up?"

"I don't know. Maybe I gave him too much."

"The place is a mess."

"I was getting ready to clean it up, but—"

"Just get him and let's go," I said. "Grandma will help!"

"No, CeCe. She can't and you know it."

I paused. Nina was wrong about Grandma; I knew that Grandma would have known exactly who to call and what had to be done to help out. But I had stolen Grandma's car keys and broken my promise in coming here. I'd been trapped in the house by this horrible man, and only my insane courage had gotten me out. At that moment I wasn't so sure that Grandma would agree to get involved, because at that moment, Nina's appearance suggested that everything the townspeople believed about the Prices was true.

Nina was desperate to make me leave. She certainly didn't want to be alone with DeAndre, but she also needed me to go in order to try and repair the damage I'd done.

I had to leave. It was the simplest solution, even if it was the cruelest.

"Okay," I said softly. "Okay."

She nodded.

"You going to be okay?" I asked.

"Just go," she said in a low voice. A teardrop spattered on her slipper. I wanted to fold her into my arms. I wanted to decorate the yard with DeAndre's blood.

But instead I turned away. I hadn't gone three steps before I heard him hit her.

He struck her so hard that I felt it, too. She gave a little yelp in the language of my mother, Brenda Berniece Johnson Castle.

I twisted around to find Nina on her knees, where she'd fallen from the blow, and DeAndre standing over her, savoring the moment.

Before I knew what was happening, I'd swung the bat with all the force in my lean little monkey body, connecting squarely with that fucked-up, abusing, punk-ass rapist swine's back.

He flew forward, landing with a thick thud face down on the ground by the door. His pink embroidered shirt billowed up over his hairy white back, and I raised the bat above my head and swung hard a second time, narrowly missing (perhaps by unconscious design) the center of his skull. The bat glanced off the side of his ear and struck his shoulder, and he growled in pain as his ear sprouted blood.

I hit him a third time, in the ribs, and wondered whether I should kick him there, too, like my father kicked my mother.

Nina was back on her feet, both hands pressed against her mouth in horror, blood from a cut below her eye smearing the side of her face.

"Listen, motherfucker," I said, panting as I raised the bat a fourth time, "don't you ever let me see a mark on her again. If I do, I'll put this entire bat up your motherfucking ass." With that, I struck him with all the force I had left, on his other side, hearing a sickening, satisfying *crunch* as something shattered.

I must have looked ridiculous—a womanchild, barely five-foot-three in height, beating an enormous, much older man. But then again, I had learned from the best, and I would do everything in my power to protect my sister.

Now I did turn to go, because I knew he was in no condition to touch her—at least not on *that* day. Maybe he'd think twice before he *ever* put his hands on her again.

These were my thoughts as I ran up the crest, my rage draining with every step. My exhaustion, sudden and terrible, felt like I was wrestling my way out of quicksand. I had to get to the car, get the car down that muddy path and make my way home. By now Grandma would be more than worried.

But the car was blocked. DeAndre had deliberately parked a rusting pickup in front of Grandma's car. The only good thing about the situation was that he hadn't managed to dent it.

With the remaining energy in my body, I got behind the wheel and began backing the hulking car off the road, praying I wouldn't find myself stuck in the thick muddy ditches and trapped within DeAndre's reach. Sweating, nearly panting with fear, I steered the car forward and backward in a maneuver that seemed to take an hour—but probably only lasted a couple of minutes—until I had enough clearance to inch my way past the truck.

During my desperate angling I expected to see his figure come staggering through the bushes and down to the vehicles, but even when I looked back as I pulled away there was no one to be seen.

Grandma was standing in the backyard when I pulled in, and by her posture I knew I was first-degree busted. Despite everything that had happened in my twenty-two months in Blissfield, I had never been dishonest with her, so I steeled myself and turned off the motor.

She walked out to the car.

"CeCe, come in the house."

"Grandma, I—"

"Come in the house."

I watched the set of her shoulders as she made her way over the thick roots of the ancient oak tree and opened the rear screen door. I got out and shut the car door, unaware until I reached the threshold that I was carrying the bat. Suddenly self-conscious, I laid it down in the dirt, wiped my hands on my jeans and went inside.

She didn't stop until we had walked the length of the house and into the front room, which was the coldest room in the house. Though she'd put in central heat decades before, we only warmed the rooms we lived in—the kitchen and our bedrooms.

She sat down on the stiff, embroidered sofa, but left me standing.

"Where were you?" she asked, her voice weirdly neutral. It occurred to me that I'd never seen her really angry, not even at the church people on Easter Sunday, or at nosy, stupid Mrs. Mitchell, or at least, she'd never let it show. Now her anger was in her gaze, which was piercing and unyielding.

"I went to Nina's house," I said.

"You promised you wouldn't go there."

"I know."

"You took my car without my permission."

"Yes," I said, trying not to look away. "I did."

"Why?"

"Because—because I was afraid you wouldn't let me go."

"Have I ever stopped you before?"

"No," I said.

"So what was different this time?"

"She—she called, and she didn't sound right."

"'Right'?" Grandma repeated.

"I mean, I know Nina, and I know when something's wrong."

"Did she ask you to come?"

"No." For the first time I dropped my eyes. "She told me not to."

"But you went anyway," Grandma said.

"Isn't that what friends are supposed to do?"

"Bethany, friends help friends, but they do it the right way. Do you suppose there was a reason why she didn't want you there?"

"Yes." If there ever was a time to lie, it was at that moment. But I couldn't, because lying to Grandma was the same as lying to myself. "Yes, Grandma, but I wouldn't have found out if I hadn't gone—"

"Found what out?" she said.

"Social Services are planning to take Ben and she was there all by herself and the place looked really terrible and I could tell she was terrified because she was wearing this strange stuff and she looked dirty and her hair—"

"Where was Gideon?" Grandma cut in.

"At work, and—" Suddenly I was sobbing like the worst idiot in the universe.

She watched me cry. I wiped my face with the butt of my hands, but the tears just kept on coming. I was surprised she didn't move, didn't find a tissue or a handkerchief or open her arms to me.

And then I realized she wasn't looking at me. She was looking at the traces of Copley, who was looking back from inside of me.

"Everything's different," I said, furiously wiping away my tears. "Nina's different, Gideon's different, and I can't do anything about it."

She stirred, moving her head just enough to let me know she was paying attention.

"The worse thing," I said, "is that I can't do anything to help them. Last summer it seemed like just being together made us happy. Now it feels like I'm their enemy. They won't talk to me. Nina doesn't even want to see me. And then—then in the Goodwill store, I saw that man, and Nina was so afraid of him!"

"Bethany, I think it's better if you stay away from them for a while," she began, but I cut her off.

"He came to the house while I was there. He didn't see me at first, but he called Nina inside and told her to—to—"

I didn't have to finish the sentence. Grandma was suddenly on her feet, standing just a few inches from me.

"What happened, Bethany?"

"I—I thought she was in trouble," I said, "so I made a noise outside to stop him. Then I went inside to try and get Ben—"

"You went into the house with that man?"

"And he said he would do the same things to me." I said.

She leaned in and grasped my upper arms. "Then what?"

"I saw Gideon's baseball bat by the mattress and I picked it up. I told him I'd bust him up and he laughed. Then he went after Nina and hit her really hard in the face, so I—"

"You what?" Grandma said.

"I did what I said." Exhaling, I heard the words pour out of me like a dying breath.

Her mouth opened, then closed. Her grip on my arms tightened so much it hurt.

"Is he still breathing?" she asked in a very low voice.

"I don't know," I whispered.

"But you hit him?"

I nodded.

"More than once?"

I shrugged and, turning, sank down on the sofa.

"Did you see him get up?" she asked.

"No. I didn't stay to see how bad it was."

"Did you hit his head?"

"I tried," I murmured, "but I missed and only got him by his ear. Then I hit his back and I think I got his ribs. I don't remember exactly."

"That's why you had that bat when you got out of the car," Grandma said, mechanically turning to stare at the street. For a moment I imagined red and blue lights outside and a heavy knock on the door. I think she was imagining it, too.

"You think I'll get in trouble?" I said.

"Princess, you already are," she answered without looking at me.

"With the police?"

"No," she said. "Worse."

"Worse?"

She walked out of the room and went down the hall to the phone. I heard her lift it and dial a number. She spoke for a time in a low voice. I could only make out some of the words.

When she came back, her face was set. "That man—DeAndre—is pure evil, Princess. I suppose that, knowing what I knew, I should never have let you get involved with Nina and her brother. Even though I don't agree with the mistreatment those children have been subjected to by the townspeople, there are reasons why Blissfield steers clear of them."

She shook her head. "You see, DeAndre is involved in all kinds of criminal things—things he probably couldn't do if he wasn't protected by people who really should be enforcing the law. What he did to Nina and Gideon's mother when she was just a child is only the surface of what he's into. Unfortunately, Nina is now about the same age her mother was when he stole her life. I've been afraid for that child out there, with no one to protect her, but I really didn't have the means to do more. I'd hoped the teachers and the principal might make a genuine effort to help her out.

"For now, " she continued, "you need to understand this: what you saw at that house today—the fact that this man is probably abusing your friend—is something he can't afford to let you share with anyone. He knows that if you tell me, or a teacher, or if you manage to find even one honest policeman, he could spend the rest of his life in prison."

"Do you think one of his cop friends will come after me?" I asked.

"No, baby, I think he's going to make this personal, and there are all kinds of ways he can come back at you."

"You mean, he could hurt *you*?" I said.

"He could try, but I'm not afraid for myself. I'm afraid for you."

"You think he'll come here?"

"He doesn't have to," Grandma said. "Even if I put you under lock and key he'd be able to find you. You've got to go to school. You need to be able to leave the house."

"I'll be super careful—"

"It wouldn't matter," she said, her face sorrowful. Suddenly she was sitting beside me, holding my arms once again. When I looked into her face I saw something I'd never seen before: powerlessness, and this was the moment I became truly afraid.

She got up and walked down the hall to the kitchen. I could hear her moving around, restlessly, as if she couldn't bear not to be moving. The room no longer felt cold. Framed photos of generations of Castles peered at me, wondering why, of all the traits I could have carried forward, I bore my father's mad hunger for the unique pleasure of violence. My eyes fell on the glass cabinet containing the porcelain figurines. One of the little glass people, a shepherdess wearing a sky blue scarf, two lambs at her feet, smiled mockingly.

I sat in silence for a long while, unable to focus my thoughts. Copley was long gone, replaced by that familiar fuzziness that I'd overheard Grandma describing to Mr. Saunders as "vacant."

When she returned her face was oddly empty. She settled beside me on her embroidered sofa, and when she spoke I knew she had already come to a decision.

"Bethany, your momma asked me to protect you from what was going on in your home. I was more than happy to do it, because I know my son and what he's capable of, and there was no other way to keep you safe. Now I see I've failed. What can happen here is potentially much, much worse than what could happen in Akron—"

"But Grandma—"

She raised her voice. "Listen to me, child! There are people in this town who respect me because I taught their children and grandchildren. But no one in this town would be willing to protect you and me, with the exception of poor Mr. Saunders, and I cannot ask him to risk his life against an animal like DeAndre Manning."

"Maybe he won't do anything," I said.

"Maybe you're right. When I called Mr. Saunders, I asked him to check around and see if anybody's heard anything. Some people are still out food shopping, or getting ready for service tonight. He'll call me back as soon as he's got any news.

"In the meantime," Grandma said, "you need to know this: DeAndre has been pimping women for the past thirty years. He likes young girls, usually those from broken or very poor homes, because they're hungry and need a place to live. Once he has them out there, working the motels and truck stops on the highway, he beats them if they try to get away. One or two women have turned up dead, but their bodies were so rotted the coroner could hardly determine their identity, much less find any evidence proving DeAndre was involved."

"That's why everyone is so mean to Nina and Gideon?" I said.

"Unfortunately, everything you've heard is true," Grandma said. "Their mother has been on the street for twenty years. She's also an addict, which is another way that DeAndre keeps women under his control. She barely knows where she is or what she's doing. It's a miracle those children have managed to make it this far."

"Does he really pay for that house?"

"Probably, and that may be to provide some shelter for Benedictine. If the government steps in and takes him away, DeAndre's interest will likely turn to putting Nina on the street. In fact, he may see this as his rightful payback for the money he's already given them. I don't know. I can only guess."

"Can't anybody help her, Grandma?"

"People could help, but they won't. DeAndre has ties to people who bring drugs into this area, which means he can always find someone to clean up any mess he makes. This is also why he will have to retaliate for what happened today. If word gets out that he was beaten by a girl with a baseball bat, can you imagine what that does to his reputation?"

"Nina's not going to tell—"

"No, but he's not to going let this go."

She looked out the window again. "The real problem is, I don't know whether you'll be any safer in Ohio."

"Ohio?" I shouted, jumping to my feet. "I'm not going back to—"

The phone ringing in the hall sent Grandma on a swift walk to the rear of the house. This time I followed her, intent on listening.

I could hear the rise and fall of Mr. Saunders's voice on the line. Grandma listened, mostly without speaking. She nodded once or twice, though he clearly couldn't see her, then turned to look at me. Her face was fixed, grim, decided. When she hung up, she spoke firmly.

"Pack enough cold weather clothes to fill a single suitcase. I'll box up the rest and send it the day after tomorrow. You should have it by next week."

"Grandma," I said, "you can't be serious."

"I'm not going to have you beaten, raped, or murdered by that man or one of his associates. He's already put the word out in town, asking for girls matching your description," she said.

"That doesn't mean he'll find me."

"Bethany, this is Blissfield. How long do you think it'll be before someone tells him that Nina and her brother came to church with Corinthia Castle's grand-daughter?"

Struck dumb, I stood stock still, trying to figure out what to say. Grandma, however, was far from adrift. She took my arm and pulled me down the hall to my bedroom.

"Bethany, if you can't decide what to pack, I'll do it for you."

"Grandma, I can't leave."

"The bus leaves in ninety minutes. We have to hurry."

"I don't want to go," I said.

"Get moving, Bethany."

"Can I say goodbye to—"

"No. There's no time, and no way to contact them, in any case."

"Gideon may be at the store," I said.

"The store's closed. It only opened until noon on Christmas Eve."

"Grandma, I—"

Moving with sharp precision, she raised her hand and slapped me so hard the sound echoed through the house.

Stunned, I took a step back, holding my face.

"Mr. Saunders will be here in fifteen minutes to take us to the bus station," she said. "Get moving."

I had no idea what I took, how I packed, when I finished, or what happened next. Suddenly I was in a car, and we were moving silently along the black tongue of road between towering pines, the red earth now the color of drying blood. When Roanoke Rapids crawled out of the winter darkness, I realized how stupidly fond I'd become of Grandma's favorite clothing store, now festooned with silvery decorations that matched the headless silver mannequins. I did not see the Good-will, because the bus station was closer, and when we pulled up in front of it I was oddly pleased that nothing about it made me think of Nina or Gideon. The ache in me was as if my skin was burned away, and my flesh was as raw and bloody as that of a slaughtered animal.

I found it impossible to think of anything at all.

Mr. Saunders went into the station, and I sat in silence, staring blindly from the car window into the black evening light. Neither Grandma nor I spoke.

When he returned he opened the trunk and pulled out the dufflebag. The car door opened beside me. I didn't move. I didn't breathe. Then Grandma was standing there, her hand outstretched to help me out.

"I'm sorry," I said quietly, not moving.

"I know," she answered.

"Please, please don't send me away."

"Let's go," she said, reaching forward to pull me firmly from the back seat.

"Grandma—"

"Beth—" It was then that I heard the tears in her voice, and I knew that she would never let me stay.

I climbed out of the car, barely breathing. We walked into the station, our backs straight, and I thought for the thousandth time that I was but a younger version of my grandmother.

The bus was purring in its stall, the two other passengers already seated. At the door Grandma kept her eyes on me as Mr. Saunders handed my duffle to the driver. Then, ever sensitive, he stepped away, not even saying so much as goodbye.

Grandma reached up and stroked my hair. She looked into my face with indescribable sadness, and I looked back, realizing how much I wanted to say, and how much would go unsaid.

Then the driver told us it was time to go. Grandma handed me a paper bag that smelled of tuna sandwiches, and leaned forward to kiss me on the same cheek she'd struck an hour before. Somehow I was up the stairs. I felt the rough upholstery and smelled the sickly sweetness of the seat. I looked out the window, which was heavily tinted, and saw only an unfocused version of her face. Then the bus exhaled a violent lurch of diesel, bounced backwards, and she grew smaller as Mr. Saunders stepped forward, slipped his arm around her and pulled her close. Her face vanished into the crook of his shoulder.

I never saw my grandmother again.

VII.

akron, ohio.

2001

twenty-two.

BeBe Johnson was so frail I hardly knew her.

Her gentle face brightened when I stepped down from the bus into the snow, then, as I took in her home-knitted scarf and men's wool overcoat, I slipped as if I had never walked on snow before.

She hugged me for a long time, but her shoulder blades were sharper than Nina's, and there was a slight, permanent trembling under her skin.

She asked about the trip, and I lied, telling her that I had slept, rather than wept, for most of the sixteen hours. She looked into my face and I realized she was still several inches taller than me. I also discovered that her eyes had died, or maybe I was seeing the reflection of what no longer lived in mine.

Because everything that remained of the sweet girl Grandma tried to nurture to life died somewhere around Washington. She was six feet under by the time we hit Pennsylvania. The woman that climbed down from the bus may have *looked* like Grandma's Princess, but my soul was gutted, and I felt absolutely nothing.

We walked to a bus stop outside the terminal while I shivered in my heaviest jacket, which was wholly unsuited for the Ohio winter. To my surprise, we did not go back to our house. My mother had moved to the upstairs flat in a run-down duplex a few blocks from my childhood home. We climbed down from the bus, my mother carrying my bag, and made our way along a street of identical, wooden two-family duplexes, their paint peeling and, in most cases, the windows boarded up. She did not speak as we negotiated the icy porch stairs and entered a narrow foyer that smelled of grease and damp and cold. We mounted a steep narrow staircase single file, and she unlocked a door that stuck until we pushed hard on it.

The front room held a few pieces of furniture I recognized: a wooden table with three chairs, a stained, threadbare sofa covered with flowered fabric, and a rocker. A large painting of a black man, naked except for a loincloth, embracing a similarly scantily clad black woman, hung on the paint-chipped wall above the sofa. An empty glass ashtray was the only other decor. My mother had lain out dishes and silverware and plastic cups. A two-foot plastic Christmas tree made of aluminum foil stood in the corner. I had forgotten it was Christmas.

The room was cold, and I noticed she was wearing a heavy sweater beneath her coat. I kept my jacket on, having no sweater. Trying my best, I managed a weak smile.

"Thank you very much." My voice was much stiffer than I intended.

"For what?" she asked softly, her eyes seeking approval in mine.

"For coming to the station," I said.

"Oh. I almost didn't recognize you. You grown up so much."

Not recognize me? That seemed crazy, because we both knew that over the past two years I'd come to resemble my father more than ever.

I really looked at her then, my mother. I saw the dark liquid and guileless gaze, the full lips, now cracked, and the natural gracefulness of her carriage. She had lost so much weight that she might have been my sister rather than my mother, and I thought with a pang that perhaps she often went hungry.

Involuntarily I glanced toward the kitchen and she said, "You must be starving," as if she had read a command in my gaze.

Embarrassed, I followed her. "Can I—can I help?"

"You don't have to. You home, now," she added shyly.

"No, Momma, I'd really like to help."

It seemed as if a veil was swept away, then, and she really smiled at me. I noticed that two of her lower teeth were missing. She immediately covered her mouth with her hand, so I looked away. There wasn't anything to say.

We cooked pasta, with meat sauce from a jar, which had been my favorite dinner when I was a kid. I didn't tell my mother that Grandma didn't believe spaghetti was real food, and I hadn't eaten it in two years. I didn't need to tell her, because it didn't matter. I wasn't in Blissfield anymore.

We sat together and ate, and I talked a little bit about school. I talked about the teachers I liked, and learning to drive and working in the garden beside Grandma.

I didn't tell her about DeAndre, and she didn't ask. I didn't mention Nina, because I couldn't. And I did not even think about saying the word "Gideon," because Gideon was an open, aching wound that felt larger than my heart.

Momma and I shared a bed because the other bedroom had no furniture. It appeared that she had moved only the most important of her meager possessions, and my childhood bed had already been too small for me before I left for Blissfield.

Though her bedroom was cold, we were warm enough, snuggled together beneath the covers. I slept almost immediately and woke up in the middle of the night, thinking of Nina's face when DeAndre hit her, and Gideon's voice when he held me in his arms.

A frigid dawn came slowly, with snow drifting lazily from a steely sky. Momma woke up suddenly and peered at me in surprise. I knew what she was feeling: it had all happened so quickly that neither one of us was sure the other was real.

"I'll turn on the space heater," she said. "Stay in bed and it'll warm up in a little while."

"Do you have to go to work?"

"The cleaners is closed today."

"Oh. I could come with you tomorrow. I mean, do you think they'd give me a job?"

Her face registered her surprise and pleasure, before clouding.

"It would be fun, but I don't know if they can pay another person. There ain't much business in this neighborhood, and since I don't have a car, I can't really work anywhere the buses don't go at night. Anyway, you'll be back at school in two weeks, so there's probably no point in you trying to get a job."

"I don't have to go to school right away. I mean, the semester's almost over and Grandma won't be able to send my school records until after New Year's. The term won't start till the end of January, right? It would make more sense for me to get a job and help out with things."

She paused, clearly unused to making decisions on her own. I could see her trying to decide what to do.

"I don't know what your Grandma would think about you missing school, even for a few days," she said quietly.

"Grandma would understand. She understands pretty much everything," I said.

"Yeah, but her being a teacher and all," Bebe J said.

"I'll go back when the new semester starts. But for now —"

We looked at each other. She spoke before I did. "Beth, did your grandmother tell you anything about—about your dad?"

"She said he got in trouble and had to go to prison. Why didn't you tell me, Momma?"

"I—well, I didn't want you to worry."

I looked away, thinking how stupid it was for him to bring his shit into our home. Mistaking my silence for concern about my father's welfare, she began speaking more quickly. "Well, he gonna have a parole hearing in a few more weeks, and they might release him."

"So?" I said.

"So I don't want to do nothing to upset him."

Her words made me want to both laugh hysterically and to weep. After so many years with Copley, didn't she know that something would *always* upset him?

"He already gonna be pretty mad that I couldn't keep the house," she continued. "It was just too much for me, and I didn't like being there by myself. Sometime people came looking for him — you know, people who didn't know what happened, and sometime they didn't believe me when I said he had went away."

She was trying to convince me that she had a good reason to move, but I really didn't care. That house had been a monument to my father's abuse. At least this apartment had no memories for me.

"It's okay, Momma. I think this place is nice," I said.

She brightened. "Well, this is our home for now. I just hope your father will understand."

He won't, I thought, but there's no point in worrying about that right now. "So, what if I got a job in a store or something?"

"You serious?"

"I don't have any money."

"Oh," she answered. "I thought maybe Miss Corinne—"

"No." I said firmly.

For a moment neither one of us spoke. Then I had a sudden, completely unexpected insight: *I was more intelligent than my mother.* I couldn't expect her to make decisions for me, or to protect me in the days to come. In fact, I'd be lucky if I could protect her, or myself, from what would surely happen if my father came home.

God knows I hadn't been able to protect Nina.

As I cleared the table, one eye on the snow swirling beyond the window, I began to understand that my childhood was over. And, unless I got very, very lucky, I might not make it back to North Carolina any time soon.

My mother came into the kitchen holding something in her hands. It was a pink mohair cardigan sweater.

"I got this for you for Christmas," she said in explanation, "but I get off work so late I didn't have time to mail it. I never dreamed you'd be back so soon."

I took the sweater, which looked heavy, and was surprised at its light weight. I slipped it on over my tee-shirt. It was too large and I knew it, but I played along when Momma said it was perfect for me. I knew the sweater was forgotten merchandise from the dry cleaners, and the coat she'd been wearing the night before was, too.

"Thanks, Momma. I really love it. I'm sorry—I don't have anything for you."

"*You're* my Christmas gift, baby! I'm so glad you're home!"

For the rest of the day we watched *The Sound of Music*, which with commercials went on for at least four hours, on Momma's little black and white TV. We didn't talk much. I did everything in my power not to think. I could see her watching me every time I got up to pee, trying to anticipate what I needed. By the end of the evening the shock of the new climate, coupled with my grief, had turned my brain to sludge, so I went off to bed. BeBe J's voice woke me up an hour or so later, though she was talking softly.

"Yeah, yeah, she here. Your mother sent her. No—she not in no trouble. She just came for—no, she not going back. Not right now, I mean. Well, I—she didn't say much about—

"No, she didn't give her no money. I axt her, but—no, I didn't look in her bag. No—well, she say she want to work. Yeah, I know, but she could work after school, if—if you okay with it."

She paused for a few moments. "No, baby, she don't eat much or take up no space. She real nice, baby, and so polite! Wait till you see how she grown up—she so pretty, too! She look exactly like your mo—

"Okay, baby. Baby, there something I need to tell you 'bout the house. It—well—I—"

Her voice went silent for a long time. I thought maybe she had hung up, or maybe the line had gone dead, but then I heard her speak.

"How much? I don't have—I don't—I can't pay it right now, but—okay. Okay. I'll find a way to get it to you next week."

There was another long pause before she said, "Yeah, okay—the thirty-first of next month. Okay, baby."

Now I was sure she had hung up. The silence in the apartment was broken only by some rapper yelling something from a car on the street below. I knew she was moving around, but my mother made no sound. She barely existed.

Because even when he wasn't there, he was there. Even though *he* was behind bars, she was also in prison.

Which is why, as I lay in bed my second night in Akron, I decided I would find a way to make my mother leave my father.

* * * * * * *

The following morning I asked my mother what restaurants, fast-food places and stores were within walking distance of the duplex, and I set out soon after she left for work. She'd reluctantly admitted that she'd been evicted from our house, and when the owner locked her out, he'd put most of our belongings on the street, which was why she had little to no clothing. I'd outgrown the stuff that was left behind, so I knew I hadn't lost anything in the process. But my father was going to go insane when he learned that she was only able to salvage as much from the house as she could remove on the day of the eviction. Fortunately, her employers had been kind enough to use the company truck to move the bed and living room furniture from the house into the duplex. She was so scared about this that she jumped at any unexpected sounds, including the voices of the people who, I suspected, were squatting in the flat below. I also suspected she feared being discovered in her new dwelling by my father's associates, who felt he still owed them money.

I knew, then, that my offer to work really *was* most welcome, though she had no way of realizing that I had zero intention of helping her pay off Copley's debts. My intention was to raise enough money to get myself, and my mother (if she could bear to leave my father), on a bus back to Blissfield. I figured that even if Copley followed us there, he would never do anything to hurt BeBe J and me in front of Grandma.

So I had five weeks until the start of the new semester, which is when my mother wanted me to enroll in the local high school. Five weeks until Copley's scheduled parole hearing. Five weeks to find three-hundred fifty dollars: the price of two Greyhound tickets south. Five weeks to talk my well-intentioned, but dumber than fuck mother into coming with me, though I knew a lifetime of being told what to do by my father meant she wouldn't want to listen.

Still, I had to try. All hell was going to break loose in Akron once Copley got out of the joint. Maybe DeAndre would have moved on by the time I got back to Blissfield.

I dressed myself in layers, carefully descended the steeply pitched stairs and went out onto the street. The cold was like a blow, and by the time I got to the end of the block my hands and feet were already on fire. What would Nina say about this?

First I asked the guy working behind the plexiglass at the corner liquor store if they were hiring. "What are you, twelve?" he snorted, looking me up and down. The manager at the pharmacy across the street was slightly more polite, but equally uninterested. I tried a Chinese carry-out down the block, but the woman behind the counter just shook her head as if she didn't understand English.

I hit the Poppy's at the next intersection, but it was nearly lunchtime, and the greyhairs working behind the counter were running like mice in a maze. I needed a job pretty bad, but I knew the heat, grease and intensity of a fast-food place would probably incite me to hurt someone. And since when did folks as old as Grandma work in fast food places?

By the time I got to Tony's Supermarket, I didn't expect much. The store, which was clean, but tastefully decorated with cracked linoleum tiles on the floor and stained ceiling tiles overhead, was the only source of meat, fruit and vegetables within a mile of my mother's place. Tall food compartments hummed louder than the corny Christmas carols sung by chipmunks over the store speakers. The manager, a paunchy, fifty-five-ish, dark-eyed guy with unnaturally black hair, looked me over carefully before asking me if I'd ever worked in a food store before.

"Yes, in North Carolina."

"Doing what?"

"Stock. Inventory. Sometimes checkout."

"You're kinda small for that."

"I'm stronger than I look."

"You got kids?"

"No!"

"How old are you?"

"Seventeen—but I'll be eighteen in a few days."

"That's nice, but I need someone reliable."

"Pardon me?"

"You'd have to work evenings and maybe nights, too. You can't do that with kids."

The guy needed a shave or something like it. His curly black hair also needed washing, and his hands, large and chapped, were stained.

"No kids," I repeated, remembering to be polite. "I'll be here day, night, whenever you need me."

He grunted and I caught a glimpse of myself in one of the security monitors behind his desk. He was right—standing there in my too-small jacket, my two-inches-past-my-shoulder-length hair pulled back in a ponytail, I might have been any one of the teen mothers who should have been in school, but was instead walking a tightrope over homelessness.

"I never seen you around here before," the manager said.

"I've been living with my grandmother in North Carolina."

"You still in school?"

"Until last week."

"And now?"

"I'll start again when the new semester begins next month. For now, I'll work as much as you let me."

The ballpoint pen in his hand hovered over the open book on his desk. He'd been writing when I walked up, and I got the impression that he really was proud of sitting in that glass booth, keeping track of the orders and accounting, while the other employees stocked, rang up customers or cleaned up messes in aisle five.

"You really gonna show up?" he said. "Most kids your age—"

"I'll be here."

He considered me a long moment. Strangely, I didn't see anything like lust in his eyes.

"I can give you six hours a week right now."

"Six hours? Please—I need more than that," I said.

"You start at six and we'll see how you do."

"Let me start at *twelve* and show you what I can do. *Sir.*"

He looked me over again and something in my eyes made him do a quick bouncing nod, eyebrows raised.

"What's your name?"

"Bethany Celeste Castle, but you can call me 'Annie.'"

"Annie Castle, huh?" His brows came together thoughtfully.

If Nina had been there she would have guffawed at 'Annie' ("that a *white* girl name!"), but this was a new day, and being 'Bethany' hadn't brought me much luck, lately.

"Alright," he said. "I don't know why I'm giving in, but if you wait here for a minute, I'll get someone to explain things to you. You can fill out the application during your break."

He got on the intercom and his voice echoed weirdly through the store. An older black woman who'd been watching us from her post at a checkout sidled up. She, too, looked me over like I was on an auction block.

"LaNell, start her out in inventory, and let me know when she can handle more," he said with the disinterest of someone who was used to workers coming and going like customers.

"Yeah, alright, Tony."

LaNell turned off the light at her station and motioned for me to follow her. Short like me, she had picked up a hundred pounds at some point and now rolled her enormous hips, belly and butt from one side to the other as she walked. Looking at her was like making a mental note to avoid chocolate and potato chips as if they were nuclear waste.

"Where you from? I ain't seen you round here," she asked over shoulder.

"North Carolina."

"What's your name?"

"People call me Annie."

"Annie?" she said. "Sound like a white girl name" (I could hear Nina howling). "My name 'sposed to be LaBelle, like Patti, but somebody made a mistake at the hospital and my momma just let it go."

"That's cool," I said. *That's messed up*, I thought.

She gave me a long red apron whose ties wrapped three times around my waist.

"You are *little*," she remarked, rolling her eyes. "Working here, that won't last long."

That morning I counted canisters of oatmeal, packages of lima beans, boxes of macaroni and cheese, and cans of tuna as if they were the crown jewels, though my soul screamed every time I glanced up to find a security camera mounted over me.

During my break I sat with the other workers in a grey cinderblock room in the back, drinking asphalt coffee from a stained machine while the other women feasted on outdated triple-layer cakes, Krispy Kreme donuts, peanut butter cookies and Moose-Track ice cream. Not wanting to alienate them, I worked very, very hard on the job application, and jumped up to turn it in rather than joining in the feast. I didn't want that stuff because it seemed to distance me from Nina, Gideon and my mother, who never had enough to eat. The others made it clear that while I was allowed to eat as much as I could cram down my gut during my breaks, I wasn't allowed to take any of the food home. Tony said the vendors would hold him accountable for the missing food, and that was grounds for getting fired.

I quickly found I could do my new job without using much of my mind, which was more of a curse than a blessing. Now I had hours to ponder how to make contact with Nina and Gideon. They had no address, or at least, it didn't seem like that house could be connected with an actual street address, and though they'd had a phone, my mother didn't have enough money to afford rice and beans, much less a bunch of long distance calls. I finally decided to write to them in care of the high school. I prayed the secretary would give the letter to Nina: after all, she worked for them, didn't she?

I found, however, that when I tried to get my emotions into words, I didn't know what to say. For starters, what if I really had hurt DeAndre? What had he done to her as payback? He probably assumed she knew where I'd gone, which, of course, she didn't. Would he go after Grandma? Was she safe, alone in that house? Was it smart to let anybody down there know where I was living now? Would Nina resent me for escaping DeAndre and making it to this new, momentarily safer life?

After thinking about it, I took a single sheet of paper and wrote a few lines:

December 27, 2001
Dear Nina and Gideon,
    You probably know by now that my Grandma made me leave. I'm back in Ohio with my mother. I am working now and will save money so I can get back to Blissfield ASAP. I'm incredibly sorry for what happened and I pray that you are both okay (Ben too!). I miss you both so much! PLEASE write back to me!
    I'll see you real soon,
    Love, love, LOVE,
    CeCe

I slipped the letter into an envelope and wrote Nina's name, care of Booker T. Washington High School, Blissfield, North Carolina. When I put it in the mail, I reckoned she'd receive it by the end of the week. I gave the house where I grew up as the return address, thinking that if she wrote back, the post office would forward the letter to our new place, and no one in Blissfield would know where we really lived.

Then, with the hopefulness of a seventeen-year-old, I waited.

Every day I got up at 5:00 a.m. and reported to the supermarket before 6:00 to help stock the shelves. The owner, whose name really was Tony, watched me with curiosity, as if waiting for the day he'd catch me sucking whipped cream from the canisters, sipping wine coolers in the employee toilet, or making out with one of the delivery men. He didn't seem to believe that someone my age really would show up on time and work herself to exhaustion, and occasionally I saw LaNelle, or Rasheeda, one of the other women, eyeing me distrustfully. I didn't react, because I really did need the money, though Copley, who prickled just beneath the surface of my skin, secretly urged me to confront them.

Copley only lost that fight because of Nina and Gideon. Their faces and voices kept me calm, focused, silent, no matter how long the shift. I ignored the pallets of fruit the others left for me to move from the stockroom to the shelves, the mountains of empty boxes that needed to be cut down for recycling, and the sour, cold coffee that waited for me when I finally found time to stop by the roach-infested break room. None of it mattered, because it was part of the dues I had to pay to get back to Blissfield.

After five days Tony called me over to the manager's booth near the cash registers.

"You learn quick. Why aren't you in school?"

"End of the month, when the new semester begins."

"Night school?"

I paused. It hadn't occurred to me that I could go to night school, like Gideon. "Yep," I said. "Why?"

"I was thinking about giving you an additional shift. You been working how many hours?"

"You asked me to do twelve, but I already did twenty this week. I could do more," I said.

"Okay, we'll take you up to thirty," he said. "You can come in on the weekend?"

"Sure."

"Good. I'll get LaNelle to show you how to work the cash register. But listen to me, Annie: if even one penny goes missing, it's your smart little tail. You understand?"

"Yes," I said, and once again he gave me that little bouncing nod.

When I got paid I took the check to a bank about two blocks from our house and opened an account. The bank noted that I was a few days shy of my eighteenth birthday, so I took the paperwork to Poppy's, the fast food joint, and forged my mother's signature while drinking the cheapest, hottest thing I could get—some bitter black coffee. I didn't tell my mother about the account. She cashed her checks at the corner liquor store, but Grandma had made it clear to me that you need to establish a bank account in order to properly manage your funds.

And then, I remembered my mother's phone conversation with my father the night I came home. I heard her tell him I hadn't brought any money with me. That she would have a look through my things. Though it made me sad to think about it, in all honesty, I was coming to understand even more disappointing things about my mother.

So when Bebe J asked me when the supermarket was going to pay me, I explained that the store was only giving me a 'training wage' for the first six weeks. This sounded like bullshit, even to me, but she couldn't seem to tell I was lying.

All the more reason my father walked all over her.

The day before Copley's hearing she started cleaning the duplex over and over again. She startled easily and sometimes stared out the windows for long periods without speaking. Finally I tried to talk with her.

"Has he called back?" I asked.

"Your daddy?"

"Yes. Do you know when he's coming home?"

"In a few weeks." She spoke wearily, as if exhausted from thinking about it.

"Are you going to get him?" I said.

"I don't have a car."

"I know, but does he expect you to come?"

She was quiet.

"Is there somebody else?" I asked, thinking that one of Copley's gambling buddies might drive up to Cleveland to bring him home. But something changed in my mother's face.

"It don't mean nothing," she said.

"What?" I said, confused.

"He love me," my mother said, "but she just wouldn't leave him alone."

"Who?"

"Her name Cynthia. She stay in the projects over behind the Goodyear plant."

"Wait—are you saying Copley's got another woman?"

"Don't call him—"

"Answer me, Momma."

"She ain't got no kids with him or nothing like that," BeBe J said.

"So, are you leaving?" I asked very softly.

"Leaving where?" she echoed, her eyes growing rounder.

"Leaving Copley."

"What?" she said breathlessly. I watched as she sank down on the flowered sofa and clasped her hands in her lap. "I can't."

"You can't what?" I asked, moving closer to her.

"I can't leave. He your daddy."

"So? He doesn't act like it."

"What do you mean?" she said. "He always did for you."

"He beats you."

"I made him mad sometimes."

"That's no excuse," I said.

"I'm not excusing it. I'm just saying I should of been a better wife."

Momma—" I sat down beside her. "—I saw all the shit he did and I thought it was normal. I didn't understand until you sent me to Grandma that men aren't supposed to hit women."

She was silent.

"He's wrong, Momma. He never, ever should lay a hand on you."

"He didn't really hurt me," she said, looking away.

"Yes he did!"

"I'm okay," she said, standing up. "I love your father."

"He doesn't love you," I said.

"We been together twenty years."

"And you've been his punching bag for twenty years."

"You don't know what you talking about," she said.

"I was there, Momma. I saw it."

"You don't remember what you seen."

"I remember everything," I said. "I just didn't understand it."

My mother shook her head. "You *still* don't understand. Copley not a bad man. He went out every night and brought his money back—"

"He hit you, slapped you, choked you, and yelled and screamed at you so long that now you're almost scared to breathe. You haven't even told him we don't live in our house anymore!"

"You just be quiet!" she cried, her face contorted. "You are a *child*! You cannot talk about your father this way!"

"Are you serious?"

"Shut up!" she shouted.

I had literally never seen my mother become angry. Never. I was stunned that she would turn her anger on me, when I was only trying to help her.

"Momma," I said, getting to my feet, too. "I don't want you to get hurt."

"Nobody going to hurt me," she insisted.

"Then why are you so scared of him?"

"I'm not scared!"

"Yes you *are*!" Without meaning to, I was shouting, too. She backed away, her hands up. I must have looked like my father at that moment, and it made me very sad.

"I'm sorry, Momma," I said. "I don't mean to scare you, but I'm telling you—you don't have to live this way."

"I don't know what you mean," she said.

"You're like a cat in a room full of pit bulls. That's how he wants you to feel."

"You need to stop, Bethany."

"He wants you to be too afraid to do anything," I said.

"He my husband—" she wailed.

"He's not your master!"

"You sound like you crazy!"

"He's the one who's crazy! He beat on you for years, and as soon as I got old enough to think for myself he started beating on me, too."

"I never saw him hit you," she said, her voice belligerent.

"What?" I said, stunned.

"That's a lie. He *never* hit you, Bethany."

"Then—then why did you send me away?" I said.

"I sent you away because—because we didn't have the money to give you what you needed."

"Are you serious?" I asked, my voice now low with rage.

"Your grandmother said she could send you to school, and teach you piano, and you could have nice friends and—"

"Oh my god!" I said. "You *know* I called Grandma after I fought with Copley and—"

"That never happened, Bethany! You're making it up!"

I was silent. She stood a few feet away from me, her eyes full of tears and her hands shaking. I would have felt sorry for her if she hadn't been lying about things that were so crucial to my life.

"You going to lie for him?" I asked quietly.

"You his daughter and you owe him your respect!"

"*Respect?*" I said. "You want me to respect a man who sells drugs, has another woman, and who's been beating you for years?"

"That's between me and your father."

"Until he came after me, too!"

"Your father never hurt you and he never will," she said.

"So I'm supposed to just watch him beat you when he gets home?"

"I expect you to mind your own business."

"Damn, Momma," I said softly. "If it wasn't bad enough that he kicked your ass every day, what kind of mother stands by the man who beat her daughter?"

Bebe J and I stared at each other. I could see her struggling to work out an answer. I could see she regretted what she'd already said. But she didn't regret it half as much as I did, for I realized at that moment that I would never be able to trust her again. No matter how badly he treated her, she would always choose her abuser over her child.

Worse than that, my anger was so intense that if I had let things go any further, I might not have been able to trust myself.

I wished with all my heart that I could go straight to Grandma and tell her what was happening. Then I remembered that my father was her son. That he grew up in her house. That somehow, she played a part in the man he'd become—and the woman I was fast becoming.

I also remembered that when faced with our own catastrophe, rather than fight for me, Grandma had simply put me on a bus back to this septic tank of a life.

So I turned around, went into the kitchen, took my jacket from the peg on the wall and walked down those treacherous stairs and out into the night.

Into the late December, northern Ohio cold.

Ice caked the sidewalks; half-melted snow formed ankle-deep tire tracks in the streets. Wind slapped the naked tree branches back and forth, and without a hat or gloves, I might as well have been naked. I had nowhere to go. The libraries were closed. Poppy's waited, greasy and crowded, on the next block, but the fluorescent lights and soiled plastic booths repelled me like a police interrogation room.

Because my thoughts were dangerous. I had wanted to hurt certain people in my life, and taken great pleasure in hurting them, but I had never before wanted to hurt my mother.

The fact that I was out on the streets to stop myself from going Copley on her scared the shit out of me. The fact that I shared his contempt for her meant that I had no right to judge him. But it also meant that I had no responsibility to save her. After all, she was spitting on my desire to protect us.

I was two days' shy of my eighteenth birthday. I couldn't go in any bars. I couldn't get a hotel room, even if I went and withdrew money from the ATM at my bank. I could ride the bus all night—I knew there were buses that went to the outskirts of the city and came back—and I could go to a homeless shelter.

I was motherfucking cold. My feet, in gym shoes, were freezing and wet. My fingers had no feeling. My ears and nose felt like they were made of glass. Even my lungs were starting to hurt.

But nothing hurt like my soul. Because I was genuinely afraid of myself as I walked through the Akron streets that night.

Miraculously, about ten blocks from my house, I passed a church that, against all odds, was lit up. The building, a stone structure with a soaring roof, stained glass windows and a separate Gothic bell tower, had once been beautiful. Though I wasn't surprised that the sign in front was bright—*St. Barnabas welcomes you!*—I was surprised to see the sidewalk beside the north entrance completely salted, cleared, and lit with gas lamps. It was like Jesus opened a Motel 6 just for me.

Expecting nothing, I made my way up the sidewalk and pushed on the heavy wooden door. I was met with a gush of hot, damp, meaty air. The black linoleum floor was mud splattered, and the foyer opened up to a long corridor with a number of stained glass doors. I listened and heard distant voices.

For a moment I hedged. I was still very, very angry, and anybody with any skill at reading body language might think I was walking away from a crime. I knew my eyes would show it, even if I did manage a smile. But I was also very cold, so I made my way down the hall.

I found myself in a small square room in which a group of some fifteen people sat in a circle. There was nothing remarkable about the room or the group, which included white and black men and women between the ages of about thirty, to, say, sixty. They were dressed casually, but their faces were serious when they looked over at me.

I hesitated, trying to understand what was going on. A bald-headed man stood up and walked toward me. I saw in his face that he was not an easy man, but I recognized his determination to meet me with some semblance of politeness. I couldn't blame him for being annoyed: it was late and this gathering was obviously private.

"Welcome," he said as he arrived at my side. "Are you here for the meeting?"

"Ah—yes." Behind the circle was a table with coffee and hot chocolate. He saw me looking, and glanced over his shoulder.

"Help yourself. We started about ten minutes ago."

I wandered over to the table, trying to appear nonchalant, while listening intently to their conversation. A man about Copley's age was talking, with some agitation, about leaving his wife.

"It was the hardest damn thing I ever had to do," he said, and I saw him reach up to wipe his eyes. "But she wouldn't stop asking me to come to her friends' houses and watch while they got messed up—or she invited them over and—and she couldn't stand that I wasn't going to do it with her anymore. So I had to choose: either leave her, or let her fuck me up..." He ran out of words, and the man sitting next to him patted him gently on the back.

264

Several people made affirming noises, nodding their heads in agreement.

"So," the man concluded, "I left. I left her, my house, my dog, all my friends, everything."

"*We're* your friends," someone said, and now the whole circle was agreeing.

Suddenly I got it. I had heard about these groups for years, even seen them in movies and television shows. I just never believed they were real.

After pouring myself a hot chocolate, I sat in a corner of the room in the semi-darkness. Huddling there, trying to warm up, I blew on my cup and waited for the rest of my body to come to life again.

Somebody looked over. "Hello," she said. "Please join us."

"That's okay."

"Um, this is a closed meeting," the bald guy man said. "You're welcome to join us, but if you're not in the Program, you have to leave."

"Oh," I said. I glanced at my chocolate and looked around awkwardly.

"Are you experiencing doubts about yourself?" the woman asked.

"Doubts?"

"It's always tough the first time. For many of us, the first step is the hardest."

"The first—?"

"Admitting you're powerless over your addiction."

"Oh, right." Every person in the circle was now staring in my direction. The woman, who was white and probably in her forties, stood and walked over to me. "Don't be afraid, sweetheart."

I let her lead me to the circle, and she pulled up a chair.

"How old are you, anyway?" the bald man asked.

"Eighteen," I answered, almost honestly.

"When did you start drinking?" he asked suspiciously.

"Damn, Martin—cut it out," the woman said. "She's here. That's what matters," another woman said.

"But she—"

"Welcome," the woman repeated, more forcefully. "What's your name, baby?"

The others remained silent as I sat down gingerly on the folding wooden chair.

"Bet—Elizabeth."

"Hi, Elizabeth," the entire group said, as if with one voice. I felt like I was in an X-ray with all those eyes vised on me.

"You don't have to say anything," the woman continued. "Just listen and participate if it feels comfortable."

That sounded perfect to me. I settled in, despite the hardness of my seat, and allowed myself to relax, my anger momentarily at bay.

The conversation shifted as several other people shared tales of similar distress. Though at first it seemed like I was in a room of whining weirdos, I quickly found myself identifying with lots of things I was hearing: broken families, beatings, fear, hunger, betrayals.

Well, just goddamn. Even though years of living with Copley had pretty much taught me to hate the smell and taste of alcohol, I had no doubt: These were my people.

The meeting ended after a time and they all began to rise. I quickly put my cup in the trash and zipped up my jacket.

"Is that all you have to wear, Elizabeth?" The same woman eyed me critically. She was putting on a fuzzy purple and pink plaid coat that looked really old, but really warm, and fit her perfectly.

"Not really. I just left home in a hurry."

"You didn't want to be late?"

"That's right."

"You can't possibly go out in this cold dressed that way. Come with me. We have a clothing exchange next door."

I followed her dutifully into another room. When she turned on the light, I found myself surrounded by rack upon rack of clean, pressed, neatly hung clothing.

I hesitated in the doorway.

"It's okay. Usually we ask people to leave something, but it's so cold you should just take a coat. Get a hat and some gloves, too.

It didn't take me long. The woman, who told me her name was Paula, stood by the door, watching.

As I was zipping myself into an oversized, gray down jacket and pulling a heavy red knit hat down over my ears, she stepped closer. I could smell her odor of warm patchouli oil, perhaps mixed with something like sandalwood.

"Do you have somewhere to stay tonight?"

"I—"

"It seemed like you were really lost when you came in."

"I had to get out of my house."

"Are your parents home?"

"My momma's home, but—" I hesitated to open up, feeling instinctively that I shouldn't tell anyone above our private family business. But there she stood, her eyes radiating intense, sincere interest.

"My father's in prison," I said, looking at the floor. "He's about to get out, or at least it looks that way, and I'm really scared about what's gonna happen when he comes home."

"Has he done something to hurt you?"

"He hurts my mother, mostly. I mean, I haven't seen him for a couple of years. My mother sent me down to North Carolina to live with my grandmother so he couldn't get to me."

She continued to look at me thoughtfully. I could smell the dry rot of the clothing, the distant scent of church incense, the coffee and hot chocolate from the room next store.

"I'm a social worker," she said. "Because you're eighteen I can't do much to intervene in your family situation, that is, unless your mother asks for my help."

"Actually, I'm still seventeen," I said. "I'll be eighteen in a couple more days."

"I thought so," she said. I looked up and was surprised to discover that her face was shrewd, but open and non-judging.

"Are you hungry?"

I shook my head.

"Want a ride home?"

I thought about it. It was late; the church was closing. I could hit Poppy's, or keep walking. I'd be warm enough in the down jacket and hat. I really didn't want to go back to the duplex, or to deal with my mother.

"No thanks. I'll be okay."

Paula nodded. "I'm going to give you my office number, Elizabeth. You call me tomorrow, or anytime if you need anything, alright?"

"Yes, thank you so much," I said, remembering to be polite.

"Elizabeth, it's hard enough dealing with these things when you're *my* age. The worst part of being your age is not knowing what to do, who to turn to, or what choices you've got. Listen to me: you have the right to be safe. You have the right to be warm and have enough to eat. Call me if you need my help."

She didn't touch me, try to hug me, or ask me where I was going. In a crazy way I realized that when I left that church, I really was alone in the world. My mother was not capable of doing for herself—or for me. Where I went and what I did was entirely on me, now.

But I did go home that night. The front door was unlocked, and when I climbed those narrow stairs I almost felt sorry for my mother. Almost.

The house was cold. I balled up on the sofa in the down jacket and slept for a few hours, then got up and went to work before dawn.

* * * * * * *

I worked a full shift that day, then stayed an additional shift for one of the other women. I'd been taught to handle the cash register, conduct inventory with the barcode scanner, and to manage stock in the storage areas in the back. The other workers were polite, but kept a distance, as if I came from a different country or something. I didn't care. I knew their names, but when I talked with them I'd suddenly forget what to call them, or what they'd told me about their families, or anything more than the fact that they worked there, too. I didn't chat, share their jokes, or meet them in the break room to eat the crap that no one in their right minds wanted to buy.

In other words, I was more than alone.

Late that day, as I was cleaning up the candy displays, my mother appeared at the end of the aisle. She was wearing her woolen man's coat and the knitted scarf, along with a pair of heavy boots. She walked hesitantly toward me, her face down. She was holding a brown bag.

"I brought you something to eat," she said so quietly I could barely hear her.

I stood up and smoothed my apron. "Thanks, Momma, but this is a food store."

"Oh," she said, looking around as if surprised. "I—I didn't know if you was allowed to eat."

"I can buy food, just like you."

"Yeah, I guess that's right." She looked a bit lost. "Do you have money?"

"Sure," I said, no longer ashamed I'd lied to her about my pay.

"Oh," she repeated. "Well—you okay?"

"I'm fine."

"I waited up for you last night."

"I got in pretty late and didn't want to disturb you," I said.

"I wouldn't of cared."

"I did okay on the couch."

"You not still mad, are you?"

"Should I be?" I asked.

LaNelle passed at the end of the aisle and stood there, eyeballing us.

"Hey, Mom, I can't do this right now. If they think I'm messing around I could lose my job."

"Will you be late tonight?"

"This shift ends at ten. I'll probably get something to eat with my coworkers and then be home afterward." I was lying, but I didn't care.

"I have to be at work at seven tomorrow morning," she said.

"Well, if I don't talk to you tonight, maybe we'll have time tomorrow night or the next day."

I turned back to my shelves and she stood there a moment, then slowly walked away, still holding the brown bag. LaNelle stared at her openly, without the slightest pretense of politeness, and anger flared up in me. Yes, my mother was wearing a man's coat, and yes, I'd treated her like little more than a stranger. But it didn't give this cow the right to look at her like that.

When my shift ended that night I found myself walking in the opposite direction from the duplex. There was no point in going home. My mother had told me she had to start work early the next day and I figured she was already in bed. Even if she was up, I didn't want to hear any more of her bullshit.

I wasn't hungry. I was almost never hungry, and though physically exhausted, my thoughts were sharp as shards of broken glass and painfully, surgically precise.

I ached to see Nina and to hear Gideon's voice. The past two years loomed like a dream, almost a fantasy, and I couldn't bear to think that I would never return to the yellow frame house, the enormous Buick, the dinner table set with good food, the simple decent clothes, church on Sundays, the shaded backyard and most of all, the people I loved. I still hoped against all hope that I might get a letter from Nina, telling me DeAndre had been arrested, or maybe stabbed or shot dead, and that it was safe for me to come back home.

I walked into Poppy's and ordered a coffee. I knew I looked like a fool in my oversized down jacket and ridiculous red hat, but I really didn't give a shit. The girl in the hideous orange and yellow uniform smirked as she handed me the Styrofoam cup, and when I tasted the muddy brine she rolled her head to let me know she'd had a shitty day and *really* hoped I'd give her some backtalk so she could mess my evening up, too.

But I was only there to escape the cold and to keep from climbing those narrow steps to the top floor of the duplex.

I crammed myself into one of the plastic booths, the fluorescent lights buzzing overhead as I warmed my hands over the steaming cup.

"Damn, girl, you look like you from another planet," someone said.

The voice was low and neither too young, nor exactly too old to try to hit on me. Though I didn't want to dignify the comment with a reaction, my instinct for self-preservation told me I'd better have a look.

The man was everything smooth. His almond skin was brushstroke fine, with neither blemish, nor the trace of a beard. Conversely, he sported a carefully-trimmed moustache that poured glossy and black over his full brown lips. I had never seen such onyx eyes: eyes without a hint of seriousness, yet without the slightest humor. He was seeing his life through a lens that was unknown to me, and I knew in an instant it was better left that way.

He was wearing a black knit cap and an earring glinted from an uncovered lobe. His jacket was some kind of silvery fabric that looked expensive. I saw he had on black jeans and dark boots. Not the typical street thug. Maybe a master player, unlike my stupid, wanna-be gangsta father.

Without so much as blinking, I slid out of the booth and walked to the rear corner of the room. The five-six other customers didn't so much as glance in my direction, as if pretending not to see immunized them from what was going down.

I sat so I was facing the drive-through. I was close enough to the kitchen door to call out if I needed help, and just adjacent to the women's bathroom, which might serve as a refuge, if Mr. Smooth decided not to leave me the fuck alone.

Within seconds, I watched as his reflection rose and sauntered over, taking a seat in the both next to mine.

He addressed my mirrored image as I stared steadfastly at the cars lining up for the drive-through.

"That wasn't a joke, baby. You wearing that messed-up coat make it look better than any other woman on earth."

Glancing toward the bathroom, I calculated how long it would take me to get there after splashing my scalding coffee in Smooth's face.

He continued. "You really want to lower the temperature up in here? It's already below freezing out there."

Still refraining from answering, I zipped up my collar so it hid the bottom half of my face.

"You know I ain't trying to hit on you," he said. "Can't nobody even see you with that hat pulled down to your nose and your collar pulled up to your ears."

I glanced around for a security guard, and found none. The place would close shortly, and both this man and I would be expelled to the streets. I was pretty sure I didn't want him following me, so I decided to get rid of him as soon as possible.

"What the hell do you want?" I said without turning my head.

"Wow—she can talk. Maybe she *is* a member of the human race."

"I don't have shit to say to you, and I don't want to hear whatever shit you trying to say to me."

"And she knows her rights."

"Fuck you."

"Right now?"

The conversation had moved altogether too swiftly into a zone I was unprepared for, so I stood and threw my coffee in the trash. I then went into the bathroom, peed, pulled my hat low and carefully zipped up my coat. I had enough money for a taxi, though I didn't want to spend it, but if he was still hanging around when I went outside I'd have to find a cab to get back to the flat.

Predictably, he was now sitting on the table with his feet resting on two of the chairs. He had unzipped his jacket, which sported the logo of an expensive brand of outdoor sports clothing, to show me a University of Akron tee-shirt underneath.

"Okay," he said. "I scared you. I didn't mean to. I thought you were a student. Now I realize I was mistaken. Don't call the cops or anything. Since they're about to close this place up, I thought the least I could do was offer you a ride home."

I walked past him and, without looking back, launched myself into the night. Freezing rain stung my face and almost immediately began to saturate my jacket. The streets had a thick icy sheen that sparkled in the streetlights, and the sidewalks were a skating rink under my thin shoes. Few cars were out and there was nothing that resembled a cab in sight. I decided to catch the nearest bus, ride wherever it was going until it was so late there was no possibility that my mother would still be up.

Arcs of ice-blown light ringed the pitch-black streets. If I hadn't been so afraid of falling, I would have found an unlit path or alley to navigate, rather than risking the exposure of the street. But it was on the open street that I was probably safest if the man decided to try and follow me.

A bus stop was less than a block away. I had to walk like I was ninety years old, my arms lifted for balance, feeling every step out before planting my weight on the ice. I had only made it a few hundred feet when a midnight-black SUV with fully tinted windows slid up beside me. The driver blew the horn and rolled the passenger window down.

"Hey, girl! Get in! It's fucked up out there."

I ignored the voice, focusing instead on my feet.

"Don't be scared," he called. "I'm not an ax-murderer or anything. Just let me get you to the bus stop, or to your place or whatever."

I kept sliding forward, struggling not to end up on my ass. Beside me, the truck's engine purred menacingly.

"Jesus!" he shouted. "I'm not going to hurt you. I just want to give you a hand."

He drove alongside me, keeping pace with my uncertain steps.

"Hey," he said in a mocking sing-song, "it's warm and dry in here!"

Valiantly, even desperately, I continued to ignore him.

"Listen: I apologize for spooking you. I really didn't mean to freak you out in there. You didn't need to take off like that!"

"*You* listen, asshole," I yelled, finally raising my head. "I'm calling the cops if you don't leave me the fuck alone. I don't need your help. I don't want a goddamn ride, and I'm not getting in your motherfucking truck."

"How about if I apologize again for that stupid shit I sa—"

He had turned on the interior cabin lights, and I could see him peering back and forth between the road and me so he wouldn't hit any parked cars.

"Listen, dickhead," I shouted, "I don't know what your problem is, but it's late, I'm tired, and you do *not* want to fuck with me."

"I'd like to drive you home," he said.

"Leave me the fuck alone."

"Okay. But first, let me get you somewhere safe."

"Fuck *off*, asshole!"

"Baby, I'm trying to protect you."

I attempted to walk faster. The bus stop was less than half a block away and I could see the lights of a bus approaching through the thickening sleet.

"I'm not going to hurt you," he yelled.

"I'm calling the motherfucking cops," I shouted, pretending to pull out a phone I didn't have.

"You don't need to call the cops," he shouted. "I *am* a cop."

His words stopped me cold. He drove on a short distance, then halted, too.

I began jogging clumsily and waving my arms in the hopes of alerting the bus, which was just pulling up to the bus stop. My right foot slipped and I went down heavily on my hands and knees, icy water splashing up my shins, soaking my jeans and saturating my gym shoes.

Ignoring my slamming heart and the shock of painful cold, I climbed back to my feet and kept on running. Breathless, tears of pain and frustration running down my face, I arrived at the stop just as the bus pulled away. I leaned against the metal frame of the shelter in the darkness, my shoes, jeans and jacket sopping with ice-water.

Then the purring was beside me. The blackened window slid open once again.

"Look," the guy said, "you really don't have to afraid. I actually *am* a cop."

"So the fuck what?" I said, my breath exploding in clouds of ice.

"You're not safe here. Let me help you."

"Why would you want to help me?"

"I know you're okay," he said. "You work at Tony's. I've seen you there."

I didn't answer. I'd never noticed him in the store. But then I never noticed anyone. My mind was in Blissfield as I stacked the shelves and slid people's groceries across the scanner.

"This is my final offer," he said. "I'll drive you home if you want. I promise you're safe with me. I'm holding up my badge so you can see it. Look!"

I couldn't think of what to do or say. I was so cold I thought my heart might stop. I felt like lying down, right there, and never taking another step.

The driver's door opened, and he emerged, coming around to open the passenger door for me. He held out his hand. "Get in."

No one knew where I was. No one cared. I didn't know if I was selling my soul, or what was left of it, but I stepped off the icy curb, walked through the gathering snow, and let him help me into his vehicle.

twenty-three.

His apartment was the shit.

I had never even imagined anything like it. We drove through the blizzard to the industrial edge of the city, a district of empty steel and cement buildings, and just as I resigned myself to death and dismemberment, we pulled up to a grilled entrance, which opened when he swiped a card through a box at his window. In contrast to all that yelling on the street, we hadn't spoken a word during the entire trip, and remained silent as the grill slid open.

We rolled down a short ramp into a spotless underground garage, and parked in a numbered space, surrounded by other cars. He came around to my door, and when I climbed out he began by brushing the remaining ice off my shoulders and the top of my hat.

"You okay?"

I stood like a statue, looking at his chest. The minute I got in his truck I'd reverted to the Bethany Celeste from Copley Castle's world, and, exhausted and scared, I was running on killer-instinct now.

He gestured toward an elevator in the corner of the garage, then locked the car with a flick of his wrist. I moved slowly, mechanically, every sense on high alert. We got into the elevator and he pushed a number. I didn't see which number. I was too busy watching his hands.

When the elevator doors opened we were facing a dimly lit cement corridor with two or three shining metal doors. We walked the length of the virtually silent corridor, and he unlocked a door which was unmarked except for a peephole, and walked ahead of me into the apartment. A light switched on and he said, "welcome to my castle."

I entered a single enormous room with floor-to-ceiling windows looking out over the city. A kitchen of gleaming steel appliances was wrapped around one wall, with a wide, acid-washed cement counter (as he explained later), rising across from it. The polished cement floors were covered by large area rugs that sectioned the remaining space into a dining area with a rough wooden table, a living area with a long leather sofa flanked by a couple of armchairs, an enormous television on a black metal stand, and, in the far corner, a three-person bed. A series of folding doors signaled closet space and, behind a glass brick wall was, I figured, a bathroom.

I had never seen a loft before, so my confusion grew. I turned back to look at him as he locked the door and shrugged out of his coat.

"How about some tea?" he said.

I hadn't moved more than two feet from the threshold. Looking him over swiftly, I was now surprised to find him leaner and taller than I'd imagined in the fast-food restaurant.

When I didn't answer, a note of annoyance crept into his voice. "Hey. You don't have to stay. I'll call you a cab, if you want. But if you're willing to stay, please let me dry those wet clothes. You're leaking all over my floor."

I looked down at the muddy sleet dripping from my pants, socks and shoes.

"Here—" he held out his arm. "I'm not going to touch you, okay? Just take off the hat and coat and those kicks. I'll get you some dry pants. Alright?"

I exhaled slowly. It was way too late to do anything but comply.

He crossed the room and returned with a pair of clean socks and some sweat pants. Still standing by the door, I soon found myself stripped of my coat, shoes, hat and socks. He loaded my clothes into a dryer behind one of the folding doors and placed my shoes on a radiator beneath the windows.

"Those pants are going to be way too big," he said, "but at least they're dry. The bathroom's over there, behind that glass. Help yourself."

I moved slowly across the room, listening intently to see if he was following me. Instead, I heard him rummaging around the kitchen. He ran water, turned on the gas and set a kettle on the stove. As I dressed he opened and closed cabinets and the fridge.

The bathroom was small and efficiently built, with double sinks along one wall, a double-wide glassed-in shower, and a commode. I didn't bother to turn on the light, because plenty of light was coming in from the main room, and I didn't want the mirror to show me how bad I looked.

I came out slowly, grasping a handful of the sweat pants at the waist because, though I had pulled the drawstrings tight, they still slid down over my hips.

I was still wearing a long-sleeved tee-shirt under a sweat shirt, clothes I'd found piled in a corner of BeBe J's place. The supermarket was always cold, particularly back in the stockrooms. I knew I looked even more like my father, but I wanted it that way. Nina's fashion sense had taught me a thing or two, after all.

The guy was standing behind the counter, pouring hot water into mugs. A scent of warm cinnamon filled the room.

Cut lean, like the runners on our high school track team, his shoulders and arms were rounded and muscular, his thighs at once thick and stringy. His black tee-shirt and jeans fit him well, but were still loose enough for him to comfortably wear a shoulder belt with a walkie-talkie device, and, I could see, a holster.

So he really *was* a cop. Something inside me both relaxed and tightened.

"This," he said as he slid the mug across the counter, "is called *chai*. Ever tasted it?"

"Is it spiked?"

"That would be a waste of good tea," he answered drily. Two bar stools were pulled up to the counter. "Sit down," he said, holding up three fingers. "You're safe. Scouts honor."

I slid one hip onto a stool and looked at the tea. He lifted a carton of Half and Half and said, "You're really supposed to drink this with cream. Is it okay if I give you a shot?"

"A shot?" I asked.

"Only cream," he answered.

I didn't react and he laughed. "Okay—full disclosure: it's Half and Half. That is, half milk and half cream. Less dangerous to the waistline."

Once again he laughed alone. He pursed his lips. "Either you're froze solid or I'm seriously not funny."

"What do you want from me?" I asked coldly.

"She speaks," he said, his eyes measuring. There was another pause while he worked at getting the right expression on his face. "What do I want? Absolutely nothing."

"Then why am I here?" I said.

"You're the best person to answer that."

"Why didn't you just leave me alone?"

"It was a dark and stormy night. You didn't seem to have anywhere to go."

"So you're some kind of Daddy Warbucks?"

He really laughed this time. "Well, I see she knows the comics."

"I'd appreciate an answer."

"Look, whatever your name is, I thought I was being a good citizen. I'll call you a cab right now. Please remember that I offered, but you refused to tell me where to take you."

I looked down at the tea, which smelled both peppery and sweet. He poured a bit of cream into it and I watched the color change from deep red to a soft orangey white.

"Please give it a try before it gets too cold," he said.

I lifted the mug and brought it to my lips. The tea tasted like a cinnamon drop stirred into vanilla ice cream.

"What do you think?" he said.

I nodded, staring at the mug. When I looked up he was smiling.

"You hungry?" he asked.

I shook my head.

He held out his hand. "The name is Jesse. *Not* Jesse James—Jessie Brantley. Graduate of the University of Akron and the State Police Academy. Twelve-year veteran of the Akron police force. Savior of lost ladies on dark and stormy nights."

Ignoring his hand, I drank some more of the tea, then set the mug down on the counter.

"Okay," he said, dropping his hand to the counter. "You don't do meet-and-greets. You won't tell me what you want or need. If I didn't know any better, I'd be a little bit scared of you."

Good instincts, I thought with my own inward smile.

He was still wearing the knit cap he'd had on in Poppy's. Now he pulled the hat off, revealing a perfectly bald head. The apartment was warm and despite the huge, naked windows, quite comfortable.

The tea was calming me down, too.

"Okay," I said. "Thank you for getting me out of the snow. Thank you for the dry clothes and the tea."

"Good manners, too," he said approvingly. "So what *were* you doing in Poppy's, during an ice-storm, at this time of night?"

"Having a coffee, till you messed that up."

"Were you waiting on somebody?"

"Yeah," I said. "My fairy godmother promised to drop by with some spare benjamins."

"You got nowhere to go?" he asked.

"Nowhere I want to go," I said. "And by the way, I wasn't trying to go on any 'dates,' either."

"Never crossed my mind, with you looking so fashion-forward," he said.

"That's hard to believe," I said, "you being a cop and all."

"Are you willing to tell me your name?"

"In exchange for what?"

"Your rear on that barstool."

"Sure," I said.

He waited a beat. "Could you share that bit of information now?"

I took another look at his coal black eyes. "My name is Bethany Celeste Castle. I've been living in North Carolina for the past two years. I got back here a few weeks ago. My father is named Copley Castle. He's in prison in Cleveland. I haven't seen or heard from him since I left. He's due home in about two weeks. My mother is named Brenda Berniece Castle. She works in a dry cleaners over on Hawkins."

Jesse fell back against the sink as if pushed by a strong wind. "Wow," he said quietly. "Once you get her started she don't hold back."

"Just saving time and energy," I said.

He stepped forward again and leaned down on the counter. "Why are you out on the streets, Bethany?"

"Call me Celeste," I said. "Nobody ever calls me Celeste."

"Alright, Celeste. Why are you on the streets?"

"Because my father beat my mother, and then he started to beat on me, and my mother continues to protect him."

"But you said he's not back."

"He will be," I said, "and I can't live that way anymore."

"Does your mother know you feel like this?"

"Yes, and she doesn't care."

"Maybe she just doesn't know what to—"

"So you're a therapist, too?" I said.

For a long moment neither one of us spoke. I realized that his apartment was absolutely silent. No sound filtered up from the streets, and nothing could be heard from the apartments above or below.

"Listen," he said, "if you need some support from Social Services I can —"

"Nobody's making my mother change her mind," I said. "Believe me, I've tried."

"Sometimes," he responded with a gentleness I didn't expect, "people don't understand their lives can be better. She probably tells herself that he needs her."

"Bingo," I said.

He paused. "You really don't want to be at home?"

"My home is gone," I said. "My mother lost our house. She's living in a run-down duplex on a street full of boarded-up buildings."

"Where?"

"Over off of Exchange."

"Does your father know?"

"She's afraid to tell him."

I saw him looking at me again, gauging whether to humor, cajole, or simply speak his mind. "You're not making enough money at that store to take care of yourself," he remarked.

"I'll figure it out," I said.

"And in the meantime you're sleeping in fast-food joints and bus-stops."

"In the meantime I'm working, watching my paycheck and trying to stay away from creeps in cars."

"How's that working out for you?" he asked.

I paused. "You don't have to worry about me."

"Just pointing out the obvious," he said.

I glanced around me. "Speaking of obvious, how can you afford this?"

"It's only one room, if you look carefully."

"One expensive room."

"It would be," he said, "if people with money wanted to live down here. Fact is, these apartments were empty for two years before the builder gave up and lowered the price. Now it's full of lecturers from the university and journalism interns from the *Beacon Journal*, and everybody loves having a cop for a neighbor."

"So you've got this nice place," I said, "but you still prefer hanging around Poppy's at night?"

"There's been some shady shit going on in there, so I go in and take a look around every once in a while."

"A look for what?" I asked.

"Whatever needs to be seen."

"And some things that don't."

"That's the job." For the first time his voice gained an edge, as if the nice-guy act was starting to tire him out.

"So," he said, standing up and taking our mugs to the sink, "it's getting late and I've got to get in early tomorrow. That couch looks hard, but I'm told it's really quite comfortable. I'll get you a sheet and some blankets, okay? I'm going to trust that since I plan to leave you here in the morning, I won't come back and find any of my shit missing."

"You don't have to count the spoons," I said. "I've got to go in early, too."

I slid off the barstool and walked over to the sofa, sitting on it gingerly. The cushions were unexpectedly soft. The snow had stopped, and my attention was drawn to the headlights climbing the city's distant hills. They seemed to be in a different world.

I looked up to find him standing beside me, a bundle in his arms. He set the bedclothes down on the sofa.

"Why are you helping me?" I asked for what must have been the fifth or sixth time.

"You looked lost."

"That simple?"

"Was for me."

He walked away. I listened as he went into the bathroom and closed the door. The shower ran for a long time. Then he brushed his teeth and the toilet flushed. He came out and walked straight to his bed.

"All yours," he said.

I heard him stretch out. He turned the kitchen light off with a remote, then settled into the black silence.

I waited for a while, then slowly stood. My body was warm and comfortable, and I wanted to let go of my anger and fear. But it had been a while since I hadn't been angry and afraid. Anger and fear seemed like the safest, most normal place to be.

The polished cement floor shone in the distant lights. It was warmer than I expected, even through my socks. When I got to the bathroom I found a clean towel and washcloth on the counter. I closed and locked the door, then turned on the shower.

The flow from the showerhead was so strong it hurt. I turned the temperature up as high as I could stand it, and stood there, feeling the water strip off my mother's blankness, Grandma's sad determination and Nina's stammering surrender. The lint brains and *burtle* went down the drain, along with that idiot woman who watched Grandma's house from across the street. The only person who stayed under my skin was the person I most wanted to see. As I stood naked in the hot, steaming water, I would have opened my veins to touch, hear or lay my eyes on Gideon.

Suddenly I ducked my entire head under the water and pulled open my braid. I hadn't washed my hair in days, and my scalp nearly screamed in the pleasure of the hot water. I didn't care how I'd look the next day. I didn't care if my curlynappy mess turned into dreads. I didn't care about anything at all.

I didn't have a toothbrush, and he hadn't left one out for me, but I did what I could to clean my mouth. Then I stood in front of the mirror and examined myself.

I had no idea how old I looked. I mean, my face was, despite my teenage boy's body, still slightly rounded. My skin was clear, though I no longer ate Grandma's good food, and my hair, now towel dried, had become a rough, tangled mess.

I glanced at the rest of me. There wasn't much to see. I was thinner than I'd been in the past two years, with little bumps for breasts and a fine ribbon of hair between my legs. Dulled with exhaustion, I wiped the counter dry and hung up my damp towels. I slipped into my underwear, then had second thoughts and put all the clothes on, in case I'd need to make a swift departure.

The loft was filled with night. Akron blinked and winked below. I stood by the glass wall, looking at the big room and the shape of the man under the covers. Barefoot, I went to the kitchen and slid one of the steak knives out of its wooden stand.

I walked over to the bed. The cop didn't move, and for a moment I thought he was asleep.

"What do you need, Celeste?" he said.

I thought about how different his low, clear voice was from Gideon's.

"I just wanted to let you know," I said casually, "that I will fuck you up if you come anywhere near me."

"You don't have to worry about either one of those options," he said.

"I mean it."

"So do I."

He turned on the lamp beside the bed. When he sat up the sheet fell away. He was actually wearing flannel pajamas.

"Listen, Celeste," he said. "I'm not a predator. I didn't bring you here for sex. I'm just trying to help you out." He pointed to the sofa. "Wrap up in those blankets and go to sleep."

I stared at him, still trying to make out if he was lying.

"How old are you?" he asked.

"Do you want to know the truth?"

"Yes."

"I turned eighteen twelve minutes ago."

"Sheeeeit," he whispered. "I figured you were young, but not *that* motherfuck-ing young. I'll tell you what, Celeste: you take my bed and I'll make do on the couch tonight. Tomorrow we'll look for someplace better for you to go."

He threw back the covers and stood up. "I got it all warmed up for you. Go on and get under the covers. Do it now. It's late and I'm tired. Do you under-stand?" His voice had hardened and I knew he was serious, so I did as I was told.

I felt his annoyance as he walked over to the couch and unfolded the sheet and blankets. He spread out the sheet and sat down, pulling the ends over his legs. He then covered himself with two blankets and turned on his side. With his legs folded, his feet didn't stick out over the end of the cushions.

"Turn off the light, Celeste. Good night."

* * * * * * *

The morning was also coldly polite. I awakened to a half-flattened curlynappy afro and the smell of coffee. He was already in a black tee-shirt and black jeans, but today he'd added a suit coat to his look.

"There's coffee in the pot," he said. "You want some oatmeal? It's brown sugar- cinnamon."

"What's with you and cinnamon?" I asked from his bed.

"I think the correct response is 'thank you.'"

"I wouldn't want to miss a chance to be correct," I said, standing up. The loose sweatpants began to fall and I caught the waistband. "So in order to be cor-rect," I continued, "please let me borrow a belt tonight."

"There won't be any tonights," he answered. "I need my own bed and so do you. If you're not going home, we're contacting Social Services to see if we can find you a group home or halfway house."

"I'm of age," I said, walking to the doors that hid the washer and dryer. "I don't have to go anywhere."

"Well, you can't stay here."

"I could clean," I offered.

"You can't stay here."

"I'm not a bad cook."

"You're still a kid and you can't stay here."

"I'm not a kid. I told you last night."

"What you said is what convinced me you're a kid," he replied. "I've told you three times you can't stay here. If I say it again, you'll turn back into a frog."

I removed my clothes from the dryer and went behind the glass wall to dress. When I came out he was putting on his coat.

"You've got two minutes," he said, "or you'll have to find your own way back across town."

"But my hair—"

"Not my problem."

"Could I at least get a coffee?"

"One minute fifty seconds."

I ran back into the bathroom to try and pull myself together while he poured the java into a small thermos. When I came out he was looking impatiently at the floor.

"Twenty seconds."

I jogged the last few steps. He opened the door and followed me out.

"Thank you," I said as he locked the door behind us.

"For?"

"For not arresting me for anything. For getting me into your car. For the dry clothes. For introducing me to *chai*. For letting me use your shower. For giving up your bed. For being a good citizen."

"And?" he said with a half-smile.

"And for trying to help me find a better place to stay, Officer Brantley."

"And I have to thank you for not carving me up in my sleep with that steak knife you 'borrowed' from the kitchen," he said.

He smiled harder as he led me briskly down the hall. "You're something else, Ms. Bethany Celeste Castile."

"That's 'Castle.'"

"I know," he said. "Just making sure you were paying attention."

* * * * * * *

Though he said he wanted to help me, I honestly never expected to see him again. He dropped me off at Tony's and kept on driving without so much as a backward glance.

Around noon, while I was stocking fruit, Tony called me via the store intercom. I came up to the front, flushed with embarrassment, to find my mother standing there once again.

"I'm going on break," I said to Tony, who was eyeing my mother with a mixture of clear lust and clearer distrust. The woolen men's coat that incited LaNell's attention the day before really was becoming on her shapely body, but its bulk invited shoplifting the way a kangaroo's pouch hid her joey.

Taking off my apron, I led her to the front of the store—as close to the door as I dared without the entire staff thinking I was passing her merchandise or money. I looked into her face, ready and perfectly willing to lie.

"You didn't come home last night."

"No, and I won't be back, except to pick up the stuff I brought from North Carolina."

"Why, Beth?"

Her face was filled with pleading, and I felt a wave of shame, followed by frustration at my realization that she simply refused to understand.

"When's he coming home?" I asked.

"Your daddy? He called last night. He thinks he'll be out a week from Friday."

I calculated quickly. His release was ten days away. She had ten days to convince me to stay with her, in case he didn't take the loss of the house very well. Ten days to arrange for my presence, and the fact that I had a job, to serve as a buffer between her body and his rage.

"Momma, I love you, but I just can't do it."

"Do what?"

"Stay there and watch what's going to happen," I said.

"Nothing's going to happen, Bethany. Your father's glad to be coming home."

"Did you tell him about the house?"

She hesitated. "Not yet, but it'll be okay." Her eyes were wide open, honest in their own way, and filled with desperation.

"I'm afraid," I said to her.

"You don't have to be, baby. Everything's going to be alright."

I turned to look at the snow twinkling under the Nordic blue sky. Though I loved the mild winters in Blissfield, sometimes I'd missed the pure, diamond-steel winters of Akron.

"I'm not coming back," I said, making the decision final even as I said it.

"But—"

"Somebody's helping me find somewhere else to live," I said. "I've got my own money, now. I can take care of myself."

"But we a family," she whispered, as if saying the words quietly enough might protect us from the truth.

"We can still be a family," I answered, "if Copley behaves. It's just going to be a new kind of family, where I live someplace else."

"But what about school?"

"I'll get back to that in a little while."

"You can't just quit!"

"*You* did."

"And look what I have to do to put bread on the table!" She glanced at the clock over the manager's station: her lunch break was almost over.

"All the more reason for me to be taking care of myself," I answered, tying on my apron.

"What would your grandmother say?" she asked, taking her last best shot.

I considered my answer for a moment. "I figure she'd say 'good luck and good riddance.'"

I turned to go and my mother grasped my arm. "Will you at least come home tonight? It's your birthday."

I laughed. "Thanks for reminding me. I actually forgot."

"But Bethany—"

I walked away, not because I wanted to hurt her, but because I didn't want her to see the tears in my eyes. I returned to the fruit section and went back to work with almost insane purpose, refusing to think about Copley, Bebe J, Grandma or Nina. I focused my mind on Gideon. Always, hanging around in the shadows of my heart, his voice a rough whisper, his touch liquid fire, was Gideon.

Again I took a double shift, and as the afternoon slipped away I began thinking about where I would sleep, since my options were so very brilliant. I wondered if I could slip back into the church and find a way into the sanctuary, where I might curl up on a remote pew. Poppy's wasn't going to work, because the cop might show up there again. The buses seemed my best shot. I'd heard in passing that it was possible to stay warm and safe as long as the driver didn't decide to be an asshole and throw you off—or worse.

I really did need to get some fresh clothes, too. My mother normally worked during the day, so I planned to go by the duplex and pack up some clothes the following morning. Getting in the house was a problem I'd deal with once I arrived.

So I really was surprised when Jesse Brantley walked up as I straightened the cereal shelves, his watch cap pulled low, his expensive gunmetal jacket velcroed tight against the cold. He walked with just a hint of a dip, like any good man of the streets, and his black eyes were ever cold and watchful.

"Celeste, I see you're pulling a double."

"Double the money, double the fun," I said dryly.

"You planning on going home tonight?"

"Nope."

"Hotel?"

"I don't know," I said.

He sucked his teeth. "You trying for Poppy's?"

"Hell no. I heard a cop's hanging out there."

"Where, then?"

"I don't know—the busses, maybe."

"No, baby. That's how you get robbed, raped, or your very own obituary."

"Then what do you recommend, as a career rescuer of lost women?"

"There are shelters, but in this weather they fill up by six or seven o'clock. When do you get off?"

"Ten," I said.

"Too late."

"Don't you have some pull?"

"Full is full," he said. "They have to respect fire laws and such."

"So what do you think I should to do, Officer?"

He paused. We were speaking in low voices, neither of us particularly friendly or cordial. But there was something personal in the way his eyes continually appraised mine. I guessed that much of his success as a cop depended on him being good at reading people. I felt that he was reading and re-reading me, like I was a book that got more interesting or complex each time you opened it.

But then again, maybe he was just using his interrogation skills to lead me toward the conclusion he wanted.

"So," I repeated, waiting with some annoyance for his answer, "what do you want me to do?"

"First of all, I want you to get out of those funky clothes," he said in a new voice, one that was less commanding, "and into something clean. I can smell you from here."

"Can't do a damn thing about my smell," I said, after lifting both arms and taking a quick sniff. "I left my little black dress and Chanel No. 5 in the back of my limo."

I caught his smile, which vanished as fast as it came.

"Second," he continued, "I want you to eat some food so you don't go on resembling one of the walking dead."

"Keep the compliments coming," I said.

"Third, I really need you to figure out how you want to spend the evening of your eighteenth birthday, because Celeste, this place just ain't getting' it."

I shrugged. "Better than Poppy's or the back of a bus."

He shook his head. "I'm going to speak to Tony now. Go put your apron away and meet me at the front. You've got—" he looked at his watch "—exactly seven minutes."

"But I need the mon—"

"Six fifty-five."

I looked into his face. "Hurry up," he said. "It's too damn hot for me to be standing here in this coat and hat, and I sure as hell don't want to be stankin' like you."

* * * * * * *

I didn't dare ask what was really going on as we drove through the early evening streets toward the industrial district and his loft. He put some jazz on in the car—a woman was singing a really sad song about flying away—and he didn't so much as look my way during the entire trip. He took a couple of bulging bags from the trunk and carried them up, checking his phone messages in the elevator and as we walked down the corridor to his door.

The loft was even more impressive in the fading light. He had a beautiful view of the sun setting over the graceful suspension bridge that tied the west end of the city to downtown, and the wintry light cast the entire apartment in a faint pinkish glow.

He came up behind me. "Look: I'm no good at buying women's clothes, but you need something warm to wear. Head into the shower and get yourself cleaned up. You can keep whatever fits, but don't take the tags off anything 'til you've tried them on. And Celeste—*do* take that shower, first." He handed me four bags and walked back to the kitchen, where he began doing what he seemed to love best: making tea.

Though everything in my past was telling me I was being lured into some kind of trap, I was willing to take the bait. I *knew* I stank: I was coming to understand that my odor might repel a would-be assailant, and it was also a strange, but powerful reminder that I really was alive. Two days without any kind of home had already shown me how hard it was to hang on to my self-worth, or to remember why I had to keep on fighting.

The shower was, once again, life-changing. I came out of it with my hair even more tangled, but to my surprise, there was a wide-tooth comb and a bottle of detangler in one of the bags. I actually laughed out loud as I worked the cream into my hair and wrapped a towel around my head.

There were two pair of jeans in the other bag. One pair was much too large but the second fit alright. He'd also bought several women's tee-shirts and two vee-necked wool sweaters. They weren't high-fashion, but they were clean and, as he noted, warm. I found a package of bikini panties in the bag. He hadn't purchased a bra. He was right: I didn't really need one, but it seemed sort of insulting that he was pointing that out, too.

When I washed out the conditioner I was actually able to get the comb through my hair, and I plaited it into a French braid that I twisted into a neat ball at my neck.

I wiped the counters, mirror and floor, and put the too-large jeans back in their bag. When I stopped to glance at myself I was surprised. Though still compact, wary, certainly ready to defend myself, for the first time a woman, with no trace of a child, looked back.

He was watching ESPN when I came out, a mug of tea on the table at his knees. He looked around and nodded as if satisfied.

"Okay, Celeste. Let's get going."

I stood by the glass wall, stung by his abruptness. He rose and walked to the kitchen to rinse the mug, then noticed my face.

"Something wrong?" he asked.

"I—do I look okay?"

"You look exactly the way you're supposed to look." His answer, frank and honest, didn't give me what I needed.

Suddenly he chuckled. "Wow—I'm sorry. Let me start over again: Celeste, you look very nice this evening."

I shook my head. "If it's *that* hard, don't bother."

"I thought you already knew."

"Knew what?"

"You're a pretty girl and you clean up nicely."

"I'm not a girl."

"Then stop acting like one."

Another barb. I brought the bags across the room and set them on the counter. "Thank you for the clothes. I'll pay you back as soon as I get my check."

"No payback required. They're part of your birthday present."

heather neff.

"I don't need any presents."

"Sure you do. You only turn eighteen once."

"I don't even know you," I said.

"You don't have to. Just enjoy my gifts."

"I'll pay you back," I insisted.

"Not necessary, Celeste. Now, why don't we get going?"

"I don't know if I want to."

"Well, if it's a choice between Poppy's or celebrating in the back of a bus, let me step up with a better offer."

Weirdly, I couldn't decide whether he was genuine or mocking me. He smiled, his eyes measuring my reaction. "Where would you like to go?"

"I don't know. I haven't lived here in a long time."

"Two years isn't so long."

"Like you pointed out: I was a girl back then, and I'm not a girl anymore."

He laughed again. "I'll tell you one thing: no matter how you look, you certainly don't think like a child."

"I'll tell you something else: I lost that choice a couple of weeks ago."

He went over to the sofa and picked up our coats. He helped me into mine, then looked away. "How about a hamburger and a movie? That sound alright?"

"Long as it's not Poppy's and the bus to get there."

He laughed again and raised his eyebrows. "Good god: what have I got myself into?"

* * * * * * *

The burger place was unexpectedly high-end, with sandwiches costing way more than ten dollars. The mountain of fries they brought out was ridiculous, and he ate one or two while watching me put the food away. Once he murmured, "Slow down, baby. There's plenty more where that came from."

I swallowed and hit the oversized Coke he'd ordered along with the food. He ate a salad with grilled salmon, his eyes occasionally taking a quick professional tour of the room, while I feasted on as much grease as I could put in my body. Who knew when I'd get to eat like that again?

"Okay," he said when my expression signaled that contentment and heartburn were playing tag in my belly. "We can hit a movie, but only after we talk."

"Oh, no," I said. "Things were going so well."

"Serious rarely gets a day off," he answered. "Please worry less about coming up with the smart-gal answer, and more about actually hearing what I have to tell you."

"Alright," I said, though I wasn't happy about it.

He had taken his hat off after we sat down, and he now rubbed his hand back and forth over his naked head, as if searching for nonexistent stubble.

"I could tell you some crazy, made-up shit," he began, "but I think you're old enough and bright enough to hear the truth."

"And if I don't want to?"

"You need to," he said, glancing at the people sitting at the table over my shoulder.

"Okay. Listening."

"When I went in to work this morning I started asking around for a halfway house or group home that might take you. It occurred to me that I should check on your family to see if you're eligible for any kind of public assistance."

"So was I switched at birth with a rich kid?"

"Celeste—for *once*, please listen."

The warning in his voice was more or less explicit. I tried to calm myself down—all that food had made me feel like I was actually flying—and really focus on what he was saying.

"I had to look your parents up, Celeste, because you're nowhere in the system."

"There's the downside of good behavior," I said, holding my right hand up to match his Boy Scout salute. "I'm invisible to the Law."

When I saw his face, I apologized. "Please excuse me, Officer."

"Celeste, pay attention: Your father is trouble."

"Big surprise."

"Actually, it may be."

"Whatever he did doesn't matter," I said. "You guys got him. He's locked up right this minute."

"That's about to change, and my sergeant, my colleagues, the dispatch coordinator, and even the garbage man think you need to be out of his way when he gets home."

"That's why I'm not going home."

"No, you don't understand. You probably shouldn't be in Akron."

"Already working on it," I said, picturing the Greyhound arriving at the Roanoke Rapids bus station.

"Celeste," he said, "I'm serious."

The relaxed voices of the other diners seemed to swell at that moment, so I leaned closer to him.

"What's going on?" I asked.

"Copley Castle only got a few months, but the prosecutor wanted to see him put away for life."

"Life? For selling *weed?*"

"Celeste," Jesse Brantley said, "we believe your father committed a murder."

"Murder?" I echoed, suddenly completely serious. "Who——?"

"A guy we found floating in the Cuyahoga River."

"Then why is he serving time for drugs?"

"Not enough evidence. He was holding a small quantity of smoke when we picked him up, so he's only serving the minimum."

"But my mother never said——"

"You were safer *not* knowing."

"Was she involved?" I asked.

"She was at work when the guy disappeared, but it looks like your mother and this man were friends."

"Friends? If you're saying she was cheating, that's bullshit. She doesn't breathe without my father's permission."

Jesse shifted restlessly in his seat. "Celeste, today I talked to both my Sarge and my captain, and we're thinking Copley Castle's going to come out believing he beat the system. His ego is going to tell him he won't get caught again. He's going to be mad as hell when he realizes he no longer has that house to conduct his business in. And finally, there's his greatest liability."

"That would be——?"

"You already know: your mother."

"He's definitely going to be very pissed at her," I agreed. "Has my father——I mean, are there records about things he——he did to her before?"

"Yes, though in every case she refused to press charges. In fact, she was hospitalized two winters ago after supposedly falling down the basement stairs. Do you remember that incident?"

"When was it?" I asked.

"Late February," he said.

I shook my head, looking at the floor. Clearly this was Copley's retribution for Bebe J sending me away. My thoughts turned guiltily to how I'd ignored her pitiful letters.

Jesse went on speaking. "Though we could get you into one of the group homes for young people who've aged out of foster care, we——that is, my captain and I——believe you'd be better off——" he hesitated, as if trying to determine exactly how to say it—— "in a protected environment."

"You're locking me up?" I said, making a stab at a joke.

"No, Celeste. You haven't committed any crimes," he answered, completely serious.

"Then where?"

"With me, until something else opens up."

"*You*?" I repeated, surprised.

"I spent the afternoon talking to my colleagues, and no one else had the space or was willing to take you in."

"And the halfway house solution?" I asked.

"There'd be no security, and since you're not really a witness, we can't offer you official protection."

"How long would it be?"

"Only until we can get things under control with your father."

"Under control?"

"Until we can see what he's going to do."

"How long will *that* take?"

"Not long, if we're right about him."

"Meaning?"

"He'll either report to his parole officer as required, go to his job training courses and apply for work, or he'll do something stupid, and we'll take over from there."

"And then what?"

"Then," Jesse Brantley said, "you can get on with your life."

"You mean I'm supposed to stay with you until Copley fucks up?"

"You can stay in my crib," Brantley said, "but not as my girlfriend, daughter, goddaughter, stepdaughter, cook, maid or jester."

"Then as what?" I asked.

"As someone who might need a safe place to sleep until things get straightened out between her parents."

"And in the meantime you're just going to let Copley do whatever he wants to my mother?"

"I'm going to keep an eye on their place, but Celeste, we can't help your mother unless she agrees."

"Shouldn't I be staying with—I don't know, someone else?"

"You mean a female officer? Yes. But we'd have to send you to Cleveland or Columbus."

"I don't want to go to—"

"I know, and I couldn't force you, anyway. Your boss at the supermarket is an old friend, so this will probably work out best for everyone concerned."

"You think I'm safe at work."

"I think so. Tony's got a pretty good view of the store from his booth."

"But if Copley wants to see me," I said, "Tony can't keep him out."

"No, but he can call the cops. It won't take us long to get there."

"And if Copley tried to get me at the store, you'd have—"

"—A pretty good reason to pick him up again," Jesse said.

"So in other words," I said, "I'm the bait."

Jesse eyed me thoughtfully. "I could lie and tell you I'm not concerned about how your father might behave. But honestly, Celeste, though he's a dangerous man, I don't think Copley Castle has ever been stupid."

"I'm the bait," I repeated.

I watched him watching me. "Are you okay with this?" he asked quietly.

"Are *you?*"

"I'm okay with getting a killer off the streets."

"This is pretty shitty witness protection."

"Howso?"

"You're betting my father won't manage to hurt me," I said, "but you're kind of hoping he'll try."

"I promise to look out for you," Jesse said.

"You sure you can do that?"

"If you'll let me," he answered.

I knew very well he wasn't telling me everything, and there was something very difficult and complicated that he didn't want me to know. But all my life people had been trying to keep the truth about Copley as far away from me as possible, so I shrugged it off. And anyway, his room high above the city, with its echoing, empty space, seemed the perfect sanctuary for my battered soul.

"Happy Birthday to me," I said, raising my Coke, "Ms. Bethany Celeste CeCe Annie Elizabeth Castle."

He raised his brows but didn't ask me to explain. "How about that movie?"

"No," I said. "I'm beat and I need to get up real early for work tomorrow."

"Now she's talking like a grown-up," he said, only half smiling.

"Thanks for the encouragement," I said. "I'll try not to disappoint."

* * * * * * *

I called my mother from the loft and asked her to leave her key hidden somewhere, so I could get into the flat to pick up my stuff the following day. Brantley, who was making himself a before-bed cup of tea, pretended not to be listening.

My mother bleated and moaned about my decision, then asked how she could reach me. When I told her to come to Tony's to find me, her mother-instinct kicked in:

"You going with a man?"

"*Going* with— ?" I repeated blankly.

"Are you doing something with a man?"

"What man?"

"I don't know. The man that own the store?"

"Tony? Oh, hell no. He doesn't even talk to me."

"Then who?"

"Nobody," I said, quite honestly.

"You met a man in the store?"

"No. You can come and ask anybody."

"Then who you stayin' with?"

"I told you," I said.

"No you didn't."

"It really doesn't matter. I'm not doing anything wrong and I'm old enough to make my own decisions."

"Not if some man doing something to you."

"You don't have to worry about that," I said, Nina's shadow crossing my mind.

"You shouldn't be out on the streets," she said.

"I'm not on the streets," I answered, thinking it was much too late for her to step in and try to tell me right from wrong.

"Then what you doing?"

"I go to work and go home. That's all."

"You can do that here."

"Not if Copley's there," I said.

"Don't call him that. He your father."

"I'm not having that argument again."

"Then don't. Just come home."

"Why?" I said.

"Because you belong here."

"No, Momma."

"You want to be out there with strangers?"

"When does he get home?" I asked.

"Probly next week."

"Then leave the key so I can get my stuff."

"I don't want you to go," she said.

"I know."

"Beth, it's not right. This here is your home."

"Not while he's there."

"Beth—"

"Leave the key somewhere, Momma. I need to get my stuff."

She finally caved in and told me she'd leave it beneath a loose board on the opposite end of the front porch.

Relieved, I hung up to find Brantley staring at me.

"You handled that like a pro," he said dryly.

"I've had two years to think about it."

His mouth smiled, but his eyes didn't. "Lying come natural to you, Celeste?"

"Evidently," I answered.

"If you really don't want to be near your father," he said, "why'd you come back to Ohio in the first place?"

"Absence makes the heart," I answered, walking toward him. I suddenly felt strange in his enormous, neat, empty room, and the interrogation wasn't making me feel any better. Standing stock still in front of him, I stared up into his black eyes.

"You want me to go, Officer?"

"I've gone to a good bit of trouble to get you here."

"I didn't chase your truck down the street."

"Look—" he began.

"No, *you* look," I said, feeling Copley smirking behind my words. "No matter what you're about to say, I know you're not doing this to be cool. You want something from me, and it must be something important. There's no way you'd let me into this room if there wasn't something in it for you."

"Meaning?"

"Stop acting like you're some kind of action hero," I said.

He lifted his chin, still looking at me. His face broke into a genuine smile.

"You'd make a good cop."

"You're not a cop," I noted. "You're a detective, right?"

"Right."

"Working a case," I said.

"I'm always working a case."

"Working *my* case," I amended.

He actually laughed. "Not *your* case."

"Then my father's," I said slowly. "You're working my father's case."

He reached up and wiped something out of one eye, then yawned.

"You need a nap?" I asked.

"Don't get an attitude with me, Bethany."

"Don't call me Bethany," I said. "That's what *he* calls me."

"Changing your name won't get rid of him."

"Making me think about him won't, either."

"Then why come back to Ohio in the first place?" Jesse asked again.

"My grandmother made that decision."

"You in some kind of trouble?"

"No, but two of my friends were. My grandmother wanted me out of the way."

"Trouble seems to like you, girl," Jesse said.

"You seem to like me, too."

"Don't get confused."

"Don't *you* get confused," I said sharply. "I'm just doing what I can to make it through another day."

He raised his brows. "Good job, baby. You've learned the first law of survival: take what's necessary to survive."

"Don't put this on me. I'm here because *you* brought me."

"That's true," he conceded. He walked across the room and sat down on his couch. "You want some tea?"

"No thanks. I'm tired, though."

"Oh, pardon me," he said, standing up. "Unless you were planning on my bed again."

"I'm more than happy to take the couch, as long as you're straight with me," I said.

"About what?"

"About everything."

"Everything I can."

"That's not good enough."

"Everything I can," he repeated firmly.

* * * * * * *

The weekend came and went, with no word from Bebe J. I'd gone by the duplex on Thursday morning and cleared out the few articles of clothing I'd brought from North Carolina, bringing them with me to work, then on to the loft. While I walked through my mother's flat, looking for my things, I tried to get a handle on how I felt about everything. All I found inside me was emptiness.

I was about to leave when I noticed an envelope sticking out from under a phone book. I recognized Grandma's writing.

My mother had torn open only enough of the envelope for her to stick her hand in without pulling out the letter. I knew she was looking for money. She didn't even care enough about what my grandmother wrote to read it. Incensed, I stuffed the letter into my bag and took it with me.

When I got back to the loft that night I took it into the bathroom and opened it. It was dated the day after she'd put me on the bus.

"Dear Berniece,
I know what Bethany told you, but the truth is that what happened was entirely my fault. I should have done more to protect her from situations that put her in danger. I'm sorry she had to leave so suddenly, but I feel this was the best decision under the circumstances. Here is some money to help her get started in Ohio. I know she will

need warm winter clothes. Please get her enrolled in school right away and do your best to keep her safe.

Love,

Corinne

I hid the letter in my clothes and said nothing to Jesse Brantley, who was already in bed with the lights turned out when I walked across the room to the couch. He said nothing to me and remained perfectly silent while I sat down, then stretched out and lay beneath the blankets, my fist in my mouth so he wouldn't hear me crying.

I don't know why it mattered so much that he couldn't hear my sobs, which were violent enough to move my whole body beneath the blankets. I bit my hand so hard that the teeth marks were still visible the next morning. I couldn't hold back the rage, sadness and gaping ache that filled my heart.

Jesse Brantley drove me to work that day, and he showed up punctually when my second shift ended that night. I'd worked so much over the previous days that the paycheck Tony handed me actually shocked me, and as a result I offered Jesse Brantley some rent money.

"I told you this is official, not personal," he replied.

"I'd have to pay rent anywhere else," I said.

"You're not my tenant."

"I'm not your guest."

He was standing in front of one of the folding closet doors, hanging up his shirt. His smooth chest gleamed in the low lights.

"Your expenses are being covered," he said.

"By who?"

"Does it matter?"

"It does to me," I said. "I don't want to wake up one morning owing anybody anything."

"Just trust me, Celeste," he said.

"Sorry. I'm a little low on trust right now."

"Understandably." He slipped into a sweatshirt and grabbed his pajamas. I watched him walk behind the glass brick wall and vanish into the bathroom.

I'd written a letter to my grandmother during my break that day, but I knew I'd never send it. In the letter I tried to civilize my feelings enough to get them down on paper, but I found I couldn't really describe my fear, grief and loneliness.

I also discovered that deep down inside I harbored a terrible, consuming rage that she'd sent me away rather than fighting for me to stay with the people I loved. Did she really believe that Copley was less dangerous than DeAndre, or that I was better off with my stupid, weak mother?

I concluded that Grandma didn't deserve to know how I really felt, because it was her fault I was here. Her fault that Nina and Gideon were lost to me. Her fault that I would have to watch my father continue to beat my mother, or, if I was stupid enough to move back into the duplex, risk getting myself hurt, too.

If my anger and resentment toward Grandma weren't enough, I also sensed she'd never give me any real information about Nina and Gideon. She wouldn't want me to send them my address or phone number, or even let them dream that they could escape Blissfield by coming north to live with me.

Still, I ached to see my grandmother and hear her voice. I ached to sleep in a bed that smelled of sundried sheets, and to eat the good meat and potatoes from her kitchen. I wanted to play the piano in the sunny front room, dust off her porcelain figurines, and read books at the picnic table beneath the sweeping oak tree. Every cell of my being wept to be back in Blissfield.

I supposed I could call her, but then I'd have to tell her I wasn't living with my parents or returning to school. I'd have to lie about the loft—and the cop. And if Grandma called my mother, Bebe J would never tell her she'd stolen the money that was meant for me. She'd never admit that she'd defended Copley and denied to the police that he'd beaten her. She would never tell my grandmother she didn't even know where I was.

None of it mattered, anyway. All that childhood shit was over. I had to make my own decisions, now.

"Everything alright out there?" Jesse's voice from the bathroom fell like a hammer on my thoughts.

No, *I thought.* "Yes," I said.

"Don't lie to me, Celeste."

"I'm not."

"You're too quiet."

"Nothing to say."

"That never stopped you from talking before."

He began brushing his teeth with his electric toothbrush. The low whine, would, under any other circumstances, have annoyed me. But that night the sound was familiar and reassuring, as if I was living in a normal home. Although who the hell even knew what *normal* meant anymore?

He emerged in his pajamas and signaled by pointing over his shoulder that the bathroom was clear and I needed a shower. He didn't speak again.

Wearily I walked across the cement floor and closed the bathroom door behind me.

When I came out, the loft was lit by moonlight. I was still trying hard not to think when I heard his voice.

"You okay?" he asked quietly.

"Why?"

"I'm getting worried," he said.

"You pretending to care?"

"Don't have to pretend."

I sat down on the couch, pulled the blankets over my legs and looked out into the night. The sky had the iron coldness of late January.

"You like the view?" he asked.

"I like the quiet."

"That's something new."

"Why don't you just let me *be*?" I asked, unable to hide my sadness.

For a long time neither one of us spoke. I watched the blackness with its flickering distant pinpricks of light, and somewhere far away, the wintry crescent moon.

He surprised me by getting out of bed and padding across the room. He stood beside me for a moment, then said, "Scoot, Celeste."

I slid sideways on the couch and he sat down beside me.

"You thinking about your folks?" he asked.

"I'm trying real hard not to think about anything."

"That would be good if it was true."

"You don't know what's going on in my head," I said.

"I can guess."

"I doubt it."

"How about this?" he said softly. "You left somebody down there in North Carolina."

"I left a bunch of people down there."

"You left somebody special."

I glanced up at him. Was it possible he actually knew something about Nina and Gideon?

"So," he said, "I'm right."

"What difference does it make?" I said. "I'm here. He—they're there."

"He?"

"*They,*" I said firmly.

"That makes it a lot harder to get straight."

"I'm never gonna get straight."

"You're home, Celeste."

"No, I'm not," I said. "This will never be my home."

"It's your home for now."

"No. Blissfield's where I belong."

"Then," he said quietly, "it must be hard to be in this room with me."

I shot him a look. His body was straight, disciplined, never at rest, and his dark eyes were hard, when I needed them to be soft. I should have been afraid of Jesse Brantley, but I wasn't.

"There she is," he murmured. "The warrior princess."

"So what?" I asked, defiant.

"I like her. I like that part of you that's always ready to fight."

"Because it's easier for you when I've got my armor on," I observed.

"That's possible," he conceded.

"Before I left Copley's house two years ago, wearing armor seemed normal. But now I know everyone doesn't live with weapons hidden in every corner of their lives."

He grew very still, his eyes intensely observant. "I can't believe you're only eighteen."

"Sometimes," I said, "neither can I."

He stood up and, careful not to touch me, backed a couple of steps away. "Try not to think too much, Celeste."

"I have to think," I said, "to stay ahead of you."

"We both know you're not thinking about me."

"Of course I'm thinking about you. I'm in this room with you. You're keeping me from landing back on the streets, or back in my father's house."

"But don't start thinking of me as a man," he said.

"What difference would that make?" I said. "I'm only eighteen and we all know I'm too young to really love someone."

"Who told you that?"

"He did."

"The guy you love?"

"The guy I love."

"He didn't believe you love him?"

"He didn't care that I love him," I said, my voice bitter.

"I don't believe that," Jesse Brantley said gently. "He might have been afraid, or he might not have known how to love you back. But I don't believe he didn't love you."

"Nobody loves me."

"He does," Jesse said. "And the other person—or people you left behind? They love you, too."

"I don't know why," I said. "I'm really not pretty and I don't have any kind of body and I'm broke and homeless and—"

"Easy does it," he murmured.

I knew if he didn't shut up I was going to cry some more, and I didn't want him to see me cry.

"Hey, little one," he said, "it's gonna be okay. Really."

"It's never been okay," I said, shaking my head.

"It will be soon."

"How? I can't go back to Blissfield. I can't go back to my mother. And you and I both know I shouldn't be here."

"You're safe here, Celeste."

"For today, maybe."

"Nothing's going to happen," he said in the gentlest voice he could find. Beneath the gentleness I could hear the man, and the man was bothered by how gentle he'd become.

"Something's going to happen," I said so quietly I could barely hear my own exhausted sadness. "It's going to happen and we can't do anything to stop it."

"I'm going to stop it," he said, and I sensed his wavering struggle.

"You can't, Detective Brantley."

"I can, little warrior."

"How?"

That's when he did it. He walked forward, sank down and lifted me like a doll into his arms. I didn't resist, and he held me close. I pressed my face into his chest and inhaled. He smelled of clean, clear strength.

He didn't smell of Gideon.

I was glad.

He stared at me for a long moment, his eyes fixed on my face. He stared and stared, unblinking. Then, very gently, he covered me with the blanket, and returned, alone, to his bed.

twenty-four.

It was morning. A Sunday. And still weird.

"So you and this guy down south never——?" Jesse asked.

I shook my head.

"You were waiting until you got married?"

"*He* was waiting," I said.

"Religious guy?"

"No. In fact, we took them to church for the first time."

"We?"

"Grandma and me."

"Them?"

"Gideon and his sister, Nina. My best friend. My sister."

"Oh." Jesse Brantley walked to the kitchen, wearing his sweats, and poured water into the kettle. I had put on one of my new tee shirts and sweaters, and now wandered over to the windows. Snow had fallen on the city beneath us and I could hear the wind moaning outside. For the very first time I tried to make out the part of town where I'd grown up. The street. The roof of the house.

"So you liked this guy," Jesse said. "How did his sister feel about it?"

I was surprised at how telling the cop even a little bit about my life seemed to have broken down a great big fence. Suddenly he was treating me like a person, not a problem. But that led me to a whole new challenge: I didn't want to answer Jesse Brantley's questions. I didn't want to think about any of it.

"You alright?" he asked.

"No. I don't want you in my business," I said.

"Just trying to know you better."

"You're trying to get inside my head, and that's not your territory."

"Don't want me to talk to you?" he asked casually.

"Not about Gideon," I said. "Never about Gideon."

"Because?"

"He's the only good thing I have."

Brantley didn't answer. Instead, he poured two mugs of hot water before taking out a canister of whatever tea he felt like drinking that day. It was weird watching a man make such a big deal about tea, but I figured he wanted something to make him different. Something that lifted his life above the people he put in the joint. This loft was part of it. So was I.

"What's he like?" Jesse asked.

"Who?"

"The guy in North Carolina?"

"I told you——"

"Okay. What's his sister like?"

"I don't know," I said honestly. "I used to know, but not anymore."

"Because?"

"Because she changed. He did, too. I mean, I know it wasn't their fault, but they wouldn't let me do anything to help them."

Brantley dripped a dollop of honey into my chai and pushed the cup across the counter. "So, what was he like?" he asked again.

"Simple," I said without wanting to. "He just wants everything to be simple."

I could feel the cop studying me. "Sounds like a puppy."

I laughed, remembering when Nina said the same thing. "Yeah. He was something like that."

"And good looking?"

I glanced over at the cop, knowing he couldn't stand the idea that he wasn't the finest man in my life. "Yeah, he's beautiful," I said. Gideon's face bloomed in my mind, along with his smell, his taste, and the feel of him. The ache worsened in my belly.

"Sounds like he was just about perfect," Jesse said.

For a moment I saw a football arching silently over a hot blue sky. I left the window and walked over to the counter. Brantley went back to putting a pinch of Earl Grey into a tea ball. He kept his eyes on that stupid ball and chain.

Though he seemed at home and at ease, I was aware of his careful, if nonchalant scrutiny. He missed nothing, though he never seemed to be looking. So I decided to do a little digging, too.

"Who was she?" I said, climbing up on a stool.

"Who?"

"The woman who turned you into Robocop."

"Is that who I am?" He looked up with a cool smile.

"Who you're trying to be."

"Why do you ask?" he said.

"Because some part of you wants me to know," I said.

He laughed. A deep laugh—the way, I would learn, a man laughs when he's uncomfortable with being read.

"Maybe it wasn't a she."

"Not likely," I said.

The sun was high and the icicles over the windows were dripping. We were both hungry, but neither one of us was scheduled to work, and it felt way too cold, and way too much trouble to go out to eat.

"Now you're trying to get inside *my* head," he said.

I shrugged. "I guess neither one of us is getting in without an invitation."

He sipped his tea and laughed. "Eighteen?"

"How old are you?"

"I'd rather not say. I'm embarrassed enough already."

"Why?"

"Because this should be strictly business, and I'm talking to you like you're my little sister," Jesse said.

"*Sister?*"

"Okay, like you're my goddaughter."

"Or maybe a girlfriend?" I looked him squarely in the face over my teacup.

"Never," he said, "in a thousand years." He gazed at me for a long moment. "Celeste," he said gently, "sounds like that guy down south is pretty cool. You deserve a man who'll treat you like a princess. When you find one, try to keep him."

For a moment I pictured Gideon standing in his place. I pictured Gideon coming around the counter and lifting me into his arms. I pictured—

"Can I make us something to eat?" I asked, pushing the vision away. "I'm so hungry I'm hallucinating."

"You looking to put me to work?" Jesse said.

"I'm looking to eat something better than outdated microwave macaroni. I'd be happy to cook if you'll let me get behind that counter."

He grumbled as he showed me where to find the pans, utensils and spices, but I knew he wasn't genuinely incensed. Jesse Brantley, like me, was more comfortable in confrontation than he was at making peace. He sat on the couch while I prepared some salmon and brown rice. He didn't have any fresh rosemary, which Grandma put on everything, but he had some dried basil. I cut the stems off some broccoli I found in the back of the fridge and steamed it over the rice pot. I wiped off the table and set it. Jesse was sitting on the sofa, the sound low on the TV. We'd found an easy rhythm: no speeches, fake friendliness or particular politeness required.

We both sort of liked that.

After we ate he padded over and turned to a football game with the sound still muted. I loaded the dishwasher, enjoying the hot whoosh of the faucet as I rinsed the dishes and their clanging as I loaded the rack. The great big windows steamed up and the loft smelled warm and wet and stupidly safe.

"All of the above," he suddenly said, his eyes fixed on the screen.

I looked across at his huge form, settled beside my blankets on the couch, his thin-thick legs perched on the coffee table, his lower back cushioned by my pillow.

"Excuse me?" I said.

"She was all of the above."

"Who?"

"My ex-wife."

"How long were you together?"

"Most of my life. Childhood friend."

"I see." I glanced around the handsome, empty room. "You got this for her."

"For us, when there was an 'us.'"

"She booked?"

"Fell in love with another man. Said being with me so long never gave her a chance to grow."

I didn't answer. Not because I couldn't, but because no answer was needed. He was wounded and willing to admit it. I was wounded and admitted it, too.

We understood each other very well. Both Jesse Brantley and I had nothing left but memories.

I closed the dishwasher and started it, walked over to my suitcase and began dressing in layers.

"Going out?" he asked, watching without watching.

"What do you need besides eggs and bread?"

"There's no stores around here."

"I got a license."

"Not for my truck."

"I'll walk."

"It's twenty-two degrees out there."

"Coat's warm."

"It's way too far to a store."

"Seven-Eleven?"

"Nope."

"Liquor-Lotto?"

"That, either."

"So I'm stuck here?"

"Just think of it as a couple of quiet days."

For a shining instant I experienced Copley shifting in my belly. I recognized it as the beginning of the kind of feeling I didn't manage well. He didn't see it; he'd gone back to his game.

Restless, anxious, I wandered back to the kitchen and wiped down the counter. I found some Ajax under the sink and cleaned the stovetop. When I got out the Lysol and started toward the bathroom he called out to me.

"Hey Celeste, I pay somebody to do that."

"Just staying busy," I said.

"Come and relax."

"I am relaxing."

"By cleaning?"

"By staying busy."

He understood, then. He stood up, turned off the game and came across the room just as I began wiping the fridge handles, and caught my arm. "What's wrong?"

"Let me go, Brantley."

He sighed. "I'll come with you."

"No."

"Celeste—"

"I just need to take a walk, okay?"

He dropped his arm and took a step backwards. "You're good," he said.

Outside the sun had fallen like a dunked basketball. The wind cut my face, but it was perfect and settled the animal in my belly. The streets were blank and gray, the eyes of empty factory buildings fading into the black night. I didn't care. I figured anybody looking in my direction would see a guy in his mid-teens walking to the nearest liquor store for some pop and chips. I didn't even look old enough to smoke.

Not a thought came into my head as I slowly made my way out of the neighborhood and across the long suspension bridge, battered by angry winds, and into an old residential area of the city. My father had driven through this area during my childhood, but never slowed down long enough for me to get more than a glimpse of the streets.

Most of the houses were hunkered down, blinds drawn, steel gates locked, lights out. Thin wisps from the chimneys said that pulses still beat behind the weathered shingles and mid-century aluminum siding. Occasional dogs, and by their baritone barks, very large dogs, greeted my footsteps. I neither sped up nor slowed down, because I was too close to empty to be bothered with fear.

Eventually I hit the outer limits of my emotional rubber band and I stopped for a while, enjoying the ache in my frozen, gym-shoed feet, before making my way back to the loft. I had no interest in time, and couldn't say whether I'd been walking for one hour or three, but my feet, hands and nose had progressed from ice-cold to inferno. This was how saints must have felt when the executioner lit the match.

Jesse Brantley was standing in the foyer in his fancy jacket and watchcap when I rang the outer doorbell. He let me in and stood sheepishly, car key in hand. "I was on my way to look for you."

"Why?"

"Shit happens."

I moved past him into the enormous room, his silent figure at my heels. I saw that he had cleaned up, made his bed, and even swept and vacuumed.

"See anything?" he asked, his voice determinedly relaxed.

"Darkness."

"That's all?"

"What else would I see on a frigid Sunday evening in the bowels of Akron, Ohio?"

"Just wondering if you ran into anybody."

"Like who?"

"Like anybody."

"Like, maybe my dealer?" I said. "Newsflash: I don't do drugs. My mother? She's somewhere worrying about getting her ass kicked in the next couple of days. And my father?" I laughed darkly. "At this very minute my father is fantasizing about how he's going to kick my mother's ass in the exact same time frame."

Jesse made a quick, unstudied move, like a cat when a flea bites. "You scared he'll come looking for you?"

"Sure. He's gonna be pissed off as hell that I'm out of his control." I lifted my chin, Nina-style, and squinted in Jesse's direction. "So why are you asking about Copley?"

He whistled softly. "You, Celeste, are a mystery. Sometimes it looks like you're one second from breaking, but then you turn around and talk like you're solid steel."

He was standing very close to me as he said this, and I felt like I was seeing his face very for the very first time. There was uncertainty in his eyes, and his mouth was softer than I'd realized. He worked hard at being hard, but I'd already broken through his thickest walls, though I hadn't realized it until that moment.

"I'm sorry," I said, speaking to the man beneath the façade. "It's called cabin fever. Sometimes I overheat and need a few clicks to cool off."

This wasn't entirely true; I'd been overloaded with thoughts and emotions for weeks, but now I knew what he needed me to say.

"Thank you again, Detective Brantley," I added in my best imitation of Miss Corinne's granddaughter. "I know you're just trying to protect me. I don't think I can get through this without you."

He grunted softly, trying to get that hardness back onto his face. But I'd already seen his eyes. I knew, now, that something else was going on.

He pulled my coat away from my shoulders and took it, with his, over to the closet.

"Officer Brantley," I said, "why do you care so much about me and my father?"

He didn't answer as he hung up my coat.

"Do you have a history with my father?" I asked.

"Celeste—"

"A simple yes or no would be cool."

"Listen—"

"Jesse," I followed him to the closet, "what's going on between you and Copley?"

He towered over me when we were this close.

"Look, Celeste, it's complicated," he said.

"I can keep up."

"Okay. Come over here and let's talk."

We ended up facing each other over the kitchen counter, where he quite predictably made me wait while he brewed more tea. Irritated, I kept my eyes riveted on his face, which was once again safe behind his detective's mask.

"The man who ended up face-down in the Cuyahoga River—that man your mother knew—he was my partner. We'd worked together since I was a rookie. I'd followed him into investigating. I'm his son's godfather."

"Wait—how could a cop be friends with my mother?" I asked.

"He was working undercover, trying to find out what was up with your father."

"I can't believe they're letting you investigate this case," I observed. I'd watched enough *Law and Order* episodes to know that much.

"No," Jesse said. "Someone else is in charge of the case. You being here is already pushing the absolute limit of what they'll allow."

"Then," I said, almost intuitively, "it was amazing luck that you just happened to be in Poppy's when I came in that night."

"Sure was." He raised his mug and sipped his tea, calmly returning my gaze.

"You were following me."

"Let's just say I was checking you out."

"Since when?"

"Actually, we never stopped watching your mother. We don't think she was involved in your father's shit, but we wanted to know if his buddies were still hanging around her," Jesse explained.

"Were they?"

"Far as we can tell, your mother did everything she could to get away from those people."

"What about me?" I said.

"You weren't even on our radar. As far as our records showed, you were just a kid when your father got caught. We didn't know where you went or what you were doing. We pulled your mother's phone luds, but her calls to North Carolina made perfect sense, considering Copley's mother was paying for his lawyer. We certainly didn't know you were there, or that you came back to Ohio. I probably still wouldn't know if you hadn't gone to work for Tony. Like I said, Tony and I go way, way back."

"And—"

"You were a minor, so you had to put your parents' names on your application," Jesse said. "Tony recognized Copley's name and called me. I stopped by the store and watched you work. And then one night you turned up at the burger joint."

"And you just happened to be there," I said.

"I told you I was trying to stop some other sh—"

"You're a lousy liar for a cop."

For a long moment neither one of us spoke. Then he shrugged. "Alright. Tony told me you were working double shifts and showing up in the same clothes. He figured you were living rough, so yes, I wasn't too far behind."

"But why?" I asked.

"Celeste, I didn't know how close you were to your father, or why you'd left his house. What you knew about his business. Whether his friends were threatening you or your mother. Or whether—sorry, baby, but I have to say it—whether you'd gone to work for them."

"Doing what?"

"Taking orders, running shit, or whatever else your mother needed to raise some money for your father."

"None of the above," I said. "I left that fucking house because she won't."

"Now I get it," Jesse said. He lifted his mug again. My mug remained untouched, the hot steam drifting lazily upward.

"So," I said, "this has never been about protecting me. It was always about finding a way to get to my father."

"No, Celeste. It was also about protecting you from your father. I'm figuring he won't be on the streets very long. He's going to do something stupid and we'll get him, or his associates will catch up with him and we won't have to. You and your mother will be safe, and then you can go home."

"That's over for me," I said.

"You need to finish school."

"First, I need to survive."

"I'm not going to let it come to that," Jesse said.

"I hope not," I said.

* * * * * * *

302

And that's the way it went: early in the morning Jesse Brantley dropped me off at Tony's Supermarket, where I worked hard until around eight at night. He picked me up and brought me back to the loft, where we ate, watched TV, talked, argued, showered and slept in separate beds. Almost like we were married.

He let me put all my money in the bank. He said I'd need it later, when all of "this" was over. I couldn't picture a time when "this" would be over. When anything would be different. I couldn't imagine what that future could possibly look like. So I didn't try.

He came home one day with a flip phone that was small enough to rest in the palm of my hand. He told me it was programmed with two numbers: his cell and 911. "I want you to always keep it on you," he said without smiling. "You never know when you'll need it."

"I thought you're keeping an eye on me," I said.

"Celeste, he said quietly, "This is serious. Take it everywhere, alright?"

The days unwound, and I almost relaxed. And then one afternoon when I was unpacking apples I glanced up to find my father, Copley Nehemiah Castle, standing by a display of oranges, not three feet away. He was still short, tense and deadly as a ready-to-spring animal trap. But he had nearly doubled in muscle mass. Under his stained down jacket I could see the G.I. Joe shoulders and ballooning pecs. Even his neck, heavily veined, had thickened.

He stared at me with a gaze of unfamiliar familiarity. I knew he saw both himself and his mother in me, but he must have also been keenly aware that he was no longer looking at a girl.

I straightened up quickly and an apple bounced off the display and rolled, of course, precisely to his feet. He didn't bother to pick it up.

"You not in school?" he asked by way of greeting.

His voice was deep for a small man. His eyes had withered, with a tangled circuit of fine lines and a permanent shadow beneath them.

"Bills," I answered, and went back to the display.

He took a step closer. "You crashing in the city?"

I nodded as I worked. It struck me that anyone who saw us would instantly know we were related, though we didn't touch and I refused to meet his gaze.

"Why you not with your momma?"

I shrugged and he grabbed my arm. I twisted away, stunned that he would put his hands on me in public.

"Look at me when I speak to you," he said.

"What do you want?" My voice was ragged. Two or three customers stopped to stare.

"What's wrong with your momma house?" he spat.

"Nothing wrong with my momma house."

"You doing something you don't want her to see?"

"I'm old enough to be on my own," I said.

"Girl, you ain't old enough to wipe your own ass."

"It's been two years, and the best you can do is come here looking for some shit on me and my momma?"

"What she doing?"

"Leave me alone," I hissed, the fingers of my free hand groping for the phone in my apron pocket.

"Who do you think you are?" he replied, his spongy odor of cigarette and cheap cognac washing over me.

One of the other girls, a Mexican called Mila, suddenly appeared from the back, pushing a pallet loaded with pears. She stopped just beside me and glanced at my father. Copley let go of my arm.

"Could we switch breaks?" she asked, her eyes coming to rest on me.

"Ah—yeah," I said, surprised.

"Cool," she said, nodding her head toward the manager's booth. "I'll go tell Tony."

The diversion helped. I looked back at my father. His gaze shifted between Mila's departing back and me, calculating something.

"Don't," I said. "Whatever you're planning. Take it somewhere else."

His eyes narrowed. "You don't tell me what to do."

"I work here," I said. "I need the money."

"You need to be home."

"I'm eighteen. You don't get to tell me what to do anymore."

"I'll slap the shit out of you—"

"If you touch me again they'll call the cops and put you right back in the hole."

"You think I'm scared a you?"

"No. I think you're scared of *them*." I nicked my head toward the booth and my father lifted his head and followed my gaze.

"Listen, you little bitch—"he growled. His smell was so strong I nearly tasted him. He filled the space with his malice, his desire to wound. "I should've finished what I started before I let you get on that bus two years ago," he said.

"You had nothing to say about me getting on that bus—"

"You think I didn't know she was sending you down there? Your momma don't do nothin' less I say so!"

"Fuck you!" I spat before I could help myself.

This time he grabbed me hard, just above the elbow. Our eyes locked and for a moment we became one person, sealed with hatred.

Tony's voice suddenly crackled over the intercom. "Annie, need you at the registers!"

I jerked my arm out of his grasp.

"Who the fuck is Annie?" my father snarled.

"Let me work," I said.

He stared at me a long moment, then turned and stomped down the aisle, vanishing into the cold.

Bending to pick up the apple, I was suddenly aware of the tight smooth skin and sweet jeweled smell of the fruit. Grandma's face came to mind and I wondered if Copley ever missed the deep red earth of his home.

Only then did I realize my underclothes were drenched with sweat.

I had survived my first adult encounter with my father.

* * * * * * *

Things were really tough that night in the loft.

I didn't feel like talking, so I said nothing to Jesse Brantley at all. But he knew. I guess Tony had seen it from his glass booth. Or maybe it just showed all over me.

I made eggs and ate at the counter while Jesse sat in front of the TV. I could tell, now, when he was looking in one direction and watching me at the same time, and that night I felt his detective's gaze all over me.

He was reading when I flicked off the bathroom light and walked toward my couch.

"This is pretty good," he said, showing me his novel. "You ever read any Stephen King?"

Nina's image sprang up like a shard in my heart. I missed her in my bones. Missed listening to her talk about books and teachers and papers and other stuff. I missed her calling me crazy. I missed her brother. I missed his voice. His eyes, His touch. I missed being a girl. A student. A granddaughter.

Jesse set down his book, pulled the covers away and stood up.

"Come here," he said gently.

I shook my head.

"Please," he said.

I sat on the edge of the sofa and wrapped my arms around myself.

"Let me do that," he said. "I promise it won't hurt."

"It always hurts."

"Not this time. I promise, Celeste."

I couldn't move. He came over to me.

And, though at first it still hurt to let him hold me, I did.

* * * * * * *

But then I had the dream. Once again I was in a darkened room. I could see the woman's legs as she lay on the bed, and the man was cutting or burning her while she moaned, her puppet legs bouncing in agony.

I cried out and sat up suddenly, the images more real than Jesse's flat in the darkness. I found myself on the sofa, a blanket wrapped tightly around me.

"Hey, hey," Jesse murmured, crossing the room and again taking me in his arms. His body was hard, hot, smelling of flesh and laundry and sleep. "You're safe, Celeste. I'm right here, okay?"

Obediently I nodded, but when he held me close I couldn't close my eyes.

"He can't get in here, baby," Jesse said.

"He doesn't have to," I said.

"I won't let him hurt you."

"Too late for that."

"Would it help to cry?"

"Do you want me to cry?"

"Only if it would help."

"How would it help?" I said.

"Sometimes it helps."

"What would I cry about?"

"I don't know," he said quietly. "Your mother. Your grandma. Maybe that guy down south."

"That," I said, "would be pointless."

"Baby," he said hoarsely, "you don't have to be at war all the time."

"Yes, I do," I said.

"No you don't, Celeste," he whispered. "Not here. Not now." There was nothing in his touch that reminded me of Gideon, and though our bodies were warm, I felt miles away from desire.

"So what's he doing?" I asked into the darkness.

"Who?"

"You know who."

"I've got other cases, Celeste."

"But you knew he came to the store."

"Tony called."

"So what's my father doing?"

For a long time, the detective didn't speak.

"Please, Jesse," I said. "I need to know."

"Couple of my guys stopped by your parents' crib last night," he said quietly.

"Did they arrest him?"

"You mother sent them away."

I sat in silence, my heart beating heavily. "So how are you going to get him?"

"Don't worry, Celeste: Tony's watching. If he comes back Tony will let me know right away."

"You don't get it," I said into the darkness. "I'm not afraid of my father. I'm afraid of what I'll do to protect myself from my father—"

"Tony will call me," Jesse said. "I'm never more than a few minutes away."

"Jesse—"

"I'm never more than a few minutes away."

* * * * * * *

And this is how we crawled through February, repeating the same pattern day in and day out. I didn't talk much, and Jesse accepted that this felt right to me. The dream came regularly, but I didn't wake him up. The weather was miserable. I saw nothing of my mother—or Copley.

And then it was March. The weather broke and we were into the ugly cold days where the winds still fought January's battles, though the earth was trying to create new life. When I looked through the huge plate glass windows at the front of the supermarket, the parking lot was a desert of drifting trash and eerily un-moored shopping carts. The other staff, having heard that something seriously toxic was up between me and that Marvel-comics guy with the mean bright eyes, kept a careful distance. They all greeted me, as Black people do, but they made themselves busy on different aisles from whenever LaNelle sent me to work.

I kept my mind clear by battering my body. I stacked. Inventoried. Cleaned. Swept. Moved entire displays. Worked the checkout for three or four hours without a break.

I kept my mind at peace with letters. I wrote them on my break and during my lunch hour. Sometimes two or three each day. And I addressed them to the high school, the Piggly Wiggly, to anywhere I thought Nina or Gideon might be found. I didn't say much, because there wasn't much to be said. I just hoped that somehow they would write back to me in care of the store. I needed them to know how much I needed them. They needed to know how much they were loved.

When Jesse picked me up after work I was zombied. We spoke little in the car, cooked and ate in a healing silence, then laid down on opposite sides of the room. In the mornings we moved in rhythm and even genuinely laughed once or twice. I tried to make myself believe that with Tony and Jesse watching, I was safe. But I sensed Jesse's tension and knew I wasn't.

I can count back, now. The last nine days, with me feeling it in the air, like the barometer in my soul was spinning too fast. The thing coming toward me and me not being able to do anything about it. Like I was strapped into a roller coaster clicking up a mile-high track that would soon plunge me straight to earth.

And Jesse Brantley knowing, too, but not knowing. He could watch me when he could watch me, and ask other people to watch me when he couldn't. But he was counting on Copley coming for me or going after my mother, and he wanted to see it without being seen. He thought Copley would be too sly to try it in daylight, in the store, in front of so many people, and he thought he could be with me every other second of my life.

Because he had started to care for me, though neither one of us knew what to do about it. He was scared to let himself love anyone, and I was unwilling to love anyone but Gideon. Jesse might have been willing to keep me, take care of me, make me the woman in the loft, except that I couldn't let him do any of those things—not, at least, while I needed my love for Gideon to prove that some part of Grandma's Princess was still alive.

Day four of the nine was a Sunday, and Jesse put me in his truck and we drove twenty miles outside of the city and into the still-yellowed cornfields that rolled and pitched between splintering barns. Horse-drawn buggies holding families in black clothes slowed us down, and he explained that these people lived without our poisons.

"They're Amish," he said. "They don't use electricity, cars or any technology at all."

"And that's because?"

"They believe our world is sinful."

"I can't imagine why," I said.

I had never known that people like this lived so close to us, right outside the boundaries of our madness. We stopped at a crossroads with no building in sight and bought a thick apple pie from two children sitting in a carriage and dressed like they'd missed a century, then we started back down a narrow highway bordered by lines of sprouting poplars.

"Ever been out here before?" he asked as I stared out the window, thinking of Blissfield.

"No," I said simply.

"You like it?"

"Oh, I don't know."

He didn't look at me, and I understood he'd wanted to offer me a bit of Blissfield, though Blissfield never felt as cold and barren as Ohio on that March afternoon.

"We can have a picnic when it gets a little warmer," he said, and I wondered where that idea came from. "I'll take you to Cedar Pointe. Ever been there?"

"Once, with my fifth grade class. My mother was supposed to chaperone, but she had a black eye and didn't go."

"Well, we've got to get you back to Sandusky before you're sixty." Ignoring my comment about my mother, he spoke in a matter-of-fact voice, as if he was talking about going to the cleaners or washing the car.

"I'm not a kid anymore," I said.

"That's too bad. Bet you were cute. Nicer, too."

"Yeah, and look where it got me."

He didn't answer and we drove for a while. Then suddenly he pulled over to the side of the highway and jerked up the handbrake. All we could see in any direction was broken yellow corn stalks and the weird, ice-blue sky.

"Alright," he said.

"What?"

"Your turn to drive."

"Where?"

"Anywhere. Just take the wheel, Celeste."

Before I could resist he was out of the car and into the cold, his watch cap pulled low and his dark glasses reflecting the courageous early spring sun. When he opened my door I slid into his arms.

"You know, you need to get some height on you," he murmured, his voice strangely thick.

I had never driven anything like his big black truck. Grandma's old Buick floated on the roads; Jesse's contraption handled hard, like an ox straining against its yoke. The steering wheel disliked me immediately, and before I could measure exactly how much weight to put on the accelerator, the truck tried to leap into a field. Jesse laughed and grabbed the wheel.

"See what I mean?" he said. "Too little."

"Am not!"

"Then let me see what you got, Peewee."

That set my jaw out of whack. I put all my concentration on bending the vehicle to my will, and soon we were flying down those gritty two-lane roads like they were laid out for me, and me alone.

I don't know if I frightened him or not. It must have taken Herculean self-control for him to let me drive like that. I fought to keep the truck exactly where it belonged, in the center of the lane, but I didn't slow down when the hills got steep, and more than once we took a rise so fast we went airborne and I felt my belly fly up into my throat, and I liked it. The strain of forcing down the accelerator hurt all the way up to my hip, and my shoulders ached from the tension of mastering the steering wheel. But it was clean, good pain, and the sheared stalks flew by like razors sluicing through the weeks of rage and fear.

And I began to laugh. Hard, deep, and harder still. The laughter shook my spine and belly and arms and then my face loosened and I was howling, with Jesse howling right beside me. I laughed until tears ran down into my lips and open mouth, then dampened my legs and the seat between my legs.

Finally I eased off of the pedals and let the car drift more and more slowly, until we coasted into the yard of an ancient and roofless farmhouse and a barn that had half-collapsed under the weight of the late-winter snow.

Without a word I climbed across the seat and into Jesse's arms. He held me close, rocking me gently, then got out of the car and back into the driver's seat.

That night he made us dinner.

"It's strange," he remarked as he took a rare sip from a bottle of beer, "how I never thought I'd be able to share this space with anybody."

I thought you bought it for a woman."

"*With* a woman," he said. "That's different."

"But—"

"It was the loft that drove her away," he said. "After she lived here a few months she decided she wanted a picket fence. A bunch of babies and a family room and a yorkie. I wanted to be here, in a space where I could see every corner while looking out over the world."

"She wanted you to think like a husband—" I said.

"—and I was thinking like a cop." He was quiet for a little while, but I knew he needed to say something. "With you," he finally went on, "this room doesn't seem so large."

"How does that make sense? I can barely see over the counter."

"I don't know." He lifted his bottle. "Here's to cohabitation."

"We're not cohabitating. I'm a baby leopard, locked in your cage."

"Honestly, Celeste: I don't know what you are. Neither do you."

I looked at him and I knew he saw the fear in my eyes.

"Easy does it," he said softly. "It really is going to be alright."

"How is it going to be alright?"

"We'll get him, baby. We'll get him before he gets to you."

"And before he gets to her?" I asked.

"That's something no one can control. She can use the phone, like anybody else," Jesse said. "She can walk into a store, a hospital, or even into a school, post office, gas station or supermarket, and someone will help her."

I looked at my half-empty plate. Jesse reached over and took my hand. "You can't carry this, Celeste. Do you hear me? You can *not* carry this."

That's when I knew he really was starting to care—though knowing it didn't mean I could let myself feel it.

We went to our separate beds, but that night I wanted him to do more than hold me. "You don't have to carry all of this alone," he'd said, but I *did* have to carry it. Jesse didn't know how hard it was for me to be civil, to be reasonable, to be *normal*, when all I could think about was how to be ready when the moment came. Copley-ready. Bad-ass enough to survive whatever was about to happen. Because I knew it was going to happen.

I just didn't know when. And I didn't know how.

twenty-five.

Day five rolled by, my bones aching by the end of my second shift, the black truck waiting outside. Day six and seven and eight were the same. Tony's Supermarket was a world inside of a world, a world in which I could work to exhaustion and pray that the eyes of the public and the other workers would keep Copley on the periphery of my life.

On the morning of day nine, Jesse's phone chimed at daybreak. He was in the shower and I picked it up, knowing I shouldn't. I took a breath, listening to the spray behind the glass wall.

The message was simple: *"Jesse, we got him last night. Arraignment at nine. See you there."*

My heart exploded.

I set the phone down. The water stopped; I went into the kitchen and began the morning coffee. Jesse padded out with a towel around his waist.

"What was it?" he asked.

"What?"

"I heard it ring," he said, gesturing to the phone.

"I didn't touch it," I said.

"Come on, Celeste."

I shrugged and began filling our mugs. My hands were shaking and I prayed he wouldn't notice. He scooped the phone up and listened to the message. His expression shifted, but he didn't speak. His glance at me a few seconds later was so distant we might have been strangers.

"Want some coffee?" I asked.

"No time," he said, walking swiftly to his closet.

"You always have coffee."

"Got to get to the station." He took out a shirt and tie.

"What happened?"

"We need to get going," he said.

"Who's going to be arraigned, Jesse?"

"I thought you didn't listen."

"Of course I listened."

"You shouldn't have."

"Is it Copley?" I asked.

He strode over to the kitchen, the shirt tails flapping. Despite what he'd said, I knew he would drink the coffee and toast a couple slices of bread. He would turn on the radio and listen to the national and local news headlines, eating while standing. In precisely twelve minutes he'd be putting on his suit jacket, adjusting his tie, buffing a quick shine onto his shoes.

He would not be talking.

I went into the shower and came out quickly. I pulled my hair back into a simple braid. While I was in the shower I heard him speaking to someone. By the time I came out, his face was even more distant.

"Toast, Celeste?"

"Not till you answer."

"Coffee?"

"Jesse, if this is about my family, you need—"

"Don't tell me how to do my job," he said irritably.

"Who called you?"

"Let's go."

"Are you listening to me?"

He stopped moving. "Celeste, I always listen to you. What you heard was a message about a case I'm working on."

"My father's case?"

"No."

"You're lying."

He was. I knew him well enough, now, to see it in his eyes. But then, I'd been lying, too.

"You're going to work," he said, "where I'll come and pick you up when your shift is over."

"Jesse—"

"It's too soon to discuss this, Celeste. Do you understand?" The coldness was back again, as if it were the dark January night when we first met. Silently I put on my jacket and went to wait by the door. It didn't take him long to join me.

The streets were wet and windy, with paper-towel clouds blowing raggedly across another cinematically blue sky. We didn't talk in the car, but I noticed he'd put on his dark glasses, though it was barely past daybreak. I also saw the bulge under his suit jacket.

When he stopped in front of Tony's, I tried one last time.

"Jesse, would you please tell me—"

"I've got to go, Celeste. Just wait for me. Do you understand? Wait for me here. I'll pick you up tonight."

For ten weeks Tony's Supermarket had been the refuge that kept me sane during the day, the way the loft kept me calm at night. Though I'd made no real friends, the staff appreciated my work ethic and the fact that I left the donuts and day-old cake entirely for them. They understood my mother's appearances, followed by my father's, because none of them had had simple lives. They understood why I'd quit high school, because they'd quit, too. They even understood my odd, distant behavior. Every single one of them had known deep, personal grief, and recognized what they saw in my eyes.

So no one bothered me that entire day, while I worked more furiously than ever. And then, around seven o'clock, three hours before the end of my shift, my mother, bundled up in her man's coat, an enormous scarf and a strange hat, jogged up to the door.

I caught her image through the plate glass windows and had an argument with myself at the speed of light. Should I greet her, or should I vanish through the employee lounge and slip into the oncoming night?

I didn't know what to say to her, and I didn't want to argue with her or hear her whining about Copley's arrest. There was no other reason on earth for her to show up on the same day Jesse got that message.

And though I wanted to flee, and knew Jesse would have told me to go, for some unbelievable reason, I didn't. I stayed. I didn't move from my cash register. I waited for her to stomp the mud from her boots after she crossed the threshold, and make her way toward me.

"Beth, baby," she began in a low, breathless, voice. She was wearing a blue wool Sherpa hat with earflaps that now swung loose, the ties hanging down under her chin. I could see traces of a purplish mark beneath her left eye.

I couldn't meet her gaze. "Hey, Momma."

"Listen, baby. I want you to come with me."

She had placed her hand on the same arm Copley held a few weeks before. I felt the slight trembling that made its way from her flesh to mine.

"I'm at work, Momma."

"I know, but tell the guy—your boss—you need to go home early tonight."

"I can't. Someone's coming to pick me up in a little while."

She stepped closer and brought her head near mine. "It's important, baby. I want you to come by my place. It'll only be for a few minutes."

"I got other things to do, Momma."

Any other night there would have been customers straggling through the store, and I could have gotten rid of her by simply pointing out that I was busy. That night, however, the store was nearly empty. Maybe it was the cold, which was unusual for that time of year. Or maybe we were both plain unlucky.

"Listen to me, Bethany. It's real important. You ain't been home in months. Just come by this evening. It'll be okay, I promise."

I took a good look at my mother. Her face, once doe-like, had softened to the point where even her enormous eyes seemed lost in her flesh. The hat held her features captive, so I could see the full lips, now split from the cold, and her nose, which was running slightly. The rest of her was bundled up so heavily she might have been a mass of flesh.

"What about your husband?" I asked.

"You mean your father?"

"Yeah."

"He won't be there."

"How do you know?"

"He— he not there."

"Momma, I don't think—"

"Beth, please come. Just this once. Come over this time and I'll leave you alone after that."

"I don't think I should," I said.

"It's okay. Really, it's okay," she said. "I have something to show you. A surprise. You'll like it. I promise."

She was pleading with me, and it was pitiful. I actually felt bad for her. A couple of the stock boys, red-faced from collecting stray carts from the parking lot, looked over at us as they came inside. I glanced toward Tony's office behind the enormous two-way mirror that overlooked the entire store. I couldn't tell if he was in there or not.

I let my heart, not my mind, make the decision. I felt sorry for my mother. I was pretty sure she showed up because Copley was gone, and the coast was clear for the first time since they'd let him out of prison. And there was something else: what if, by some strange twist of fate, Nina and Gideon had been writing to me, care of Grandma, who had forwarded their letters to my mother? I knew my mother had kept Grandma's letters from reaching me. What if she'd also kept Nina and Gideon's?

I went into the back, removed my apron, put on my down jacket. I told the stock boys, who were drinking hot chocolate, to tell Tony I was taking my second-shift lunch break, and would be back in about forty-five minutes. I figured on fifteen to walk to the duplex, fifteen to visit with her, then fifteen to walk back. I'd get back to the store with time to spare before Jesse picked me up.

"Okay," I said to my mother. "Let's go. But I can only stay for a minute."

We went out into the cold, scentless twilight. The ice was long gone, but the wind felt like a wall and we both leaned into it with our shoulders, making it nearly impossible to talk. Anyway, neither one of us wanted to say anything about Copley. It was a no exit highway to another argument.

The duplex, on a block that looked even more beleaguered after yet another winter, was now blistered and patched, with sheets of wood nailed over several ground floor windows.

"What happened?" I asked as she unlocked the street door.

"They got raided. It was some kind of crime scene and nobody can go inside."

"Did they raid your place, too?" I asked.

"Not really. I mean, they came in and looked around."

"So are you okay here?"

"Sometimes the furnace go out and it can get kinda cold."

"Did you pay the bill?"

"Maybe a couple of weeks late, but yeah, I paid it," she said.

I felt like I was talking to a child. We started up the steep, narrow stairs. "What about Copley?" I asked.

"You mean, your dad?"

"Dang, Momma. We both know who we're talking about."

"What about him?"

"Where is he?" I asked.

"Well, he was home, but he may be gone again for a while."

"Did they arrest him?"

"He don't matter, Beth."

"Momma—did they arrest him?" I stopped halfway up the stairs.

"Never mind that. Just come in."

Breathing heavily, I watched her vanish into the apartment. "Shit," I muttered to myself, listening intently. Aside from my mother's steps on the living room floor, the house was dead silent. If Copley was home, silence would have been impossible.

The place was icy cold and in a state of weird disarray. Not only was clothing strewn on the floor as if the cops had torn the place up, but dishes and glasses and bowls were everywhere, too. My heart sank. I'd never find any letters in this mess.

"What's going on in here?" I asked, looking around. Neither one of us had taken off our coats. My mother switched on a lamp and turned to face me. She opened her mouth, then hesitated, as if afraid to speak.

"I—I got something here. Look—" She crossed the room and took a plastic folder of papers out from under the seat cushion of an old armchair. The folder contained our birth certificates, her marriage license, and two Greyhound tickets for Baltimore, Maryland.

"What's this?" I asked.

"It's for us," she whispered, automatically lowering her voice.

"What do you mean?"

"I always said we would go. Now we going."

"Where?"

"To my aunt in Maryland."

"Maryland?" I repeated stupidly.

"I promised you, baby. Back then, two years ago, I wasn't ready. I—I just didn't have myself together. But I'm ready now. I got the tickets today."

I looked at her, standing there in her lumpy coat and weird hat, the strings swinging back and forth under her chin. For a moment I thought she was truly insane, but then I realized she was really proud of the fact that she'd finally managed to purchase those tickets.

"Momma, I can't just leave," I said.

"Yes, you can. That store's no kind a job. You got to get back in school."

"The only place I'm going is back to Blissfield."

"You can't go back there," she said. "Your grandma don't want you."

"Grandma loves me. She'll be glad when I get there."

"No she won't. She told me you took her car and went and attacked someone. She said you shamed her at the school where she used to teach, and at her church, and also to her neighbor. She said she tried her best to keep you from behaving like your father, but she can't handle you no more!"

The hurt caused by my mother's words was worse than any blow, and I took several steps backwards and dropped the papers on the floor beside the scuffed end table. "I don't believe Grandma said those things."

"It's true. How else would I know?" BeBe J answered.

"Even if she said them, it was because she was mad at me," I said. "She knows what happened. She knows it wasn't my fault. She knows how bad I need to come back."

BeBe J grasped my arms. "Beth, listen to me: the bus leave at ten o'clock tonight. We don't need to take nothing with us. I got some money saved up, and you can write that man at the store for your check."

"No. I'm not going anywhere but Blissfield!"

"But I been planning this for two years, Beth! *Two whole years!*"

"It's too late. I'm not a little kid anymore. I have to make my own decisions."

"But Bethany," she wailed, "I'm finally ready to go."

"You not hearing me, Momma. You can go, but I'm not going with you."

She stared at me as if she really didn't get it, but I didn't care. The only thing I cared about was what she said about Grandma.

"Look, Momma," I said, "I got to get back to the store. Before I go, I need to ask you something. Did I get any letters?"

"Letters?"

"Did Grandma or anybody else send me letters?" I had raised my voice. She was trembling, though I was several inches shorter, and much smaller than she was. *Was I that much like my father?*

"I just want to get us somewhere safe," she whimpered.

"Then go. I only want my letters."

"Beth, I'm sorry," she said, sinking down on the sofa, her hands over her eyes. "I'm sorry you had to see all those things. I just didn't know how to leave. I loved him so much."

"I don't give a shit about any of that. I just want my let—"

The door at the bottom of the stairs burst open, slamming hard enough to rattle the picture of the naked couple hung above the sofa.

My first thought was that Jesse had arrived early at the grocery store and learned from my coworkers that I'd left with my mother. I turned toward the door, intending to call out to him, when we both heard the voice.

"Where the fuck you at, bitch?"

My mother jumped up, eyes bulging beneath her hat.

"Go!" she whispered harshly. "Go!"

"Where?" I knew there was no other way out of the apartment.

"Just hide till I can calm him down!"

He was thudding up the steep stairs, the sound partnered with a series of threats. There were only two places I could go: the kitchen, which opened onto the living room, or the bedroom, which at least had a closet. I had started toward the bedroom when that other voice in my head—*Copley's* voice— spoke clearly: *No. There'll be weapons in the kitchen.*

Within seconds I was inside the arched opening that separated the two rooms. I knew I was partially exposed, but the kitchen was dark and I had on my gray jacket. My eyes went to the sink, the counters, the row of little hooks on the wall above the stove. I gently pulled open the drawers on either side of the sink. Nothing but toothpicks, a can opener, a plastic spatula—and not one, single, solitary knife. I tried the next drawer and the next, all the time listening as Copley, raging at the top of his lungs, entered the living room.

And then I knew: Bebe J had got rid of anything and everything that might be used as a weapon. There were no knives in the kitchen. I pulled the phone out of my jacket and managed to get it open. My fingers, wet with sweat, slipped over the keypad. I realized that the sharp little melody that would chime when it dialed might get his attention and anyway, it was already too late: Copley would be done with whatever it was he planned to do long before help could arrive.

Empty-handed, I flattened myself against the side of the fridge. I couldn't see my father, but I could smell him—stale cigarettes, unwashed clothes and spilled malt liquor—and I certainly heard him round on my mother.

"What the fuck did you do, bitch?"

"Nothin', baby. I ain't done nothing," she whimpered.

"Don't lie to me, fucking c——!"

"——I'm not, Copley."

"Get that stupid shit off your head!"

"Okay." I saw her reach up and pull off her hat. There was a moment's silence as she made her face naked to his gaze.

Then he slapped her. The slap rang through the apartment. She was silent, as if ready and waiting for the next blow.

"Who you told?" he said. "Who you open your bitch mouth to?"

"I ain't told nobody nothing, Copley."

He hit her again. "You told somebody. Nobody else knew shit. Nobody."

"Maybe somebody saw somethin,' baby. Maybe somebody followed you."

"Oh, you just motherfucking Sherlock Holmes, now? You going to tell me somebody been following me and I ain't seen it?"

He slapped her a third time, and this time she cried out. I remembered from my childhood that slapping her in the same place repeatedly was the way he initiated a *real* beating.

"Please, baby," she whispered. "Don't get mad. I ain't been doing nothin' but going to work everyday. I don't see nobody or talk to nobody——"

He grabbed her upper arm and pulled her so close that her face was bathed in his spittle. "Those motherfucking cops pick me up and try to tell me they got what they need to put some motherfucking shit on me. They call in some goddamn stupid court-appointed dick, then drag me in front of the judge. The lawyer say they ain't got shit for evidence, and the motherfucking prosecutor start babbling some shit and the judge tell me they don't got enough to keep me. Took all motherfucking day, but they couldn't make nothin' stick. When I find out which motherfucker talked, I'm going to fuck them up. And it better not be *you*——"

"No baby, no. I never——"

"Shut the fuck up." He shoved her away.

In the kitchen, sweat covered my face. When I peered around the corner of the fridge I could see my mother, standing in the center of the room in her man's coat, staring at the floor, one trembling hand on her cheek. By leaning an inch or two farther I could see my father, who was wearing jeans and a black hoodie, staring at the floor, his left leg bouncing tensely.

"You hungry, baby?" she mumbled. "I'll go get you some shrimp."

He glared up at her. She shifted nervously.

"Why this place so tore up?" he asked.

"You didn't come home, so I was looking for your lawyer number."

"Why?"

"I was worried."

"Why? You thought I got arrested?"

"I—no, baby. I was just making sure I had his number had in case something wrong."

"What—you psychic or something?"

"I was just worried about you," she said, voice trembling.

"You lying," he said. "I can always tell when you lying."

"No, Copley. It's the truth. I was worried about you and—"

I thought he was going to hit her again, but instead I heard him drop down on the sofa, suddenly and heavily. "Why's it so motherfucking cold in here?"

"I don't know, baby. I paid the bill."

At that moment his head turned to the papers by the table at his feet.

"What's this shit?"

"Just some stuff I found in a drawer."

I heard him pick up and shuffle through the papers. "Your birth certificate? Bethany's birth—"

He stopped talking. I knew he'd come to the bus tickets.

"Who you buy these for?" he asked.

"Those are old, Copley." Her voice was trembling.

"Who you buy these for, bitch?"

"I bought them a long time ago, when you was still in Cleveland."

"For who?"

"For—for Beth and me."

"Beth? You said she was with my mother."

"She was."

"Then why you buy these tickets?" he said.

"I wanted to go see my Aunt Vashti."

"Your *who*?"

"You know I got my father's sister in Baltimore," she said. "I was thinking maybe Beth and me could go there while you was away."

"How?"

"I was just thinking she could come home over the summer, and we could take a trip."

"That don't make no sense."

"I didn't go, baby. I was just thinking about it."

He was silent, studying the tickets. "Wait," he said, his voice rising, "these tickets for *tonight*. Who you buy this ticket for?"

"What?"

"You planning to leave with a man?" he asked, his voice rising.

"No—*no*! I got that ticket for Beth."

"Beth don't live here, you lying bitch! You ratted me out then got these tickets with the money—"

"Nobody gave me any money, Copley! I saved—"

The sound he made was fiercely incoherent, between a babble and a scream. He knew she'd bought the tickets that morning, right after she'd called the cops on him.

And the world went into slow motion.

Using all the force in his thick, compact body, he sprang off the sofa and hit her so hard that she seemed to float into the air and curve gracefully and soundlessly down to the floor. Even when her head struck the edge of the table and seemed to bounce back up, I heard nothing.

But Copley was just getting started. He threw the tickets aside and leapt on my mother's prone body, striking her in the face with his fist one, twice, three times. I heard the brittle crunch, like a cracker snapping, and watched him stagger to his feet, trading his weight from one leg to the other as he began kicking her.

I wondered why I wasn't moving, despite the voice in my head screaming at me to stop him. All those months, all those years I had become Copley whenever needed, and here I was, needing more than at any point in my life to become my father, and suddenly I couldn't move away from that kitchen wall.

I had seen my father strike my mother every day of my childhood, and I knew the brief, intense, and deliberate pattern of his attacks. He slapped her repeatedly, twisted her arms and choked her until, bleeding, weeping and broken, she begged him to stop. But this was different. Some kind of boundary had been crossed. He didn't want anything from her anymore. He wasn't beating her to cow her. He was beating her to annihilate her.

And even though I hated her for bringing me here and making me see this, and I hated him even more for making me watch this every day of my childhood, I had promised myself never to allow him to hit her again.

I could not let my father murder my mother while I stood only ten feet away.

Breaking through my terror, I ran at him as fast and hard as I could, with nothing to protect myself except my fists and my anger.

He was not prepared. My body collided with his and we both went down, even as he twisted and shoved me off of him. He was beyond speech now, as was I, and the sight of me sprawled beside him only added to his rage.

He moved like a spider, throwing one of his muscular legs over mine even as he struck me with the butt of his hand. I saw white, but grabbed at his hand and pulled it into my mouth, biting down as hard as I could.

Still, he made no sound. He let me go and scampered backwards, rolling over and getting to his feet. I struggled to rise, unable to do more than protect myself from his boots. Faster than I would have believed possible, he took aim and kicked me as hard as he could in the lungs, and I curled up on the floor, unable to breathe.

And then I heard the click of the knife and understood he was going to kill us both. We would die on the floor of that filthy, unheated apartment, on a street of boarded up houses, in the icy darkness of that March night, and he would take the tickets and leave us to be found, mother and daughter bound in death, when someone got curious about the odor of our decomposing bodies.

I've seen movies where soldiers lunge toward their enemies in battle, as if death was the purest purpose of their lives. At that moment I, too, figured that if my mother and I were going to die, I would die fighting my motherfucking father to my last pathetic breath.

So even though I was more afraid than I had ever been in my life, and in more pain than I could imagine, I rolled away, got to my feet and threw myself at him, kicking and hitting and spitting and biting, soundlessly, ferociously, desperately, ridiculously.

The knife flew out of his hand and spun across the floor. He pushed me away, but I went on kicking and biting and beating at him with all the force in my body. I got him once near the eye and his head snapped back, but his fist connected with my left breast and the pain was excruciating. Still, I fought on, pulling him into a tight embrace so he couldn't get to his weapon.

He slammed me in the forehead, and my vision skipped as if my brain was experiencing a power outage, but I leaned forward and clamped my teeth on his jaw, finding bone and unshaven flesh, and then, blood.

But he was stronger. When his fist struck my back I lost my grip and fell hard, only by some miracle managing to keep my head from striking the floor. Copley staggered backwards, holding his face, blood spurting between his fingers.

Both of us were panting. Neither of us spoke, though my flesh was screaming.

I saw him look at me. Saw the hatred in his eyes, tempered by something else: a new and completely unexpected respect for his daughter, his *Self*.

But I also saw the sense of purpose that had driven him to do whatever he chose to do every day of his life. And in two strides he crossed the room and picked up the knife. By the time he turned around I was on all fours, and as he came toward me I staggered to my feet. The voices in my head were shouting *no no no no no,* but the room was deadly silent.

I threw myself toward him, but he was faster. The blade caught my coat, slicing through the tight polyester. The fabric ripped and my sweatshirt ripped and my tee-shirt tore and the warm metal scraped then severed the skin along my collarbone across the entire front of my chest. I heard an odd *oh* escape my lips and it was as if he was gone, the knife was gone, the room was gone, the floor was gone, because the world was the blood spurting through the gash just inches above my heart.

And Copley turned away from me as I fell to my knees, took another easy step, and looked back at me with a smile as the knife caressed Bebe J's gently pulsing neck, showering me with her blood.

So as I pulled my legs up tight against my belly, grasping at the warmth pooling under my clothes, Bebe J's life splattered on my face, my hair, my own exposed throat.

The only sound I could hear was Copley's breathing.

He took a step back, surveying his work.

As I began to float outside of my body, I wondered if he was proud.

If this was the movies, the guys in uniform would have stormed up the stairs, wrestled my father to the floor, then knelt down beside me and repeated, "*stay with me, Bethany—stay with me!*"

In the movies, my softening gaze would have wavered between life and the *Light*. In the movies, I'd be given a choice to stay in that room with Copley, or to go on to the next room, with heat and sunlight and plenty to eat, with my mother.

But this wasn't the movies. And I've never been given any choices in my life.

Copley Nehemiah Castle went into the bedroom, silently got out of his bloody clothes, stuffed them into a bag from the cleaners where my mother had worked her for most of her adult life, and put on a different pair of pants and a clean sweatshirt. He then calmly removed my mother's wallet from her purse, picked up the bus tickets and walked through the living room, without pausing, to the door.

He left his wife and daughter lying in the growing pool of their shared blood. He probably knew I wasn't dead, but his rage was spent, and as he told Jesse Brantley later, he was pretty certain I would die.

I remember listening to him descend the stairs, a faint and indistinct voice warning me that those very stairs were my gateway between life and the *Light*.

When the downstairs door closed, I rolled over onto my stomach, feeling my soaked sweatshirt balloon, beneath my jacket, with warm liquid. I looked down with surprise as blood smeared through the jacket, and down into the cracks of the floorboards, beneath the waistband of my jeans and right through to my pink cotton panties. Teeth clenched, I crawled, a scarlet reptile, to the top of the stairs, followed by a smear of blood and tears and mucus. The stairwell was dark and frigid and mountain steep, but I spread my legs and let myself fall. I didn't feel pain when my ankles and knees and hips ricocheted into the crevasse of the night.

At the bottom I pulled myself up by the doorknob, opened the door and rolled out onto the porch. Somehow I managed to get the phone out of my pocket, but my fingers kept on sliding, sliding, sliding off the buttons. That must be when my hearing returned, because someone began screaming, screaming, screaming with what was left of her lungs.

twenty-six.

I was twenty-three years old when I made it back to life.
The wiki version goes like this:

> After three months in a hospital and three months in a rehab facility, Bethany Celeste Castle was shipped to a psychiatric inpatient treatment center, which was her home for more than two and a half years. She was released at the age of twenty-one, despite exhibiting lingering physical and emotional symptoms resulting from the attack. For the next eighteen months she inhabited a residential home for women who were survivors of similar abuse, but there are no recorded incidents of any violent outbursts or other maladaptive behavior. Bethany Castle was released from the home after having earned her GED, and sought gainful employment with the support of her assigned Social Worker...

But the lady, methinks, is getting way ahead of herself.
The full-length version went more like this:
I didn't regain consciousness for a full two weeks after the March night my father murdered my mother and me. I have no memory of those two weeks, except that I am absolutely sure that while I was dead on the porch, and afterward, when I was still on the borderline in the hospital, no loving voices coaxed me toward the *Light*. When I emerged from the coma I learned I had three broken ribs, a punctured spleen, a hairline fracture in my forehead, a dislocated shoulder, and a six-inch gash in my chest. The subsequent fall down the stairs snapped my right ankle, wrist, and shredded my left meniscus. With massive blood loss, shock, and hypothermia from the half-hour I lay screaming on the front porch of the abandoned house on a street of abandoned houses, I had been dead for several minutes before a portable defibrillator started my heart again.

Thus, along with having been murdered, I absolutely should have stayed dead.
Bebe J, of course, did.
They caught up with Copley at a rest stop in Pennsylvania, buying malt-liquor, a carton of Kools and a packet of beef-jerky, with his dead wife's (actually, his own mother's) money. The Greyhound driver recognized his picture on a television monitor in the rest stop lobby. Copley laughed when the cops surrounded him. He was still laughing when he was interviewed by Detective Jesse Brantley. He said he didn't give a shit if they arrested him. He'd taken care of the bitch who ratted him out. He didn't even bother to mention me when asked. He merely shrugged.

It was Jesse Brantley who (sort of) explained these things to me. He happened to be sitting next to the bed when I tuned back in after my long time out. His eyes were very black and very cold, but his voice was gentle.

"I fucked up, baby. I fucked up bad and I'm very, very sorry."

I could hear everything he said, but the braided tubes delivering top-shelf painkillers to my system kept me from making enough sense of it to respond. That didn't matter, however. Jesse needed to talk, and probably would have gone on talking, even if he'd been the only person in the room.

"I got to the store that night and someone said you'd gone out for your lunch break about an hour earlier and already should have been back. So I asked them where you'd gone. One of the other employees said you'd left with a woman who they thought was your mother. That's when I started to run. Before I was halfway there I got the call from the EMS responders."

He had taken off his jacket, and when I looked around the room I saw flowers, magazines, and even a book or two. Someone had practically moved in.

My gaze fell to the tubes in my wrists and arms. I felt no pain, but I also felt no particular need to speak.

Jesse moved closer to me and placed one of his hands very carefully on my belly. It was strange because he'd never done that when my body was healthy and whole. "Celeste, you're going to be alright. Your injuries were pretty serious, but the doctor says you'll be out of here in the next couple of weeks."

I might have nodded. His words made perfect sense, but my mind wasn't trying to respond.

"When this is over I want you to come and live with me," he said. "We do pretty good together, don't we?"

There was guilt in his eyes. I didn't know why.

"Do you need anything, baby?"

I imagine I shook my head.

"Then sleep."

When I woke up the next time a nurse was doing what nurses do. That's when I became aware of the bandages on my head and the soft casts on my left knee and right ankle.

"You're back," the nurse observed. "Feeling any better?"

I tried to shrug, only to discover my shoulder and chest hurt like hell.

"It's okay. Don't try to move. The doctor cut back on the painkillers, so you're probably really feeling those injuries. I can get you a pill if you need one."

I must have nodded. She vanished. I waited for nothing in particular. She came back and gave me something to swallow and I was out.

"Baby? Somebody's here who really needs to speak to you."

I got my eyes open. A white man in a suit was standing there with Jesse.

"We have some papers for you to sign. This way we can begin to settle your mother's estate."

He might have been speaking in whatever they speak in Burma.

"Celeste, I need you to focus. This gentleman is your lawyer. He's going to see that the bills are paid until you're well enough to take over."

I tried to lift my tube-tethered hand.

"If you can't write," Jesse said, "you can give me Power of Attorney and I'll take care of things for you."

My mouth still refused to answer, but I motioned vaguely and he put a pen in my hand. "Celeste, please focus," he said, leaning over me with a clipboard. "I need you to sign this document."

I probably should have signed, but I didn't.

"Bethany Celeste," Jesse said in a very low voice. "You know you can trust me, and this needs to get done. Do you understand?"

I nodded.

"Will you sign?"

I shook my head, then scrawled one word from my cottony mind on the top of the page: "Grandma."

Now it was Jesse who shook his head. "I'm sorry, baby. She's not here."

I stared at him, because he wasn't making sense. I pointed at the clipboard.

"No, honey. I spoke to her but she said—well, she said her health isn't good enough for her to travel."

He had never been any good at lying to me, and we both knew it. He looked away, ashamed, and that's when I understood he really *had* talked to her and she really had refused. She'd refused to come, even though her son had murdered his wife and her granddaughter, and her granddaughter, who was now trying to decide whether or not to return to the living, needed her more than anything on earth.

Jesse wanted to spare my feelings.

For some reason one of the machines beside my bed began to beep wildly. A nurse appeared in the doorway. "Gentlemen, I have to ask you to leave."

"We just need a min—"

"Sir: you both need to leave."

Grateful not to have to think, I let myself go under once again.

I didn't see them again for a while. I figure the lawyer got some kind of emergency order, and they went ahead and settled my mother's estate. Jesse came again and, sitting beside me on the edge of the bed, assured me everything was going to be alright.

But here's the thing: I really didn't give a shit.

As my mind cleared I wondered why Grandma hadn't come, and why she wasn't signing for me. I wondered what kind of "estate" remained. I wondered what they'd done with my father.

I also noticed that the grass had greened up and there were geraniums outside my window. I then realized I wasn't in a hospital, anymore. I'd been moved to some kind of rehabilitation facility. The tubes were gone, so I was no longer tethered to my bed.

Jesse still came and sat beside me, but less often. He talked, but he no longer asked me to respond. I guess he accepted the fact that I couldn't. That I could hear his voice, but there was no one left inside of me to talk with. So he talked. I didn't.

"It's all over, baby. They found the knife in the bedroom with your father's prints on it. His lawyer got him a plea deal—no trial. Life without the possibility of parole. That the way he avoided the death penalty. Murder two, as opposed to pre-meditated. Though I figure he came there that night with full intent. He just didn't know you were there."

Jesse stopped and looked at me. He was wearing a grey tee-shirt and dark jeans, and I saw that his arms were bigger and firmer than I remembered. I didn't know what I looked like. I was wearing a light robe and the athletic pants he'd purchased for me months earlier.

"Anyway," he continued, "he's gone for good. You have nothing to worry about, now." He shifted restlessly, as if he really expected me to respond. But I hadn't spoken for nearly five months, and I wondered why he didn't just accept that I wasn't going to.

"So," he said in sudden mock cheerfulness, "when are you gonna get up and out of this place? The rehab folks say you're ready to start walking. Looks like they're not feeding you, either. Let's face it, Celeste: you didn't have ten pounds to lose."

He was smiling, trying hard to make his voice warm and loving, but I heard the end of something. I knew it was just a visit or two before I wouldn't see him again.

"I wish you'd tell me what's going on in your head," he now said. "I am very, very sorry about everything that happened. I never intended for you to get hurt. I never thought he'd be able to get to you. I just didn't expect that anything like this could ever happen."

I heard in his voice that he had reached a boundary. I knew from five months of listening that there was something more, something even more terrible and shameful he had to tell me. Each time he visited he got closer to the truth, but each time he stopped himself before The Final Confession.

I really didn't care, however. Nothing he could tell me was worse than what I'd been through. Who gave a shit, really?

"I still expect you to come back to the loft when you're back on your feet," he said, the statement embarrassing, now. We both knew he was lying, but I couldn't imagine why. I would never go back to that loft. Never go back to being the womanchild who thought everything could somehow be alright.

* * * * * *

The last time I saw Jesse Brantley was in late September. I'd been moved again, out of the rehabilitation facility and into a psychiatric facility. The nuthouse looked like a motel: big rooms with wide windows and thickly carpeted corridors. They clearly didn't think I would hurt anyone, because the doors were open, and they didn't think I'd hurt myself, because my bathrobe had a belt. I attended group therapy three days a week, and sat for an hour twice each week with a nice old guy with white hair who'd been fixing broken people for over forty years. The other days I went to the gym and ran on a treadmill and used the stair climber, and I took online GED classes. I liked the classes because they gave me something to think about. That is, something other than the one and only thing I couldn't stop from thinking about: Grandma didn't want me. How would I ever find my way back to Gideon and Nina?

And then, though I could nod, shake my head, and occasionally smile, I still didn't talk. I don't know if I couldn't. I just didn't believe I should.

Jesse was wearing a brown suede jacket and a black turtleneck when he found me in the computer room, working on a Political Science assignment. He pulled up a chair and sat down beside me. He'd never been more beautiful. He'd never been more of a stranger.

"They say you'll have your high school degree by next spring. That's great news, Bethany."

I looked at him quickly, incensed that he'd used Bebe J. and Copley's name for me. I didn't know if he did it intentionally, thinking I might react by saying something, or whether calling me Bethany was a way of distancing himself from the Celeste he'd taught to trust him.

"You've really done a great job," he went on, glancing at the essay I was writing. "When I think about the kid I met that night in Poppy's—"

I flinched involuntarily. Any mention of those days was misery for me.

"Well," he said, catching himself, "I'm glad to see how good you look these days." He cleared his throat and moved a little bit closer. "I just want to make sure you know that even though I never intended to do anything more than protect you, I really did come to care for you. I enjoyed the time we had together. It was incredibly special."

He took my hand. "I'm still so sorry, baby. I thought we had it all taken care of. My team had been talking to her for weeks, trying to get her to work with us to get him off the streets. It was nearly impossible to convince her, though we told her we'd put her in a safe place until the trial was over."

He paused. "When I got the call that morning I thought everything was going to be alright. She'd given us what we needed to arrest him, and we picked him up. All she had to do was wait until he was arraigned—the prosecutor was sure he'd never get bail—but the judge unexpectedly let him go. I went to the store to make sure you were okay, but you were already gone. The fact that you were in that house—I will never forgive myself, Bethany."

My name is my own, I thought,

my own,

my own,

my own.

I glanced up at him, at his black black eyes, and understood that my mother had been so desperate to escape that for the first time in her life she'd made an independent decision. She'd decided not to let the cops protect her. She went and bought those stupid bus tickets, rather than letting Jesse's people move her somewhere Copley couldn't find her. And then she came and got me, rather than leaving me to my own damn life.

It wasn't Jesse Brantley's fault. Bebe J was just fulfilling a promise she'd made to me the day she put me on that bus when I was sixteen years old.

Well, we'd gone on a trip, alright.

And just look where we all ended up!

Jesse saw all this in my eyes. I had always been able to read him better than he could read me. "I know I messed up real bad," he said. "I promised to protect you. Hell, I promised to protect *her*. It's just that everything went as motherfucking wrong as possible."

He let go of my hand. "I didn't know how to tell you, but—the truth is that no one knew you were there, in my place. I mean, I told you I had permission to let you stay, but the fact is that I never let my lieutenant know I found you. If I had told him, he would have freaked out. He would have made you go to some clapboard motel with a female police office and stay cooped up under round-the-clock surveillance. But I really believed you would be safer with me. I was pretty sure that between Tony at the store, and me the rest of the time, there was no way your father would ever get to you."

He stopped speaking, literally searching my face to see if I understood. The problem was that I *did* understand. I had *always* understood: he used me as bait to get my mother to help him get my father.

Unnerved by what he saw in my eyes, he started up again.

"Look—I'm sorry, Bethany Celeste. I don't know what else to say. If your mother had followed my directions, things would have been different that day. If you hadn't listened to the message, you wouldn't have left the store with your mother. And if Tony had seen you leaving with her, he would have let me know right away. Shit, baby—if I could start over again, I'd put you on a plane to somewhere as far away as possible. Maybe even back to that guy in North Carolina."

Until that moment I'd managed, with the help of ongoing and regularly timed medication, not to open my mind to the details of That Night. Swift and glancing memories sometimes flitted through my head, but whenever the pressure began to build, like a vicious tightening in my chest, I was offered alms to heal my soul in the form of finely attenuated pharmaceuticals.

But Jesse had brought up something even more painful to me: '*that guy in North Carolina,*' and now, against all expectation, I found that I was smiling. I was also suddenly crying. The sound of my weeping laughter surprised me. It came from a huge echoing cavern where my spleen used to be, and felt like a gigantic balloon exploding. He looked horrified, and stood abruptly.

I watched, eyes flooding tears, still laughing hysterically. When he returned with a nurse, they found me sitting in the computer chair, hands clasped neatly in my lap, laughing and laughing. I was at last releasing a lifetime's worth of pain, brought into exquisite and precise focus by Jesse's sad confession and the fact that in my heavily medicated grief, I'd been forced to face my loss of Nina and Gideon.

The nurse asked Jesse Brantley to leave.

He left.

I never saw him again.

It would be untrue to suggest that he'd pulled the plug on my silence, because laughing absolutely is *not* speaking. Indeed, I didn't actually speak for another three months. It was during a holiday party that I found myself silently singing along with my favorite childhood Christmas song. When the rest of the room sang, "Do you see what I see?" I suddenly sang the echo out loud.

The shrink who'd been treating me for months, the nice Old Man who never, ever lost his cool, swung around to look at me. When the song came to the chorus again, I again sang the echo. He smiled, though he did nothing more.

The next morning my rusty voice asked one of the other patients to pass me the grape jelly. A dining room worker who'd been watching me for the entire eight months of my residency began to jump up and down and applaud. She then ran for a nurse.

Though I found their reaction irritating, I continued to talk. I don't know why. I just felt like talking.

Now my sessions with the psychiatrist began in earnest. Over the next ten months he prodded into my past, asking me to share everything I could remember about every beating I'd witnessed, or participated in, throughout my life. He made copious notes—I figured I might actually end up in a book— and seemed fascinated with the Castles' rise and fall.

He also asked me a lot about Gideon and Nina, and my life in Grandma's home. He asked me why I was able to control my anger in Grandma's presence, and why that control failed when I dealt with others. He asked why my Grandmother never visited, and I told him what I'd done to be exiled from Blissfield. He asked me why I did it. I said I was trying to save someone I loved, the way I'd tried to save my mother.

"Guess I won't try *that* again," I joked. He didn't laugh.

Over the many months of his questions and my answers, I grew less and less dependent on my pharma friends, finding I could think of That Night not as the destruction of my being, but instead as a simple, hideous affirmation of my determination to survive.

In some ways my life fascinated me as much as it fascinated him. He seemed very interested in the details—the way Copley doted on me while abusing my mother; the way Grandma glossed over any discussion of my father's behavior, and the way I grew up to become the perfect blend of both of my father's violence and my grandmother's love.

He asked me to keep a journal detailing how each episode of violence had affected my life. Well, even with the stuff I could no longer remember, there were lots of episodes to write about. We talked about my ability to ignore my mother's suffering and the suffering of people I'd hurt—he called it "dissociation," and I remembered Grandma saying I seemed "vacant." We spent lots of time on how I'd been a student of my father's behavior, and how I might avoid his lessons in the future.

The doctor was very focused on my future.

My. Future. What an amusing idea!

So I turned twenty in the nut house, and was still there, and still talking and journaling, when I turned twenty-one. I completed my GED and was told that, in the eyes of my doctor, I was just about ready for "reinsertion" into everyday life. I disagreed, but I suppose the funds for my unique vacation were running out.

So one day, after a great deal of coaxing from the good man, I agreed to consider moving into a halfway house. I was instructed to dress and wait in my room for the social worker who'd take me to look at several possible sites.

Though I knew I should be happy to go, part of me was utterly terrified to leave the hospital. So when the door opened I was unprepared for the woman who stepped inside. I remembered the coat, an unusual purple and pink plaid, before I remembered her face.

"Hi! My name's Paula, and—" she paused. "Wait: I know you. Let me see—" She stared at me a long moment, considering. "Ah. Yes. Now I remember. About a year, no, two years ago. Very cold night. At the church, right?"

She was almost correct, and it surprised me.

"Yes," I said. "That's about right. You took me into a room and gave me a coat and hat. Actually, it was about three and a half years ago."

"That long? Let me think: wow, it *has* been more than three years!"

"How did you find me?" I asked.

"Find you?"

"Yeah. How did you know I'd be here?"

"I didn't. This is my job, sweetheart."

"Oh." I was oddly disappointed. She'd been kind to me the night I'd wandered into the AA meeting.

"Well," she said brightly, "don't look so down! Seems like you're getting out of here very soon."

"Why?"

"Because everyone agrees you're ready."

When I didn't answer, she came and sank down on the edge of the bed beside me. "Look, sweetheart: you're too young to give in to the things that put you in here. If you need meds in order to face the outside world, you take them. If you need fifty more years of therapy, you do it. Life is too short and too precious to waste. You've got plenty of happy days ahead, but you've got to fight for them, okay?"

This was a strange speech coming from a near stranger, and I hated what she said. But I looked into her plain, open face and realized I liked her. It was a surprise for me to like anything.

So I got up and followed her outside the hospital, into a crisp, cool April afternoon. My first time out of a hospital of some sort since That Night. I kept close to her, unsure how I'd react if I saw something that reminded me of my parents. She seemed to sense this, because although she said nothing, she walked close beside me. I had an unexpected sense that I could tell her anything, even the things about my past that months of therapy with that sweet Old Man hadn't pried loose.

The air was wild with the scents of wet earth, old leaves, freshly cut grass and shouting flowers. I also smelled car exhaust, cigarette smoke, new asphalt and a trace of stale patchouli.

"So, I saw on your chart you've finished your GED. Well done, Bethany. And by the way, weren't you going by a different name when we met that night at the church? Wasn't it Elizabeth?"

"*Beth*any, Eliza*beth*. Who cares?"

"I don't," she said honestly.

"I can't believe you remember," I said.

"I'm one of those people."

"That's pretty crazy."

"You're telling me. Sometimes I wish I *could* forget stuff. Anyway, back then you wanted to be Elizabeth. What about now?"

"I don't know."

"That's okay. Sometimes when we're in a tight spot we just improvise. Let me know what works best for you."

"Isn't it, I don't know, weird to keep changing my name?" I asked.

She considered the question. "Well, women often change their name when they get married. It reflects a change in their social status. In other cultures, people change their names after going on a religious pilgrimage. It's a mark of honor. I think your name should reflect who you are at any given point in your life. So you should decide what you want to be called," she said, reminding me painfully of Nina.

I thought about the way she'd stood up for me at the church. Suddenly I wasn't afraid. With Paula beside me, I was going to be okay.

Paula didn't mess around. She found me a clean, well-ordered transition house for women who'd been through crazy shit. The other girls were young, angry, rough. Most had suffered trauma not unlike mine, but few had been lucky enough to swing two years in a psychiatric hospital, with plenty of food, clean sheets, and hours and hours of therapy. For that reason alone, they went their way and I went mine. It wasn't bad, however: I had a nice room with a closet, shelving and a window overlooking the backyard. I could shut my door and have some peace and quiet. No one fucked with me and I didn't have to fuck anybody up. It was exactly what I needed at that point in my life.

It occurred to me soon after moving in that someone must have been taking care of the bill. So one day when Paula came by to check up on me I asked her about it.

"Just out of curiosity," I said, "did my mother have any insurance?"

"Your mom? I don't think so, Bethany."

"Then who paid for the hospitals? My rehab? Who's paying for this room?"

"Well, your records say a lot of it was covered by the State, but there was another person who asked that their name not be shown in the paperwork."

"Why?"

"First of all, it turns out you were led to believe you were under official police protection when you were assaulted. My understanding is that one of the detectives told you he had permission to let you live in his home. Not only was that untrue, but quite clearly, he failed to protect you."

I thought about it before speaking. "While I was recovering from my injuries, the detective came to my room several times with a lawyer."

"I see," she said.

"He asked me to sign some papers, but the nurse made him leave."

"Good. He should never have approached you while you were in the hospital." She tucked her brown hair behind her ears. "I suspect, though I've never seen those papers, that he was trying to get you to sign something so you wouldn't sue."

"I could have sued him?" I asked.

"You could probably have sued the State for what happened to you, Bethany. Perhaps you still can." She looked at me with her practitioner's eyes. "Did you and the detective ever——?"

"No."

"But you lived with him."

"I slept on his couch from January till March," I said.

"And he never——"

"Not even a finger."

"But did he try?" she asked.

"He never figured it out," I said.

"What?"

"What he really felt." For a moment I was very angry at Jesse Brantley. It pissed me off that he couldn't decide whether he wanted to be my father, my big brother, my guardian or, yes, my lover. I thought about how he'd struggled with it almost every moment we were together.

Then I realized he *had* figured it out. That's why he'd brought the lawyer. Why he kept on apologizing. Why he kept on visiting me. He figured that if people realized he'd fucked it up so spectacularly, he stood to lose his beautiful loft, shiny black truck and promising career. At the end of the day he had chosen that shit over me. He just wanted to get on with his life.

I thought about how it would feel to sue the city. I figured I could get myself a house, new car, and a couple of trips to warm and sunny places. But then, I decided, Copley had already destroyed three lives. Why should he also have the chance to destroy Jesse Brantley, who'd only been trying to keep my father from hurting us all?

"You okay, kiddo?" Paula's voice cut through my ruminations.

"Yeah," I said. "At least, I think so."

"Got any more questions?"

"No, Paula. I think—it's weird, but I think I'm going to let it go."

She smiled. "Sure?"

"Pretty sure. I mean, I just don't feel like going back to That Night, and I'd have to spend some serious time there if I tried to sue."

"That's true." She touched my hand. "But I want you to know I'm proud of you. Sometimes letting go of the past is the best way to welcome the future."

"Doesn't feel like it."

"That's what happens when you're living in an aquarium."

"Aquarium?"

"Listen, love, there's only so much they can do to fix you," she said. "After a while you're just something for them to observe and write articles about. Your goal is to get out of the aquarium and back into the ocean, where you can be free."

"But what if I can't?"

"Can't what? Eat, sleep, go to work, watch TV, dream? You did all those things until that one messed up night, and you've done them ever since. Now the only thing you have to decide is whether that one messed-up night is going to be your excuse to avoid challenges, or whether you're going to go out and create a new life for yourself. I believe your future is still waiting for you."

"What if I mess things up?" I said.

"Then you go back to the doctors and let them fix you up again."

What if they can't?"

"Well, we'll cross that bridge when we get to it." She paused thoughtfully. "Tell me something, sweetheart: that night we met—the night you came to the meeting at the church—you were just trying to get out of the cold, right?"

I nodded.

"I thought so," she said.

"Then why'd you let me stay? That other guy wanted to kick me out."

She smiled sadly. "Part of our mission is to save others who might need us. You needed us, Bethany. I'd like to believe we did something good that night."

"Every time I try to do something good, somebody gets fucked up," I said.

"Life doesn't make us any promises, Bethany. We just have to keep doing the best we can. For now, just remember: Easy does it."

I continued my weekly sessions with the Old Man from the nuthouse, but I also began to attend an assault survivor meeting at Paula's church. Though I rarely spoke, the others' life stories calmed me. They seemed very close, and sometimes had meals together or celebrated each other's birthdays, but I told myself I didn't want to hang out with other damaged people. I had enough trouble managing my own shit.

Paula, who herself had eighteen years of sobriety, still met with me regularly to talk things through. She didn't let me whine—in fact, she reacted with strict practicality to everything I said. But she always tried to help me deal with whatever was bugging me.

Secretly I wished she'd invite me to her home, or take me shopping or just treat me like a daughter. But she wasn't into that. She was always 'by the book,' and drew the line when it came to her free time. I'd had a mother, and she was dead. I had a grandmother, but she was lost. I had a sister, but she'd vanished along with the others. And I'd been in love, but...

"You need to learn how to live with other people," Paula sometimes said, "but you've also got to learn to be alone."

I was alone. What was left to learn?

And as for other people—let's face it—other people were overrated.

* * * * * * *

You ask yourself how you can lose track of the years.

The truth is that time swallows us alive.

At least, that's how time played me.

Aside from generally feeling like shit, with aching joints, sore scars, and a non-ending headache that might have made me an addict if Paula hadn't convinced me to stick to over-the-counters, I found that lots of things I should have remembered were more like a muddy smear.

I listened to a lot of music—and it helped, particularly when I stumbled on a song that took me away from That Night and led straight me back to Nina and Gideon (Al Green: *"...spending my days, thinking about you, girl..."*). But then, it hurt like hell to go there, too, and I couldn't sleep when I had them on my mind, and I couldn't focus on much, either.

So I read a lot of books. I started with the stuff Nina used to talk about—the Classics, so to speak. I imagined us discussing Cathy and Heathcliff out on the moor ("bet that heather real scratchy when you sit on it!") and Gatsby's green light ("He such a dummy! That stupid cow couldn't hardly talk and she already married the first guy for his money!"). I was sure we'd have argued a lot about which house I'd have been placed in at the magic school ("with you, CeCe, it depend on the day of the week!"), and whether Beloved really was a ghost ("you better hope not, CeCe. Your daddy already crazy enough while he was alive!"). I read and read, sometimes consuming several books a week.

Paula found me a job as a custodian at Cuyahoga Community College. After six months I could enroll in a class for free, so I took a Great Books course and found myself meeting up with the Brontës and Poe, among other old friends. I dropped out, however, after the instructor, trying desperately to tie Dickens to modern life, led a conversation about Nancy's loyalty to Bill Sykes—that is, until the night Bill beat her to death.

Too damn much loyalty for me.

So I kept pushing the broom, and eventually graduated to food services, where I ate very well despite the pathetic pay, and then moved on to a job at the Student Center, where I sold coffee mugs and tee shirts bearing the college logo.

I took a couple of personal defense classes so I could manage the walks from the Student Center to the bus stop, then from the bus stop to my apartment, without sweating through my clothes. I carried a hunting knife that folded neatly up into my coat sleeve, and never left home without it.

* * * * * * *

Every once in a while I'd get brave and use a library computer to make a half-hearted attempt to find Nina and Gideon. In the years since I'd left Blissfield I'd heard from neither the brother nor the sister. I asked one of the other women in my house to teach me how to look for people on the Internet. It was no surprise that they were ghosts on social networking sites: hell, if I didn't have a 'homepage,' why should they? It only made sense that Gideon—who'd chosen to become an auto mechanic, and Nina, who'd fully expected to do menial work to support Ben, had little or no access to a computer, either.

There were no phone numbers in any directories. Had the phone they used been in their mother's name? Or had everything—their rent, water, electricity and phone—been paid for by the man I'd tried to kill that Christmas Eve, years earlier?

With no other means to make contact, I returned to letters. As I wrote and wrote, sometimes daily, I began to share my deepest feelings. I told them about my life in Akron, my work and the things I learned in my support group. It took a while, but I finally managed to write about That Night. I didn't want to dwell on it; I just decided—with the full support of the Old Man—that it was better to get it out, at least once, fully and completely. I prayed that having done so, I would never have to talk about it with anyone again.

I sent every letter. Every single one. I once again wrote to them care of the high school, the Piggly Wiggly, even General Delivery. I figured that someone, somehow, would know how to find them.

I never got a single answer.

After talking it over with the Old Man, my group, and with Paula, I finally broke down and wrote to Grandma. The letter was factual and brief: I told her I was working at a college, living in a decent place, had a good support network, and hoped she was well. Never mind that my pay was barely enough to cover my room in the halfway house and my support network primarily consisted of paid practitioners and other abused women, and that I was monumentally pissed and extremely hurt that I'd heard nothing from her since that Christmas Eve five years before. I just wanted to make contact with the one family member I had left in the world.

But no answer came. I tried to call, but the old number was disconnected and no new number was listed. She clearly had no presence on the Internet, and I had neither a car nor money to fly across the country. In short, she was as lost to me as the Prices.

The women in my group urged me to accept what I couldn't change. The Old Man asked me to think about how I should deal with my feelings of frustration and powerlessness. Paula told me that the situation was toxic, and it was best for me to close the door, both literally and emotionally, on that chapter of my life.

Just after my twenty-sixth birthday I took a job as a junior manager in a young women's clothing store at Summit Mall. Though I believed a position in retail management was the start of my ascent to Trumpdom, the job was about as beneficial to my future as a stall is to a racehorse's escape.

Many evenings, arriving home after ten at night, legs aching, worried about shoplifting, low sales numbers, the incessant turnover of salesgirls, and, of course, my insufficient salary, I told myself I needed to go to college and complete a degree. I told myself I needed to stop writing stupid letters, and just make the trip to Blissfield. I told myself I needed to stop comparing the men I met either to Copley—which stopped things cold—or to Gideon, who in my imagination was an insane blend of Denzel Washington and the Dalai Lama. My girlfriends, who worked as managers at the other teen shops in the mall, told me I needed to find an ordinary guy and have lots of sex (something that was definitely not on my table), go to Disney World (definitely not in my wallet) or buy a flashy little car—they recommended a Jeep.

A couple of years into my sentence of life without parole in retail management, I started rooming with my co-workers. Our apartment quickly filled up with cheap furniture and shiny appliances. Our closets filled up, too, with cheap trendy clothes and expensive running shoes. We joined a gym and worked out every day. We had off-brand laptops and tablets and smartphones. We had knock-off designer purses and a twelve-cup Italian espresso machine. We got along fine, as long as we didn't talk about anything deeper than how to split the water bill.

My roommates dated guys they met online, and that worked for me—as long as their riffraff didn't try to get into my bed. Most of the men were in and out of their lives in a matter of weeks. They seemed to accept this as the nature of internet dating. They believed they had to kiss a bunch of frogs to find a prince. I watched from a distance, because I'd already found mine—I was just in exile from our kingdom.

And with each passing day I slid farther and farther away from Bebe Johnson's little girl, the teenager Miss Corinthia Castle took to church every Sunday, the reader who shared her love of books with Nina, and the fragile young woman Gideon once loved. It was like the gold plating, painted so carefully by my past, steadily chipped off to reveal the cheap metal underneath. This new woman was hard, dented, distant, tough, and just happy to survive.

Survival, it seemed, was the only thing left for me to do.

I quit my support group and stopped seeing the Old Man and Paula. My only tie to the past was the letters I continued to write and mail to Nina and Gideon, using my best approximation of their address from Google maps. Since no letter ever came back, I wrote out of dogged stubbornness. It wasn't much, but it helped me survive.

I didn't date. I didn't go anywhere near men, in fact. I avoided bars and clubs and parks. I continued to read a lot of books and, since I volunteered to work the late shifts and rarely got home before ten p.m., six days a week, I managed to arrive too exhausted to think about my father.

I know now that this so-called "ordinary" life was a kind of anesthetic, which explains why I genuinely lost my mind when, after seven years, my last roommate moved out, taking her array of adult male sex toys along with my financial stability.

I had blown my credit cards on shit, and I lost my job while going to court to deal with my debts, so I could no longer pay the rent on the apartment. So much had been purchased on credit that after everything was repo'd or left on the street, I was reduced to sleeping in the car.

Until the voice of a stranger who worked in a morgue announced that my grandmother, Corinthia Bibb Castle, was dead.

VIII.

blissfield, north carolina.

2016.

twenty-seven.

The cicadas screamed all night like the world was on fire. The pre-dawn darkness found me sitting at the kitchen table, elbows glued to the vinyl tea kettles and pies, smoking the last of my Camels.

I was beaten.

The day of reckoning had arrived.

The Akron chapter of my life was over and there was nothing left for me in Blissfield.

It was obvious I was going to lose Grandma's property. Even if the will left her house to me, I had no money to pay the taxes or make the needed repairs. I had no job, and there were none to be had in this backwater town. My future was bleak, and the past, always hanging out in the shadows, merely echoed my present: No family. No love. No friends—well, except for the two thin benjamins hiding in my pocket.

And Gideon was right: though I desperately wanted to believe differently, a blind man could see I no longer knew the Prices. He was also right about my arrogance. Why *did* I believe they'd spent the past fifteen years waiting for me? After all, what had I done beyond bringing yet more violence into their already fucked up young lives? How could I have frozen them in time, believing Nina was still my goofy best friend, and Gideon was that doe-eyed teen who refused to make love with me because I "deserved better"? Was I out of my mind?

Miserable and ashamed, I weighed the benefits of throwing my few belongings into the rear of my jeep and making my home wherever I ended up when the tank was empty. How would it feel to land in a place where no one had ever heard the Castle name? A place without memories or regrets, where everything was possible?

I found myself listening for an answer in the breeze creaking through the rafters, branches tapping the metal roof and the mad choirs of birds ushering in the dawn.

Which suddenly ceased.

The tree branch tapped again, and the breeze caressed the rafters.

But the birds were no longer singing.

I rose from the table and walked to the front of the house. The dim street outside was bathed in damp mist. I made my way back down the main hall, peering out of each window as I passed.

At the rear door I stopped. The wide fenced backyard was a vision of silvery blue, caught between the moon echo and first rays of the sun. An intricate spider web laced the edge of the picnic table where fifteen years before I'd often sat with Nina. My jeep, parked in the red earth driveway beside the house, wept dew tears.

And then a blur of pure white caught my eye and he was standing, ghostlike, in the driveway at the side of the house. If I'd been a superstitious woman, I might have barred the door and gone looking for Grandma's bible.

Instead I stepped blindly into the mist and let the screen door slip between my fingers, where it whispered shut behind me. The air was cool, clean, unburdened with the spongy heat that would erupt with the rising sun.

He took his time as he moved toward me, head up and thick arms unnaturally loose at his sides. His tee shirt was damp, his work pants stained. It looked like neither one of us had slept.

If I hadn't grown up with Copley I might have thought his gait relaxed, but many years of watching my father had taught me to recognize well-masked rage, even in an apparently easy-going man. My knife was in the house, next to my bed. I hoped I was reading him wrong.

"Gideon," I said, when he was an arm's length away.

He stopped moving and stood tense and still, his features soft in the vibrant, blue-grey light. Reaching up, he broke a low-hanging twig from a branch of the sprawling oak tree. He held it like a crop, one end resting in his open palm.

"I didn't think I'd see you again," I said uncertainly.

"I need to apologize," he said, and my brain leapt to the fact that men never apologized unless they wanted something. But what could he realistically want from me?

His fifteen-year older voice had deepened, but I still marveled that his throat could produce such a gnarled sound.

"—And," he added, "I got some shit to explain."

I gestured toward the house. "You want to come in? It might be yours, anyway."

"For thirty years I was never welcome inside that house, and I'm not trying to change things now." He glanced around the shadowy yard, then tipped his head toward the picnic table. "That okay?"

"Sure."

Though the sun would soon rise, the air still shimmered with a dampness that reminded me of old age, loneliness and death. At that instant I was piercingly aware of Grandma's presence somewhere nearby.

"Damn," Gideon muttered as he caught sight of the spider web. "Guess I wasn't the only one up all night."

"That makes three of us," I said.

He swept his hand along the tabletop, splattering the dew, and sat down with his feet on the bench. His muddy shoes left red prints on the chipped grey wood.

I stood a few steps away, remembering that, shamefully, I still had on yesterday's clothes, had raccoon eyes and brambled hair. I probably smelled pretty ripe, too. But I reckoned it was way too late for a celebrity makeover. And, frankly, it was nothing he hadn't seen before.

Over the years I'd never been able to picture Gideon a day older than his fifteen-year old self. Now, in the swelling brightness, I could see new scars on his corded forearms, inexplicable ridges beneath the thin cotton of his shirt, and, again, the place where his jaw had been sliced to the bone.

I shifted my weight, watching his hands without watching them. He wore no watch, and no jewelry except a silver band on his right ring finger. Watching Copley had taught me a lot about what a ring can do when decorating a fist—even Gideon's fist.

Gideon watched me watching him. He gave me time to look him over and decide just how close I wanted to stand. After a few moments he spoke.

"The other night in Whelan's—"

"—So it *was* you," I said, and he raised one hand, gesturing me to silence.

"That night in Whelan's—well, I heard you was here, but I wasn't sure it was true, " Gideon said. "I mean, fifteen years is a long-ass time. So I drove here first and saw a light on. Then I took a little tour 'round town."

"I'm sorry you had to see what happened with that man," I said.

"I'm sure Gerry got what was coming to him."

"Why didn't you speak to me?"

"I got history with Brandon—the guy working behind the bar," Gideon said. "I was married to his sister."

Though this was a blow, Nina's words now made sense. Though it was barely dawn, I knew that hurt and, yes, jealousy were visible on my face.

"I didn't speak to you," he continued, "because I needed some time to get my head around you just showing up. Nina said from the start you was never coming back. After a while I figured she was right."

He paused. "I thought all that was over. But you being here, well, it bring shit back."

I watched as he blindly studied the twig, turning it over and over in his huge, chapped hands. "I know you seen my sister."

"Yes."

"What she tell you?"

"Nothing."

"Normally she never stop talking," he said with a dry laugh. "All of a sudden she lost her voice."

"She—" I hesitated "—she said it was for you to tell."

He laughed again. "It's not a thing you tell people, but after what you said at the lawyer's place, I need you to know the truth."

"Okay," I said guardedly.

He tossed the twig on the ground and used both hands to push himself off the table. I moved a couple of steps away as he turned to face the rising sun, bathing his face in the silken, lukewarm light.

"Yesterday," he began, "you said I wasn't man enough to take care of DeAndre. But CeCe, I *did* take care of him. A few weeks after you left I came home from night school and found him on my sister. I had a box cutter from work in my pocket. We fought over it and he cut my face. I got it out of his hand and returned the favor. Missed his face, though. Got him right across the neck."

"Shit," I whispered.

"Nina called the cops, but when she told them it was DeAndre they got lost trying to find the house. By the time they showed up he was gone."

Gideon bent his head in my direction. He didn't exactly look in my face, which was a good thing. My mind was scrambling to keep up with his words, and I have no idea what was in my eyes.

He laughed quietly. "Even though they knew he was a motherfucking dog, they still arrested me. I guess they figured they got two niggers for the price of one. I could've told them what he'd been doing to Nina, but hell, she been through enough. My mouthpiece kept saying I'd get off if I described what I saw when I came in the house, but I just couldn't do that to my sister. They found me guilty of manslaughter, but because I was still fifteen when I killed him, I only got six years."

"*Only* six years?" I said.

"The prosecutor wanted twenty-five, no chance of parole."

"But you were just a kid."

"A kid doing a man's work."

"But they knew he was..." my voice trailed off.

"I guess the judge knew some of it," Gideon said, "'cause instead of putting me in the hole, they sent me to the psychiatric wing at Butner. Said my momma was a junkie and I probably had some kind of brain damage from her being high when I was in her belly. Most of the inmates was doped stupid and sat around drooling on themselves. After they kicked my ass a few times to make me respect them, they put me to work in the yard, so I got to be outside all day. Funny thing is, for the first time in my life I had warm clothes, clean sheets and enough to eat. They even let me take classes. I was actually sad when I hit twenty-one and they kicked me out."

"Don't they believe in juvenile detention down here?" I asked.

He looked away, then a genuine laugh rumbled from the center of his chest. "No Black man with a crackhead momma, pimp daddy and a murder rap going to juvenile in North Carolina. And the folks in the hospital was actually pretty cool. When the guards heard what I done, they treated me like some kind a hero. They'd all heard about DeAndre. They said I performed a service to the community."

"Your lawyer didn't try to get you out?" I said.

"Yeah, well, my mouthpiece did what he could, but hell, the whole motherfucking thing was fucked up, and somebody had to pay."

"I'm sorry for what I said, Gideon."

"Why? It was true. After you tried your damn hardest to kill him on Christmas Eve I knew I couldn't walk away anymore. All those years he was beating my momma and raping my sister, and I took Benny and marched up and down the road, pretending not to know what was going on in that shack. It took you about two minutes to decide to do what I should of done years before." He grunted. "I ought to be thanking you for the inspiration."

"I never should have gone out there that day," I said. "I didn't want to hurt anybody. I was just worried about you and Nina."

"Nina wasn't scared for herself, CeCe. Hell—she knew what was coming whenever DeAndre showed up. She didn't want him to get a look at *you*. She was afraid of what he would do if he caught you alone somewhere."

Gideon paused, then looked directly into my eyes for the first time.

"My sister loved you, CeCe. She loved being with you, riding that old bike with you and sitting on that log in the schoolyard with you. She loved going to my games with you. And she *loved* talking about books with you. I figure it was them books that got her through all of it. She always said a book could take her anyplace in the world. Especially when she was in the room with him."

I rarely cry. I mean, I hadn't cried about Blissfield since that night in Jesse Brantley's loft, after I found Grandma's letter in BeBe J's bedroom. Yet Gideon's words broke something inside of me. I literally heard something break, and my eyes exploded with tears. Holding back my sobs, I sank down on the muddy bench and covered my face with my hands.

It came to me in a flash that while I was being murdered by my father, Gideon was killing the man who might have been his. While I was coming back to life in a nuthouse, he was serving time in a nuthouse of his own. Copley had taught me to hurt people, but he hadn't taught me quite well enough. If I had managed to kill DeAndre that Christmas Eve, I would never have made it back to Akron. Maybe my mother would still be alive, and Gideon's childhood could have been spared. In the end, I hadn't done shit with the past fifteen years: I might as well have taken his place in prison.

He waited until I wiped my eyes. Turning very slowly, he again lifted his head so that the sun, having risen, shone fully on his face.

"After I went away," he continued in his rough whisper, "my momma put a bunch of shit in her arm and didn't wake up. Nina and Ben moved in with my aunt and Nina started working at that retirement home. Ben quit school when he was sixteen and enlisted the day he turned seventeen. He in Japan, now. I'm pretty sure he not coming back to Blissfield."

"When I got out the joint," Gideon said, "my PO found me a job working on cars at this gas station in Roanoke Rapids. Bruce and Brandon sister used to stop in to fill up every few days on her way to her job at the Walmart. One thing led to another, and after a while we got hitched. She already had two kids and was ready for more, but I wasn't trying to go down that road with nobody."

He smiled inwardly, remembering something private.

"We made it for three years, then I just couldn't do it no more. She hated my guts in the end, but she just wouldn't let me go. When I finally took off she sent her brothers after me. They don't go looking for trouble, but they didn't turn down the chance to kick my ass good, just to make her happy."

He glanced down at me.

"You know the funny thing?" he said. "I never fought nobody, not one single time, before I put that blade in DeAndre, and I ain't never touched nobody since. Not even when they was 'breaking me in' at Butner. I took it all because it was my due for what my momma and sister been through. Even when Bruce and Brandon came to get me, I let it happen. I 'spose I had it coming for what went down with their sister, too. So do that make me a hero, or a clown or just another damn fool?"

"I'm so sorry," I repeated, not knowing what else to say.

"Stop acting like this on you," he said with irritation. "Anybody in town could have stopped it. But nobody tried to help us out because they loved it. They loved watching it, talking about it, making fun of it. At the end of the day, every hick motherfucking backwater town need at least one pimp that deal rock to his pathetic ho and rape his own pathetic stepdaughter."

"You think my grandmother knew?"

"I'm sure she knew what folks was saying. You saw how they acted at that church."

"Did she ever try to help you?" I asked in a small voice.

"When?"

"After she made me—after I left."

He shrugged one shoulder. "Somehow she dug up our number. She called the house one time and talked to Nina. Said she wanted to see if Nina was straight."

"What about you?" I asked.

"She never came to the court, but I think she might of paid for the mouthpiece," Gideon said. "While I was in lockup this young cat—a *real* lawyer from Raleigh showed up. Not some court-appointed suit. He came into the courtroom acting like we was on TV. Went after the police for taking so long to get to the house. Told the judge DeAndre died because no one came to help us. We was two kids alone in the woods. Our momma was a ho, and DeAndre beat her, and I had to quit school to help with Benny, and so on. The jury was staring at me like I belonged in a zoo, but I guess he managed to make one or two a them feel sorry for me. That's probably the only reason I didn't end up with twenty-five."

For the first time I forgave my grandmother, just a bit, for her silence. It didn't explain why she threw me away, but at least she hadn't completely abandoned Gideon and Nina.

He shifted restlessly and the air seemed to shimmer. I felt his tension humming like a cord strung taut between us, and I realized I'd known all along why he'd come to the house that morning—and exactly what he came for.

Gideon had given me his confession. Now he was waiting for mine.

I glanced at him. Our eyes met and I looked away, speaking in a monotone.

"So you want to know the real reason I'm back in Blissfield," I said. "I told you the truth. I came back to find you."

He exhaled sharply, his voice gaining an unexpected edge. "That sound crazy, CeCe. You disappear for fifteen years, show up when Miss Corinne die and want to pretend it's about us—not her money?"

"It's never been about money," I insisted. "I just want to have the two of you in my life."

"There something you need to understand," he said gravely. "I can't be that guy you hoping for—that guy you dreaming about. People change, CeCe. None of us the same as we used to me. But that don't matter," he added softly, "'cause both of us know you scared of me. Don't you think I see it?"

As if to test his words he took a casual step toward me. I got off the bench and, though I tried to stop myself, moved beyond his reach.

"There it is," he murmured, shaking his head slowly.

It was an insane moment. For fifteen years I would have walked through fire to be standing beside Gideon, but now I felt as naked and defenseless as a child. Maybe, I thought, I *still* can't function if Copley's not in charge.

Gideon watched me with cool impatience, clearly thinking he might as well leave. I couldn't blame him. Seeing my behavior at Whelan's and in the lawyer's office would convince anyone I was still wired for quick detonation—not necessarily someone you should rush to believe. This was my last chance to make my case to be forgiven for leaving, but he and Nina were primed to keep it moving, with or without me.

So I struck an ugly bargain with myself: I would go against my years of work with the Old Man and walk Gideon through my own valley of death. I'd take him on a tour of the landscapes I avoided every minute of every day. I knew that telling him about the last fifteen years might open up some wounds and welcome back some nightmares I worked to keep at bay. It might not change a damn thing in the way he felt about me. But I knew I'd regret it the rest of my life if I didn't at least try to make him understand.

"You're right," I said, feeling a thread of sweat instantly emerge along my hairline, "I'm scared. But not for the reasons you think."

Glancing around the yard, I pictured Mr. Saunders' car and the womanchild emerging from the back seat in her worn pink track suit, eyes swollen from crying, a small bag held like a shield in front of her.

"You remember what I was like when I first came to live here?" I said, my voice still flat. "That was the Bethany Celeste of Copley Castle's world. Folks say my father was fast and tricky on the football field. Well, let me tell you something: he was also very good at creating misery. I can't even begin to describe the things I saw him do to my mother. I remember the concentration on his face and how his muscles pulled and flexed when he hurt her. To tell you the truth, to me it was a kind of art."

Gideon's brows came together, but he didn't speak.

"By the time I was seven or eight I'd learned Copley's methods," I said. "I didn't give a shit about my mother, and I never did a single thing to help or protect another living soul, because given a choice, I figured it was better to be like my father than to be his victim. We didn't go to church, talk to our neighbors, and god knows I was never anything like a Girl Scout, so there was no one to tell me any different. The fact that I didn't have enough to eat, or clothes that fit me, and our house was falling down around us—well, all that went right by me. The only thing I thought about was pleasing him."

I risked a glance at Gideon and saw intense focus—and dawning comprehension in his eyes.

"Everything went to pieces when I turned fifteen. Overnight I changed from being Copley's little darling to someone he had to master. He made up crazy reasons to yell and scream and beat me, too. But imagine his surprise," I said, "when instead of me being like my mother, he met up with a female version of himself. My mother was too scared to defend herself. I was scared as hell, too—but I was ready to fight him to the death. Once or twice I even tried. My mother put me on a bus to Blissfield to keep him from literally tearing me apart."

Gideon's gaze sharpened. In all the hours we'd spent together, I'd never told him, or Nina, how fucked up my childhood really was. I couldn't have done it back then if I'd tried—I hadn't understood it myself.

"So when I arrived in Blissfield," I continued, sweeping my arm with mock graciousness around the yard, "for days I could hardly speak. Grandma got me out of bed, fed me and made me work in the garden beside her. She didn't say much—she just watched me the way you watch a dog to see if it displays any sign of rabies. Looking back, I think my shrink would diagnose me as—" I raised my fingers to make air quotes— "'suffering from the effects of acute, prolonged trauma.' As for me, I'd simply say that without Copley's constant threat I had no idea how to live."

I shifted my weight, feeling tension collect in the base of my spine.

"Grandma enrolled me in Booker T and asked the teachers to give me some time to cool down. They did, for the most part. I can't remember much about those first few weeks. Everything comes into focus the day I attacked those two girls in the bathroom. I won't lie: getting Bree and LaToya was the purest, deepest pleasure I'd ever known. Not only did I take care of my enemies, release some of the stress I'd been carrying since Akron, but I really enjoyed talking my way out of trouble after it was over.

"Of course, Grandma didn't buy any part of it. She took one look at me and knew exactly what I'd done. She told me she'd let me go that time, but I could never allow Copley to take control again. The thing is, Grandma didn't understand that I couldn't hear her. I felt safest when Copley was calling the shots. I mean, I went along with what she wanted me to do, but that was just theater. The *real* world was Copley, and it was just a matter of time before I hurt someone else. A clock was actually ticking inside my brain."

Gideon watched me with the same wariness he and Nina had shown on the day we met. Just as they waited, perched on those rocks while I stood there holding those plates, he now adopted the preternatural stillness of an animal assessing a potential threat.

"And then," I said, holding my voice as steady as I could, "we went to church that Easter Sunday and I met you and Nina. I will never know what made me cross that field, but it changed everything. Nina didn't even know me, but from the start she stood up for me. She taught me how to survive in this world, and even though she saw how damaged I was, she didn't walk away. She forgave me when I hurt her and did her best to keep me from hurting you. And lord knows she was right—I had no idea how to get along with other people, or how to be anybody's sister, much less anybody's friend."

An image of Nina whipping her own twig back and forth as she showed me the way to the stone hut passed through my mind. That was the day she declared I was her best friend—and the day I agreed to be her friend, too.

"I was watching," I said. "I saw how you trusted each other and looked out for each other. You protected Ben. You cared about your mother, even though she couldn't be there for you. Blissfield did its best to mess you up, but I never saw either one of you do anything to hurt anybody. Believe me," I chuckled softly, "that was a whole new way of thinking for me.

"For the first time," I continued, "I started to understand that my father was truly crazy. I began to feel incredibly guilty that I never tried to help my mother. I got real scared of the parts of Copley that still lived inside me. And the worst thing was that even though my grandma was always good to me, I wasn't sure I could trust her. After all, my father grew up in her house. She raised him. She showed him how to live. Sometimes when she got mad I could even see him there, pacing around in the shadows in her eyes.

"So I started questioning things. I asked her about Blissfield in the 'olden times,' our family history and what her life was like when she was young. Most of all, I kept asking her what happened to make my father so goddamn evil.

"My grandmother seemed willing to talk," I said, remembering Grandma eating animal crackers at the kitchen table, while speaking calmly about the Castles. "I mean, she told me long, detailed stories about her parents, their farm and all these adventures from her childhood. But she never told me what I really wanted to know—what I *still* need to know, Gideon: what made my father become such a sick, sick man?"

Letting my breath out in a long, rough sigh, I drew a line in the dirt, the red earth staining my toes. A sparrow landed on a branch near Gideon, drawn by his stillness.

"I do know one thing," I said. "Grandma definitely saw the difference you and Nina made in my life. It didn't take long before Copley's vicious little hand grenade was replaced by someone new—this girl called 'CeCe'—a person who was capable of kindness, patience and caring about somebody other than herself. I mean, I started talking like a normal person, getting good grades and helping out around the house. I learned to laugh, cook, sew, drive the car and even to dream—something I'd never done in my life. Nina and I talked for hours about what we were going to do in the years to come. What we were going to study. Where we wanted to live. How we would take care of each other.

"And then there was you, Gideon. You never raised your hand or your voice to me. You never threatened me or called me names or tried to make me jealous. Hell—you even asked for permission before you kissed me! I'd never seen a man behave that way before. You made me feel like I was the most beauti—"

He looked up sharply. "CeCe, I—"

"—You must be the only guy in the universe who refused to have sex with his out-of-her-head-in-love-with-him girlfriend," I said softly. "You told me time and time again to wait, because I deserved something better than the back seat of a car. At first I couldn't understand what you meant by that. Now I know you cared more about me than I cared about myself."

He glanced away, troubled.

"Gideon," I said, "your sister was the first and only true friend I've ever had. You and Nina are the only people on this earth, even to this day, who've ever told me to my face that you love me."

He made a low, complicated sound deep in his throat. He removed a crushed pack from his pocket and pulled out a cigarette. Though I wanted to have something to do with my hands, I shook my head when he offered one to me. If I was going to do this, it was going to be raw: No crutches. No props. Nothing to hide behind.

He struck a match against the table, and when he exhaled the ribbon of smoke, I saw that he, too, was steadying himself for the rest of it—the thing, like he said, that you don't tell people. The thing I'd never shared with anyone except the Old Man, who had listened, over the course of many months, to every god-damn, unbearable detail.

After all, That Night was nothing to share. But then, Gideon knew all about evil and how it maims and warps the soul. He had the right to know why I hadn't come back—after I'd sworn I'd never go.

Making an effort to calm myself, the way the Old Man taught me, I walked over and took Gideon's place on the table, shoulders hunched, breathing deeply and slowly. Gideon stood a few feet away, drawing deeply on his cigarette and vising me with his dense, impenetrable gaze.

"Ten weeks after my grandmother sent me back to Akron," I said quietly, "I did something incredibly stupid. I was staying with a cop who was trying to protect me from my father. The cop made me promise to steer clear of my mother, but I let her talk me into going to her place one night. There were no neighbors on the street and no one knew I was there. They'd arrested my father and we both thought we were safe.

"Suddenly Copley showed up. The police had let him go and he was completely out of control. I had fought him when I was a kid, but there'd always been a stick or something I could use to defend myself. But that night was different. I didn't have a baseball bat or a box cutter, a gun or a knife—but my father did.

"He got to my mother before I could stop him. He cut her throat right in front of me. I didn't have anything but my fists, but I fought him anyway. I did my motherfucking best to kill Copley Castle, but he won. He stabbed me, then beat me and left me lying in my mother's blood. When the cops found me my heart had stopped. The doctors literally brought me back from the dead."

I wiped the sweat pouring down my face, gluing my clothes to my body. Gideon remained rooted to the spot, the lazy thread of smoke the only sign he wasn't made of stone.

"They caught Copley the next day. They gave him life, but they might as well have put me in the hole, too. It took me five years to graduate from the hospital to a rehab place, then to a psychiatric facility, then on to a halfway house. I guess my shrink needed all that time to make sure I didn't pose a threat to the general public. Even then, for months I couldn't go outside after dark. I eventually managed to make it across a parking lot—as long as I was carrying a hunting knife—but I've never been able to date anyone. For the past ten years I've worked bullshit jobs for almost no pay. I finally lost everything and ended up sleeping in my car."

Glancing toward the house, I spoke as much to Corinthia Castle's spirit as I did to Gideon.

"So there are lots of reasons I couldn't come back," I said. "I was broke and I was broken. I didn't speak a word for almost a year. I was wound way too tight to be around other people. But most of all, I wrote hundreds of letters to you, Nina and Grandma. I never got a call, message or a letter in reply.

"I figured you hated me for what I did to DeAndre that Christmas Eve. That's what my mother told me that night, just before my father showed up. She said Grandma didn't want me back because I attacked DeAndre. When I never heard from anybody I thought it must be true. I couldn't face the possibility that my mother was right. So I didn't come back," I said, "until after Grandma died. At least that way *she* couldn't reject me."

Raising my hands, palms open, at last I looked directly into Gideon's eyes. "So yes," I said, "I'm scared. I'm scared to think, scared to remember, scared to trust, and to be completely honest, since the night my father killed me I've been scared to live. Even if you don't believe a single word of anything I just told you, please understand this: You and Nina are the reason I survived. Believing in you is what got me through it. I don't care about my grandmother's money. I don't care about this house. My stupid and completely ridiculous hope that you might still want me around is the one and only reason I made this journey back to Blissfield."

Wearily I got to my feet. I was awash with sweat and my joints hurt like someone had thrown me off the roof.

"So that's it," I said, gesturing toward my soiled clothes, make-up-smeared face and uncombed hair. "You're looking at all that's left of the CeCe you used to know."

Gideon took measure of me, his face pensive, judging. I saw his gaze flicker from my bare feet to my too-thin frame, then up to my starved, exhausted eyes. The silence between us seemed deafening despite the joyous babel of birdsong in the trees. The air, heavy with the blood-scent of the earth, held a tang of grass after rain.

After what seemed like a lifetime he inhaled deeply, dropped his cigarette and pressed the butt into the ground with the toe of his work boot.

"What do you see when you look at me?" he asked softly.

I straightened my back to meet his haunted gaze. "I see a man who's still here despite everything this fucked-up place put him through," I said.

Fifteen years earlier he would have taken me in his arms. That morning, however, a stranger looked back. He raised his arms and showed me his hands.

"You still searching for the past, like it might save you," he said, his voice strained and low, "but you already know, just like I do, that dreams don't always come true, CeCe. I am truly sorry about everything that happened to you. Truly. But you looking for a echo. A shadow. You have to accept that I'm not that guy. You want too much, and I truly got nothing left to give."

"I—"

"Nothing," he said with finality. Then, with a move that recalled the athletic grace of his youth, he turned away.

I watched him, wordless, recognizing both regret and resolve in the set of his shoulders. He had already reached the drive when it hit me like ice that I might never see him again. Before my mind caught up with my body I was running over the roots of that giant tree, my bare feet reddened by the dirt. I caught up with him as he reached the front of the house. Throwing my arms around his waist, I buried my face in his chest and breathed him in as deeply as I could. For a few seconds his arms hovered over my back. Then, as if out of curiosity, he finally gave in and held me close.

Our bodies were different, and the flesh recognition I'd dreamed about for so long vanished like a whisper. His chest was in the wrong place, his head now inches above mine. Though I was still compact and firm, my breasts felt thick and strange against him. Even his heart, which once raced at my touch, was steady and indifferent.

That's when I knew he wasn't lying. Though he looked and smelled like the man I loved, this man was not my Gideon.

Every woman likes to believe her first love will love her forever. I'd held onto this illusion literally my entire adult life. The idea of Gideon had glued me together, even in my darkest moments. But now it was time to let all of that go.

He carefully loosened my arms, his gaze focused on some point far away, and without a word turned back to the road. Heart skittering, I watched until, moving swiftly, he vanished at the end of the street. Then I returned to the backyard and stood very still, arms hugging my chest in the pitiless sunlight. I looked at the yard, the overgrown flowerbeds, the empty cinderblock garage now wreathed with weeds. I stared at the house that had welcomed me, protected me, loved me and lied to me. The house in which my father, my murderer, was born and raised. The biblical house of Bethany: my house of sorrow. My house of song.

Finally, I understood.

I had to come back here.

If only to make it possible to leave.

twenty-eight.

Struggling not to think, I showered for a long, long time. I washed my hair, combed it out and tied it neatly away from my face. I put on the one clean tee-shirt I had left and climbed into a pair of jeans I pulled from the bottom of my duffle. I was ready to face the next chapter of my life.

Everything else was packed in about five minutes. I went through the house and swept, closed the blinds, bolted the front door, and unplugged all the lamps and appliances. When I got to the kitchen I turned off the fridge and blocked the door open. No matter what happened to the property after I left, I didn't want the cops—or the lawyer—coming after me. At the last moment I lifted the urn with Grandma's ashes and took it with me. I didn't know what I'd do with it, but I figured I was proving something just by treating her better than she'd treated me.

Locking the door behind me, I slid the key back into the little wooden niche beneath the front window. I then walked over to my car with the duffle on my shoulder and the urn cradled in the crux of my arm. I threw the bag on the back seat, then anchored the urn carefully on the floor.

I had backed all the way up to the street when it came to me: Everyone knew everything that happened in Blissfield. I knew what I needed to know, but I'd been asking the wrong people all along. If I couldn't do anything to change the way Nina and Gideon felt about me, at least I could drive away from Blissfield with all my questions answered.

The cicadas went silent as I strolled across the already-hot asphalt. Mrs. Mitchell's door was open before I made it to the top of her steps. Her bungalow, a faded eggshell blue, had elaborate, peeling white gingerbread trim along the eaves. It looked like she and Grandma had once been in a dead heat over who lived in Blissfield's most charming home.

"Well, Princess, you're up early this morning," Mrs. Mitchell said, eyeing my hair and clothing. "I'm glad you finally came to visit. Come on in out of the sun."

Weirdly, I couldn't remember ever having set foot in her house before. I breathed in the generations of fried lard, sweet pork, and greens marinating in vinegar. The parlor had been rosebud pink maybe sixty years ago, and the main hall had delicately fading wallpaper with ships sailing on a Delft sea. Old electric fans churned frantically in every room, stirring the lacy curtains she hid behind while watching Castle lives. It was strange seeing my grandmother's house from this stealthy perspective, but then, that's precisely why I'd come.

She sat me down at her kitchen table, fittingly covered with a flowered table-cloth that matched the curtains at the small-paned window. A percolator stirred on a sixties-era, avocado-toned electric range, and when she poured coffee into a yellowing Martin Luther King mug, it looked exactly like thick, hot gravy. A square of pie, a fork and a paper napkin appeared in front of me. Though a gospel choir roared on her ancient radio, the words to an old song about backstabbers looped softly through my head.

She settled beside me in a cloud of rose-scented talc. "I'm sorry Princess, I hope you don't mind this leftover apple cobbler I made for church last Sunday," she said.

"Thank you, Mrs. Mitchell. I really don't have time to eat anything," I said. "I just wanted to say goodbye."

"You leaving already?"

"Yes, I'm all packed and the house is closed up, too."

"So everything's settled," she said.

"As settled as possible."

"You've decided to sell?"

"Not quite yet."

"Well, these things can be very complicated, but I'm sure your grandmother would have wanted you to keep the house in the family."

"Yes," I said, blowing on the steam rising from the mug. I lifted the cup and sipped the sludge.

"The house *is* coming to you?" she asked, unable to stop herself.

"Well, the lawyer—"

"—You're speaking of Richard Armitage, your grandmother's attorney?"

"Yes," I said, no longer surprised by our lack of privacy. "He expects it's going to take some time for the will to clear probate."

"I see," she said, looking at the tablecloth. Her eyes returned to mine. "I've been meaning to ask you whether, by chance, you ran into that brother and sister you used to spend so much time with?"

"Who?" I asked.

"Those Price children. I remember you were friends with them when you lived with your grandmother."

I figured, as I took a reluctant bite of the sickly-sweet cobbler, that she'd seen someone she suspected of being Gideon either coming or going that morning.

"Well," I said pleasantly , "I really haven't—"

"Thank *goodness!*" she exclaimed, pressing her hand to her chest. "I am so very relieved to hear that! The Prices are nothing but trouble. I hear the girl is living above the pharmacy, doing some kind of menial work, but the brother—that's something else entirely."

She said this in one long breath. I don't know how, but I must have managed to hold onto my polite expression because she rattled on, delighted to share what she hadn't told me before — now that this might be her last chance.

"Of course, sometimes bad things just happen," she said. "Their mother started so young, and there's only so long that anyone can get away with taking those drugs. Sooner or later the mind just gives out. She was blessed to be attractive for so long, under the circumstances. But then again, her beauty really was her curse. And it certainly was visited on her older son, if not the daughter. I guess you could say the girl was lucky she didn't have her mother's beauty, because God knows, that man her mother took up with might have had her out on the highway, too. As it was, she was more useful to him to watch over her brother, and then that unfortunate baby. It was a miracle the little one wasn't retarded, considering what his mother was doing when he was in her belly. How he didn't get into *real* trouble, like his brother, still floors me. But maybe it was because his older brother was away in the penitentiary while he was growing up, and his aunt took him in with the girl after it happened."

"After what happened?" I said, curious to hear Blissfield's version of what happened to Nina and Gideon.

"You don't know?" She leaned toward me, her voice so low I could barely hear it. "Corrine never told you what he did? That young man—the Price boy—well, he committed murder shortly after you went back to live with your mother!"

Her hand returned to her chest and she pushed her chair back for dramatic effect. "It was horrible—absolutely *horrible*! The entire town was up in arms over it!"

"Really?" I said. "What happened?"

"He attacked their mother's consort with some sort of knife. Ambushed him and stabbed him in the chest over twenty times. Then he and his sister refused to call anyone for help, so even though the man—evil as he was—might have been saved, instead he died on the doorstep of their shack. And do you know what's worse? He had been paying the bills to keep a roof over those children's heads ever since they were babies. He was the closest thing to a father they had ever known."

She gazed at me, triumph in her eyes. "*That's* why I didn't say anything about them when I brought you those vegetables last week. Your grandmother wouldn't have wanted you to have anything to do with either one of the Prices. They live like animals and you, Princess, were raised to be a lady."

"You're right, Mrs. Mitchell," I said. "That's exactly what my grandmother would have wanted."

Mrs. Mitchell smiled. "Corinne was so concerned they might try to contact you, or even follow you after you went back to your mother. Especially the young man. That's why she made sure they wouldn't find out where you'd gone. It took some convincing, but she finally got Joe to agree."

"Of course," I said with unbelievable self-control. "That was a very wise decision."

Encouraged by my response, she placed her hand on my arm and nodded vigorously. "Your grandmother wanted you to build a new life for yourself in Ohio. To get to know your parents again, make new friends and enjoy your final years of high school. I know you went through a difficult period, but you did eventually go on to college, didn't you?"

"So to speak," I said, thinking of my years as a custodian at the community college.

"Well," Mrs. Mitchell said, "we all heard what happened between your parents. We were so sorry things ended up that way, but then, your father wasn't the same after he found out the truth. That's why he enlisted and went off to fight in that terrible war! And he wasn't the only veteran to have problems when he came home. They even have a name for his condition—PTSD—but don't expect me to tell you what it means! I'm absolutely sure your father never meant to hurt anyone. After all, Copley was such a lovely child!"

I didn't react fast enough to hide my confusion.

"I'm sorry—" she was staring at me intently "—your grandmother shared this with me in the strictest confidence."

"Of course," I said. "I just didn't realize anyone else knew."

"Well, you know I was just like a sister to her. We're all one big family in the end."

"That's right," I murmured. I was still smiling, but my nails were cutting into the palm of the hand I'd placed politely beneath the table.

Her gaze wandered to the window. "You know, after it happened Corinne never was quite the same again. Bless her soul, it looked like she aged thirty years overnight. She was always a leader in our community, but after your father hurt you and your mother, some part of her just died. To tell you the truth, she felt very guilty for sending you back to—where was it again?"

"—Akron—"

"Yes, that's it. She told me once that she knew she should visit you, but she just didn't have the strength. She said she'd already seen so much death. She stopped serving on the church guild. She let the house go. She didn't even tend to her roses anymore, and you know how she loved her roses! It was sad to see, but I did everything I could to make sure she was alright."

"Thank you for that, Mrs. Mitchell."

"Of course, she still tried to help you as much as she could. I heard her talking about it with Joe one day when I stopped by with some fresh greens from my garden. She said she hoped the money she sent was enough to help with some of your medical expenses."

"Yes," I said, "it did."

"And it's perfectly clear you're just fine now. You must have a good job up there in the north, or you wouldn't have that lovely car. Am I right?"

I nodded.

"But I don't see a ring! Don't tell me you don't have a husband hidden away somewhere. You're just as pretty as your grandmother was when we were young!"

I made myself laugh. "Well, I have one or two serious candidates. And," I said, pushing back from the table, "that's precisely why I have to get going. Someone special's waiting for me, and if I'm gone too long he might get away."

She giggled stupidly. "Well, I am so glad we had this time to chat. I hope you'll stop by the next time you're in Blissfield. Don't make me wait another fifteen years!"

She ushered me to the door. I descended the steps on trembling legs. I didn't look back as I drove away, though I knew she'd be waving.

* * * * * *

The highway stretched oily and black beneath the wheels of the jeep. The deep drainage ditches on the sides of the road were bearded with cattails, now stiff and brittle with the end of summer. I passed the Castle farm with its ancient, listing fence surrounding our private cemetery—the final remnants of Redmond's dream. With no more than a glance toward the past, I drove on.

The pure white steeple of Holy Redeemer Baptist Church appeared like God's compass on life's endless highway. Though it was a Friday, and I had no right to expect anyone to be there, I knew the answer to all my questions waited here. I pulled off the road in a swirl of red and parked beside the barge-like Buick, polished to a sheen despite the dusty roads.

The church door was open and I walked inside, all the way down to the place where Grandma died.

The sanctuary shimmered with scents of heat, shellac and aging mums. It also smelled of Easter picnics, choir exultations, of trust in something true. My purpose had nothing to do with my lost faith, but I couldn't help but slip down into the pew, which was bathed in pure white light shining in through the windows.

"Bethany?"

The old man was standing in the doorway behind me. His carefully pressed shirt and clean-shaven face belied his stooped gait, which bore easy witness to his eight decades on earth.

"Mr. Saunders." I was on my feet, moving quickly toward him.

He smiled, his entire face opening with pleasure. "I'm happy you're back."

"I have something to ask," I said, stopping just short of touching him.

"What is it, Princess?"

I paused, wondering whether there was a right way to do this. Then I figured the question was too important, and I'd been blind too long to waste another moment.

"Are you, I mean, is it possible that you're my grandfather?"

The color of his eyes deepened. He drew in a breath. "Why, yes, sweetheart. Yes, I am."

The world tilted a little and I sank down on the nearest pew. Mr. Saunders shuffled forward and sat down beside me.

I looked at his kind face. It was the face of everything good I remembered about my life in Blissfield. Here was the man who had taken care of me and my Grandma. Who drove us everywhere important. Ate meals with us. Went to church with us. And he was the person she called whenever things got crazy.

It suddenly made perfect sense that he was the man she loved her whole life through. He was the man who stood by her all those years, who was standing beside her right there, in that sanctuary, when she died.

It also became clear to me that only moments before I had been alone in the world. Now, even if only briefly, I had someone who shared my blood.

"Why didn't she tell me?" I asked.

"She never told anyone, Princess, though I'm sure everybody in Blissfield know."

"Then why keep it a secret?"

"I don't know. Pride, perhaps. It's difficult for a woman when her husband vanish to places—and people—unknown. We all figured there was another woman, though we didn't know who. In those days it was hard to keep track of people when they decided to pass. Just imagine what that was like for her boys."

"Pass?" I echoed, confused.

"Rumor had it that Julius preferred to live as a white man. He was fair-skinned enough to do so, and probably found life much easier that way."

"Why didn't Grandma just divorce him?"

"Things was different in our day, Princess. Fifty years ago it was hard enough for a woman to find a good job, and being divorced made it much harder. Corrie wanted her sons to bear her husband name. She always believed that by remaining his wife, her boys would inherit the land. Your grandmother was not the first woman, and she was far from the last to give up her freedom to try and offer her children a better life."

"She gave up the man she truly loved for that stupid farm out on the highway?" I said.

Mr. Saunders leaned closer, his soft brown eyes focused intently on me. "I loved Corinthia Bibb Castle from the moment I first laid eyes on her, and I still love her now. She did me the greatest honor on earth by bearing my child, and by allowing me to be part of your life. The rest never mattered, Princess. Corrie and I was closer, and stayed together much longer than most people who walk down the aisle. Over those eighty years we never, ever waivered in our love for each other."

"If she wanted to protect her family," I said, "why did she abandon me?"

"Abandon you?" His eyebrows went up in surprise. "Your grandmother never abandoned you, Princess. When you went back to Ohio she tried her best to get your mother to take you as far from your father as possible. We don't know why your mother didn't do it, but after her death your grandmother got you the best medical care she could afford, and she followed your progress first through your doctors—"

"And then through my letters," I said, unable to hide my bitterness.

His dark eyes held mind for a moment, then he looked down at his hands.

"We talked a long time about what should happen with those letters," he said. "I was a postman in this town for almost fifty years, and I got my nephew a job sorting mail at the post office. Corrie asked him to get a hold of your letters when they arrived and to keep them for her. At first she was afraid that man, DeAndre, would come after you if he found out your address. Then, after the boy was sent to prison and the girl went to live with her father sister, your grandmother just hung onto them. Reading those letters let her know what you was going through. They let her know you was getting better and having a decent life. To tell you the truth, Princess, I think those letters was the only way she found some peace with what our son done to you and your mother."

"If she cared so much, she could have come to get me."

"Oh, baby." He moved a little closer and grasped both my hands in his twig-like fingers. "Bethany, I want you to listen hard to what I'm about to say.

"Your grandmother heart broke in two when she put you on the Greyhound that Christmas Eve, but she was afraid to let you stay here in Blissfield. That man was involved with some very dangerous people. To save face and preserve his reputation he would of found a way to hurt you.

"At the same time, your grandmother knew the situation between your mother and father was dire. Your mother was deathly afraid of Copley, and with good reason. Copley learned his violence from his older brothers, who'd learned it from their own father."

"Julius hit them?"

"Yes, and Julius often struck their mother."

"Grandma?" I whispered.

"Yes, baby. It began soon after they was married and went on the entire time they was together. Julius was a peculiar man—cold, distant, and he hated Blissfield. Being married to a woman he didn't love, and a Black woman on top of that—well, he must of felt like he was trapped. She tried her best to be a good wife, but he took his anger and frustration out on her. That's why, when he decided to leave, your grandmother let him go and never made no effort to find him."

"I can't believe it," I said, struggling with the idea that Grandma had once been like my mother.

"She wouldn't want me to tell you this," Mr. Saunders went on, "but maybe it's best you know the truth. Julius never believed Corinne was good enough for him, so he didn't see no reason to treat her with respect. I remember stopping by the house to deliver a package one summer morning—something Julius had ordered, if I remember right—and I found your grandmother out in the garage, sitting in the dark with a dishcloth full of ice pressed up against her face. Her arms was covered with bruises, and one of her eyes was," he paused, looking down at the floor, "I'll just say she couldn't go out in public for days.

"I told Corinne I would find Julius and make sure he never touched her again, but she was afraid of what he might do. Julius hired a number of men to work his land, and she reasoned that he would pay them to come after me. Princess, I couldn't stop what was going on in their home, but I made myself a promise that I would stand by her and do anything I could to help her for the rest of my days.

"Unfortunately," Mr. Saunders continued, "Corinne's older boys saw all of it—the police didn't care to get involved when a colored man was beating his wife—and years later, Jeremiah and Paul was often unkind to your father in similar ways. They blamed your grandmother and Copley both for their father's absence, though Copley's birth had nothing at all to do with it. Julius was long gone before your father came along."

"Why didn't Grandma tell me these things? I said. "I asked her again and again what went wrong in our family."

Ms. Saunders' gaze traveled over my shoulder to the window, his eyes reflecting the blank blue of the sky.

"It can be real hard for any person who been treated like dirt to risk loving somebody," he said. "After Julius left and Paul and Jeremiah died, Corinne had a hard time showing your daddy how much she cared about him. I think, though you had to look real close to see it, that in her heart she was very, very afraid to let anybody know she loved them."

The old man's gnarled hands trembled gently as they held mine.

"Bethany, you coming down here all those years ago was a gift from heaven. Your grandmother adored you from the moment she first set eyes on you, that time Copley brought you down when you was just a little girl. Imagine how she felt when you was more like her the next time you visited. I never seen her happier than when your mother sent you here to stay. Corinne loved having you in the house. Loved having a reason to cook and clean. Loved getting out her sewing machine and making things again. She believed God gave her the chance to fix what Julius had broken. You being here made up for everything that happened before."

"But she never told me the truth," I said, shaking my head. "Copley might have had less power over me if I'd understood what made him so sick."

"She couldn't bear to tell you that her husband treated her like she was a dog. Or that her older sons ran away as soon as the Army would take them, and that everyone in Blissfield knew Copley was headed for trouble. She didn't want you to see her as a failure, Princess. I think she just wanted you to love her."

"But what about Gideon and Nina?" I asked.

He leaned his head to the side, and his voice softened, as if I were a child. "One thing is sure," he said quietly, "your grandmother never could stop herself from being kind to those kids. She was so proud of you that Easter Sunday when you walked across that field with those two plates of food! She loved the model you set for the other church folk, who never did anything for those Price children. And your grandmother was very glad those kids was in your life. She especially liked the girl. Always said that girl was good for you."

I looked away, fearing he'd see the frustrated tears pressing against my eyes.

"So believe me," he continued, "it was a terrible thing when we put you on the bus to Ohio that day. She cried all the way back to Blissfield. I never seen her cry like that, even when her older boys died. She told me DeAndre had killed your childhood, and now Copley would destroy the rest of your life."

"Then why didn't she send for me after DeAndre died?" I said.

"Do you think she wanted you here when they arrested that Price boy and found him guilty of murder? It would have drove you crazy, sweetheart. And then, it wasn't more than a few days later you lost your own mother—"

"—You mean, my father murdered my mother."

"Princess, after you went back to Ohio your grandmother sent your mother a good amount of money so the two of you could leave. We will never know why your mother didn't just gather you up and go when she had the chance. The only thing we know is sometimes people believe love is meant to be painful. They live for the approval of the person that hurts them, without ever understanding that hurting them is the only way that person can feel powerful."

"Grandma never came," I whispered. "She never called or wrote to me."

"That's true," he said. "In time she realized that was a mistake. Your grandmother often talked about going up to Ohio, or bringing you back to Blissfield, but she decided you had a better chance of starting over if you wasn't trapped in a place like this. None of us knew what was going to happen to that boy and girl, but we both knew how people would treat you. Blissfield lives in the past, Princess, and she wanted you to have a new life—a better life."

"I needed her, Mr. Saunders."

"None of that was in your letters, Princess. She thought from your letters you was doing alright."

I closed my eyes on the bitter irony that the letters I'd written, designed to mask my desperate hurt and longing, had convinced my Grandma that life in Akron was okay. Copley was gone and she was paying for my rehab, the nuthouse and my shrink. In her mind, Akron probably seemed to offer me a more promising future than the backwater hopelessness of Blissfield.

"Come out here with me," he said quietly, and we walked together through the church and out onto the red clay of the yard. We went to his car and I watched as he opened the trunk. Inside was a large cardboard box sealed with packing tape.

"The day she died I went and got this," he said, "and took it to my home so no one would mess with it. When you came here last week I wanted to tell you, but it just didn't seem right. I hoped that God would give me the chance to let you know how very much she loved you. I love you, too. And even when you was gone we was thinking about you and praying for you every single day."

He drew a penknife from his pocket and, cutting the tape, opened the top to reveal a cache of carefully folded papers, tied with rubber bands and fitted into neat piles. Someone had divided them by date, each packet holding some forty to fifty letters, organized chronologically over the lost years of my life. I pulled one of the envelopes out and held it up to the sun. It was postmarked fourteen years earlier, when I was a patient in the psychiatric hospital. Hands shaking, I opened the letter.

> Hi Gideon and Nina,
> Where are you guys this XMas?
> I'm still staying in this place and I would really like to tell you about it. I never stop thinking about you. I have'nt heard from you but I hope your busy taking care of Benny and going to your mechanics classes. ~~My~~ If you see my grandmother let me know. I never hear from anyone so I hope you write I miss you very very much.
> XOXO CeCe

The letter on the top of another packet, dated a few years later, captured a different stage of my recovery.

> November 12, 2006
> Dear Nina,
> Are you still living in the same place? I've been looking for some other address for you and I can't find anything anywhere. I've been writing to my grandmother to but she doesn't write back. Are you all in the twilight zone or something? It has been so long but I still ~~want~~ need to know how you are doing.
> The other girls in my house are okay, but sometimes they really get on my nerves, so I just stay in my room. My social worker, her name is Paula, says I should be happy to have my own, but I figure their scare to put me in a double. I don't have a TV so I go to the library

and pretend I'm with you. I take out so many books they think I'm crazy (just like you always said). God I miss talking to you about books. What are you reading right now? Have you read those books about the kids at the magic school? Sometimes the things in the books remind me of you and me and Gideon. I always wonder what you would think of them.

So write me back. My address is on the envelop. I'll will write you again tomorrow and I am going to keep on writing until you give up and answer me. I miss you guys so so so much.

Say hi to Gideon.

XOXO CeCe

Sinking to the edge of the open trunk, I crumpled the letter against my chest and wiped my streaming eyes with my other hand. The frail old man sat carefully beside me, gathered me in his arms and swayed gently back and forth. I hadn't expected it to happen, but the dampness along my hairline told me he was crying, too.

We cried together for a long, long time. I never dreamed I could cry so hard. I never dreamed I would cry in the arms of my grandfather.

At last our tears subsided. Mr. Saunders took out a handkerchief and gently wiped my face. "I wish I played a greater role in my son's life. I wish I had raised him to be a better man."

"I wish he'd never been born," I said.

"No, Princess, no. If he'd never been born you wouldn't be here."

"Is my life a fair trade for all the people he hurt?"

"That depends on how you choose to live out the days that's left to you. Remember, Bethany: you make choices every day. When you help others, things often work out. How else can you explain that sister and brother? They came to you when you needed them as a child. And now, after so much pain, I'm sure you'll find each other again. There's been more than enough sadness, Princess. Now you must find your way to joy."

I looked up. "Mr. Saunders—"

"Grandpa," he said gently.

"Grandpa, would you come out to the farm with me? I think—and you'll have to tell me if this is right—Grandma would have preferred to rest there."

"Yes, Princess," he agreed. "And she would have been proud that you thought of it."

twenty-nine.

Three cars were parked in the diagonal spaces in front of the pharmacy. I knocked on the side door, balancing the cardboard box on my hip, since there was no bell. No one answered, so I walked around the building and entered the store. A middle-aged woman looked up from the center aisle as I came in. She turned her head, making eye contact with someone else, and I figured that Brandon the bartender had been right about the pharmacist's interest in Nina's visitors.

It smelled like the pharmacy of my childhood—bitter, medicinal, moldy—and the shelves were filled with foot creams, knee braces, old-fashioned soaps and toothpastes. Hundreds of small boxes were locked behind glass doors, with a wide stone counter separating the customers from the pharmacist. Two Black couples so old they had prunes instead of faces sat on straight-backed chairs along the wall, decaying even while they waited for their medications. A plaid-shirted white man fingered a packet of powder that claimed to turn muscle into fat, and the clerk, whose peroxided hair was the only color in the place, again turned to someone in the back.

"Ms. Castle?" the pharmacist, who looked to be about fifty-five, said. Though the white coat was supposed to inspire trust, he had the look of someone who sold meth under the counter to make ends meet.

"That would be me," I said, tired, tired, tired of everybody thinking that just because they recognized me, they already knew me.

He glanced at the box, then back at my face. "You looking for that girl up-stairs?"

"I'm here to visit Nina Price, if that's who you're referring to."

He looked me over with the expression of someone who hated niggers who thought too highly of themselves. But then again, I was Miss Corinne's grand-daughter, and for all he knew, insane like my father.

"Played pool with your daddy," he said with dead-on intuition.

"I'm sure you never won," I said.

"How's that?"

"You're still alive."

He threw back his head and roared with laughter. The other customers looked up apprehensively. I wondered if he really was in the Klan or something.

"You got his sense a humor, too," he said, wiping his eyes.

"Never my intention."

"Well, didn't none of us choose our momma or daddy. We just got to do our best with what we got."

"So, is she up there?" I asked patiently.

"She probly sleep, this time a day. Never seen nobody work like that girl. Six-seven days a week, all night long and she never seem to properly eat nothing. Don't put out no trash and never seen her go to the store, neither."

"Her phone working?" I asked.

The guy shrugged and looked at the blonde woman, who shrugged, too.

"Can she hear the door when somebody knocks?"

"Probly not."

"So how do I wake her up?"

"You probly can't. Not if she deep under."

"But I need to talk to her."

"Then go on up!" he motioned loosely toward the ceiling. "I know you ain't about to take nothing. We seen you already!" Again he burst into idiotic laughter.

The whole store was eyeballing me now, but it hardly mattered. Everyone in Blissfield who had any memory of the Castles was already clocking my every move. A few more eyewitnesses might mean that the gossipers would at least get it right.

Once back outside I discovered that, indeed, the door to the upstairs flat was open. I pushed it slowly, the cardboard box in my arms, and made my way carefully, again struggling not to think about the steep narrow stairs. Inside the apartment the air was close, scented with vanilla candles, but the quiet was filled with peace.

I set the box down on the leather sofa and looked around the room. I hadn't realized how many books she'd collected—there were shelves, and crates, and books on every flat surface, including the floor. I saw Gatsby and *Great Expectations*, *The Prisoner of Azkaban*, *Invisible Man* and *The Bluest Eye* stacked beside a medical dictionary, Julia Child's *The Way to Cook*, and an etiquette book that had been read so often the cover had come loose from the pages.

I walked to the door of the kitchen. The plates and dishes were washed and put away. A half loaf of white bread sat on top of the fridge. A large bottle of lemonade stood on the corner of the counter. There was no visible sign of alcohol, though I smelled stale cigarette.

A sudden movement startled me, and she was standing in the bedroom doorway, a wild look in her eyes, her hands fisted and held stiffly at her sides.

"What do you want?" she said gruffly.

"Nina—I'm sorry. I knocked and nobody answered. The guy downstairs told me you were probably asleep and I should come on up."

Her hair was mashed flat on one side of her head, and her faded nightgown, a few sizes too large, made her look like a Victorian governess. She stared at me, then blinked and turned away.

Nina—wait —"

"*You* wait. I need to pee, for heaven's sake."

I went back into the front room and sat down, wondering if she'd be pissed if I opened a window. The heat and the smell of those candles were almost too much to bear.

She appeared a few moments later, her eyes traveling from my clothes to my face.

"So you leaving," she said. "You got that I-can't-take-much-more-a-this look."

"I'm broke," I said, getting to my feet, "and I need to get myself someplace where there might be a job."

"That won't be here," she said.

I searched her face for some sign of the boyish girl who defended me in the schoolyard seventeen years before, but Gideon had made it clear I was chasing shadows.

"Even though things didn't work out like I hoped," I said, "I'm not sorry I found you, Nina, and I'm glad you and Gideon are doing okay."

She lifted her chin and narrowed her eyes. "What do you want, CeCe?" she repeated coldly.

"Tell me to stay, Nina."

"Can't do that."

"Why?"

"Did it a whole bunch of times before and it didn't make one bit of difference."

It was now afternoon and sunbeams flooded the room, swirling lazily in the dust.

"Well," I said, my voice oddly scratchy, "before I leave, there's one other thing I want you to do."

She tilted her head expectantly. I put my hand on the box. "Please open it," I said.

She walked forward and lifted the lid like she thought a snake might pop out. At first she just stared at the stacks of paper. She leaned a little closer when she recognized her name on the top envelope. Picking it up, she turned it over, brought the date closer to her eyes, then peered at me, a question in her gaze.

"Nina," I said, "she did it. My grandmother. She took every single one of them and kept them for herself."

"How?" Nina muttered, reaching deeper into the box and lifting out a stack of fifteen or twenty letters.

"It was her friend, Mr. Saunders. His nephew works at the post office and—"

"That's against the law," Nina said.

"There's something else, too," I said. "It turns out Mr. Saunders is my—"

"No, CeCe," she said very calmly. She placed the letters back in the box and closed it firmly.

"No *what*?" I asked.

"Just no."

"I want you—I mean, would you please read them?"

"Why?"

"Because I want you to know how I felt after my grandmother put me on that bus."

"What's the point?" she said. "It's the past. It's done."

"Not for me," I said.

"It is for me."

Nina hoisted up the box and held it out toward me until I stood up and took it. "I hope you make it to wherever you going," she said.

"Nina, please——"

"Please, *what*? You come back here and think me and Gideon 'sposed to care? *Hello*, CeCe! We got to go to work while you driving up and down the road. We got bills while you chilling at Miss Corinne house, waiting to find out what's in her will. Now you know you may not get anything, so you want me to feel bad because you leaving?" She shook her head. "Don't you hear right, CeCe? Gideon and me: *we don't want you no more.*"

The world went into a kind of slow motion. Nina's face slammed shut and I saw that her eyes, already the eyes of a woman who worry and loneliness had destined to a premature and solitary old age, were filled with rage. I recognized that rage because I'd carried it too, buried deep inside my body, for most of my life.

And, perhaps for the first time in my life, I didn't meet rage with rage. I suddenly understood what the Old Man with the white hair meant when he talked about accepting things I can't change. Even *that* idea once filled me with anger. This moment, however, was different. This was the moment to surrender.

"Okay," I said. "I'm sorry. I understand why you feel that way."

Drained, I moved the box onto my hip. It seemed much, much heavier than only moments before. Nina turned away, staring coldly out the window, her gaze fixed on the near-deserted street below. She didn't turn her head when I stopped at the top of the stairs.

"There's only one reason I brought these to you," I said without looking back. "I wanted you to know how much I loved you and your brother, even after my grandmother sent me away."

"That's nice," she said bitterly.

"You may not believe me, but it's the truth. And I'll tell you something else: I loved my mother. I loved my grandmother. I loved Gideon and I loved you."

She grunted dryly.

"My father, Copley Castle, didn't want me to love anybody but him," I said. "And DeAndre, that man who hurt you and your mother, wanted you and Gideon to believe nobody would *ever* love you."

I paused. "But I loved you and your brother, Nina. Do you hear me? I *still* love you. Even when I was damn near dead, I laid in that hospital bed thinking about you. When I didn't have a dime I drove myself crazy trying to figure out how to get back down here to you. Loving you made it possible for me to keep living when everyone and everything else was gone. And maybe—hell, I don't know—maybe in some crazy way my love helped you and Gideon survive, too."

I didn't really expect her to react. Even years ago, when we were close, she'd always needed time to get right with her feelings. Her brother had made it clear I was a closed chapter in his life. So though I knew I might not ever see them again, I wanted to leave some truth in my wake.

"Take care of yourself," I said as I turned to go.

I was halfway down the stairs when I heard the voice.

"Hold up, CeCe."

He appeared from the shadows like a ghost version of himself. He was dressed in the same white tee-shirt and smelled of oil and sweat, smoke and fading cologne. An unlit cigarette was tucked behind his ear, forgotten. I knew from the look on his face he'd heard every word Nina and I said.

Nina spoke quietly to her brother. "Let it be, Gid."

"No, Nina."

"Gid, you need to let her go."

Ignoring her, he descended several steps toward me. We looked at each other a long moment. He held out his arms and took the box. "Come back up, CeCe. I need to get something to eat."

Though the tension in the small flat was palpable, I followed him back into the kitchen, again noticing the closet-like room tucked beside Nina's.

"You live here?" I asked as I sat at the half-moon table.

"Naw. I got my own place over by my job. I just stay here sometime when Nina not right."

"Does the guy downstairs know?"

"He know enough."

I watched as he fried eggs and bacon for all three of us, moving slowly, but comfortably around the kitchen. In the full daylight I could see he protected his left hip by shifting his weight to his right, and more than once he leaned briefly, but heavily against the counter. When he bent down to look for a pan, a tremor crossed his face and, beneath his rolled-up sleeve I saw a scar that extended up his arm.

He turned on the radio, and we caught Stevie Wonder's gentle tenor: *"then the winter came, love could not be found..."*

Gideon's face remained a study in emptiness. We didn't speak or look at each other, though for me, just being there with him, no matter the circumstances, was a kind of bliss.

He called Nina when the food was ready, but she went into her room and shut the door. He knitted his brows, then pushed her food back into the frying pan and calmly placed her plate in the sink. Sitting across from me, I was surprised when he bent his head in silent prayer before picking up his knife and fork.

We ate in silence, eyes on our plates, and I thought of the gentle boy who'd followed me on his skateboard as I walked my bike along the street, saying nothing at all. Our knees touched beneath the table and he looked up as if prepared to apologize.

I smiled. "You're a good cook."

"This about it."

"Well, at least I don't have to worry about you starving."

"You don't have to worry about us at all."

"I've never stopped worrying about you," I said.

His gaze sharpened. I could see how close to the surface his anger still paced.

"Take it easy," I said, "I'm not trying to piss you off."

He stood to reach for the old-fashioned percolator. When he turned back, I understood it was curiosity, not trust, that led him to invite me to stay.

I cleared the table and washed the dishes, my back turned to his silence. I heard the cardboard box open, followed by the rustling of dried paper. The silence deepened. He didn't speak. After a few minutes the rustling began again. I knew he'd moved on to another letter.

When I finished washing up I went back into the front room and sat on the sofa. Nina, dressed in another odd combination of sweaters, slacks and a pair of slipper-boots, emerged from her bedroom. She exchanged a few words with her brother, then walked to the threshold of the living room, a plastic lunch bag in her hand.

"I hope you gone before I get back in the morning," she said.

Darkness fell. I sat for a long time, listening to the cicadas shrilling, a night bird calling, the muted radio in the kitchen and the occasional thrum of a car in the street. One of the windows was open, filling the room with the sweet perfume of a southern summer night.

Head cradled in my arms, I dozed off, curled up on the sofa. Suddenly I jerked awake, startled by the sound of an engine gunning at the stop sign below. Glancing at a clock above the TV, I saw that I'd been asleep for nearly three hours. I stood up fast—too fast—and had to put my head down and breathe deeply to stop a rising wave of vertigo. Never, in the fifteen years since That Night, had I fallen asleep anywhere without either locks on the door or a weapon by my side. Nina's little living room, walled with books and smelling of Grandma's kitchen, felt unbelievably safe.

I went back to the kitchen door and found Gideon hunched at the table beside a saucer full of smashed butts, still reading intently. He moved steadily from letter to letter, taking them in order, opening the brittle pages carefully with his large, scarred hands. His eyes moved across the pages and sometimes his lips formed the words, opening to a brief smile, then closing tightly, suppressing a sound.

Without a word I sank down across from him. He looked up and gazed at me for a long moment, his expression thoughtful and appraising. Then his eyes flickered down and he returned to his reading.

He'd taken the letters chronologically, beginning with the hardest and saddest days of my life. He now knew all about Bebe J and the boarded-up street, Jesse Brantley and the loft overlooking the city, and the full details about That Night.

The letters from the hospitals lay beside those written from the halfway-house, and later, from the apartments I shared with other women. He was now learning how I'd spent the past few years, when I'd lived with little purpose, direction or meaning.

I watched him as he read and smoked, still guarded, or guarding himself, his eyes both too empty and too complex to be deciphered. I had no idea what he was feeling. I hardly knew what I was feeling, myself—except the pure relief of knowing that Gideon could finally see these words, which were always meant for him and Nina alone.

A few minutes after midnight he reached the bottom of box. He leaned back, looking at me, and it took every ounce of courage I could find to look right back. So much had changed in his face, and yet so little. So much had happened to me, and yet I was sure that nothing mattered as much as this moment. My soul lay open before him, expressed with the full and complete honesty of desperate love. What else could have driven me to write and write, through the loneliness, hopelessness, fear and indescribable pain?

Gideon sighed and leaned forward, reaching for one of the final letters in the box. Opening a tightly folded square, a sudden rough sound escaped his throat and he pushed back hard from the table. Startled, I looked first at his stricken face, then down at the paper. He was holding an oddly stained page.

> Dear CeCe,
> How are you? I hope your day is going good. Did you do okay on Mr. Greens test? Nina said his test are very hard and he dont grade too fare. I know you can take care of him if you have to! (smile). I think your a very good student so it wont be a problem for you. Are you coming to the game friday night? I hope we can win against Chowan because they usually beat us. If coach will let me play my game I know I can make a few touchdowns. I will make a touchdown for you! WISH ME LUCK, OKAY?
> Have a good day.
> Your friend Gideon Price

I looked from his hand to the bottom of the box, and there they were. Many—perhaps all of the letters he'd written to me when he was a manchild, all gathered from their hiding place—a shoebox I'd been forced to leave behind when I was sent into exile from Blissfield.

For a long time neither one of us spoke. The intensity of our silence was so great that it drowned out the drilling cicadas and twittering birds outside.

Then his gaze, filled with almost unimaginable sorrow, rose to meet mine, and I knew that I was looking into Gideon's naked soul.

"I heard what you said to Nina," he murmured. "You said DeAndre wanted to us to believe nobody would ever love us." He drew on his cigarette, exhaled slowly. "You right."

I watched as he slowly pressed the cigarette into the saucer. It hissed softly and died.

"And you right about something else. You said when you was little you couldn't think about nothing but your father. Well, that's how we was with DeAndre. He gave us that shack and just enough to get by so he could keep control of every second of our life. The only thing that mattered to him was for us to take care of his son. We was less than dogs in his eyes."

He paused, looking searchingly at me.

"CeCe, I never gave much thought to why you was so ready to fight when you came here. I never axt you to tell me the real reasons your momma sent you away."

He lifted his hand and let it drop to the table. "To be honest with you, when I got out the joint, Nina and me—we could of gone anywhere. We never said a word out loud about it, but we never gave up hoping you would find you way back. You was the one that really cared about us, CeCe. The only one."

He reached across the table and opened his hand to mine.

Gingerly, as I had so many years before, I pressed my palm against his, feeling the hard callouses on the oil-stained skin. My heart leapt at the warmth of his touch.

He smiled slowly, almost shyly, and I could see in his eyes that he finally trusted the thing he hadn't dared to believe: Never had he *ever* been unloved.

"You still scared? he asked.

* * * * * * *

When he stood waiting before me, I found gouges on his calf from linebackers' cleats, a jagged slash on his thigh from a rusted truck fender and the bone-deep slice along his jaw, the echo of his single fight with DeAndre. A cobalt tattoo of an Egyptian eye lay over his heart, its graceful hook sweeping just below his nipple. I touched the tear that fell from the eye, mirroring both eternal sorrow and protection from everything evil.

On me he found a pearl-stitched necklace that sealed the pink gap on my chest, growing wider above my heart. He found the raised scars where doctors removed my damaged organs, rebuilt my crushed frame and repaired my shredded knee and torn shoulder. He saw the shadows that never seemed to leave my eyes, and the bones emerging from the skin, starved from so many years of being alone.

His eyes, calm and dark, considered me, even as his hands lay open at his sides. Then, with exquisite tenderness, he reached up and drew his fingers from my temple to the point of my chin. He lifted my face and brought his lips to mine.

The kiss was soft, chaste and seemed to go on for a lifetime. I felt an aching that bloomed in my core, exploded in my bones and nearly scalded every inch of my body. With one hand he stroked the hair away from my face, while his other hand found the small of my back. Lifting me carefully into his arms, he held me breathlessly close, as if I was infinitely precious. As if he knew how difficult being touched might be for me.

He lowered our bodies carefully to the mattress, keeping his weight on his good right hip, and settled me against him. He drew the sheet over us and we lay there, heartbeat to heartbeat, breath to breath. He pressed his lips against the crown of my head and sighed.

He was giving me time.

Making me a promise.

Telling me with the patience of his flesh that this was to be a bond made in love.

And we both let ourselves remember.

Quietly he began to weep, as if from the very depths of his being.

* * * * * * *

Late in the night I woke and found Gideon beside me, his head resting on his folded arm, his lashes still, lips soft, chest rising and falling. I had never seen him sleep, so I held myself very still and studied the hills and valleys of his face, silhouetted by moonlight filtered through a tangle of branches outside.

From the day of our first meeting seventeen years before, I recognized that Gideon emanated a serenity that complemented the naked logic of his sister, but until that moment I had never understood it. The two years we loved each other—yes, in the way children love each other—tested his spirit again and again, but he never broke. He had never been unkind to me, to Nina, to Benedictine, or to any of the adults who failed him. As I lay there, looking at his face and body in repose, I understood how unnatural it was, and how desperate he must have been to attack DeAndre. I also realized, as I made out the Egyptian eye tattooed over his heart, that he would never be at peace with the person he'd become to save the people he loved.

Now, because of my many months of work with the Old Man, I also understood the price I had paid to do the same—not in Copley's tearing of my flesh and breaking of my bones—no, my price was the burden of violent fear that Copley seared into my spirit when I was just a small child. I had to die in a filthy stairwell on a frigid night before I could be given this chance of a new life—a better life than I had ever known before.

A lone car passed on the street outside and Gideon shifted slightly, but he didn't wake. I thought of the reasons why he and Nina might have kept their distance when they learned of my return. Nina's last sight of me had been on the muddy path outside their home that Christmas Eve, standing over DeAndre with a bloody baseball bat in my hand. After fifteen years of silence, neither of the Prices could possibly have imagined what kind of woman I'd become, and they loved each other too much to invite a rattlesnake into their lives.

I had failed at so many things. I had no education, no work, no savings, no home and no friends. And yet, as I looked at this man—the first and only man I had ever cared for—I realized that I had survived all of it so I could be right there, at that moment, beside him. For the first time since that distant winter morning when my father first struck me—I truly wasn't afraid.

Gideon's eyes opened and gently, silently, calmly he smiled.

He reached for me. His thumb stroked my face, the scar that ringed my chest, then his fingers moved on to my breasts, the nipples springing to life, and then on to my belly, where his hand gently kneaded and pulled, kneaded and pulled.

I made no sound, not even when took my tongue into his mouth and sucked it softly, as he had when we were young. Everything ceased except the salty, wood-earth smell of him, the apple-charcoal taste of him, the smooth taut strength of him, the indescribable relief of my complete trust in him.

We had taught each other the ways of pleasure before we understood the price we would pay for it. It had been so easy in the tall grasses beside the stone cabin, behind the wall in the schoolyard and in my grandmother's giant old car.

The heat of our bodies, our kiss-chapped lips, our hands wet and sticky with curious touching. My desire—no, my *need* for him. His eyes black. His voice raw with wanting.

How could we have known we were charting maps that no one else could follow? During the wandering years the geographies of our flesh had shifted, even as storms move cities and forests and sands. Here, in a room so small the single mattress barely fit, was the man who'd forced us to wait, certain one day we'd reach this moment.

He took my hips and shifted me carefully beneath him. Leaning up on his forearms, he braced his legs against the inside of my thighs. "You are so beautiful, CeCe," he whispered. "I can't hardly believe my eyes."

He pressed in slowly and my body, trembling, arched to meet his. But something passed through him—a sudden intuition—and he pulled back, locking his eyes with mine.

Because he knew. Somehow he knew. Of course he knew.

"CeCe?" he said, asking without asking the one thing I hadn't told him.

"Yes, Gideon." I paused. "I deserved better. So I waited."

"You — ? "

"It was the best way I could love you."

For a very long time he didn't speak, but when he did, I heard the love in his words.

"You sure this is what you want?" he said.

"I'm sure," I answered, because he was all I'd ever wanted, and when we became one, I wanted nothing more.

* * * * * * *

Later, still, we woke again.

"When I was in the joint," he said, voice slow and rough and thoughtful, "they made me talk to one of their guys. I didn't want to at first, but they said if I did it I might get out sooner."

He shifted his weight to hold me closer.

"I never knew no other way to live, CeCe. I didn't know all men don't hit their women and kids. I didn't know what it did to me to walk away with Ben and leave Nina in that house with DeAndre."

I listened.

"CeCe, I never seen nothing when I looked in the mirror. I was a ghost. I wasn't even a boy I was so empty. All my life I was a outline of a living thing, like a old cartoon, with nothing filling me up inside.

"You was the first person that looked at me and Nina and seen *somebody*. You walked away from those people that Easter Sunday and made us feel like we was alive. No one in this town ever done nothing for us before. And you didn't care that we wasn't in church, or that we didn't have shit to wear, or that we must of looked like two mongrels in a field of dirt on the Lord's holiest day."

I felt tears flood my eyes.

"You let my sister be herself," Gideon said. "You never made little of her because she love to read books. Remember when you helped her make that yellow dress? It was the first time in her life she had something that didn't come from a resale store."

He was quiet for a moment.

"And then, during lunchtime on the first day of school you was looking at me. *Me.* Nobody ever looked at me like that before. I didn't know what to do. I didn't know how to feel. Your eyes settled on me and you wasn't seeing a cartoon. You was seeing a *person.*"

He laughed gently, and through my tears, I laughed, too.

"I felt like I was drunk," he said. "Like I couldn't get enough. Nothing in the world felt as good. I showed up at your classes, hoping it would happen again. Then I looked for you in the schoolyard at lunch and in the bleachers during football practice. I started coming with Nina in the mornings, just so I could see my face in your eyes."

"Oh, baby," I whispered.

"It's true," he said. "I couldn't think of nothing else. I started acting so stupid that Nina damn near lost her mind. I couldn't talk, couldn't think—like I had brain damage or something. Still, it only took her a second to understand. And then she got real scared. See, nobody ever really cared if we lived or died. Much as she loved you, she was scared you was going to hurt me. So she tried to change your mind. Then she tried to change *my* mind. But it was too late."

We both laughed quietly. Tenderly he pulled me closer. "Those afternoons —those days by that old cabin—they made me start thinking about what I had to do to escape from this place. To become the man you deserved. To be able to give you something. I knew one day you would wake up and realize I didn't have shit, and wasn't going to have shit, and then you would move on. After all, you was Miss Corinne granddaughter—a Castle—and no Price boy could ever be good enough for you."

"You know I don't think like that," I said, slipping out of his arms to lean up on one elbow. "I've never thought that way."

"It don't matter, baby. All of them—all the ones that would of kept us apart—they all gone, now."

"Except Nina," I said. "She won't even look at the letters. She refuses to believe I never stopped caring about you—"

"She can't help it, CeCe. She was the one who carried the weight for both Benny and me. She was the one he slapped around and forced to lie down. And then he was dead and our momma was dead and she was still here in Blissfield. She had to walk down these streets every day and deal with these people. She had to live here with her memories. Hell—me sitting in a prison nuthouse, planting rose bushes—that was easy. I even got help with the shit going on in my head. What Nina been through is enough to make Jesus crazy.

"So you see," he said, "I can't leave her behind. I got a place near my job, but I stay here some nights because she need me. I don't know what she might do if she alone. Sometime DeAndre still show up, even if we both know he dead in the ground. She hear his voice and feel what he done all over again. I put on some music and get her to sing, or we watch some stupid movie, and then, when she at peace she stand up and say good night. It might take one hour or it might take all night."

He was still staring into the darkness.

"So when I hooked up with Macey—Brandon and Bruce sister—I could never really be her husband. I had to look after Nina, and when I was at Macey place my mind was still over here. Macey tried to pretend I was with some other woman, but that was some bullshit and she knew it. In a town like this you can't be with nobody without everybody knowing—specially *her* brothers—but she wanted me to let Nina go. She even said if Nina want to take herself out, I should let her do it. To be honest, that's when I knew I had to let Macey be."

I nodded, any lingering jealousy I felt fading away.

"You were right, CeCe. Nina looked out for me and Benny all those years," he said. "She was our momma and our sister and our teacher. She made all the food and washed all the clothes. She worked so hard every day and she never complained. Now I feel ashamed. I didn't get it when I was a kid. She never had no kind of childhood. The only thing that saved her was those books."

My heart turned over. Even when I rode bikes with her, ate lunch with her, went to the library with her, I hadn't understood.

Now, despite the darkness, I felt his gaze on me.

"I bet you trying to feel guilty, right? Well, Nina never wanted you to know. She was happy you liked her just the way she was. You was the closest thing to a friend—wait," he said, reaching out to touch my face, "—I meant to say that you was the only friend *she* ever had, too."

He clasped my hand and brought it to his lips. "We can't carry this, CeCe. We can't change a thing about what happened to us when we was kids. We got to move forward or DeAndre and your father get what they wanted."

"I know you're right," I said, "but sometimes I wish—I wish I'd done better by my mother."

"There's a whole lot I wish I done better, too."

We were quiet a long time. I could see Bebe J's face and hear her voice as she tried to reason with my father. Maybe, I thought, she let him hurt her to protect me. Maybe that was the best way she could love me.

As if he could hear my thoughts, Gideon spoke. "We got to forgive ourself, CeCe. We done the best we could then, and we going to do the best we can now."

"Gideon, sometimes—" I had begun to talk before thinking it through, and my voice hit a wall mid-sentence.

He was listening intently, his hand absently stroking the length of my arm.

"—sometimes I still feel him inside of me." The confession was so soft, even I could barely hear it.

"I know," he answered. "I seen it the other night in Whelan's. But baby, I also seen your grandmother in you when you tried to tell me how you feel and what you want for us. I know your father come out when you scared and fighting to survive. I know you doing your best to control that part of you, even though it can be real hard."

"But what if I can't control it?"

He made a low sound. "To tell you the truth, I knew you was in town probly five minutes after you arrived. But I was scared, too, CeCe. I thought if I came to you, and if you was only here for the money—well, it would of seemed like everything had been a joke, even the things we felt when we was young.

"You was the best thing in my life, CeCe—the one thing I got right back then. And I been in love with you since that Easter Sunday in that field. I never stopped loving you, baby. And if you let me, I will do what I can to make sure your father never need to show up again. And if he do show up, I promise you won't have to deal with him alone."

thirty.

Richard Armitage rose from behind his desk when his receptionist showed us in. His eyes moved quickly between us, trying to measure what had happened since we'd left, and what was likely to happen in the following minutes.

His gaze rested momentarily on Gideon. "How are things, Mr. Price?"

"Just fine, Mr. Armitage, but I'm ready for this weather to cool down some," Gideon said, making small talk as he folded his long frame into the same seat he'd taken before. He was wearing a white collared shirt and clean work pants, and I'd put on the navy dress I'd worn to this office on my first visit. The lawyer looked us over quickly, then nodded in my general direction, politely avoiding my gaze.

"I must confess that, considering our last discussion, I'm somewhat relieved to see the two of you walk in together," Armitage said lightly.

"I apologize for that," Gideon said, touching my arm with the small finger of his left hand. "I think we worked some things out and we're ready to hear what you got to say."

The lawyer at once sank into his chair, set his shoulders, and brushed off the cover of my grandmother's folder.

"Before sharing these documents with you," he said, "I'd like to reiterate my deepest condolences on the loss of your grandmother, Ms. Castle. She was a true gift to this community, one we'll certainly never replace."

Something was about to happen. I glanced at Gideon, but his eyes were focused directly on the lawyer.

"There are histories in this town so complex it would take a chess master to figure them out," Armitage continued as if delivering a rehearsed speech. "Some of these stories go back all the way to slavery. Others are just, well, the product of people behaving like people everywhere. Fortunately or unfortunately, depending on one's perspective, we have some equally complex laws for these situations," Armitage added, "so I will ask you both to bear with me."

I shifted in my chair and Gideon reached over and laid a calming hand on mine.

Armitage opened the manila file which was secured by a metal clasp. Once freed, the folder expanded to reveal a number of documents. The lawyer removed a yellowed paper, opened it carefully and spread it flat on his desk.

"Many years ago," he began, "a farmer named Samuel Redmond purchased a relatively large parcel of land at a greatly reduced price from a man who decided to take his chances with an industrial job in the north. This sale elevated Sam Redmond to one of the most prosperous Black landowners in the area. Soon afterward he legally changed his surname to Castle, which appeared to block his siblings from having any rights to his land."

The lawyer removed another fragile paper from his folder. It was a deed to the properties along Route 58. An uncertain script marked Redmond Castle's uncertain signature, showing that despite his ambition, he had little formal schooling. Gideon remain stone-faced, but I saw a vein pulsing near his temple and my own heart was racing.

"Redmond Castle," Armitage continued," raised his son Julius to be a gentleman. He sent him to Greensboro to attend North Carolina A & T in the hope, we can assume, was that his son would gain the technical knowledge to keep the Castle properties profitable, and, of course, to carry on the family name."

Now Armitage took a third document from his folder. It was a diploma from 1948, awarding Julius Redmond Castle a degree in Agricultural Management.

"Julius returned from Greensboro and appeared to go along with his father's wishes that he run the Castle estate. What Redmond did not know, however, was that while he was away at college, Julius had engaged in a relationship with a young woman, whom he married, I assume in secret, when she became pregnant."

"When Redmond learned about the wedding he was evidently quite displeased. The marriage was quickly annulled, and soon afterward Julius married Corinthia Bibb, the daughter of a teacher and a highly regarded farmer here in Blissfield."

The lawyer produced my grandparents' marriage certificate, dated August 3rd, 1950.

"How did you get these documents?" I asked, incensed at the number of hours I'd spent searching Grandma's house.

Armitage responded calmly. "I'm your grandmother's attorney, Ms. Castle. She entrusted them to me, believing I would keep them secure."

For the thousandth time I wondered if I had ever really known Grandma.

"As you know, Ms. Castle, while she was married to Julius Redmond, Corinthia Bibb Castle gave birth to three sons: Jeremiah, Paul and Copley, your father, who was some years younger than his brothers. The older siblings died in a tragic accident while serving in the military. Obviously I need say nothing about your father."

Armitage went on. "So this brings us to the most complex and difficult parts of the story. I must ask you both to be very patient."

I looked at Gideon, who now also glanced at me. In his eyes I saw a world of emotion, which vanished with a simple blink. I remembered the blankness I'd often seen in his face as a teenager, and for the first time I understood how masterfully he'd hidden his true emotions.

Armitage cleared his throat. "Ms. Castle, I don't know exactly when your grandmother first became aware of her husband's previous marriage, but it's possible that it was only upon his death in 1969. Naturally when he died she believed herself to be the sole heir to the entire Castle estate. Instead, when the will was read, she learned, along with her sons, that he had left everything to an unknown older child from his brief first marriage."

Armitage's eyes moved from Gideon's face to mine.

"Your grandmother, Ms. Castle, was understandably quite upset. She engaged me to try and determine the identity of this heir. After an extensive search of her deceased husband's personal records, the truth about this first marriage, as well as the identity of his eldest child, Abraham, was revealed. Furthermore, she now discovered why her husband spent so much of their married life living in another city, where he claimed to be conducting business. He had, in fact, returned to his first wife, Anna."

"But if that's true," I said, "why didn't he just divorce my grandmother?"

"There's a simple explanation for that," Armitage answered. "Redmond Castle's will made Julius' inheritance contingent upon him remaining married to Corinthia. Redmond seemed determined to keep the entire property under Castle control, no matter what the cost."

"But Julius already had a son," Gideon said in a quiet voice.

"Yes," Armitage said, "and this is where things become even more complex. It was tragically ironic that the only way Julius could leave anything to Abraham was to remain married to a woman he didn't love. We know that he returned to Anna. We know that they lived together as a couple until Julius' death."

"He didn't care about the sons he'd fathered with my grandmother?" I asked.

"He sent money to your grandmother throughout his life. I have no knowledge of the details of his relationship with Corinthia, nor whether they had come to some kind of arrangement. I do know, however, that Julius and his first wife, Anna, were both extremely, shall we say, fair skinned, and chose to live as whites on the outskirts of the Winston Salem community. Living as a white man meant that having a Black wife and two Black sons was, especially during that time, extremely inconvenient."

Gideon's reaction was no more than a shifted eyebrow, but I had to grit my teeth to stop myself from speaking.

Armitage spread a thick document comprising a number of pages on the desk. The print was small, and it contained many signatures, but it was immediately clear that it was Julius Castle's will.

"Julius wrote this will in 1952, immediately after the death of his father. He left everything in his possession to his firstborn son, Abraham Price, who was just five years old at the time."

"*Price?*" Gideon glanced at me as if to be sure we were hearing the same thing. His hand tightened on mine.

"Yes," Armitage said. "Though Julius was his biological father, he was no longer married to Abraham's mother at the time of his son's birth, and the court therefore determined that the baby would bear the surname of his mother, Anna Price.

"Mr. Price," the lawyer continued, "I don't know how much you've been told about your family history, but it appears that Abraham Price was your grandfather. You are a direct descendant of Julius Castle, Corinthia Castle's husband."

Gideon's silence spoke to his bemused disbelief. The lawyer continued.

"Abraham became involved with a young white woman named Rosamond Vickers while they were still in their teens. They married against their parents' wishes, and when Rosamond became pregnant her family forced them apart. Rosamond was sent to live with her mother's relatives in Louisville, Kentucky, where in 1963 she gave birth to a daughter she called Miranda Leah Price. Soon afterward, Abraham died while swimming in a local pond. Though the circumstances of his death were unclear, the police ruled it an accidental drowning. He never had the chance to know his daughter."

Leaning forward in his chair, Gideon blinked something from his eyes.

"Mr. Price," Armitage said, "I am correct, I think, in my belief that Miranda Price was your mother. She spent her entire childhood in the care of her maternal relatives, but left home at fifteen and found her way here, I suspect, because she had some notion that her father's family came from the area. As she had no means of supporting herself, she fell into, shall we say, a very difficult way of life.

"Abraham died without a will, but as her lineage was preserved by her mother on her birth certificate—" Armitage drew the paper out of his folder, "—there can be no contest to the fact that after the death of her grandfather, Julius Redmond Castle, and her father, Abraham Price, Miranda Price became the single legal heir to the Castle estate."

Gideon began to shake his head. "I don't under—"

"Your mother could have taken possession of the land years ago, had she sought counsel," Armitage said. "I believe, however, that because of her youth and the kind of life she was leading, she was reluctant to approach any representatives of the law."

"How long have you known this?" Gideon asked, his voice rough.

"I'm sorry," Armitage said, "but no one in Blissfield had any way of knowing. Even when Corinthia hired me to find out why she was not entitled to her husband's estate, none of us could have imagined that his heir was the out-of-wedlock daughter of a stranger named Abraham Price, a girl who'd been raised as a white woman in another state. Miranda Price was only a teenager when she arrived here. She joined no church, was enrolled in night classes for only a few weeks, and never formed any relationships with the townspeople. How could anyone have guessed she was Julius Castle's grandchild?"

Gideon and I peered at each other. His anger and disbelief were mixed with an expression of carefully hidden sorrow. Only someone who knew him well would see how deeply he was hurting.

"So my grandmother," I said, "simply went on living as if the estate was hers?"

"Abraham died intestate, and because no one knew about his daughter, the estate came back to your grandmother. Of course," Armitage said, "Corinthia chose not to sell any part of it, or to glean profit from it in any particularly way. She saw herself as a kind of steward, or caretaker of the property until her husband's heirs could be identified. This might have cost her the life of her older sons, who enlisted in the military as soon as they came of age. Your grandmother confided in me once that when they realized they would never inherit the property, they saw no further reason to remain in Blissfield. In the end, her honesty and decency in relation to the estate, even after she lost her sons, were further proof of her extraordinary character."

Well, I thought, here it was: the final thing Grandma hadn't wanted me to know. Everything she'd gone through—her husband's abuse and abandonment, her struggle to raise her sons alone, the fight to keep living despite her grief, her unselfish dedication to the preservation of the Castle estate—all of it had ironically led us to the night when her surviving son murdered his wife and tried to destroy his only child, the last member of the Castle family line. It was as if a whirlwind had begun generations before, snatching up broken glass and nails and strips of metal, growing in ferocity until it became a hurricane that swallowed all of us up, leaving nothing but shattered lives in its wake. Leaving nothing but Bethany Celeste, a Castle without a castle, a beggar squatting in a house built on lies.

"So how does this end?" I asked calmly, already knowing the answer.

"Well, Ms. Castle, first of all, it ends with you, and once again, please excuse me for being so frank—having no claim whatsoever to the Castle land. Your father has a partial claim on the value of the house because it was jointly purchased by Corinthia and Julius' fathers and given to them as a wedding gift. Half of the value of the house will go to Copley."

"But my father's in prison for life—"

"Yes, and this is where Ohio law intervenes," Armitage said. "Many states require inmates to forfeit bequests in payment of their incarceration. Ohio is one such state. The house will be sold and your father's portion of the proceeds will go to the Ohio Department of Corrections. The other half will be returned to the Price family."

Armitage looked at Gideon, who nodded once, signaling he understood.

"So, Mr. Price," the attorney concluded, "the only documents I need are birth certificates for you, your sister Leah, and your brother, Benedictine. When you give me permission, I will order these documents from the State. I suggest you speak to them as soon as possible."

"Wait—" I said suddenly. "Is there anything in those papers that would make it—" I paused, stumbling over the words, "—*illegal* for Gideon and me to—to—" I glanced shyly toward Gideon.

Armitage smiled. "Your grandmother told me many years ago that Copley Castle is not Julius' son, meaning that your father shares no biological connection to the descendants of Abraham Price. In short, there are no barriers whatsoever to anything you and Mr. Price might be planning."

"Thank you," Gideon said, holding his hand out to the lawyer as we stood.

Grasping his palm, Armitage paused for a moment. "Mr. Price," he said, "if you'll excuse me for saying this, I just want you to know how glad I am that things have worked out. You won't remember this, but I was in courtroom the day they brought you in, years ago, when you got in trouble for defending your sister. Corinthia called and asked me if I could help you. Well, I couldn't do much—you see, I'm really a contract lawyer. But I put a call in to my roommate from law school, Hank Peterson. I believe he's one of the best criminal defense attorneys in the state, and he was more than happy to come up from Raleigh and take your case. He worked *pro bono*, as a matter of fact. Like me, he doesn't believe that minors should be locked up with adults."

"I appreciate that," Gideon said with dignity. "It likely saved my life."

"So," Armitage said, "the final thing I should add is this: to be perfectly frank, Mr. Price, the property your family has inherited is very valuable. You have several thousand acres of farmland, an additional fifteen-hundred acres of untouched timber and a number of plots suitable for development as business or residential sites. There are many potential uses for the land, depending on what you and your siblings decide to do. If you're interested, I would be more than happy, when the will clears probate, to assist you in making your business arrangements. Managed properly, the estate could provide your family a generous income in the years to come."

Despite a sheen in his eyes, Gideon remained composed as we left the office. He followed me out of the house, his fingers pressed gently against the small of my back. We stopped just outside the gate.

"Well," he murmured, "I guess this is what my great-grandfather always wanted. But Jesus—everything we went through: you, me, Nina, your momma and my momma—all that pain had to happen for us to be standing here now? That can't be right."

Taking his hand, I brought his fingers to my lips. "It's not wrong or right," I said. "It's Blissfield."

afterwards.

I stood at the window, looking out over the deserted main street and listening as Gideon explained things to his sister. I could hear her guffawing exclamations over the weirdly tragic story with its unexpected ending. That morning Nina and Gideon Price woke up near-destitute outcasts; that night they would go to sleep the heirs of a long-dead ancestor, and perhaps among the wealthiest inhabitants of the town.

Nina sat on her sofa, her back straight, her fingers grasping the ends of her boney knees. I wanted to go over and sit down beside her. I wanted to wrap my arms around her. I wanted pick up a comb and detangle her hair while she told me about the book she was reading. But her attention was fixed on her brother, who'd pulled up a kitchen chair and was sitting directly in front of her.

Gideon's rusty voice lulled me into a kind of peace, and I longed with all my heart to remain there forever, in that quiet room, with the two people I loved.

After a while I looked around, realizing the apartment was silent. Gideon and Nina were gazing at me. He was taller than his sister, but the two might still have been twins, so similar were their faces. Their eyes, always careful, measured, measuring, met mine with newly untroubled gazes. After a moment Nina smiled. That made me smile, too.

"See, Gid?" she said in a stage whisper. "I told you she still crazy."

"That's cool," he said, "long as she crazy with us."

* * * * * * *

We didn't have to go as far as I thought. Elizabeth City is less than two hours away, and it sits on the mighty Atlantic. We had never seen the ocean before Gideon drove us there, and when he cleared the last row of houses and came out on the causeway I forgot the heat, what was playing on the radio, and even his hand resting on mine.

Though I hadn't been swimming in years and wasn't sure I still knew how, I ran like a five-year old to edge of the roiling surf, raising my arms as if, like the gulls wheeling overhead, I could fly.

Soon Gideon and Nina were there beside me, our arms laced around each other's waists as the waves tried to knock us over. We held on tight without speaking. We didn't need to, and the roaring sea would have drowned us out if we'd tried. Some stupid part of me wished the Old Man, whose name—Dr. Baldwin—suddenly bloomed inside my head, and Paula, my die-hard social worker, had been there to see us. Another deeply buried part of me wished I could share these moments with Bebe J and, above all, with my grandmother.

We settled down to lunch on the top of a powdery sand dune. We'd struggled to climb the thing in the afternoon heat, our feet getting trapped and sucked down beneath our sweating bodies. Gideon reached out and tried to hold onto us both, only to fall flat on his back to our belly-aching laughter. It felt like a lifetime since I'd laughed that hard. Even Nina, who had a Ph.D. in Stubborness, let herself go. For an instant she looked like that gangly girl who sat on the log beside me such a long time ago.

When we started to eat she became my Nina again. "I'll let you make bologna sandwiches, but you don't know a thing about deviled eggs, coming from wherever it is you come from, Ms. Bethany Celeste."

"I know just as much as you, cause my Grandma taught me how to make them."

"But you northern folk can't learn right. Can't talk right, either."

"Okay," I said, suppressing a laugh. "I guess I'll let you teach me that, too."

"Wasted effort. I'll just have to go on pretending to understand your horrible accent."

I glanced at her, seeing that although she was gazing toward the water, a smile sneaked along the edges of her mouth. "I see you, Gideon!" she snapped. "Don't try to act like you not part of this conversation."

"You never told me your secret recipe either," he said, "so I know I got nothing to say." He leaned back on his elbows, absently shaking the sand out of his hair, and stared out to sea.

We drove down the coast and climbed up to the monument on Kill Devil Hill, where the Wright Brothers flew the first plane. Nina thought they were crazy to try something like that so close to the water, but she loved the way the hot wind whipped our shirts up around our faces.

"I guess if you crazy enough to try to fly in something made of plywood and glue," she said as we read the bronze dedication, "you might as well enjoy the view as you die."

* * * * * * *

That night we had barbeque in a family diner. I'd combed Nina's hair out and plaited it into a neat French braid. She had on a new yellow sundress and flat leather sandals, and kept looking down at herself as if she'd just arrived on earth from another dimension. Gideon glanced at her, then smiled at me. I had on my red dress and I felt happy—a feeling I almost didn't recognize. All three of us were getting to know each other, and ourselves, in new ways. Good ways. Full of promise ways.

The people at the next table were talking about things going on at the college.

"We got to go back to school," Nina observed, politely wiping her mouth as she finished her dessert of peach cobbler with a scoop of vanilla ice cream. "I always did want to get my college degree."

"You going to study English?" I asked, moving my straw in slow circles in my milkshake.

"I like books too much for that," she said, "and anyway, look like these days we need to know something about the law."

Gideon took a sip of his beer. "I took some computer classes in the clink. Maybe I'll follow up in the free world. We could put some tourist cabins on our property and rent them out online."

"Well, managing clothing stores for eight years," I said, "better serve for something. I need to get a business degree. If all goes well, we might end up with a lawyer, a programmer and a money-manager in the family."

"If they try to cheat us we'll just tell them *the Price is right*," Nina said, eyes twinkling.

Gordon and I groaned. "First thing you got to learn is not to be so corny," he said.

"And then you can show me how to cook," I said.

"Totally impossible, CeCe. You'll be walking with a cane before you learn your way around a kitchen."

"I could teach you how to sew," I offered.

"Miss Corinne already done that. And besides, if we take care of our business we won't need to sew no more."

"We could still do it for fun," I said.

Nina smiled. "You know what, CeCe? It's going to be nice to have some fun for a change."

"Think the three of us can handle that?" Gideon asked me, his expression unexpectedly serious.

"We can learn that, too," I said.

"What if all that other stuff get in the way?" Nina said, glancing away.

I touched her arm and to my surprise she looked at me with open, trusting eyes. "Well," I said after a pause, "back in the day I spent a whole lot of time talking with a guy—this man with white hair. At first it was pretty hard, but after a while I managed to get a lot of my stuff out. He didn't say much—every once in a while he asked me a question, then gave me time to work the answer out for myself. I guess it helped, because sometimes just thinking about him keeps me from acting as crazy as I used to."

"What about me?" she asked. "You think I should talk to somebody?"

"Couldn't hurt," I said gently.

She threw her arm around my shoulder, hugging me awkwardly. "Remember how we used to make plans for the future?" she said. "For all we know things may still work out."

"That depends—" Gideon said, lighting a cigarette to hide his smile.

"On what?" she asked.

"On if CeCe can put up with us," he said, lacing his fingers through mine.

"Neither wild horses nor monster trucks could drag me away," I said, smiling right back.

"Seriously?" Nina said, rolling her eyes dramatically. "And you say *I'm* corny? That came straight out of one of those dummy books people read up in Ohio!" She turned to her brother. "We need to get her to a library, so she can start talking like our CeCe again."

"I was thinking," Gideon said diplomatically, "that as soon as things settle down we could check out some other parts of the world, too."

"Sounds good to me," I said. "What do you think, Nina?"

"Never had the chance to travel. I'm willing to give it a try."

"Well," Gideon said, "where do you all want to go?"

"Hawaii," Nina and I said, almost simultaneously. We peered at each other. Nina shook her head while I laughed.

"Why not?" Gideon said.

The three us looked to the cobalt horizon.

And we thought about it.

* * * * * *

About the author.

Heather Neff was born in Akron and spent her teen years in Detroit. A graduate of the University of Michigan, she went on to study at the Sorbonne and the University of Zurich, where she earned her doctorate in English Language and Literature.

Neff worked as a language teacher, corporate trainer and translator before beginning her career as a Professor of English at Eastern Michigan University. She has received Eastern Michigan University's *Distinguished Faculty Award for Excellence in Teaching*, the EMU Alumni Association *Teaching Excellence Award* and was named a *Michigan Distinguished Professor* by the Presidents' Council of the State Universities of Michigan. Neff currently serves as Director of the Eastern Michigan University McNair Scholars Program and edits the EMU *McNair Scholars Research Journal*.

Neff is the author of seven novels, including *Blackgammon*, an intricate tale of the intertwined lives of Chloe, a celebrated artist making her life in Paris, and her fiery friend Michael, a scholar living in England; *Wisdom*—designated an Honor Book by the Black Caucus of the American Library Association—a thriller about the search for ancestry on a Caribbean island; *Haarlem*, which follows a man's search for his lost mother while he struggles to maintain his sobriety after years of addiction, and *Accident of Birth*, a life-long love story between an Black American woman and a Liberian student.

Leila: The Weighted Silence of Memory and its sequel, *Leila II: The Moods of the Sea*, recount the story of a girl sold into human trafficking at twelve years old. To learn more about Heather Neff's work, visit: www.heatherneffbooks.com .

Also by Heather Neff

Blackgammon

Wisdom

Accident of Birth

Haarlem

Leila: The Weighted Silence of Memory

Leila II: The Moods of the Sea

Redemption Songs: Protest in the Poetry of Afro Americans,

    1760—1865 (*nonfiction*)

Vespers (*poetry*)

Whittaker Road Works I: Departures (*editor*)

Whittaker Road Works II: Taking Flight (*editor*)

blissfield.

Made in the USA
Columbia, SC
19 January 2019